Whispers Through Time

Kim Murphy

*To Kathleen,
Best wishes,
Kim Murphy*

Published by Coachlight Press

Published by Coachlight Press May 2008

Coachlight Press, LLC
1704 Craig's Store Road
Afton, Virginia 22920
http://www.coachlightpress.com

Printed in the United States of America
Cover design by Mayapriya Long, Bookwrights Design

This is a work of fiction. Names, characters, places, and incidents either are the product of the author's imagination or are used fictitiously, and any resemblance to any actual persons, living or dead, events, or locales is entirely coincidental.

Library of Congress Catalog Number: 2008902633
ISBN-13: 978-0-9716790-7-8

*To Joan, who encouraged me at an impressionable age,
and Mystic*

Also by Kim Murphy

Whispers from the Grave
Promise & Honor
Honor & Glory
Glory & Promise

Chapter One

Near Charles City, Virginia
October 2013

A FLOORBOARD IN THE HALL CREAKED. Rubbing tired eyes, Geoff glanced up from the computer screen. *Just the house settling.* Another creak. From the rug beside the desk, his wolfish-looking black dog pricked his ears in the direction of the sound. Someone was definitely there. The door cracked open, and Mosby wagged his tail.

"Daddy . . ." Clad in seahorse-patterned pajamas, his seven-year-old daughter entered the library, clutching her spotted stuffed pony.

"Sarah, it's one in the morning. What are you doing up so late?"

Tears streaked her cheeks as she scurried over to the desk with red locks flying behind her. She climbed onto his lap and clung to him. Her cries intensified. "Daddy!"

"Sarah?" Wiping the tears from her face with his thumb, he hushed her and rocked her. "What's wrong?"

She stared up at him with blue saucer-like eyes and sniffled. "I thought you were gone."

It was the second time in a week, and the sixth time in a month that she had complained about the dream. Her description never varied. She kept seeing him lying in a pool of blood on the ground or floor, she wasn't certain which, choking to death. After a consultation with a psychologist, he had been reassured that his daughter's nightmare was caused by their recent loss of Mosby's sire, Saber. At seven, children were becoming aware of the finality of death, and Sarah had transferred her fear from the loss of a pet to a parent. But how could such a young mind envision graphic details of a lingering death, especially since Saber had died peacefully in his old age? Geoff would have expected more typical childhood fears of going to sleep and not waking up. "I'm fine, Sarah. There now—see, there's nothing to cry about."

Another sniffle. Calming slightly, she touched his face to reaffirm he was real. "Will you read me a story?"

"You pick one out, while I let Mosby outside."

Sarah scampered over to the bookcase, where the children's books were arranged on a lower shelf.

He strode to the door at the far corner of the library and held it open. "Mosby."

The dog raced across the room and out the door. He returned to Sarah, who was waiting with *The Black Stallion* under her arm, and resumed his seat. Unlike his son, Sarah was easy to calm. Neal was at that difficult teenage stage. At fifteen, he had his learner's permit, which he thought entitled him to special car privileges. Earlier in the evening, they had engaged in a stupid argument and exchanged heated words. He'd have a talk with Neal and apologize before the boy left for school in the morning.

Geoff drew Sarah onto his lap and began to read. After he had read several pages, the scent of honeysuckle drifted over him. He sucked in his breath. Unlike Saber, Mosby hadn't shown the capability of alerting him to an impending seizure, but then, he had gone nearly three years without one. The dog had only been a puppy at the time.

"Sarah, can you run and get your mom?"

She dashed for the door leading to the hall, but stopped short and screamed. His ex-wife stood in the doorway.

"Beth . . ."

But she kept staring at Sarah. Finally, she took one of Sarah's red curls between her fingers. "You're a lot like my little girl. George . . . I thought Georgianna was . . ." She glanced up at him. "You're not George." In her hand, she held a gun.

Not Sarah! Geoff hurtled across the room, shoving his daughter aside. Landing on the floorboards beside her, he heard a gunshot. Blood spattered over Sarah's pajamas. "Sarah!" Burning pain spread from his chest to his back. It wasn't Sarah's blood, but his own. *Her dream. She had foreseen his death.*

As his gaze met with Beth's violet eyes, she shouted, "Stay dead this time!" She vanished from the doorway.

Gasping for breath, he rose on an elbow and checked Sarah. Although paralyzed by fear, she seemed physically unharmed. His vision blurred. *Don't die in front of her. Not like Mom.* For a fleeting second, he was five. Glass shattered, and his mother's bloody head slumped over the steering wheel.

He felt the warmth of blood filling his shirt. Lightheaded, he struggled to remain conscious. "Sarah . . ." Losing the battle, he sank to the floor. A fog drifted over him, and he had no idea how long he lay there when panicky voices surrounded him. Gentle hands rolled him onto his back.

"Geoff!" His wife grasped his hand. "Please be all right."

"Chris? Sarah, is she . . . ?" he asked weakly.

"She's fine. Help is on the way."

In an attempt to slow the blood flow, his father applied direct pressure to the wound in his chest. Geoff gasped in agony. Unable to catch his breath, he tasted blood at the back of his throat. He reached out. "No . . ." Ignoring him, his father continued with his futile lifesaving efforts. Geoff clamped his fingers around his father's wrist. "Please . . . stop." Their gazes met, and the pressure lifted from his chest.

"Dammit, Geoff." Tears welled into the older man's eyes.

He had never seen his father cry before, and it seemed strange, even now. He coughed—more blood. Finally, another breath came.

Chris cradled him in her arms and whispered, "Hang in there, Geoff. Help will be here in a few minutes."

Her fingers stroked his hair, and she hugged him tighter. As he fought for another breath, his hand encircled hers. "I . . . love . . ." Unable to force another breath, he gulped back the blood. He choked and sputtered. His lungs were exploding. Suddenly, he felt incredibly light. He drifted. His mother waved at him. He had forgotten her gentle dimpled smile. Alongside her, Saber waited. Rejuvenated to his sleek, youthful form, the dog wagged his feathery tail and barked excitedly. Near a soft light stood a woman with black hair cascading the length of her back. *Margaret . . .* He now understood. His death had been a terrible error in judgment.

"Geoff! Geoff!"

He turned to Chris's voice, summoning him back to life.

"He's gone, Chris," said his father, weeping unashamedly.

"Noooo!" She dug her fingernails into her palm and moaned.

Geoff struggled to touch her cheek to let her know that he was all right, but his arm remained frozen at his side. He tried to speak. No words came out. She bent over him and began sobbing. Then he saw—a crimson patch covered his chest, and his own eyes stared up, sightless in death.

Granite spires and headstones covered the grounds of the family cemetery. A four-foot brick wall with an iron gate marked the perimeter of the old section. Cameron names surrounded Chris. Geoff's mother, Sarah, lay nearby. An empty plot remained beside her, where his father, Winston, would eventually rest. To keep unwelcome guests and the curious away, the funeral had been limited to family members—Winston; Geoff's sister, Judith, and her husband David; his uncle, T.J.; Chris's own parents; and Geoff's fifteen-year-old son, Neal, from his first marriage. What must the boy be feeling? His mother had been responsible for Geoff's death.

Chris had placed Saber's ashes in the casket alongside Geoff. Until the dog's death, the pair had been inseparable. A massive red-hued oak shaded the grave with ruddy fall leaves. The tree would keep them cool in the summer, and leafless branches would let the sun through to warm their faces during the winter. What was she thinking? Geoff and Saber were dead, not just sleeping, and she had joined the ranks of widowhood. So numb—when would she wake up?

"Chris . . ." Winston grasped her arm and led her to the waiting car. When she turned her back, the coffin would be lowered into the sandy ground of the land that Geoff had loved. A stable hand drove them the mile to Poplar Ridge. As they approached the three-story, red brick house with two adjoining two-story wings, she thought of her first trip to the estate nearly ten years before. After her car had a flat tire, Geoff had met her on the road to Poplar Ridge and helped her. Because of his casual attire of faded blue jeans, she thought he had been a stable hand himself.

The car reached the circular drive in front of the cascading steps and came to a halt. She barely noticed Winston escorting her to the drawing room and the tapestry sofa. She stared at the crackling flames in the fireplace. It was here that Geoff had sat beside her and told her about his epilepsy. They had both realized complications of the disorder could be life threatening, but she hadn't expected... *Not like this!*

"Chris, would you like me to look in on Sarah?"

Chris blinked and glanced up at Judith. Her friend's blue eyes were puffy and red as if she had been crying. "She hasn't said a word, since... since..."

"I know," Judith whispered, placing a tissue to her eyes.

All morning Chris's tears had remained at bay, but she felt them working their way to the surface. "Sarah had dreams this would happen. We kept reassuring her that things were all right. What do I tell her now? She keeps drawing pictures of Geoff."

Judith sat beside her. They hugged and cried. After a long while of holding each other, Judith said, "I'll go check on Sarah now."

Chris dried her tears and stood. "I'll look in on her. She needs her mother now, more than ever." Near the far wall, Mosby curled on the padded dog bed. "Come on, Mosby. Let's go see Sarah." The dog followed her with a lowered head and his tail down. Even the dog grieved. If it had been night, the brass sconces would have lit the west wing's wood-paneled hallway, like on the night that Geoff had died. The gunshot and running footsteps echoed in her mind. Beth had dropped the gun outside the library. Chris placed a hand on the knob.

Unable to go inside, she went up the stairs to Sarah's room. Outside her daughter's door, she heard a squeal of giggling laughter. "Sarah?" Although she couldn't make out the words, Sarah responded with lively chatter. Another giggle. Neal must have found some inner strength and managed to draw her out of her shell. Relieved for even that small measure of victory, Chris went inside.

Besides Sarah, the room was empty.

"Sarah, who were you talking to?"

Her daughter stared up at her with innocent-looking blue eyes. Their color and mischievous spark reminded her so much of Geoff that it made her ache. "No one," Sarah finally answered.

"Sarah . . ." On Sarah's table was another drawing. Until now, the artwork had been her daughter's only mode of communication. Expecting to see another graphic picture of Geoff lying in a pool of blood, Chris drew in a sharp breath. Geoff was depicted as sitting behind the desk with acorn carvings in the library and Sarah was on his lap. He was reading her a story. Beside the drawing lay an open copy of *The Black Stallion*, the book Geoff had been reading to Sarah on the night he had died. "Sarah, I told you not to go into the library."

"I didn't."

"Sarah . . ." No, the little girl had suffered enough. Chris decided not to scold her. "If you need anything, I'll be resting in my room."

"Okay, Mommy," she responded cheerfully.

Relieved that Sarah was talking again, Chris trudged to the room she had shared with Geoff. Upon his death, her first inclination had been to move to another bedroom, but she felt closer to him among the leather furniture and aged wood that still reflected his quiet masculinity. Not the interior decorating type herself, she had never added any feminine touches after they had married.

His jeans still remained folded in the drawers and his shirts hung in the wardrobe. It was almost as if he were away on a trip. Because of his seizure disorder, he rarely left Poplar Ridge. Even in death, he was a part of the estate. A family photograph rested on the dresser. It had been taken in late fall a couple of years before. The day had been much like this one. After a picnic in the meadow, Neal had watched Sarah, while she and Geoff had slipped off to the cottage. Her fingertips stroked the glass as if caressing his cheek. But Beth had shattered the dream. The fact that she had been caught and institutionalized failed to be of any comfort. With a scream, she hurled the picture across the room and heard the tinkle of breaking glass.

"Dammit, Geoff, how could you do this to me?"

Surrendering to her grief, Chris sank to the floor. Mosby curled next to her, and she hugged the dog closer, weeping into his thick, black fur.

"Chriiiis . . ."

Like a whisper in her ear, it was *his* voice. She clutched Mosby tighter and sobbed on the dog's shoulder.

Day and night jumbled. Chris reached to the opposite side of the bed, expecting to touch Geoff's finely muscled arm. But the empty spot was cold. Had it been two weeks since they had buried Geoff? Or four? Beside the bed, Mosby gave a gentle bark. Her eyes snapped open. Fully awake, she sat up with her heart racing. The early light of dawn filtered through the window, and she spotted a shadow looming at the end of the bed. "Who's there?"

Mosby whimpered a greeting in familiarity. *Someone I know.* The shadow approached her. "Who's there?" she repeated. Mosby's tail thumped rapidly in excitement. The apparition bent to her level, and she blinked. "Geoff?"

Like a misty veil, his blue eyes stared at her intently.

"Geoff, it really is you. I had an awful nightmare that you were dead. Please hold me." Without saying a word, he extended an arm. Longing to touch him, she reached for his hand. Their fingers nearly intertwined, when his image wavered—thinner and thinner—until it vanished. With an anguished howl, Chris pounded a fist into her pillow. She struck it again and again.

"Chris . . ."

Chris heard running footsteps, and Judith was beside her, taking her into her arms and brushing her tousled hair away from her face.

Tears fought their way to the surface. "I saw him," Chris insisted. "He was kneeling beside the bed, right where you are."

"Chris, it's only been a month. It takes time to come to terms with these things. You want to see him, so your mind conjured up an image. I know. Even though he was my crazy brother, I miss him too." Judith handed her a tissue.

Collected again, Chris dried her tears. "Mosby wagged his tail at him."

"Mosby got excited because you were," Judith corrected. "Geoff wasn't here."

Judith's words reminded Chris of similar conversations with Sarah. The psychologist had told her that Sarah's imaginary friend was a healthy outlet in accepting what had come to pass. She wondered if the same would be true for her. "I'm fine now, Judith."

Judith rubbed her on the back. "If you're not, I can delay my return home until later." For nearly a month, Judith had been away from her family in northern Virginia to be her constant nursemaid.

"Your family needs you. I can manage from here on out."

"Are you sure?"

No, but she certainly could give the illusion that she was coping. She had intruded on Judith's life long enough, and she was grateful to her friend for helping when she had been in such dire need. "Yes."

"If you insist."

"I do."

"Very well." Judith stood. "I'll see you at breakfast." After a few steps toward the door, she glanced over her shoulder with a worried frown.

"I'm fine, Judith."

Her friend nodded and closed the door behind her as she left.

Determined to get on with living, Chris went over to the wardrobe. First, she'd call the law firm and let them know that she'd be returning, then . . .

Geoff's shirts hung inside the wardrobe.

She swallowed. Maybe going back to work wasn't such a good idea yet. No, she could do it. Geoff wouldn't want her sitting around the house and moping forever.

Choosing a dark gray jacket with a matching calf-length skirt, Chris changed into business casual attire. She had lost weight. The jacket bagged, and the skirt's waist was enormous. She pinned the skirt. Over by the mirror, she brushed her hair. She dabbed on a little makeup to add some color to her cheeks before making her way down the stairs to the east wing. In the breakfast room, Judith had already arrived, and Winston stood as Chris entered. After she sat in a spindle-backed chair, he took his place at the head of the table.

"Judith tells me that you plan on returning to work." She gave a nod, and he cleared his throat. "Chris, I'll be seventy next spring. I'm much too old to resume taking on the responsibilities that go with running a working plantation again. I had hoped that you might consider taking over the farm business."

Give up her job as an attorney? "I don't think . . . ."

"Please don't dismiss the idea outright. Give it some thought. I realize that you're a woman who needs a career, but you know what it takes to keep the farm going. Neal is old enough to help with some of the physical labor, and, hopefully, he or Sarah will see fit to take over when they're capable."

What would Geoff want her to do? Very little had been more important to him than Poplar Ridge. No longer a city girl from Boston, she had grown to love the land as well. "I'll think about it," she promised.

"Good. Thank you."

Was it her imagination or had the wrinkles grown deeper in Winston's face over the past month? "I'll hold off returning to the firm until I've made my decision." As he nodded his appreciation, she caught a glimpse of his eyes growing moist. The African-American maid, Laura, entered the room carrying plates with eggs and toast and set them on the table. Suddenly no longer hungry, Chris shoved the plate away. She got to her feet. "I've decided to visit Beth today."

A plate slipped from Laura's hands and crashed to the floor. "Sorry," she said with a waver in her voice. "I'll clean it up right away."

Both Judith and Winston gaped in her direction. The elder Cameron stood, and his gray eyes met hers. "Is that wise? Even Neal doesn't wish to see her."

"I must. I need to know why."

"I doubt they'll let you in."

"They will," she insisted. "You forget that I'm an attorney. I have ways."

Concerned, Judith got to her feet. "Not illegal?"

"Of course not. But I'm certain they'll see things my way, when I explain it to them."

"I'll accompany you," Winston added.

"On my own," Chris stated firmly.

An hour later, after seeing Sarah and Neal off to school, Chris gave Judith a goodbye hug, telling her to drive carefully on her return trip home, then climbed into Geoff's classic '67 Mustang, taking Route 5 to Richmond. Scattered swamps dotted the countryside. As she got closer, high rises mushroomed. She turned off before reaching the tall buildings, and on the outskirts of the city, she halted at a hospital in a park-like setting. The facility sprawled over several hundred acres with red brick buildings surrounded by woods. Trees shaded sidewalks and buildings, making the grounds look more like a college campus than a psychiatric hospital.

Upon entering the clinic, she signed in at the registration desk with a request to see Elizabeth Carter. After leafing through out-of-date *Southern Living*s and *Reader's Digest*s for forty-five minutes, a nurse escorted her into an office. The portly, bald-headed man with glasses behind the desk stood to greet her with an outstretched arm. "Mrs. Cameron, I'm Dr. Daly. Please, have a seat."

Shaking his hand, Chris did as he instructed and sat in a chair across from the desk.

Reseating himself, he placed his hands over his rotund belly and leaned back in his maroon leather chair. "Your request to see my patient is highly irregular. May I ask why?"

"I don't intend on harming her if that's what you're asking, but I need to know what she was feeling . . . when . . . ." Her voice cracked. "When she shot my husband."

His jowls jiggled when he shook his head. "I can't allow it."

"Dr. Daly, for your information, I'm fully aware that Beth has no family besides her son, who's a minor. Even though she had been divorced from my husband for several years, he continued to pay for her medical care out of a sense of duty, not because of a court ruling. Two years ago, someone at this hospital decided that she was fully competent to reenter society. My husband is dead as a result of that error in judgment. I aim to find out who issued her release, and why the fact that she had regressed to the point of requiring hospitalization again was missed. In any case, because my husband believed that she was indeed better, he made no provisions in his will for her continued medical care. Their son will not come of legal age for two and a half years. I am his guardian. I am also in a position to continue Beth's medical treatment at this facility. In spite of what happened, I know my husband would have wanted it that way, but before I can consent to it, I must speak with Beth. The alternative is for her to become a ward of the state."

Dr. Daly fidgeted with a pen, then straightened in his chair. "I'm aware that you're an attorney. You've won your case, Mrs. Cameron. However, I must insist that I accompany you."

Relieved that she had won her first battle, Chris exhaled slowly. "That's acceptable."

He removed his glasses and rubbed his eyes. "But first . . . when my patient was released from this hospital two years ago, her schizophrenia *was* in remission. It is my professional opinion that she has suffered a relapse and was delusional when she shot your husband. I don't believe that she's aware of the events that have transpired, and I insist that you maintain a professional decorum as well as silence until I believe she is strong enough to accept the truth. If she divulges anything that would aid in her treatment, I will intervene."

"Of course."

"Very well, I'll make the arrangements."

"Thank you."

"If you'll return to the waiting area, I'll escort you to see Beth shortly."

Chris shook hands with the doctor once more, and upon returning to the waiting room, she flipped through *People* magazine. Her hands trembled. She hadn't seen Beth in seven years, since right before the woman had been committed to the hospital. *Schizophrenia?* At the time, Beth had been possessed by the ghost of Geoff's great-grandmother, Margaret. How many other people had similar experiences that were dismissed as mental illness?

Sympathy? Not quite. After what had happened to Geoff, she couldn't quite bring herself to forgive.

"Mrs. Cameron." A willowy nurse stood beside her, holding a manila folder. "Dr. Daly had a phone call and will join us. I'll escort you to the patient." The nurse led the way outside, across a grassy area, to another red-brick building. "This is where our longterm adult patients are housed."

As Chris stepped inside, she thought the polished floors and tiny rooms resembled a college dormitory. The nurse halted at a desk where another nurse was stationed and checked over a chart. Fifteen minutes passed before Dr. Daly joined them. He showed her to a door. "Let me tell Beth that you're here." He placed his security card in the lock and stepped inside.

With locks to keep the occupants inside, these rooms definitely weren't dormitories. Chris's heart pounded, and a minute passed before the doctor allowed her to enter. Beth's long black hair was tied in a ponytail, and she sat near a window covered with wire mesh on the outside. A blank stare remained on her face while she looked out the window and rocked in her chair. Suddenly sick to her stomach, Chris feared that her visit had been a dreadful mistake. But Geoff would have wanted her to discover the truth. Standing her ground, she persevered. "Beth . . ."

The rocking motion stopped, and Beth glanced over her shoulder. Her violet eyes lit up. "Chris? Come in and sit down. I haven't had any visitors since I've been here. How are Neal and Geoff?"

She doesn't remember. Chris sat in an empty chair, leaving only a small table between them. "Neal's fine, but Geoff . . ." A lump formed at the back of her throat, and Beth's eyebrows knitted together in concern. The doctor shook his head in warning. "He hasn't had any seizures."

Beth's brow relaxed. "And Sarah?"

"She's fine. Beth . . ." Her face. Chris couldn't rid herself of the image of Beth running down the hall away from the library leaving Geoff to die in a pool of blood. "Beth, does Margaret still talk to you?"

Beth paled, but her face held a child-like innocence. "Margaret? She hasn't spoken to me since . . . not since . . . years. I had a gun. But Geoff was all right. He came to visit me. I didn't mean to shoot him. He understands. Margaret thought he was the scout."

Convinced that Beth remembered nothing of the most recent shooting, Chris stood. "I must be leaving." Her throat tightened, but she managed to whisper to the doctor so Beth wouldn't overhear. "We'll continue to see to her care, but I wish to be informed if she recalls what happened."

"Yes, Mrs. Cameron."

Chris's mind was numb. She took a walk along the canal in downtown Richmond before returning to Poplar Ridge. By the time she arrived, most of the day had passed. In an attempt to avoid encountering anyone, she made a beeline for the stairs in the west wing. Each time she passed the library door, she shivered. Once upstairs, she heard a peal of laughter emanate from Sarah's room. Her daughter had made a habit of sealing herself inside after school. Imaginary friend or not, living in seclusion couldn't be healthy. Chris decided to invite her to go riding. Anything to draw her out. "Sarah," she said with a knock to her door.

Still dressed in the denim pinafore that she had worn to school, Sarah opened the door. "Mommy, you're home."

As Chris had guessed, Sarah's room was empty. She had secretly hoped that her daughter might have brought a school friend home to play. "Sarah, you've never told me what your friend's name is."

Sarah pursed her lips and shuffled her feet as if afraid to respond.

On Sarah's table, Chris found another drawing. Geoff was saddling Sarah's pony. Beside the drawing rested *The Black Stallion's Courage*. Each day the drawings varied, but the theme was constant—Geoff and Sarah. The books changed more slowly, but she could see a steady progression through the *Black Stallion* series. "Sarah?"

"Daddy," she responded softly. "I thought you might be angry if you knew that he was reading to me."

"Sarah . . ." With tears filling her eyes, Chris drew her daughter into her arms. "I know how much you want to see him. I do too, but he's not coming back."

"But he was here," Sarah insisted.

The tears spilled down Chris's cheeks. "No, Sarah. He died that night. He won't be home again."

Instead of crying, Sarah grew red-faced with anger. "Daddy was here! He explained it to me. He says death isn't the end, and you should know that because of Margaret!"

Margaret? How had Sarah known about Margaret? Unless . . . No, it was impossible. Geoff was dead. But after being dead for over seventy years, Margaret had possessed Beth. Could Sarah know something about Geoff? "What else did he say?"

"He tells me that I shouldn't be sad and reads me stories."

Like he had in life. "Does he read to you often?"

Sarah picked up the book from her table and went over to her bed, sitting on it cross-legged. "When I start to feel sad, I look at the pictures, then he starts reading."

"Do you mind if I wait to see if he visits with you now?" The little girl shrugged, and Chris waited while Sarah flipped through the pages of the book. Five minutes. Nothing. Ten. An hour. She was a silly fool for believing. Geoff *was* dead. No amount of pretending otherwise would bring him back. She'd call the psychologist later to see what she should do for Sarah. "I'll check on you later, Sarah. Let me know if Daddy visits again."

With Mosby trailing behind her, Chris went into the hall to her room and switched on a light. Except for the dog, she was alone. "Dammit Geoff, what in the hell am I supposed to do?" Funny, but she had almost expected an answer. And what would he say if he were here? Exactly what Sarah had said—not to be sad.

Chris stepped over to the dresser and looked in the mirror. Her appearance had become worn and haggard, and her cinnamon-colored hair had gone mousy looking. Then she noticed. On the finely polished wood of the dresser rested a crystal pendant on a gold chain. Her necklace, a family heirloom. Geoff had given it to her before they were married. She had buried it in her jewelry box and hadn't worn it since he had died. Laura must have mistakenly left it on the dresser when she was cleaning.

She held the chain up to the light. The crystal cast a rainbow onto the wall. She clutched the necklace to her body and curled on the bed. She lay unmoving until a scratching sound caught her attention. The clock on the nightstand read 10:02. More time had passed than she realized, but then most of her days seemed to pass without much notice. Mosby undoubtedly needed to relieve himself.

Dragging herself to her feet, she crossed the room and opened the door for the dog. Winston or Neal were likely still awake and could let him outside. Mosby occasionally spent the night in Neal's room anyway. As the dog trotted down the stairs, she felt guilty. She needed to make more time for Neal. The boy had essentially lost both of his parents with Geoff's death. Even if Beth eventually recovered, how could he ever forgive her?

Exhausted from the stressful day, Chris went into the adjoining bathroom and readied for bed. Would she ever get used to the loneliness? She placed the necklace on the counter and switched off the lights. Quietly returning to the bedroom, she slipped between the sheets. All of her tears must have been cried. Her pillow remained dry.

After tossing and turning for nearly an hour, she drifted. Half asleep, she felt the weight of someone on the edge of the bed beside her. Geoff's fingertips stroked along her cheek to her lips. She was dreaming. *So what? Don't spoil it. He's here with me—now.* His lips met hers. On the verge of waking, she kept her eyes clamped shut and floated through the layers.

The silky smoothness of her nightgown went over her head. Afraid that if she opened her eyes the dream would end, she settled against the mattress. His hands touched and caressed, gently exploring the length of her body. She murmured his name as he clutched her hips and drew her to him. She imagined his familiar weight atop her. Twisting a little to better receive him, she parted her legs in anticipation.

His fingers intertwined with hers as he slid inside her and settled into a rhythm. She luxuriated in his warmth as his kisses tingled her bare skin. Blood coursed throughout her body, and she felt an intense rush. He whispered in her ear, "Go back."

Go back? Chris opened her eyes, and the sensation of making love with Geoff faded. It *had* been a dream. An intensely real one— she was stark naked—but a dream, nonetheless. Overwhelmed by sadness, she gripped the crystal necklace in her hand. But she could have sworn that she had left it on the counter in the bathroom.

Chapter Two

THE FOLLOWING AFTERNOON, Chris decided the time had come to face the library. In the far west wing, she took a deep breath and opened the door. Bookcases full of hardcovers lined the walls. Behind the massive oaken desk with acorn carvings was where Geoff had often spent his evenings, tending to bookwork. She could almost imagine him sitting in the black leather chair, tapping away on the computer keyboard.

Finally, she gathered her courage to look at the floor. Dark blotches stained the wood. She sank to the floor and ran her fingers across the mottling where Geoff had taken his final breath. Well into the morning, Lieutenant Jim Franks had asked questions, while his team took pictures of the body. He wasn't a body, but a living, breathing . . . The police hadn't meant for her to see the body bag.

"Laura!" When the maid failed to respond, she shouted again.

Out of breath, the pint-sized maid rushed into the library. "Yes, Chris."

Chris stood and pointed to the floor. "Why hasn't this been cleaned?"

After another gulping breath, Laura answered, "The wood needs to be stripped and re-varnished, or completely replaced."

"Why hasn't the job been done?"

"I've been waiting for you or Mr. Cameron to authorize payment."

"No one brought it to my attention. Bring me the paperwork. In the meantime, I'll thank you to place a rug over it. Geoff died here, and I'll not have the area treated like some sort of curiosity."

"I'll see to it right away." Laura ran from the library in tears.

"Chris . . ."

Staring at the bloodstained floor again, she hadn't heard Winston enter. "I'll not tolerate sloppy work."

"Under the circumstances, she's doing the best she can. We all are."

"But Geoff . . ." She swayed on her feet.

"I know." He gripped her arm to help steady her. "Parents aren't supposed to outlive their children."

His statement made her realize just how much he hurt, and she hugged him close. Then she kissed him on the cheek. "I've decided that I'll work part-time here, and part-time for the firm."

"Splendid!" A wide grin crossed Winston's face. "That way, Neal and Sarah's heritage will be preserved for them."

"Geoff would have wanted it this way." And he wouldn't have wanted her to give up her career. Compromise had been her only solution.

"Chris," Winston said in a low, but even voice, "the reason I came in here was to let you know the school called." He handed her a slip of paper to call Sarah's teacher.

Chris sighed. She might as well get the call over with and picked up the receiver. As she dialed, Winston exited the library. "Mrs. Sims, this is Chris Cameron."

"Mrs. Cameron, I realize this has been a very difficult time for you and your family, but Sarah . . ."

"Please, go ahead."

"I'm very worried about Sarah. She used to make friends easily. It's only natural for her to be sad after losing her father, especially the way . . . But she's scaring the other students with ghost stories. She says that her father still reads to her and spends time with her."

"Because of what she's experienced, I have a psychologist working with her, but I'll let her know that she's upsetting the other kids. Hopefully, that will help." The teacher hung up with an apology and a thank you. *When would the nightmare end?* Chris took a deep breath and plodded up the stairs to Sarah's room. More laughter emanated from behind the door. "Sarah?" Chris knocked on the door and went inside. As usual, the room was empty, except for her daughter. The marker in the book on Sarah's table now held a place in a different chapter from the day before. "Sarah, I just spoke with Mrs. Sims. She says you're scaring the other kids in class with your stories about your dad."

"But I'm telling the truth. You always told me to tell the truth."

"I know." Chris drew Sarah over to the bed and sat beside her. "If your dad really is coming to see you, why hasn't he shown himself to Neal or me?"

Sarah looked pensive a moment before responding, "He says that I'm easier."

The psychologist had warned Chris that her daughter was likely blocking the memory of how Geoff had died from her mind. "Why do you suppose that would be? More than anything, I want to see him too."

Sarah shrugged. "He said that he thought he made it through to you a couple of times. He was sure you'd remember last night."

Last night? How could Sarah have known, unless Geoff had said something to her. No, just fanciful daydreaming. But what if? "What did he say about last night?"

"Nothin', other than he thought you'd remember."

Of course, he would have been tactful in front of Sarah. "Did he say anything else?"

"That you must go back."

The same words Chris thought she had imagined. "Go back? What did he mean?"

Sarah shook her head that she didn't know.

"Sarah, if you see him again, will you ask him what he meant?" She nodded. "Also, no more telling the kids at school. We can't make them believe, and you're scaring them. Understood?" Another nod. "I'll see you at dinner, then. Please come down. You can't keep hiding in your room." As Chris retreated from her daughter's room, she pondered the possibilities. Geoff really was communicating to Sarah. And last night . . . she had made love to him. How could she find a way to openly speak with him?

Chris went into the bathroom and turned on the ivory handles to the claw-footed bathtub. After lacing the water with perfume-scented bath oil, she undressed and stepped into the tub, leaning against the cool porcelain. Soaking up the warmth from the water, she closed her eyes. The words "go back" kept running through her mind. What could Geoff have meant? Go back to his grave. Not wishing to be reminded by the finality of his absence, she hadn't visited the site since his burial. She vowed to do so in the morning.

Quickly finishing her bath, she dried her body and dressed. Her necklace rested on the counter. This time, she was certain she had returned it to her jewelry box. "Geoff . . ." He wanted her to wear it. She fumbled with the clasp but managed to put the gold chain about her throat. "Is that what you wanted?" No answer. If she waited, maybe he'd communicate with her. Five minutes passed. Ten. Like the time in Sarah's room, nothing happened.

Disappointed, Chris joined the family for dinner. It was the first time in over a month that the entire family had been present, and they ate the meal in uncomfortable silence. Neal kept glancing to Geoff's empty chair. She'd make a point to speak with the boy after supper. As the meal concluded, Laura brought her a phone. Chris excused herself and went into the hall before answering it.

"Mrs. Cameron, Dr. Daly here."

"I told you that we'll continue to pay Beth's medical bills."

"Yes, of course. Thank you, but that's not why I'm calling. Ever since your visit, my patient has become extremely agitated. She won't speak to me about what's troubling her."

"I was very careful about what I said," she reminded him.

"I'm aware of that, but I was hoping that you could return tomorrow. I think she may remember what happened."

Beth remembered? The phone nearly slipped from her fingers as Chris's heart skipped a beat. "I'll be there." After making the arrangements, she switched off the receiver. When she turned, Neal stood behind her with Mosby at his side. The boy's blond hair and blue eyes reminded her so much of Geoff's that it made her want to cry. "How much of that did you hear?" she asked.

His brow wrinkled in anger. "Why are you going to see *her?*"

In the past year, his voice had deepened, and he sounded very much like Geoff as well. "She's the only one who can provide us with a reason for what happened. The doctor thinks she has finally remembered. I'm hoping to find some answers. I don't know whether I can ever forgive her, but I want to know *why.*"

His brow relaxed somewhat, but he made no comment.

"Neal, I've been meaning to speak with you. I know you're angry and frustrated, but over the years, I've come to think of you as my son. I love you. We're going to get through this somehow—together."

He fought bravely, but his eyes filled with tears. "It's not fair."

"No, it's not," she agreed. She wanted to take him into her arms, but he was at that tall, gawky teenage stage, where even under the difficult circumstances, the gesture wouldn't have been appreciated.

"The last thing I said to him wasn't very complimentary."

So that was partly what bothered him. "We all say things that we wish we hadn't. Believe it or not, parents were young once. You need to forgive yourself. Your dad understood." She was uncertain whether her words helped. He breathed out slowly. "Neal, would you like to go riding with me tomorrow after school?"

"I can't." He bolted up the stairs with Mosby following him.

Spotting the tears streaking his face, Chris placed her hand on the walnut banister to go after him, then thought better of it. Riding had been the one pastime for which Neal hadn't felt too "grown up" to accompany Geoff. Only time would help him. Time was the only thing that would help any of them, and she was so weary of always having to be the strong figurehead.

On her way to her room, she checked on Sarah. As usual, her daughter sat alone at her table, carefully working on a drawing. The bookmark had moved to the next chapter, and the picture on the sketchpad . . . Geoff was holding *her* hand, not Sarah's. "Did you ask Daddy what he meant by 'go back?' "

Sarah colored Chris's dress a rusty-looking brown. The crystal necklace adorned her neck. "He said something about George." She glanced up. "Mommy, who's George?"

"Your great-, several times removed, grandfather. He lived during the time of the Civil War, and he looked very much like your dad."

Sarah giggled. "Daddy calls it the War between the States."

Or War of Northern Aggression, but Chris didn't repeat that phrase to Sarah.

"There." Sarah held up her drawing for Chris to see.

She had been mistaken. She wasn't holding Geoff's hand. Instead, he wore a long frock coat and hat from the 1800s. *George.* She was holding George's hand. *Go back.* But how? None of it made sense. She tucked Sarah in bed with a good-night kiss, then headed to her room.

"Geoff, I believe. I now know that you've been here talking to Sarah and me." She could almost hear his laughter. Talking? They had done very little talking the previous evening. "Please come see me again. I miss you."

Only the quiet stillness of the room surrounded her. Exhausted, she needed to get some sleep to face the graveyard and another visit with Beth. She had hoped to never see the woman again, but if it gave her some answers . . . She went into the bathroom to ready for bed. About to remove her necklace, Chris thought better of it. Geoff had been insistent that she wear it. *For what reason?*

A brown-tinted prescription bottle sat on the counter, exactly where Geoff had left it. He no longer needed anticonvulsants. She flushed the pills down the toilet. At least he'd never suffer another seizure. She quickly slipped on her nightgown and returned to the bedroom. Beneath the sheets, she waited—and waited.

When morning dawned, Chris hadn't remembered drifting off to sleep. To her disappointment, Geoff had made no repeat visit. She opened the drapes to a brilliant late-fall day. The poplars had shed their leaves, but the sky was a vibrant blue. She longed for a cold, drizzly rain to match her mood. Breathing deeply, she dressed in a burgundy calf-length skirt and matching jacket.

After breakfast, she sent the kids off to school, then drove to the graveyard. The wind was stronger on the flat ground near the graves than on the ridge close to the house. Chris bundled her coat around her and walked across the dry, brown grass. Dead leaves clung to the tree near Geoff's grave. Tears entered her eyes as she approached the headstone marked with his name.

Geoffrey Lee Cameron
April 13, 1974–October 15, 2013

She had read that it usually took a body up to a year to completely decompose. *Morbid.* She thought of the time that she and Judith had found a skeleton from the Civil War in the cellar. Drying her tears, Chris continued on until coming to the four-foot brick wall that marked the perimeter of the old section of the cemetery.

The iron groaned on its hinges as she opened the gate. She went through and studied the tombstones. George's parents, his brother and sister. Georgianna—*George and Margaret's daughter.* The daughter that Margaret had thought was the consequence of a sexual assault from a Union scout. The same scout who had wound up as a skeleton in the cellar. Geoff had made certain that Georgianna got a proper marker because, in another lifetime, he had been George.

Chris arrived beside George and Margaret's graves. Suffering from posttraumatic stress, Margaret had mistaken George for the scout and killed him.

Go back.

Geoff had said that *she* had been George's lover, Catherine. *How was it possible?*

She checked her watch and took a deep breath. The time had come to face Beth.

As on the previous day, the same willowy nurse greeted Chris before Dr. Daly escorted her to Beth's room.

"She won't speak to us," the doctor said, placing his security card in the lock. "In fact, she won't let anyone near her. If your visit doesn't help, then it may become necessary to sedate her."

She followed Dr. Daly into the room. Beth sat beside the window, rocking in her chair. Her hair was again tied back in a ponytail. Unlike the day before, loose strands flew in disarray, and her face was very pale. Chris's stomach churned, but she moved forward. "Beth . . ."

The rocking motion halted, but Beth continued to stare out the window.

"Beth, you wanted to see me."

Beth burst into tears.

"Beth, please don't..." Fighting her own tears, Chris handed Beth a tissue.

"Chris..." Beth dried her tears, only for more to fill her eyes. "He came to visit me soon after you left."

"Geoff?"

"Yes, he... he told me what happened." Tears spilled down her cheeks. "Why didn't you tell me that he was dead?"

Chris glanced over at the doctor standing near the door, then returned her attention to Beth. "They thought it best that I didn't say anything."

"But I... I..." Her hands flew to her mouth.

"Beth..." Chris grasped her arm, and gently pulled it away from her mouth. "Tell me what he said."

Dabbing the tissue to her red-rimmed eyes, Beth sniffled. "He says that he doesn't blame me. He knows that I've been ill since Margaret..."

The words certainly sounded like Geoff. He wouldn't have blamed Beth. "Was Margaret..." She didn't want to say "possessing" in front of Dr. Daly. "...in control of you?"

"No, it was me." Her hands went to her head as if she suffered from a severe headache. "But I still can't get her voice out of my head, and then I see the scout. Chris, I would never intentionally hurt him. You must believe that. I loved him."

"I believe you." Chris suddenly felt sorry for Beth. *Compassion?* Beth couldn't help what had happened to her, anymore than Margaret had. She was likely suffering from posttraumatic stress as a result of Margaret's possession, not schizophrenia. No wonder treatment hadn't helped. The doctors had been drugging her for a disorder that she didn't have. "Did Geoff say anything else?"

"Mrs. Cameron," the doctor said, stepping forward, "this line of questioning is not what I intended."

"Please, it's important."

The doctor backed off, but continued scrutinizing her.

"Beth?" Chris asked.

Beth placed the tissue to her eyes and dabbed one more time. "He said there's only one way to change what's happened."

"Change?" Chris's heart picked up tempo and raced. "Geoff's dead. How can we change that fact?"

"I'm not certain I understand myself." Beth gulped back a breath. "Chris, I don't expect any favors for me, not after what I've done, but if there's a way to help Geoff . . ."

Losing patience, Chris raised her voice. "What did he say?"

"Mrs. Cameron." Dr. Daly buzzed for orderlies and stepped between them. "This questioning is out of line. I must insist that you leave."

"No!" Beth howled, digging her fingernails into the palm of her hand until she drew blood.

"Beth . . ." Chris heard charging footsteps behind her, but the doctor held her at arm's length, keeping her separated from Beth. "What did he say?"

"Go back. The necklace . . ."

Rough hands seized Chris's arms, drawing her from the room. Another orderly grabbed Beth.

Chris shook an arm free from the man's grip. "Let go of me, you bastard. I'm going."

The orderly loosened his hold.

Outside the door, Chris leaned against the wall and sagged. *Go back.* Everything pointed to her venturing to George's time, but Beth had given her an additional clue. The necklace. What could it all mean? Change what had happened by going back to George's time. "How, Geoff?" she whispered.

Collecting herself, Chris breathed out slowly and returned to the Mustang. Replaying her visit with Beth through her mind, she drove the twisty, winding road to Poplar Ridge. About a mile from the house, the path narrowed to a gravel lane. In a field, black Angus grazed. She reached the zigzag fence on the ridge, when a sleek black shape darted across the road in front of her. Swerving to miss the dog, she hit the brake too late, colliding with a brick pillar at the entrance. The crystal in her necklace glowed.

Thankfully, she had been going slow, but her arm hurt. *Ugh.* She was going to strangle Mosby. What had he been doing running this far from the house anyway? For a brief instant, she thought she saw three buildings where one sweeping mansion once stood. Chris blinked. The gleaming light had been her imagination. She struggled with the door, but it failed to budge. A blond-haired man with blue eyes stood on the other side. "Geoff?"

With little effort, he opened the door and helped her from the car. His hand felt light and cold. Broken glass from the windshield lay scattered on the ground.

"I must be dead if you're here."

"You're not, but you're in a place where we can meet." His voice was as airy as his touch.

"It really is you." She threw her arms around his neck and kissed him on the lips. Stunned by their iciness, she drew away slightly.

"Chris, there's not much time." He took her hand, and they were suddenly standing on the lawn of Poplar Ridge. Rows of boxwoods led the way to the river. The grass was green, not winter brown, and the magnolias had brilliant white flowers. Rejuvenated to his youthful physique, Saber sprinted ahead of them. "I haven't been very successful in reaching you."

"Occasionally, you were. Geoff, there's so much I want to tell you. I've been so lonely, but Sarah . . ."

He placed his fingers to her lips. "Not yet."

They strolled closer to the mist-covered river. Waves lapped against the bank, and Chris felt an invigorating breeze against her cheeks. A gleam appeared in Geoff's eyes. Even death couldn't separate him from the land he loved. She breathed in the river air. "Why have you brought me here?"

"To explain." A smile tugged across his mouth. Unable to resist, he kissed her.

The warmth of his presence overshadowed the cold of his lips, and she eagerly reciprocated.

"Chris, I'm sorry for bringing you here in this manner, but I needed to make my message clear. Sarah's mind is too immature to explain what I've been trying to say, and Beth . . . well, she's too confused."

Saber had been the dog running across the road, causing the accident, not Mosby. "You keep saying, 'Go back.' I've figured out that you mean to George's time, but how? And even if I can find my way, how can I prevent what's happened?"

He held up a hand that she was asking too many questions at once, then he briefly touched the crystal pendant around her throat. "I remember everything—not like before in bits and pieces—but both lifetimes. You brought this with you."

"To George's time?"

He nodded.

She clutched the necklace. "You said it was handed down through the generations."

"But Margaret took it from you. If you keep it in your possession, you'll stay safe."

"What about you? Beth said if I go back I might be able to help you."

A thoughtful expression came to his face. "Beth sees what she wishes."

Suddenly confused, Chris asked, "Why would I go back if I can't help you?"

"I meant that I'm uncertain if you can change time. I only know you were a part of both time periods, and I loved you in each. That's meant to be, and you must go back for it to happen. You almost made it this time." He glanced at the windswept island in the middle of the river, and profound sadness crossed his features. "It's time. I'll wait for you. Use the crystal . . ." His arm stretched toward her.

As Chris reached to take his hand, his words were lost to the breeze. Their fingertips nearly touched, and his hand became a misty veil. An electrifying current shot through her when their hands intertwined. *Forever—Christine Catherine.* His lips hadn't moved, but it had been his voice.

"Forever," she whispered, then he vanished. She let out a tormented cry and kicked the car door. "Not again!"

"Chris . . ." Winston struggled with the door, but muscled it open. "Are you all right? I've called for help."

She glanced around, and a moment passed before she regained her bearings. She was back in the Mustang. "I saw Geoff. He was here."

"I think you may have hit your head." He dabbed a silk handkerchief to her forehead.

"I didn't hit my head! I'm telling you—Geoff was here."

Winston's brow wrinkled in anguish. "More than anything, I want to see him too, but he's been gone for over a month."

"Winston, you know as well as I do that people don't just disappear when they die. In the past, you admitted to seeing the one-eyed ghost, and Sarah's piano music continued long after she died. Geoff's still here with us."

His face etched in sorrow. "I'd like to believe that, but it's too much to hope for. Now, let's see if you're all right. It's probably best if you see a doctor." He helped her from the car.

Wobbly on her feet, she swayed when she took a step. Winston caught her arm to help steady her. She jerked her arm free of his grip. "I'm not seeing any damned doctor. I'm fine."

"At least let me help you to my car."

To this she agreed, and she took his hand.

"Chris, what happened?"

Seated on the passenger side of Winston's car, she was struck numb. Seeing Geoff again had filled her with such happiness, and now she felt as if she had lost him a second time. "Saber ran across the road."

"Saber?" Winston said, arching a brow.

"Did you really think he'd leave Geoff's side? I buried them together for a reason."

"Indeed." Winston's eyes grew moist and his voice, weak.

In the distance, Chris heard sirens. On the night Geoff died, sirens had been everywhere. Police had combed the grounds searching for Beth, and rescue workers had taken his body away.

"Mrs. Cameron . . ." The freckle-faced emergency technician removed a blood pressure cuff from her upper arm. "Your vitals read normal, but I think we should transport you to the hospital as a precautionary measure."

Chris blinked. She hadn't recalled getting into the emergency vehicle. "I'm not going to any hospital," she insisted.

"I'll see that she gets home," came another voice.

She blinked again. When had Winston joined them?

"Very well," replied the EMT.

In a daze, she felt someone take her arm and help her to a car. Winston climbed in behind the wheel and drove along the lane lined with poplar trees. They traveled a mile before the white columns of the brick mansion came into view. Winston parked the car, then aided her to her room in the west wing. "I'll have Laura check on you a little later. The children will be home from school soon. I had better pick them up at the gate, in case the car hasn't been moved by then."

Chris sat on the edge of the bed and kicked off her shoes. Mosby trotted in through the open door. "The Mustang was totaled, wasn't it?"

Winston hesitated before answering, "Yes."

Her hand curled to a fist. "Geoff's going to be pissed."

"Chris?"

"I'll be all right, Winston." She heard the door close when he left the room. Without bothering to change, she sank to the bed. She had no idea how long she lay there, staring at the ceiling, before the sound of small footsteps pattered in the hall and into her room.

Sarah shrieked, "Mommy, he's gone!"

Chris sat up. "Gone? Sarah, what do you mean?" She pulled Sarah to her as her daughter clambered onto the bed. Sarah's grip tightened, and she started to cry. Chris pushed straying, reddish curls away from her face. "Who's gone, Sarah?"

"Daddy," Sarah whimpered. "He promised to finish *The Black Stallion's Courage* when I got home from school today." She broke into inconsolable tears.

Oh, Geoff. Her own tears mingled with Sarah's. Chris hugged her tighter. With her daughter's words she realized what his visit must have cost him. And he had failed to reveal how she could travel back to George's time. *Stop.* She'd find a way, and the crystal necklace was the key.

A week passed. Chris had postponed her return to the firm on account of Sarah. Her daughter worried her, and she checked on her frequently. "Sarah . . ." As usual, Chris found her alone in her room, drawing. *The Black Stallion's Courage* lay on the table with the book marker on the final chapter. Without acknowledging her entrance,

Sarah continued sketching. The girl hadn't uttered a word since telling her that Geoff was gone.

Chris peered over Sarah's shoulder at the drawing. Yet again, it was a picture of Geoff lying in a pool of blood while Sarah watched him die. The psychologist's response had been a referral to a shrink, who immediately wanted to place the seven-year-old on antidepressants. Unwilling to allow the medical community to drug her daughter like they had Beth, she resisted the recommendation and had placed her on a holistic remedy on the advice of a friend at the firm. Feeling that she was running out of options, Chris hoped that a change for the better developed soon. She sat on one of the tiny blue chairs at Sarah's table. "Sarah, please say something. I know you miss Daddy. I do too, but we have to find a way to go on. Remember, he wouldn't want us to be sad."

With tears filling her eyes, Sarah looked up from her drawing. Hoping that her daughter might speak, Chris held her breath, but Sarah silently returned to her sketch. It was a start though, and Chris felt a glimmer of hope.

"Chris . . ."

She glanced around at Laura, who stood in the doorway.

"If you'd like to get some rest, I'll stay with Sarah for a while."

What would she have done without Laura's help? The maid reminded her when she should sleep and eat, although she wasn't succeeding at much of either. Chris stood. "Thank you, Laura."

Laura shooed her from the room, and Chris headed to her own bedroom. Without changing, she lay down. She was no closer to finding out what Geoff had meant than she was a week ago. Mosby jumped on the bed and curled beside her. She hugged him next to her. "What am I going to do, Mosby?"

"Chriiisss . . ."

The fur on Mosby's back ruffled, then he wiggled his tail in recognition. Chris sat up. "Geoff? Where are you? We thought you were gone. Sarah's sick. She needs you."

Another whisper emanated from the opposite end of the room. "Cottage."

"You want me to go to the cottage?" No response. Convinced that's what he meant, she changed into a T-shirt and a faded pair of jeans. After tugging on her riding boots, she went downstairs and out to the stable. Arches faced the stone courtyard. The red brick building had a cupola topped by an elaborate trotting horse weather vane.

Inside the barn, she quickly saddled Traveller, the gelding that Geoff had always ridden. She slipped on a helmet, then led the gray to the courtyard and mounted. Hooves clattered against the stone surface as she reined the gelding in the direction of a grove of oak and sycamore trees. Dead fall leaves carpeted the path leading to the meadow. In the clearing, waist-high brown grasses waved in the breeze. It had been early fall the first time Geoff had brought her to the cottage, and the grass had still been green.

She reached the grove when Traveller pricked his ears forward and tossed his head. Up ahead came the sound of drumming hooves. Without warning, the gray lurched sideways, hurling her from the saddle. She slammed to the ground and hooves sailed over her. Pain shot through her head. The crystal in her necklace glowed softly.

Left in the wake of the gelding's dust, Chris struggled to her feet. Slightly dizzy, she removed the helmet. A huge crack ran the length of it. Odd, but her necklace radiated. Her first inclination was to return to the stable. No, Geoff had told her to go to the cottage. Dropping the helmet to the ground, she continued on until arriving at an animal path through the forest. Even now, she could imagine the glistening leaves, Geoff beside her, and Saber snuffling ahead. The path narrowed until opening to a clearing. The rustic log cottage stood nestled among oaks. Lightheaded, but determined to make it to the cottage, she stumbled forward. The wooden steps were almost within her reach, when her knees wobbled.

She removed her necklace. Like the times when she held it up to sunlight, a prism reflected. On a dull, gray day, what could be causing the effect? As she got closer to the cottage, the rainbow of colors shimmered. The dancing light formed a passageway.

"Chris . . ." A silhouette stood in the middle of the light, waving her toward him.

"Geoff?"

She took a hesitant step in that direction. When she entered the passage, she felt cramped and unrestricted at the same time. Was she floating or walking? Time had no meaning. After several feet, the light grew more intense. She reached a branch in the passageway. On the path to the right, she spotted Geoff and Saber.

His voice whispered as if it drifted on the wind. "Not this way."

"But Geoff . . ."

"Go back."

Now, she remembered. Choosing the branch to her left, Chris followed the light. Her head throbbed. She halted a moment and rubbed her forehead. Continuing forward, she took another step. On and on, until she came to another branch and another. Lost in a maze of light, she groped through the passageways. "Geoff, I think I may have taken a wrong turn."

Go back. His words were in her head. She proceeded along. At each branch, she silently asked Geoff which direction she should take. He answered in her mind. Finally, the light became less intense.

Up ahead, Chris saw the cottage. *Dammit.* She had been doing nothing more than traveling in circles. The light became a flicker, until vanishing completely. The crystal pendant was also gone.

Frantic, she decided to turn back and search for the necklace. Geoff had warned her to keep it with her. Her skin prickled with a tingly pins-and-needles feeling, and her vision blurred. She whispered Geoff's name and sank to the ground with blackness engulfing her.

Chapter Three

W HEN CHRIS REGAINED CONSCIOUSNESS, she lay on the ground for what seemed an eternity. She should get up and search for the necklace. Her head pounded so much that she didn't really care. *Get up!* Her body refused to obey. A few minutes later, she managed to sit. She swayed. Her vision blurred, and she sank back to the ground. *That went well.* Hoping the dizziness would pass before trying again, she closed her eyes.

Her mind fogged, and a rugged hand supported her neck to help her drink. Water trickled down her throat. It slipped down the wrong way, and she gagged.

"Take it easy," came a gentle baritone voice. "Try again."

She sipped slowly, until her thirst was quenched. Strong arms were helping her, lifting her, and carrying her. "Geoff?"

He hushed her. "Save your strength."

With her arm around his neck, Chris relaxed her face against his chest. He smelled of leather and wood smoke. She dreamed of Geoff and smiled. He helped her on a black horse, then mounted behind her, keeping an arm protectively around her so she wouldn't slip from the saddle. He reined the horse in the direction of the meadow. Like a silent film, frames flickered before her eyes.

Instead of a forest of oak and sycamore, most of the trees had been chopped to ragged stumps. One small dogwood bloomed with brilliant white flowers. *Spring?* But it was October. The stable had crumbling bricks, and the house . . . Three buildings stood in place of one sweeping mansion. Shutters were falling off or missing. Bricks tumbled from the chimneys, and the columns were smaller, making the house appear less grand. The wings had been added in the 1920s. *1920s?*

The circular drive was dirt, not paved. Remnants of a veranda surrounding the main house fell to ruins. The section over the entrance had been restored. The man halted the stallion near the steps and helped her from the saddle. After dismounting, he tied the horse to a wooden rail.

Inside, the entry hall was barren of furniture—no hand-painted vase, Persian rug, nor oil portraits lining the walls. The walnut staircase winding to the second floor lacked polish and bore a dull stain. His strong arms were around her again, carrying her to a room on the second floor. As he lowered her to a scratchy mattress, she caught a glimpse of his blue eyes and blond hair. He *was* Geoff. She whispered his name and drifted.

When Chris woke, she was flat on her back, dressed in a plain white cotton gown. Her vision cleared somewhat, and she found herself staring into his eyes. "Geoff?" She reached out and stroked his upturned moustache to make certain he really was there. Odd—normally he had a goatee. "Geoff, I had a horrible nightmare that you had died."

"Sorry, ma'am. I don't know any Geoff."

Ma'am? Geoff hadn't called her ma'am since they had first met. "Geoff, I know you like to kid around, but I'm not finding your little joke funny. I had a dream that you had died."

Another face joined his—a woman's—and her complexion was the color of cafe au lait. Her skin tone was darker than Laura's, and she appeared to be in her late twenties. "She be delirious, Mr. George."

"George?" Chris uttered. He looked like Geoff, except he was missing the little laugh lines that had begun to develop near his eyes. "You can't be George."

"George Cameron, ma'am, and this is Tessa," he said, introducing the woman standing beside him. "I'm afraid you've hit your head and likely have a concussion. You must have fallen from your horse."

"Yes, I fell . . ." She reached up and felt a bandage winding around her head. "George?"

"Cameron, ma'am," he repeated. "The doctor's been here and seen to your injuries. He thinks with a few days rest, you'll be feeling better. Were you traveling alone, or should I be out looking for Geoff?"

Her heart thumped. He looked so much like Geoff that he could almost pass as a twin. He was thinner than Geoff—no doubt due to his war experiences—and close to ten years younger. He *was* Geoff—in a previous lifetime. "I was alone. Geoff was my husband, but he died . . ." She caught herself. " . . . in the war."

George's face wrinkled—almost in pain. "Too many died in the war. Did your husband serve the Union?"

Union? Geoff? In spite of living in Virginia for eight years, her accent must have caused the question. "No, he was a Virginian."

"And your name?" he inquired.

Name? She couldn't come right out and admit that she was a Cameron. Legend stated that George had fallen in love with *her* as Catherine. Why would she have chosen to use her middle name? "Cath . . ." Could time be changed? "Christine Olson."

"Mrs. Olson." He grasped her hand. "Pleased to meet you, although I wish it had been under more favorable circumstances."

George Cameron—she still had difficulty believing that he stood before her. "Likewise," she replied. He let go of her hand, and she lifted it to her throat. "My necklace—I lost my necklace."

"When you're back on your feet, you can show me the area where you lost it, and we'll search for it together."

"Thank you, Ge . . . Mr. Cameron."

He smiled. "If you need anything, feel free to ask Tessa."

George turned to leave, but he lingered a minute longer. His gaze locked onto hers, and she yearned for Geoff. If history played out, she and George would become lovers. She must find a way to change time, so that neither George nor Geoff would die an untimely death. Her heart pounded. What month was it? George had died in May of 1867 because Margaret had mistaken him for the Union scout.

"I'll leave you in Tessa's capable hands," he finally said, breaking the spell.

Chris thanked him again, and as he left the room, she noticed a distinct limp in his right leg. "Tessa, I'd like to thank you too." She tugged on the nightdress. "I'm sure this is your doing."

"It is." Tessa plumped a feather pillow, then placed it behind Chris's head. "You meet Mr. George afore?"

"No," Chris replied, aware that her voice wavered. "Why do you ask?"

"Just da way you look at each other."

Chris had to be extra cautious around Tessa. She had no doubt the servant's loyalties lay with Margaret. Oh God, she had yet to meet Margaret, and she had to find a way of remaining cool headed when she did.

"Mrs. Olson . . ."

"Please, call me Chris."

"Miss Chris . . ." Tessa held up Chris's jeans and T-shirt. "Where did you get dese clothes? You musta bin desperate to have bin wearin' men's trousers."

With a laugh, Chris tugged at the T-shirt. Of course, she would have looked out of place when she had first arrived. Women didn't wear pants during the mid-1800s. "I took them because I had nothing else to wear."

"I ain't got much, but I gets you one of my dresses."

"Thank you, Tessa."

"Oh, Miss Chris . . ." Tessa bundled up Chris's clothes, and as she picked up the bra, she examined it. "What is dis? I ain't never seen nothin' like it afore."

"It's a brassiere—a modified corset."

This answer seemed to satisfy Tessa, but the servant shook her head in confusion. "Now dat you awake, I get you somethin' to eat."

Chris laid back as Tessa left the room. The mattress was little more than a bed of lumpy straw, covered with a tattered sheet. With her head hammering away and hurting like hell, she had a difficult time finding a comfortable position. Adding to her discomfort, the room was cold in spite of a fire in the fireplace. A piece of straw poked her in the ribs. She turned flat on her back. Straw dug into her spine.

She lifted the sheet and tried pounding the straw back into the burlap covering. Giving up, she returned the sheet to its original spot. Judging by the position of the windows and dim light penetrating the room, she guessed that it was Judith's old bedroom. It wasn't Judith's room, she reminded herself. It wouldn't be her friend's room for many years to come. The floor was bare wood, and the room contained no antique furniture nor canopied bed. Wallpaper peeled from the walls, and there was no door at the opposite end, leading to a bathroom or the west wing.

Bathroom? With a need to relieve herself, what was she to do? During the nineteenth century people used outhouses and chamber pots. Chris checked around the mattress. No pot. She'd ask Tessa when she returned. Meanwhile, she'd remain miserable.

About twenty minutes later, Tessa returned, carrying a tray with a bowl. The bowl contained a soup of greasy broth with a few turnips and carrots. Although she was clumsy due to her aching body, Chris devoured the soup as if it were gourmet fare. "Tessa, I need to relieve myself."

"I bring you a pot, straight away." Tessa scurried from the room. After a few minutes, she reappeared with a brass pot in her arms. She set it on the floor, near the bed.

Now, how to use it. Deciding that it couldn't be any worse than a camping toilet, Chris struggled to her feet. She wobbled, and Tessa assisted her. Thankful for the servant's aid, she awkwardly used the pot, hoping that Tessa would believe her ineptness was a result of her fall. When finished, she returned to the mattress. "Why did you stay on after the war?" she asked, trying to gain Tessa's confidence.

Tessa frowned. "I ain't got nowhere else to go. Sides, Miss Margaret need me."

Of course, Margaret had never recovered from being raped by the Union scout, and Tessa . . . Chris believed that she may have suffered the same fate during the war. What made one woman so much stronger than the other? Or did Tessa merely appear as if she had recovered from the ordeal?

"You sounds like a Yankee, Miss Chris."

"I'm originally from Boston," Chris admitted, choosing her words carefully, "but since my husband was from Virginia, I came here, hoping that I could help him."

A look of overwhelming sadness crossed Tessa's face. "But he be dead."

The servant seemed to understand her grief. "Yes . . . he's dead, and now, *I* have nowhere to go."

Sadness changed to a smile as Tessa collected the empty soup bowl. "Da Camerons good people. Dey ain't got much dese days, but dey ain't da type to send a widow away wi' no place to go."

"Thank you, Tessa."

"Yes'm. I get you dat dress."

When Tessa left the room once more, Chris realized that she had been depending on George's kindness. But then, he *was* Geoff. Correction, George would be Geoff at a future time. Her first objectives were to learn what the exact date was and the location of her necklace.

Tessa soon returned with a gingham-checked dress in her arms. "When you feel strong enough, you can try it on."

Never imagining herself in blue checks, Chris touched the fabric and thanked Tessa. "I was told this area suffered heavy fighting during the war. It must have been very difficult for you. As I understand, some of the houses served as field hospitals."

Tessa swallowed noticeably. "It be difficult. Miss Margaret nursed da Yankees so dey don't burn da house. If'n you know what's good for you, you don't mention da war around Miss Margaret."

"For Mr. Cameron's sake?"

Tessa eyed her skeptically.

Chris quickly stated, "I noticed his limp and presumed he had been wounded."

"He be wounded all right. Nearly passed on, but Miss Margaret . . ." Tessa shook her head. "She don't like no talk of da war."

"Thank you for the warning."

The servant's suspicion seemed to fade. "You rest now, an' I check on you later. Hopefully, you be well enough to join da fam'ly for supper."

A little woozy again, Chris nodded that she'd take Tessa's advice. *How much time?* She had to form a plan to help Margaret to keep George from dying prematurely. Only by breaking the chain would she be able to help Geoff.

* * *

The makeshift dining-room table wobbled on uneven legs. George sighed. He would never be a carpenter. Fortunately, the James River supplied the family with most of the food they needed. He had never fancied himself a fisherman either, but the difficult times required one to be resourceful. The Yankee soldiers had taken the livestock and hunted most of the game into oblivion.

"Mr. George . . ."

George dropped the hammer to the floor and glanced up. Beside Tessa stood Mrs. Olson attired in a checked dress. He stood. Even though the dress was one of Tessa's old rags, he had a strange feeling that she would look more natural in the trousers she had arrived in than an elegant ball gown. *Nonsense.* She was a lady. Her carriage and demeanor suggested a former elite status. He took her hand and kissed the back. "Mrs. Olson . . ."

"Please, call me Chris."

Caught off guard by her immediate familiarity, he also found himself unexpectedly delighted. "Only if you will call me George."

"Of course," she agreed.

He held a chair out for her until she was seated, then took his place at the head of the table.

"I serve supper," Tessa said. "Miss Margaret say dat she just got da baby to sleep and will take supper in her room." With a curtsy, she left the dining room.

Margaret had changed. Before the war, she had been carefree and happy-go-lucky. Now, she rarely left her room. He wondered if she had even considered the impropriety of him dining with another woman alone. If that fact bothered Chris, she successfully hid it. "I apologize, Mrs . . . . Chris. Margaret hasn't been well since Jason's birth."

"There's no need to apologize. I understand. How old is your son?"

"Eleven months," he replied, happy to change the topic.

A smile tugged at her lips.

Margaret hadn't smiled since before his return, and seeing one on Chris's face suddenly brightened the shadowy, candlelit room. "You must have children of your own."

"One—a seven-year-old daughter. She's . . . away, right now." She frowned. "I had forgotten that it's March already."

Did she always speak in such a disjointed fashion? He reasoned that the blow to her head may have been more severe than the doctor had suggested. For some reason, he was intrigued by her. "In spite of the hardships, the past year has passed quickly," George admitted.

Tessa returned, carrying a wooden platter with tin plates. At one time the dishes had been imported china. Not that he really missed material possessions, but a woman such as Chris deserved finer things. A woman such as Chris? Even in the wretched tallow candlelight, he could see flecks of green glittering in her brown eyes. Her light-brown hair was neatly pinned in a chignon, no doubt due to Tessa's help, but when Chris had arrived, her tresses had fallen below her shoulders in an untamed wildness. He chastised himself for thinking of her in a less-than-ladylike fashion.

Tessa served some carrots, peas, and hard cornbread with the blue catfish that he had caught earlier in the day. The servant had thoughtfully cut Chris's fish into bite-size pieces. In an attempt to make Chris comfortable, George spoke about the year's hardships of farming with the current drought, purposely avoiding the subject of Margaret's ever-present melancholy. Chris would occasionally glance in his direction as he spoke, but quickly averted her gaze.

At the conclusion of the meal, Chris stood, and he rose to his feet.

"I want to thank you for your kindness," she said.

"It's my pleasure to help a lady in need." With a bow, he took her hand and kissed it once more. Lingering a moment before letting go of her hand, he said, "I believe we may have some brandy if you'd like to join me in the drawing room."

She frowned at his suggestion.

"Forgive me, that was highly improper."

Her frown faded into a smile. "I'd like to join you. A brandy might help the ache in my head."

"Then consider it done." He held out his arm. She stared at it a minute before she grasped it so that he could escort her into the hall.

"For some reason," Chris said, "I imagine this hall lined with por-traits."

George laughed. "We had a few portraits before the war, but I wouldn't exactly say lined." They entered the drawing room, and he showed her to the sofa, which, although the surface was threadbare, fortunately didn't wobble like the dining-room table. Even then, she shifted in her seat like she was in pain and found it difficult to get comfortable. He poured the brandy into a glass and handed it to her. At least, it wasn't a tin cup. With brandy in short supply, he poured whiskey for himself and sat in a moth-eaten chair across from her. "You haven't said much about yourself."

"There's not much to say," she said, taking a sip of brandy. "I lost my husband and home." Her eyelashes fluttered. George thought she might cry, but her eyes remained dry.

"And your daughter?"

"Sarah is with her grandfather until I can sort things out."

Again, she only revealed bits and pieces—as if she were hiding something. He didn't care. It felt good enjoying the company of a woman again. "Why did you return to Virginia when everything is in shambles?"

"It's my home."

That was a statement he could easily identify with.

"Mr. George . . ." Tessa entered the drawing room. "Mr. Tom here."

George stood to greet his younger brother. Two years separated them. While George had joined the cavalry, Tom had enlisted in the infantry and lost his right arm at Petersburg a month before the surrender. George made quick introductions and relayed the tale of how he had discovered Chris near the cottage when he was returning from his morning fishing trip. Tom bowed and took her hand in his. "It's about time this house is graced by a lovely lady's smile again. I'm pleased that your injuries weren't too serious."

"Thank you," Chris replied, standing. "If the two of you don't mind, I think I'll get some rest. It's been an exhausting day."

"Of course," George replied. They bid her good-night.

When she stepped into the hall, she glanced over her shoulder. A smile spread across her face—one of familiarity.

Could we have met before? Was she a nurse at a field hospital perhaps? He'd ask her when she was stronger.

She vanished from the hall, and Tom stared at him. "Is there something you're not telling me?"

George lowered his gaze. Why did he have a sudden feeling of guilt? Embarrassed, he realized that he was no longer longing for Margaret. "No."

"Spill the beans, George." Tom went over to the sideboard and helped himself to a whiskey. "That's not the sort of smile a lady gives a gentleman whom she's just met."

"I merely helped a lady down on her luck—nothing more."

"Nothing more," Tom echoed with skepticism, gulping down the drink. He poured another. "It's no secret that you and Margaret haven't been sharing the same bed in recent months."

His brother had an annoying way of cutting to the heart of the matter. "That doesn't mean I've taken up with the first woman who happens by."

Tom eased into the chair that he had vacated earlier and stretched out his legs. "Maybe you should."

"Not all of us are like you, Tom. Some men have restraint in such matters."

His brother eyed him a moment before laughing. "We're not talking about me. A Yankee doesn't just happen by, dear brother."

"The war is over," George reminded him. "Her husband was a Virginian. This is her home."

"Where is her husband buried? You've become rather protective of a woman who just happened by."

He had been protective, and he suspected Tom would have howled if he revealed the fact that Chris had arrived in trousers. In spite of his own questions, he trusted Chris. *Why would I trust someone I have just met?*

Maybe Tom was right, and she had aroused him.

Several stairs guided the way down to the west wing. The west wing? *Chris thought she had been transported back to George and Margaret's time. There had been no wing during the nineteenth century. Her head felt clear and the flowered wallpaper hall was lit by brass sconces. She stopped outside Sarah's room and knocked on the door. "Sarah?"*

She went inside to find Sarah at her table, drawing. The Black Stallion's Ghost *had a bookmark at the end of the first chapter, and the sketch had her daughter in the center. She and Geoff were on opposite sides of Sarah, both holding a hand. As before, Sarah was the link.*

"Sarah, Daddy's been visiting you again, hasn't he?"

Sarah glanced up with tears in her eyes. "Mommy? Daddy says he's found you again."

Chris sat beside her in the tiny chair and dried the little girl's tears with a tissue. "Found me?"

"He says when you fell from the horse that you weren't really dead."

Dead? "Sarah, I'm not dead. I've gone back in time as Daddy told me to do. I'm in George's time now. I'm going to try and right this terrible nightmare, so we can be a family again."

Tears returned to Sarah's eyes. "Daddy said it's risky."

"In what way?"

Sarah shrugged. "He didn't say."

Chris thought she heard someone call her name. "Ask him, Sarah. Will you do that?" Sarah nodded, and the voice calling her came again. Chris kissed her daughter on the forehead. "I'll talk to you later, and don't forget that I love you."

"Miss Chris . . ."

Chris opened her eyes to the morning light and Tessa bending over her. She blinked. Her headache was still there, and a definite chill lingered in the room.

"I help you get dressed."

Still trying to get her bearings, Chris blinked once more. The dream had been incredibly real. For a minute, it was as if she had been in Sarah's room. Placing a hand to her head, Chris climbed out of bed. Her back ached from the lumpy surface, and the room wasn't just chilly, but downright cold. "Thank you, Tessa."

"Miss Margaret say dat you be more comfortable in one of her wrappers." Tessa held up a rust-colored dress made of quilted-looking fabric with loose-fitting sleeves.

"Thanks, I appreciate your help." For some reason, the dress looked familiar. *With the gun in hand, Margaret backed away and stumbled, falling into the mud. The Yankee scout hurtled after her. She fired. Hit in his left eye, he tumbled backward until his head struck the mucky river ground.* Chris touched the fabric. Even though the dress had been washed many times, remnants of bloodstains remained. "She was wearing this when she shot him."

Alarmed, Tessa widened her eyes. "How do you know 'bout dat? Oh Lawd, you're workin' wi' da Yankees an' have come for Miss Margaret. Who would've guessed dey send a woman?"

"Calm down, Tessa. I haven't come for anyone." How could she explain the situation without sounding ridiculous? She couldn't come right out and say she was a time traveler. "Sometimes I see things, visions if you will, but it's bits and pieces of what's happened in the past." Concerned how the servant might accept her account, Chris held her breath.

Tessa's alarm faded. "You got da sight? I ain't knowed a white woman who had it afore."

Superstition—Chris breathed out in relief. "Yes, I have the sight. It comes to me when I least expect it."

Worry and fear crossed Tessa's face. "Are you goin' to tell da Yankees? Dey arrest Miss Margaret if'n you do."

The Yankees? Chris had studied the Carpetbaggers in school, but history class never made any mention of Northern soldiers remaining in the South after the war. She was surprised that Geoff had never told her about the aftermath. "I won't tell anyone," she assured Tessa. "I can't imagine a woman killing a soldier, unless there was good cause. Remember, my husband was a Virginian. I understand what Southern civilians went through."

"Please don't tell Miss Margaret dat you know. She think dat I say somethin' 'bout . . ." Tessa fell silent.

"About why she killed him? Tessa, why did she?"

Tessa's gaze shifted to the floor, and Chris feared that she had said too much, too soon. Finally, the servant looked up again, careful not to make direct eye contact. "if'n you as familiar wi' da South as you say, den you know a nigger gal ain't no better off wi' white men from da North."

Cryptic, but Chris easily grasped her meaning. It was also clear that Tessa would remain dutiful to the end. She would divert any potential shame from Margaret to herself as much as possible. After working at the firm for seven years, she knew she had to build a rape survivor's trust, without placing words in her mouth. "What happened, Tessa?"

Their eyes met. "It time dat you be gettin' dressed, Miss Chris, an' join da fam'ly for breakfast."

Too soon—she wasn't at the firm. Chris took the dress from Tessa's arms. "I can manage on my own. Thank you."

"If you be sure."

"I am." She thanked Tessa one more time, and the servant scurried from the room. With some difficulty, Chris changed from her nightdress to Margaret's wrapper. The dress fit her loosely, which was probably a good thing. She suspected that Margaret was smaller than she. Fortunately, Tessa hadn't brought a corset. The hooks of the wrapper were problematic enough. What she wouldn't give for a zipper. Once dressed, she glanced in the tiny, broken mirror that Tessa had supplied her with the day before. Her hair was a bit disheveled, but she'd kept the braid Tessa had given her while readying for bed the previous evening. Hopefully, as long as her hair was pulled back, it wouldn't be considered too improper.

As when she had first visited Poplar Ridge, Chris made her way down the stairs to the dining room. The chandelier had been torn from the ceiling during the Northern occupation. There was no china cabinet nor were there oil paintings of the Virginia countryside decorating the walls. At George's makeshift table sat a woman with violet eyes and black hair pulled back tightly in a chignon.

Although Margaret's face was paler than she had imagined, Chris would have recognized her anywhere. Beth *did* resemble her. But Margaret's pallid skin was almost deathly looking, and when she looked up, she didn't smile. Another item seemed lacking—she didn't wear perfume with the scent of honeysuckle. Chris gave a nervous swallow before speaking. "Mrs. Cameron, I'm pleased to finally meet you. I want to thank you for you and your husband's hospitality."

"You're welcome, Mrs. Olson." Still no smile. "I apologize for not looking in on you yesterday, but Tessa assured me that you were in good hands."

Her voice was much lighter, almost frail sounding, than Chris would have guessed. In fact, her speech sounded slightly slurred. "I was," Chris agreed.

"Please, join me."

As Chris seated herself at the table, George entered the dining room with the baby in his arms. George looked so much like Geoff that she ached to take him in her arms. She quickly reminded herself that she was a stranger here. He bid her good morning, then took his place at the head of the table. Neither the quiet family scene nor the sight of Jason brought a smile to Margaret's lips. Chris wished she could find some way of reaching her. Margaret had hidden the rape and the baby's death for so long that cover-up had become a way of life. How much did George suspect?

Tessa popped in carrying a wooden board for a tray. The servant set a tin plate of eggs and cornbread in front of her. After the others were served, Chris helped herself. Margaret picked at her food, pretending to eat, and George spent more time cleaning up after Jason. With the baby sitting on his lap, he seemed completely at ease in his role as a father. He laughed when Jason tugged on his moustache. Chris's heart melted. She wondered if he read to Jason as well. But George wouldn't see Jason grow up anymore than Geoff would see Sarah, unless she could find a way to avert tragedy.

While they ate, George relayed the adventure of Chris's arrival to Margaret. Still no emotion—she seemed incurably sad. Except for Jason's squeals, the room fell silent. In contrast, how carefree things had seemed when Chris first met Geoff. She glanced up from her plate. George was gazing wistfully at her. His face reminded her so much of Geoff's. She quickly returned to her meal.

After a bite of hard cornbread, Chris stole another peek. A smile spread across his face. As she had feared, he was attracted to her. She had to keep her wits and prevent them from becoming lovers. She had already proven that time could be changed. He knew her as Chris, not Catherine. Or did that make circumstances worse? She would hear Geoff's voice call her name and doubted that she could ignore it. For the time being, he was alive and well. Her resolve was already weakening.

Margaret continued to pick at her breakfast, either unaware or pretending not to notice. George finally glanced away when Jason spit up. From what Chris remembered reading about the nineteenth century, she expected Margaret to take the baby and clean him, but George calmly wiped Jason's face with the cloth he had been using as a napkin.

With that simple gesture, Chris understood how much George had been part of Geoff. She loved him in both incarnations.

Chapter Four

Two evenings later, George attended to bookwork in the library. His vision blurred, and he rubbed tired eyes. So much to do . . . rebuilding the veranda, mending fences, hunting for food, cutting wood, if he could even find enough to heat the house. When a knock came at the door, he stood. "Come in."

Attired in Margaret's hand-me-down dress, Chris entered the room, closing the door behind her. "George, I saw the light on and realized that I wasn't the only one who couldn't sleep."

Concerned that she might be in pain, he motioned for her to have a seat. "Is the head still bothering you?"

She approached the desk and traced her hand along the surface as though she were caressing a lover. "It's doing better. In fact, that's why I'm here. I thought maybe tomorrow you could help me search for my necklace."

"I'd be delighted."

She ran her hand along the desktop one more time. "And I'm delighted to see that at least one piece of furniture survived the war."

"The Yanks used it as their office." He pointed to several scratches on the surface. "Their spurs, but yes, it is intact, unlike most everything else around here."

"I never could have imagined . . ." She shook her head. "The only thing that seems to be missing from this room is a dog curled up on a rug near the desk."

How was it that she seemed to know him so well? "I had a dog before the war," he admitted. "Washington was a big black cur."

"What happened to him?" she asked curiously.

Months had passed before Margaret had revealed the dog's fate. "The Yanks shot him."

She frowned.

"I beg forgiveness. I hadn't meant to be blunt."

"You needn't apologize. Was he defending the place?"

"Not exactly. It seems that he revealed his true feelings for the invaders. He . . ." Hoping not to embarrass her, George hesitated before finishing. "He lifted a leg on one of the officers' boots."

Chris covered her mouth in an attempt to conceal the fact that she was laughing. "I don't mean to laugh over something tragic, but he sounds like Saber."

"Saber?"

"My husband's dog. He died a few months before Geoff. For the longest time, the two were nearly inseparable." She frowned once more.

He resisted the urge to take her into his arms. Not only would the gesture be inappropriate, she more than likely wouldn't appreciate it. "You obviously miss him very much."

"I do," she admitted, casting her gaze to the desk. She looked up again and forced a smile. "You remind me of him."

"Me?" He gestured to himself. "In what way?"

"I shouldn't have said that. Anyway, I've kept you up late enough. I'll see you in the morning."

George bid her good-night and was about to reseat himself, when she turned back.

"Could you use some help with the bookwork?"

"Bookwork?"

"My husband ran a business. I often took care of the books. Granted, he had a computer . . ."

"A what?"

She bit her lip before speaking again. "Never mind. I can help. It would give you more time to be with your family in the evenings."

More time? No doubt Chris's astute observations had already revealed that he and Margaret were experiencing marital strife. He only wished that Margaret wanted to spend time with him. "Your offer is kind, but . . ." Suddenly embarrassed, he shoved his hands in his pockets. "I have no money to pay a bookkeeper."

Her face lit up. "I don't require payment, just a place to stay. I have nowhere else to go, and I'll be happy to stay in the servants' quarters."

Even though her behavior seemed unladylike and forward, for some inexplicable reason, he was drawn to her. "If you can indeed tend to the books, I'd be happy to be relieved of the chore, but you shall remain in your current room."

With a look of delight, she bounded over to him and threw her arms around his neck. Without thinking, he kissed her on the mouth, then took a swift step back, breaking their embrace. "Forgive me. I reacted to the moment."

Acting as if nothing had happened, Chris nonchalantly straightened her skirt. "Thank you for your help. I'll see you in the morning." She retraced her steps to the door.

"Chris?"

She glanced over her shoulder.

"Would you care for an escort to the main house?"

"I'd enjoy your company."

As he made his way to the door to join her, the war wound in his leg twinged enough to make him stumble. She lent a hand to keep him from losing his balance. Mumbling his thanks, he straightened. "Why do I have the feeling that I should know you?"

She shrugged. "Until you found me near the cottage, we had never met."

Her voice was less than convincing. "A nurse in the hospital? You seem to know things about me that could only be possible if we had met."

"We never met during the war. George . . ." She placed her hand on his arm. "I'll tell you everything you want to know, but allow me some time. Please accept that for now."

"I will," he responded. Her peculiar behavior only made him more curious, but he'd honor his agreement. He held out his arm, and she hooked hers through it. Together, they stepped into the chill of the March evening and went down the library steps. With a shiver,

Chris inched closer. Lord forgive him, but he liked the way she felt next to him.

When they reached the hall inside the main house, he bowed slightly and kissed the back of her hand. "I shall see you in the morning."

A smile crossed her face, then she abruptly withdrew her hand from his grip.

George looked in the same direction as Chris's gaze. Margaret gripped the banister, and then bolted up the stairs.

"Margaret!" He charged after his wife to the room she shared with Jason and managed to keep the door from slamming in his face by shoving his foot in the frame.

She sobbed.

"It's not what you're thinking."

Struggling to control her tears, she clamped a hand over her mouth. Her voice was barely a whisper when she spoke. "It doesn't matter. I haven't been a wife to you since Jason's birth."

"It does matter." He nudged the door open further and grasped her hand. She yanked it from his grip. Maybe he was the one who had changed? He withdrew his foot from the door. "Have I become that objectionable to you? Tell me what I must do to make things right."

"Oh, George . . ." She closed the door.

Frustrated, he banged a fist against it. Her sobs came from the other side. There was no sense in trying to talk to her. She suffered from hysteria. She would have likely been happier if he hadn't returned.

The following morning, George led two saddled horses from the barn into the courtyard. Many stones were crumbling and no cupola was atop the barn. Chris had insisted that she ride astride, and now that she stood beside the chestnut mare with a flaxen mane, she wondered how in the hell women rode with long dresses. Resisting the urge to run back to the house for her jeans, she had George boost her on the mare's back.

Her skirt wrapped around her leg, making it impossible to put her foot in the stirrup. She untangled the material around her leg, while George watched in amusement. "What?" she asked, sending him a glare.

He shook his head, but his grin hadn't faded. As he mounted the black stallion, she unbunched her skirt. Relatively comfortable in the saddle, she felt a little odd without a helmet. He reined the stallion next to her. His hands had the same calluses as Geoff's, and she recalled the coarse gentleness in the way Geoff had often touched her. They used to ride out to the cottage. In a way, he *was* with her. In fond remembrance, she gave the mare a kick in the side. "Race you!"

Leather reins slid through her fingers as the mare galloped off, leaving George behind looking perplexed. The powerful muscles of a horse beneath her again exhilarated her. Pounding hooves crossed the budding spring grass of the meadow. Halfway across, she glanced over her shoulder. Another rider was catching up to her on a huge black horse. Chris coaxed the mare for more speed. Readily responding, the chestnut gave another burst, but the stallion stayed with her.

She lowered the mare to a walk and stopped with the stallion coming to a halt beside her. The chestnut breathed heavily beneath her. George swung out of the saddle. His hand reached up and grasped her arm, helping her from the saddle. His gaze locked onto hers. He obviously wanted to kiss her, and she broke eye contact. The ride reminded her of the first time she had gone to the cottage with Geoff. Only now, there was no fresh forest scent, and few fish darted along the bottom of the stream. Poison ivy clung to the stumps.

They led the horses along a path through the rows of stumps with only a tree standing here and there. "Northern soldiers did all of this?" she asked. "Why?"

"For their campfires."

The sheer number of soldiers that must have camped on Poplar Ridge's grounds was more than she could imagine. They continued walking, and the cottage came into view. No longer nestled among oak trees, the log frame appeared less weathered than she remembered. Of course, the cabin was at least 150 years newer. Geoff had brought her here soon after they had first met. It was the place where he felt secure if he knew a seizure was forthcoming.

"Do you come here often?" she asked.

George tied the horses to a hitching rail out front. "Occasionally, I do—to think. So much has happened over the past few years that I'm not certain I can comprehend it. We thought our troubles would be over when the war ended, but in many ways, it was only the beginning."

A haunted look appeared in his eyes—something she had never seen in Geoff's—making her shiver. She had never realized how much the seizures had protected Geoff from memories of war and imprisonment that he experienced as George.

"Chris . . ." The familiar friendly sparkle had returned to his eyes, and his gaze met hers. "We came here to look for your necklace."

Unable to look away, she envisioned his arms around her in the way Geoff used to hold her. Finally, she blinked and was capable of replying. "That's right."

The greening of the spring grass made nooks and crannies more difficult to sift through. With most of the trees chopped down, she wouldn't have thought there could be so many places to look. After nearly an hour of meticulously scouring under every blade of grass and notches beneath the stumps, Chris gave up. George had more immediate chores to take care of than to help her find the necklace. She'd search again tomorrow. Besides, she had her new job as book-keeper to tend to. As they went to retrieve the horses, she stared at the cottage. How often had she come here with Geoff and taken each time for granted that he would always be there?

"It's almost like you know the place," George said, interrupting her thoughts.

"My husband and I used to come to a place like this."

"Would you like to go inside?"

Uncertain about dredging up too many painful memories, Chris hesitated, but George went up the steps. She moved in his direction. No hinges groaned when he opened the door. Inside, pegs for coats lined the wall like she remembered. The room lacked the cup-board for tin plates, and there was no bed with a patchwork quilt and feather pillows. The wood floor was rotting. Knapsacks were strewn about, and coats crumbled to dust. She bent closer. The coats were faded blue. *Northern soldiers.* And George had been a Confederate officer, wounded and captured, fighting for the South. Why after all of the years of Geoff's stories had the truth never really sunk in?

"Tom and I used this place as a hunting lodge."

Before the war. Even though he hadn't voiced as much, she understood it to be the case. She went over to the fireplace and stared at the ashes. She and Geoff had made love here in front of a roaring fire. But that life was gone. *Forever?*

"Chris."

She felt George's hand on her shoulder and turned to him.

"I know you miss him."

Like he must Margaret. And he had no idea what plagued her. George was here now. Without thinking, she encircled her arms about his waist, and he drew her closer until their mouths met. She recalled times past—the comfort of his arms, kissing, and caressing. His moustache tickled her nose when they kissed again.

He was so much like Geoff. In a way, wasn't he? She was falling for him, only to create the cycle of Geoff's violent death all over again. But he *wasn't* Geoff. Geoff didn't wear suspenders or pants with a button fly. He had a goatee, not a simple moustache. What's more, he wouldn't be born for over a hundred years. With a hand going to her mouth, Chris shoved away from George.

"I'm sorry, Chris. I shouldn't have done that."

"It wasn't your fault. I'm confused. You're so much like Geoff."

Once more, he held her, and her head came to rest on his chest. In the comfort of his arms, she could pretend that her journey had been nothing more than a dream. When she woke, she'd gaze into his eyes and the world would be right again. Geoff would drop Neal off at high school, while she drove Sarah to elementary. A rumble of thunder startled her. It wasn't thunder, but galloping horses.

Before she could move, George was halfway to the door. "God-damned Yanks."

"Yankees?"

George stepped outside, and she peered over his shoulder and counted six soldiers dressed in blue as they brought their horses to a halt out front. Her heart skipped a beat. Real Northern soldiers, not pictures from some history textbook. All of them had beards or scraggly facial hair, and dust covered their uniforms as if they had been in the saddle for days. Pistols were strapped in gun belts about their waists, and rifles were sheathed in leather scabbards from their saddles.

The soldier in front of the group wore sergeant's stripes and chewed what Chris guessed to be tobacco. His piercing gaze met George's. "Cameron."

"What do you want, Sullivan?"

The sergeant spit, narrowly missing George's foot. He ogled the length of Chris's body as if he was mentally undressing her. "Lookin' for a nigger. I thought she might be with the likes of a landowner, but I see you've found yourself a mighty perty white gal."

George raised his left arm, poising to punch the sergeant. Chris latched on and held tight, when Sullivan withdrew his pistol from its holster. Even though George lowered his arm, she maintained her grip.

A haughty smile crossed the sergeant's face as he laughed to the other men. Two more soldiers on horseback approached the cottage with what looked like an officer in the lead. The grin vanished from Sullivan's face, and he reholstered his pistol.

"Trouble, Sergeant?" the officer asked.

"No, sir."

"Then I suggest you continue with your duty."

"Yes, sir." With a salute, Sullivan reined his horse around, and the other men followed, except for the officer.

When Sullivan cued his horse to a trot, Chris finally let go of George's arm and took a deep breath.

"My apologies," the officer said. Unlike the other men, his beard was neatly trimmed, but when he lowered his hat, dust flew to reveal thick black hair. He smiled warmly. "I don't believe you have introduced me to the lady, Cameron."

"Captain Rhodes. Mrs. Olson, a widow due to a Yankee bullet."

The captain ignored George's insult. "A pleasure to meet you, ma'am," he said, bowing his head slightly. He turned his attention to George. "The Negro wench stole a couple of chickens."

"Did you think that she might have a family to feed?"

Rhodes sighed. "Cameron, I long for a way to ease tensions, but I can't ignore orders. If I do, they'll only replace me with someone who won't care what happens to the citizens. Now, have you seen any Negroes at large? I assure you the wench won't be treated harshly, if I find her first."

"No," George replied. "We haven't seen anyone."

"Thank you." The captain replaced his hat on his head. "Ma'am." He rode on.

Shaken by the experience, Chris trembled. "I could never have imagined what it was like. Geoff didn't tell me."

"Rhodes or Sullivan?" George snorted a laugh. "The sergeant was in a good mood today."

"I'd hate to cross his path when he's in a bad mood."

He placed his hands on each side of her face. "Just promise me that you won't say anything to antagonize him. He has no love for Southerners, but he'd likely treat any Northerner who holds sympathy for the South worse."

"Your warning is duly noted."

Before dropping his hands from her face, he kissed her.

Resisting his advances, she drew away. "Tell me one thing, George. Were you actually going to start a fight with him?"

"I was going to beat his face to a bloody pulp."

"Because of what he insinuated I was?"

He nodded, and she shivered once more. So much like Geoff.

For the next week, Chris spent a few minutes each day scouring the area near the cottage to no avail. During that time, she had taken complete charge of George's bookwork, allotting him more time to other chores. What she wouldn't give for a good cup of coffee. The noxious potion Tessa served tasted more like tar. Still, it was better than going without a caffeine fix when she headed to the library.

Even without a computer popping figures across a screen, she could easily see that Poplar Ridge was in dire straits. Back taxes were owed. Most of the livestock was gone. Much of the land had been leased. Judith had told her the family had nearly lost the plantation, but Chris hadn't realized how desperate the situation had gotten.

And she was an extra mouth to feed. *Don't despair.* She was meant to be part of this time, and history told her that Poplar Ridge would remain in the Cameron family.

A rap at the door broke her concentration. George wouldn't be knocking, so she answered, "Come in."

Tom entered and gave a slight bow. Southern manners hadn't changed much over 140 years. Even after living in Virginia for almost a decade, she still found them quaint but refreshing.

"What can I do for you?" she asked.

"I thought George might be here at this time of day."

"I've taken over the bookwork."

Tom laughed, moved closer, and glanced over her shoulder.

She looked up and met his gaze. "Did you think a mere woman incapable of handling accounts?"

His cocky smile immediately vanished. In spite of his sandy-colored hair and heavy beard, his appearance gave away the fact that he and George were brothers. Like George, he stood close to six feet tall, and he had the same sparkling blue eyes. He always wore the same shabby gray uniform from the war with the right sleeve pinned where an arm should have been.

"And I'm delighted to be proven wrong. I was aware that things are vastly different in the North, but I hadn't realized how much. I beg forgiveness for doubting you or my brother's wisdom."

With his arrival, Chris realized that Tom must be the key person for keeping Poplar Ridge in the Cameron family. Margaret certainly wasn't in any condition to run a plantation. For some reason, Chris felt uneasy around him. Because he didn't view women with equality? Weren't most men of the nineteenth century narrow minded in that regard? *Stop dwelling on Tom.* George would die in two months time unless she came up with a plan.

"Is something wrong?" he asked.

"I was just finishing here. Perhaps we should go to the main house. George should be there by now."

He held out his arm. George and Tom always wanted to escort her everywhere. While Geoff had often been the same way, he hadn't overdone the manners. *This was a different time*, Chris thought with a sigh. She grasped Tom's arm. "If you don't think it's too forward of me, how did you lose your arm?"

"I took a bullet at Petersburg—ten days before the surrender. It shattered the bone."

So much waste. Chris couldn't fathom the country at war with itself.

As they stepped outside, a woman's shriek pierced through the air. Tom sprinted toward the banks of the river with Chris following behind him. Margaret stood near the edge, staring vacantly at the gently rolling waves.

"Margaret," Tom said in a low voice.

As Margaret turned, her eyes widened. In her hands was a pistol. She raised it.

"Tom!" Chris sprang at him with the impact of her body sending both of them sprawling. She was on her feet again, facing Margaret. "He's not the scout!"

Margaret blinked, first at Chris, then to Tom as he regained his feet. The pistol thumped to the ground. With a throaty sob, Margaret sank to her knees. She pressed her hands to her face and cried into them. Tom stepped forward, but Chris blocked him with her arm.

"Let me talk to her. I think she needs to speak with a woman right now." She grasped the pistol and handed it to Tom. With some reluctance, he returned to the path leading to the main house. Fighting the urge to withdraw, Chris held her ground. She must help Margaret in order to save George.

"Did Tessa tell you?" Margaret asked weakly.

"Tessa would guard anything you tell her with her life."

Brushing the tears from her cheeks, Margaret got to her feet. "Then George? I've seen the way that he looks at you."

George? As Chris recalled, Margaret had never revealed the rape to George. "There's nothing going on between George and me."

More tears entered Margaret's eyes. "Chris, I don't blame you or him. I haven't been a proper wife." She wandered toward the house.

"You need to tell him about the scout. What he did, and how he still haunts you. George is your husband. He will help you, not judge you."

Margaret halted, then turned slowly to face Chris. She held out her hands. "Every time I look at them, I see blood. I'm being punished for what I did."

"You shot him in self-defense, but, Margaret, don't you see what's happening? You relive the incident in your mind. What if you accidentally shoot someone else when you see the scout, like you nearly did Tom?"

Shaking her head in disbelief, Margaret said, "I couldn't shoot anyone. I barely was able to . . ." She broke off with a sob.

"Ordinarily, I'd agree, but when you had the gun in your hands, you didn't see Tom. You saw *him*."

"Lieutenant Robert Howard."

Even after all of her visions, Chris had never known the scout's name. "Here, let me help you to the house." She grasped Margaret's arm. Recoiling from Chris's touch, Margaret withdrew from her grip. Determined to help, Chris said, "Before the war, I worked with women who had been through traumatic incidents such as yours. It's not your fault that he died. Put the blame where it belongs—squarely on him." Her trial experience warned her that she must tread carefully. Margaret had to admit to the rape herself. "He attacked you."

Tears streaked Margaret's cheeks. "Don't you understand? I should have fought against him harder."

"Don't believe the nonsense that society dictates. If you had fought harder, *you* would have likely wound up dead."

"It would have been better that way."

Near the house, Tessa met them. She pulled Margaret to her and soothed her like a small child. "It be time for your medicine, Miss Margaret."

Medicine? Tessa escorted Margaret to the house, and Chris wondered what sort of medicine the servant spoke of. It might lend some explanation to Margaret's unhealthy appearance and her inability to come to terms with what had happened. Pondering the thought, she went inside.

Not surprisingly, Margaret failed to join the family for supper. After dinner, they retired to the drawing room where George thanked Chris for helping his wife. In the short time she had been at the nineteenth-century Poplar Ridge, she had already discovered that when Tom visited, whiskey and cigars were prominent among drunken conversations about the war. Geoff never smoked, and he rarely drank alcohol. She found herself a bit disconcerted seeing George puffing on a cigar while imbibing whiskey. It was very much a masculine atmosphere, but they were too polite to dismiss her. She also gathered they enjoyed her company, and having been a corporate attorney in Boston before working at the firm, she was comfortable in a male environment.

As the whiskey flowed, their tongues loosened. Tom started drinking straight from the bottle. "The damned Yank said that I needed to sign the Oath. I raised my sleeve and said, 'With what? You shot off my arm.' " He raised his stump for emphasis.

George laughed with a drunken snigger. "At least you got your pardon. I'm still waiting."

Suddenly curious, Chris leaned forward. "Oath? Pardon? What are you talking about?"

George held out his glass, and Tom proceeded to fill it once more with whiskey. "My dear, how can you have lived in the South and not known about the Oath?" asked George.

She carefully replied, "I spent a lot of time in the North—during the war."

"Every Southerner is expected to take the Yankees' Oath of Loyalty, pledging our allegiance to a united country. For all the good it does," George said with disgust. "Because I am a landowner, I have never received a pardon, nor am I allowed to vote."

She hadn't realized that some Southerners had been stripped of their basic civil rights. "What about women?"

George's brow furrowed in the same manner as Geoff's when he was confused. "What about them?"

He truly didn't know. "Shouldn't women have the right to vote too?" she asked.

Both men howled.

Chris thought better of the idea of revealing that she had voted on numerous occasions. "There's no need to be condescending."

Between guffaws, Tom snorted. "Just because a woman can keep books doesn't mean she would be able to make an intelligent voting decision."

Totally insulted, Chris sent Tom a glare. "So you think women are incapable of anything but raising their skirts for men?"

"That's a good place to start." A smile spread across Tom's face. "But there's cooking, sewing ..."

"Enough!" Chris stood. She glanced from Tom to George. At least, George had stopped laughing. She must learn to be more careful. Would men of the nineteenth century tolerate a woman's outspoken behavior?

"Chris," George stated gently, while standing. "I've heard of women pushing for suffrage in the North. It's different down here."

"How so?" she asked, once calm enough to speak in an even voice. "Think about the war. You get drunk and laugh about the atrocities. It doesn't matter which side we're talking about. Men started it, but women are made to suffer in silence." She gestured to George. "Your wife is an excellent example. The only way that things will ever change is by allowing women the right to vote and having them run for public office. Good evening, gentlemen. I have a few more entries to make in the books before retiring."

Without waiting for their reaction, Chris retreated to the hall and outside to the path leading to the library. Once inside, she lit a candle and sat behind the desk. Had she said too much? She had to remind herself that George was a product of his time. Without Geoff's life experiences, he wouldn't react in the same manner. Or was it something deeper? She had been purposely sparring with him to keep him distant.

"Chris ..."

She should have known that George would follow her. So much for him not reacting in the same manner. It was exactly what Geoff would have done.

"If I was patronizing, you have my humble apologies," he said. "You raise some notions that neither Tom nor I have ever considered." With a grimace that marked his pain from his war wound, he sank into the chair across from her. "You were right about Margaret. Her melancholy began before Jason's birth. She's suffered from it since my return." His gaze met hers. "I can only fathom what's caused it, but I fear that I am to blame."

"You? Why would you think you're to blame?"

Sadness filled his eyes. "I've changed since the war. We all have."

Tell him. She couldn't let him suffer the blame. No, she had to find a way for Margaret to come to terms with what had happened, so that she could tell him herself. "George, I overheard Tessa say to Margaret that it was time for her medicine. What is she taking?"

He stared at her a moment as if deciding whether to answer such a personal question or not. "The doctor prescribed laudanum for her melancholy."

"Laudanum," she muttered under her breath, "an opiate."

"Chris?" he asked as if not quite hearing her.

Chris waved that it wasn't important. She wished she had access to the Internet to conduct a quick search on laudanum and it's side effects. But she was willing to bet the drug kept Margaret in a semi-catatonic state. "How did she get access to a gun?"

"I don't know. As former Confederates we're not allowed to keep sidearms in this area. I've locked it away where she won't find it again."

If only that were true. Exhausted, she rubbed her eyes.

"You need some rest."

She felt George's hand on her arm. Deciding that she wouldn't resolve all of her unanswered questions in one night, she agreed. As she stood, George got to his feet as well. She came face-to-face with him. Chris caught her breath. *Geoff.* Her resolve was weakening. He bent to kiss her, and she extended an arm to stop him. "You're married. I don't think that's wise."

"I don't know what made me do that. Forgive me." He turned away slightly, then back again. "Yes, I do know what made me want to kiss you. I feel as if I should know you. If we didn't meet during the war, then I can't place how or where we must have met. But I *know* we have met before."

More than anything, she wanted to take him into her confidence. *Not yet.* "I'll see you in the morning," she whispered to cover her distress. She picked up a blank leather-bound ledger from the desk, and with a "good-night" to George, she returned to her room in the main house.

She opened the blank ledger, contemplating writing a message to Geoff. Would he find it? As she recalled, Tom had lived into the twentieth century. She might be able to persuade him to give the ledger to Winston's aunt, Greta. Greta would be alive when Geoff was growing up. Had she tried such a tactic before? She couldn't spend the next two months second guessing herself. She dipped the pen in ink and started writing.

My dearest Geoff,

Chris withdrew the pen from the paper. Her introduction sounded corny and nothing like the way she would write. Unable to erase it, she returned to the more important matter of writing her message.

I'm writing in hope that you will one day find this ledger and read my warning. Hopefully, my message will allow you to choose another path as well as prevent upcoming tragedies.

She started by introducing herself and explaining how she had become displaced in time. She couldn't help but love George because, in this time period, he *was* George. But she had to resist the temptation or history would repeat itself.

Before long, she could barely keep her eyes open. Confident that Geoff would eventually read her words, she tucked the ledger under her pillow. Dressing for bed in a cotton chemise, she vowed to write a little each day. By taking the first active step to changing time, she felt closer to Geoff.

Chapter Five

CHRIS WENT DOWN THE STAIRS *to the west wing. The door to Sarah's room was open. Her heart skipped a beat and her breath caught in her throat. Beside Sarah, Geoff sat in the little blue chair with his long legs stretched in front of him, reading* The Black Stallion Legend. *"Geoff?"*

Without looking up, he raised a hand for her to wait. He finished the last paragraph and closed the book, then gave Sarah a tender kiss on her forehead. "I must speak to your mother, Sarah." He stood and took Chris's hand.

Stunned by his hand's iciness, Chris realized this dream was very similar to when she had seen him before. "The last time . . ."

"Not yet. Bye, Sarah."

"Bye, Daddy."

Chris detected lingering sadness in his voice. His reading the final page in the original Black Stallion *series suddenly made sense. Without blinking, she stood near the mist-covered river with her fingers still intertwined with Geoff's. Saber snuffled along the edge of the bank. "You were saying a permanent goodbye. Geoff, she needs you."*

He shook his head. "I can't stay any longer, and this isn't about Sarah, but us."

"Us?"

"I am George." He reached a hand to her face and caressed her cheek. "If you are successful and change what happened in the past, then we might not experience what we shared in the present. To me, not having known your love would be more tragic than living a shorter life in either time line."

She had never considered that aspect. "Then I can change time and that's why you're here now."

He smiled slightly. "I didn't say that."

"You implied that I can. Is there a way that we can help Margaret?"

He glanced at the lapping waves of the James and clenched a hand. "I don't know. I think she might have been able to overcome what that bastard did to her if it hadn't been for Georgianna."

George and Margaret's daughter whom Margaret thought had been born as a result of the rape. In a fit of blind anger, Margaret had strangled her.

Chris closed her eyes. "I'll try to help her, but George and I mustn't become lovers."

His brow furrowed as if in pain. "No, Chris, don't try to change that."

"If we can somehow help Margaret, she won't shoot George nor drive Beth insane. In turn, you will live longer. It'll be easier to help Margaret if we don't become lovers in the past."

"Time doesn't work that simply. Chris . . ." *He clutched her hand, then kissed her on the mouth.*

Ignoring his cold lips, she placed her arms around his neck and gave him an intimate kiss.

Extreme sadness crossed his face as Geoff withdrew from her embrace and called Saber to his side. "Be aware that if you change time, there may be consequences. Make certain you can live with the results."

"A warning?"

"Yes," *he replied without hesitation.* "Be very careful what you change. Time is like a woven fabric. If it's torn, you may not recognize the result."

"Duly warned. How do I return to the present?"

"The same way you got to the past—with the crystal."

And Margaret had the crystal necklace in her possession during the early-twentieth century. "But you gave it to me before we were married."

Sadness reflected on his features once more. "I'm aware of that."

"There's no need to spare me. If I don't make it back, then I don't. I won't fail trying to find a way for you to live, and we'll be a family for longer the next time around."

"I hope you're right, but if it doesn't come to pass, I'll love you always."

"Always," *she whispered, and he was gone.*

* * *

Chris woke to peeling wall paper and moonlight beaming through the window. 1867. The candle had gone out after she drifted off. Numb and depressed, she felt Geoff's lingering presence. Certain that she wouldn't see him again, she relighted the candle, took out the ledger, and wrote about his visit.

> *You've warned me that I should be careful in what I try to change. I also may not make it back to the present until the natural progression of time.*

She lowered the pen. Living in the nineteenth century for the rest of her natural life? That thought finally hit her. Women weren't attorneys. Hell, she had argued to George and Tom earlier in the evening that women deserved the right to vote. What would her life be reduced to? Baking pies and mopping floors. How about kids? Did traveling through time somehow prevent pregnancy? Women were dependent on men to support them, and large families were the norm. Giving birth to Sarah had been tough enough. The thought of several births in a row terrified her. *Stop moping. I have an objective.* She had to find a way to prevent George's untimely death. Geoff's words finally made sense. He *was* George. If nothing else came to pass, he was here—now. She could be wasting precious time.

"George." She quickly dressed. With the ledger under her arm, she bolted into the hall and down the stairs. Once outside, she raced across the path from the main house to the library. The outbuilding was dark with no lights on inside. George must have retired for the evening. Out of breath, she pounded on the door with her fists. When there was no immediate response, she burst through. "George!"

A thump came from upstairs, then the running of footsteps on the stairs. With bare feet and a rumpled shirt, George looked as if he had rushed to make a semblance of a respectable appearance. "What's wrong, Chris?"

Like Geoff after Beth had left, George had relocated to the room above the library when Margaret had moved out of their bedroom. The same room that she had shared with Geoff. "I love you."

He blinked as if not hearing her correctly. Swallowing hard, he moved closer and his fingertips lightly tickled her cheek. "Is that wise?"

"No, but I can't help how I feel. Admit it. You've felt it too."

Lowering his arm, George gave a weak nod and withdrew the ledger from her arms, setting it on the desk. "I do love you. I'll probably be damned to hell for saying so, but I felt it when I first saw you outside the cottage. Now, are you going to tell me where we've met?"

"The time isn't right. You wouldn't believe me."

"I'd like to hear what you have to say."

"Later. Right now, I just want you to hold me." She wrapped her arms around his neck and kissed him on the mouth. His moustache tickled her nose. He put his arms around her and reciprocated. Unlike her dreams and visions, he was real with his flesh warm to her touch. He began to unbutton her bodice, and she grasped his hand. "Not here."

"Margaret doesn't come here."

Of course, she didn't. The library was where the Union scout had raped her. But it was also the place where George and Geoff would die. The bloodstains on the floorboards were imprinted in her mind.

"I see you already have regrets," George said softly.

"No regrets," she responded with a shake of her head, "but let's go upstairs."

Taking her hand, he showed her to the stairs. In the twenty-first century, the stairs were located in the wing, not at the end of the library. Upon reaching the bedroom, George lit a single candle. Chris was almost surprised to find the room contained no leather or antique furniture. Only a straw bed filled the middle of the room.

Feverishly, they kissed and touched, slowly undressing each other. George came to her bra. He stared, obviously perplexed. *Don't let him think.* Chris unhooked the back. With a laugh, she seized his hand, and they fell to the bed. While Geoff had maintained an athletic build from the farm work, George was downright thin. Too thin—most likely due to his prison ordeal at Fort Delaware. Even though he was lean, he was finely muscled. A jagged, raised scar crossed his upper right thigh.

She ran her hand from the length of his collarbone along his protruding rib cage. He kissed and touched her in an eerily familiar but delightful fashion. *Geoff.* She hoped she didn't shriek his name at a critical moment. The thought amused her, and she wondered how George would react if she took the lead.

Geoff had told her, "Southern men prefer their women like their horses—spirited." Had his motto been rooted in the previous incarnation? She needn't have questioned.

Pleased by her initiative, George lay back as she placed her legs on each side of him. How had she ever believed that she could avoid him? *Destiny.* She kissed his chest, while his hands traced the length of her back to her buttocks. Guiding him to her, she swayed her hips in a rhythmic motion. Relieved that his skin no longer felt icy like the coldness from a grave, she luxuriated in his warmth. After months of being alone, he was finally with her again. But for how long?

Tears streaked her cheeks, and she fell gently to his chest, exhausted. Time was as it should be. She and George were lovers.

In the morning light, after coupling with Chris again, George lay beside her. He should have felt guilt. Even though Margaret had left his bed months before, he had never broken his marriage vows—until now. Chris snuggled in his arms and traced a finger along the scar on his thigh.

"I received it at Spotsylvania," he said.

"And nearly died," she whispered.

"If I hadn't been near death, I would have lost my leg."

"The Union found you, and you were taken to Fort Delaware."

He could dismiss her first comment to a lucky guess. George sat up. "How do you know me so well? Chris, do you still not trust me?"

The blanket fell away from Chris's unclad body as she raised on an elbow, exposing a firm, round breast. "I do trust you, but if I revealed the truth, you would think it's a farfetched tale or that I'm crazy. Please give me a little more time."

He drew her near and kissed her on the mouth. "You just want me under your spell so that I won't question what you tell me."

She laughed. "Believe me, you'll always question what I say."

He was so caught up in her scent and fondling her nakedness that he barely heard Tom's voice call his name from downstairs. "Be there in a minute," George replied. With disappointment, he got up from the bed and tugged on his trousers. Once he was finished dressing, he headed down to the library.

His brother sat at the desk, looking over a ledger. Tom glanced up. "Usually you're awake long before eight."

"I had difficulty sleeping last night."

"Why does that not surprise me?" Tom smiled a knowing grin. "I heard a female voice upstairs—a Yankee female."

George sighed. "You, of all people, would be the last I expected to be judgmental. Or has Tessa given you a cold shoulder?"

"Tessa is as warm as always. I'm not being judgmental." Tom closed the ledger and stood. "But has Chris told you where she's from?"

"She's originally from Boston."

Tom shook his head. "No, I mean where in Virginia?" His gaze traveled to the stairway.

George glanced over his shoulder to see Chris on the stairs, leaning against the banister. "Is there something I should know?" he asked.

"Ask her," Tom replied.

His brother seemed to know more about Chris than he did. Suddenly suspicious that she kept deflecting his questions, George said, "Chris, you have put this off long enough. Where are you from?"

Joining them near the desk, she glanced at Tom, then the ledger resting on the desk. "Poplar Ridge."

No wonder she had warned him that he would think her tale to be farfetched. "How is that possible? Why are you here?"

Chris hesitated a moment. "To keep you from dying."

Had he heard correctly? "To keep me from dying?"

She picked up the ledger from the desk and handed it to him. "Since Tom has obviously read it, you might as well too."

"I think I'll wait outside," Tom said, excusing himself. He closed the door behind him as he left.

George opened the ledger to a letter that Chris had written to her husband. *A fantastic tale.* He sank into the chair and continued reading. He *would be* Geoff in a future time, and Chris . . . She must be delusional.

"Well?"

He stared blankly at the ledger. "You're right. I'm questioning your sanity."

"George, I can prove to you that I'm telling the truth."

Swallowing hard, he finally looked in her direction. "By all means."

"You married Margaret in 1861."

His patience was growing short. "That certainly proves nothing. That fact can be found in public records."

"I realize that, but you moved the wedding date forward. You weren't going to get married until after the war. On the day you joined the cavalry, you went to tell Margaret. She was alone. Her father caught the two of you . . ."

"Enough!" He slammed a fist to the desk, and Chris jumped. On the day that Virginia had announced that she had seceded from the Union, it had been spring. How could Chris have known such intimate details? George broke out in a sweat. "What else do you know?"

"After the war's end," she continued with some hesitation, "you used every ounce of strength to return home to Margaret. You barely made it. Your clothes were in tatters and you had no shoes."

The blisters on his feet had become so painful that he had barely been able to walk. He would have died before breaking his promise to Margaret. "A lot of Confederates had no shoes."

"That may be true," she agreed, "but even then, you noticed a difference in Margaret. At first, the signs were subtle because you were so happy to be home. She was constantly sad. You later found out that she had given birth to a baby girl while you were away, who died shortly after she was born. You thought the baby's death was the source of Margaret's sadness, so you made Georgianna a grave marker."

Few were aware of Georgianna's existence. How could a stranger have known about a baby that had lived for less than a week? Unless . . . "And you discovered all of this because I will be . . ." The mere thought was too preposterous. "Geoff?"

"Not exactly. The more I tell you, the more ludicrous it will sound."

She ran a hand along the wood grain of his desk, which reminded him of her first visit to the library. She had even commented on its survival. Had she truly seen the same desk from some future time? "If you really are from my future, then how is it possible that I have the feeling I've met you before?"

She contemplated his question for a minute, then shrugged. "I'm not certain, but time isn't linear. The fact that I'm here is proof of that."

Proof? He questioned her assumption but remained silent on that particular point. "So, we were destined to become intimate?"

"I tried to resist but couldn't. Don't you see?" A bittersweet smile appeared on her face. "I have loved you from the start."

The whole notion was madness. "But, Chris, I don't know anything of that world. I can't be *him*."

She leaned across the desk and stroked a finger through his moustache. "I realize that. In many ways, you're very different from Geoff, but in others, you're just like him. So you see why I can't help but love you."

Traveling through time? Impossible. But what if . . . ? How else could she know so much about him? If she spoke the truth, there was still the unasked question. "You said that you were here to keep me from dying. How . . . ?"

She shook her head. "Please, don't ask. I'm here to prevent it from happening. That's all I can say."

His death must be a violent one. Accident or . . . Her husband had been murdered, which is why she likely refused to speak further on the subject. Dwelling on one's death was unhealthy. During the war, he had controlled such dark thoughts by thinking of Margaret. What now? He was actually contemplating Chris's story as if he believed it. "Traveling through time, living one's life again. I'm uncertain that I have absorbed your words."

Chris finally came around to his side of the desk and cozied onto his lap. "Take your time."

"Do we have time?"

Seeing his question for what it really was, she smiled softly. "All of the time in the world."

He *did* love her. How strange this feeling was that he had known her for all of his life when he had just met her. Could they truly have met in another time? "Chris, is it normal for women to wear trousers where you come from?"

Hugging him close, she laughed. "It is."

He shuddered at the reason that she might have been sent to him, but he now knew that he couldn't face Margaret's melancholy alone. Chris was life, and she gave him reason to face each day again.

Granite spires and headstones covered the neatly mowed grass of the family cemetery. How similar it was to Chris's first visit when Geoff had showed her his mother's grave. Even the purple-flowered wisteria climbed along the gate of the older section. A young woman, approximately in her late teens with long auburn hair, stood near Geoff's grave with her head bowed. A gray-muzzled Belgian sheepdog lay at her feet.

As Chris approached, the woman lifted her head and smiled. She had the same color of brilliant blue eyes as Geoff. Realizing who she was, Chris caught her breath. "Sarah?"

With tears entering her eyes, Sarah gave her a bear hug. "Mom! You don't know how long I've been trying to reach you. But you're finally here."

Chris stepped back, taking a good look at her daughter. She was slender, but she definitely had more of the mature build of a woman than the girl she remembered. "How can it be? You're a woman now."

"You never came back." Sarah gestured to the graves.

Chris's heart nearly stopped. Beside Geoff's grave was a stone marked with her name. She had died the same year as Geoff in 2013. "How?"

Sarah wiped the tears from her cheeks. "You fell from Dad's horse. I know that you traveled, but it's been so long since I've heard from you that I thought your journey was unsuccessful. I haven't heard from Dad either." Her voice grew increasingly soft. "I think he's gone."

"He's not gone!" Chris demanded. Taking a deep breath, she lowered her voice. "I haven't had a chance to implement my plan."

"The ledger?"

How could Sarah know so much? *"Yes. Are you telling me that it didn't reach him?"*

"I don't think so," Sarah whispered. *"Time remains as it was."*

"I will find a way." She hugged her daughter again. *"Please believe me, I'll find a way."*

"I'll help," Sarah said, stepping back.

"How?"

"You'll understand when the time comes, but please know, in spite of your doubts about Tom, you can trust him with the knowledge of where you came from. He'll remain skeptical for a while, but he will come to believe you."

Cryptic. *But it was useful to know that she could count on having another ally. The aged dog near Sarah's feet finally struggled with stiff joints to get to his own.*

"Mosby," said Chris. *He sniffed her and wagged his feathery tail.*

"Dad wanted me to take care of him."

Bending down, Chris scratched behind the dog's ears. "He's Saber's son." *She stood again. "Sarah, I've missed you. I'm sorry for being gone all of these years."*

Her daughter smiled softly. "I know that you've found Dad again. Together, we'll try and make things right."

Chris clutched Sarah's hand. "Together," she vowed. *With the pact firmly sealed, she drifted.*

When Chris woke in the faint light before dawn, she reached for George's face and traced a finger through his moustache, cherishing the time they shared. Thanks to Sarah, they had truly been given a second chance. She kissed him on the cheek and whispered in his ear, "I'm going to return to my room now."

He muttered a goodbye, and she slipped from beneath the sheet to dress. After two weeks, the long dress was beginning to feel natural—almost. She preferred a daily shower to washing up from a tin pitcher and bowl before dressing. Real baths were even less frequent. At least, Tessa had made her a pair of baggy period underdrawers without a crotch, making going to the bathroom a much easier task. She had drawn the line at wearing a corset and didn't want to think about the fact that she may eventually have to change her mind. Finished dressing, she went downstairs to the library.

Relieved that Tom wasn't sitting at the desk to greet her, she made her way to the path leading to the main house. George's brother often spent the night at Poplar Ridge, especially after a drinking session the evening before with George. After having the dream with Sarah's message, Chris was aware that she must speak with him in the nearby future. She required allies if she was to help George. But first, she would visit the area near the cottage for another quick search for her necklace.

Bypassing the main house, she hurried across the gently greening grass of early spring to the separate building that housed the kitchen. Tessa usually prepared breakfast in the early morning hours, and the servant had promised to customize a dress for her that would make horseback riding easier. She swung the door open. "Tessa?"

No response.

Tessa must have overslept. Creeping up the stairs, Chris reached the hall with the faded whitewashed walls. Tessa's room was the first one on the right. She raised a hand to knock, but the door cracked open before she could do so. The morning light cast shadows. Tessa lay asleep on the bed. Beside her was a man with his arm across her and his hand resting on her breast. He only had one arm. Both were totally naked.

No wonder Tom often spent the night. Hoping that she hadn't been seen, Chris retreated down the stairs as quietly as possible. By the time she reached the kitchen, she heard footsteps behind her. Tessa caught up with her, only wearing a chemise. Her black hair was in disarray. "You won't tell Miss Margaret?"

"What you and Tom do is none of my business. If you care for him, then why should I be concerned that you're sleeping with him?"

Careful not to make direct eye contact, Tessa pursed her lips.

"You do care for him?"

"He be good to me."

Neat sidestepping. She'd speak to Tessa later when there was no chance of Tom overhearing. "I won't tell Margaret. Your secret is safe with me." She turned.

"Miss Chris, I got your skirt ready. Wait here." Tessa hustled up the stairs.

The table where Tessa prepared food was rickety like the one in the dining room. She missed the butcher block table and fluorescent lighting. And what she wouldn't give to talk to Judith right now over a cup of tea. *Keep busy and don't dwell on Judith.* She stirred the embers in the fireplace to get a cooking fire going, when the heavy tread of boots on the stairs warned her that Tom had risen. "Aren't such tasks as cooking and sewing mundane for a woman who travels through time?" he asked.

She whirled around. As on any other day, he wore the same ragged Confederate uniform. "And you shouldn't have been reading my personal writings. That's ungentlemanly in any time, but then, I have discovered how gentlemanly you really are."

He crossed his single arm over his chest. "I have a Negro wench, and you share the bed of a married man. Or are such transgressions considered acceptable in your century?"

His mocking tone suggested that he didn't accept her time travel story. Could she really blame him? She needed to keep her cool. Sarah had said he would eventually believe her. "I love George. Can you say the same for Tessa, or is she nothing more to you than chattel?"

A pained expression crossed his face. "Tessa is a free woman to do as she wishes."

"I shouldn't have said that," Chris quickly apologized, "but it doesn't excuse you from reading the ledger."

He bowed. "On that point, I beg forgiveness. I truly thought it was a plantation ledger."

Tessa appeared behind him, carrying a maroon woolen skirt. "I make it da way you want." She demonstrated by showing the split in the skirt like culottes.

"Perfect," Chris said, taking the skirt from the servant.

Amused, Tom raised a questioning eyebrow. "Do women from..." He glanced over at Tessa, before continuing, "...the North usually wear such garments?"

"No, but I want to be comfortable riding. Thank you, Tessa."

Tom smirked. Hoping that Sarah was right and he would come to believe her story, she left the kitchen. After changing into her new skirt and having a quick bite to eat in the kitchen with Tessa, she headed to the stable where George was readying the stallion, Raven, for his morning fishing trip. Upon seeing her, he drew her into his arms. "I missed you at breakfast."

"You know I don't think it's appropriate for me to be there when Margaret's present."

Sadness crossed his features, and he broke their embrace. "She stayed in her room this morning."

What a fool she was for loving him. No matter what Geoff had said to her in the dream, George still loved Margaret. "George . . ."

He cleared his throat. "Where are you off to this morning?"

"Another look for my necklace."

A smile replaced his frown. "Care for some company?"

"As long as your brother isn't invited."

With a bow, he kissed the back of her hand. "He's already left for home. I'll saddle a horse for you."

That's why she loved him. He was so much like Geoff.

George withdrew the chestnut mare with a flaxen mane from her stall and snapped her into a crosstie, then began to curry her coat. "Why don't you like Tom?"

"I don't dislike him," she said, remaining on the opposite side of the mare.

The currycomb moved through the mare's hair. "But . . ."

"He doesn't believe me."

Finished currying the mare, he hung the currycomb on a nail and placed a blanket on the mare's back. "It is a rather unusual story," he admitted.

"Then why do you accept it?"

He threw a saddle on the mare's back and tightened the girth before meeting her gaze. "Because we *have* met before. If not in this lifetime, then . . ." Returning to his task, he slipped a bit in the mare's mouth. "I can't say I'm ready to accept the fact that I will be Geoff at some future time, but I acknowledge that we know each other from somewhere."

After he led the horses to the outside courtyard, he boosted her on the back of the mare. The split skirt definitely gave her more freedom. George had never questioned her riding manner, and she reasoned more women had probably ridden astride than history books cared to let on. She cleared her throat as he mounted Raven. "George, did you know that Tom was seeing Tessa?"

He laughed. "I think we know each other well enough for you to say what's really on your mind. Tom has been *seeing* Tessa for years."

They rode side by side toward the ragged stumps that once had been a canopy of oak and sycamore. The landscape looked barren, and she could only imagine what it must have been like in the midst of a war. "Is that why Tessa stayed?" Chris asked.

George remained silent a moment as if pondering how to respond. "She chose to. Whether it was out of duty for Margaret or some affection for Tom, I can't answer. Hell, for all I know, she may be afraid of the unknown, and one day, she'll hightail it out of here without a trace."

Tessa struck Chris as a woman who feared little, and she doubted that Tessa would tolerate Tom in her bed if she didn't want him there.

When she and George arrived at the cottage, Chris tied the mare to the rail. George assured her that he would only be fishing a short distance away if she needed anything. On hands and knees, she searched for the necklace. Was it a waste of time? Geoff had given it to her in the future. And that's precisely why—she must have given up all hope of finding it the time before. She *could* change time.

A horse nickered directly behind her. Nearly shooting through her skin, she stood and pressed a hand to her chest.

"Didn't mean to startle you, Mrs. Olson," Captain Rhodes said astride his horse with Sergeant Sullivan beside him.

She wiped the dust from her skirt. "How long have you been there?"

He dismounted and removed his hat. "We just rode up, ma'am. Can we help you find something?"

Recovered from their sudden appearance, she attempted to remain calm. Although she didn't trust either of them, at least the sergeant made no threats in front of the captain. "No. Thank you."

"You sound Northern, Mrs. Olson," he said with a friendly smile.

Anxious to resume her search, she didn't care to engage the captain in idle conversation. "Boston," she replied in a clipped manner.

"And your husband?"

The sergeant studied her, while the captain kept her occupied. Was it a set up? "Virginian. Now, if you don't mind, I don't have time for chitchat." She called for George.

Captain Rhodes remounted his horse and placed his hat on his head. "My apologies, ma'am. I didn't mean to keep you from your chores."

Without taking his eyes off her, the sergeant spit on the ground, but they rode on when George led Raven in her direction. Breathing out in relief, she decided that it would be best to never be alone when looking for her necklace.

Chapter Six

FAIR BUT CRISP WEATHER GREETED CHRIS as the month of April dawned. More determined than before, she continued her mission of writing in the ledger to Geoff. George no longer questioned her about the journal, and as the days went on, the number of pages grew. She detailed the tragic accident that had cost Geoff's mother's life and caused his seizure disorder. *Please, Greta, if you read this, save Sarah's namesake.* She continued with how she had met Geoff, Sarah's birth, and how Beth would ultimately go mad and kill him.

George hitched the wagon, and she joined him on the two-mile journey to Tom's house. They reached a gaudy green Gothic-style Victorian house. When Greta lived there it had been off-white. Out back was a tumbledown shack. "I know this place," Chris said, clambering from the wagon before George could help her.

She followed the weed-filled path to the shack. A frayed rug hung in place of a door. As she approached, an elderly African-American woman lifted the rug, smiling to reveal a row of missing front teeth. She waved her inside to the dirt-floor cabin. "I be waitin' for you. You come from a great distance."

How could the old woman have known? "I saw you in a vision with Margaret. She came to see you . . ." About an abortion because she had been so afraid. Thankfully, the former slave hadn't agreed, and Jason had been born. "How do you know about me?"

"Miss Sarah sees and talks to da dead."

Chris's own daughter. In Sarah's time, they were all dead. "She said that she would help. Do you know how?"

The old woman shook her head. "It ain't clear yet, but she tell me when she can." The woman's gap-toothed smile widened as the rug lifted and George joined them. "You come to help him," she said to Chris before falling silent.

Chris turned to George. "George, why don't you see if Tom is home? I'll be along in a few minutes." With a nod, he left the shack. "I'm afraid that I don't know your name."

"Hester. Da missus know more dan she let on, but she know dat she cain't stop time."

A brisk wind whistled through the cracks between the boards of the shack. Chris tightened her shawl. She guessed the former slave meant that Margaret suspected her and George's relationship. "Is there anyway that we can help Margaret?"

"She see da soldier spirit. He curse her. You found da answer afore, but it too late to help her."

Why hadn't she thought of it herself? Margaret had buried the scout in the cellar, and his body wasn't discovered until the twenty-first century. Soon after he was buried elsewhere, his hauntings had halted. "Thank you, Hester. I'm sure we'll be speaking to one another again soon."

Hester cackled. "Of dat I have no doubt."

Chris said her goodbye and followed the path that George had taken. The walk that Greta had meticulously lined with evergreen shrubs was bare. Bricks were cracked, and the steps leading to the house, rotting. She knocked on the door.

Tom answered with a welcoming grin. "What have we here? The woman who travels through time."

Aware that he was mocking her, she stepped inside to a warm hearth fire. "We've been over this. You shouldn't have been reading my personal writings."

"And I have already apologized for doing so."

With his arms crossed, George stood a few feet from his brother.

"Tom," she said evenly. Sarah's words gave her the strength to continue. "I can prove to you that I come from Poplar Ridge during a future time."

"By all means." Tom gestured with his one good arm to have a seat.

Like the furniture at Poplar Ridge, the chairs were made of scrap pieces and wobbled. Once she was seated, George sat beside her. And now that she was in Tom's presence, she had no idea what to say. She had been acutely aware of many personal facts about George, but with Tom, she knew very little. Had he married and had children of his own? She couldn't even pretend to answer the most basic questions. Chris cleared her throat. "You'll live into the twentieth century."

Tom rolled his eyes, then burst out laughing. "Unless I die tomorrow that proves very little."

"If anything should happen to George or me, I'm counting on you to get my ledger to Greta."

Between laughing fits, he stopped just long enough to take a breath. "Greta?"

Keep calm. Sarah had said he would help. "Greta will be named after her grandmother, Margaret. She will be Jason's daughter. Greta will bridge the gap to my husband, Geoff."

Tears entered his eyes. He laughed so hard that he nearly fell off his chair in hysterics. "My little nephew . . . a daughter named Greta. I suppose we'll know the answer to that in twenty years."

Try a little over thirty, Chris thought, but she remained silent on that point.

"Tom," George said, finally speaking up. "Chris has given me convincing evidence that she could be telling the truth."

Still laughing, Tom straightened. "Could be telling the truth? George, don't tell me you're losing your senses because you're sharing her bed."

George sent his brother a scorching look. "She knew about Georgianna."

"Georgianna?" Tom shrugged, brushing the tears from his eyes. "What does that prove? There's a marker with her name in the cemetery."

George opened his mouth to continue. "No, George," Chris said, interrupting. It was time to play her ace. "I can handle myself. During the war, Margaret shot and killed a Union lieutenant with his own gun because he attempted to rape her. The bullet hit him in his left eye. After she and Tessa had dragged his body from the river's edge, they buried him in the cellar at Poplar Ridge."

Blinking in shock, George stared at her.

Tom sobered. "That should be easy to verify."

Chris stood. "I was counting on you to say that. I'll show you where he's buried."

"Chris?" George got to his feet. "Margaret refused to tell me what she had done with the body. How . . . ?"

"We found his skeleton—in 2004."

Both men fell silent, obviously mulling the year around in their heads.

"Gentlemen. Shall we unearth a Yankee?"

As they nodded in agreement, Chris hoped she was making the right choice. If the scout's body was reburied in the nineteenth century, then he should no longer haunt Margaret.

The stairs leading to the cellar creaked beneath their feet. George took Chris's hand and led the way with Tom trailing behind them. The tiny windows in the thick cellar walls let in very little light. At the bottom of the steps, he raised a lantern to cut through the darkness. "Exactly where is he buried?" he asked.

"We assumed that Margaret and Tessa had dragged him down the tunnel," Chris said, gesturing in the general direction of the tunnel. "We shoveled for quite sometime before giving up."

Still a little skeptical of what they might find, George continued, "I presume you mean you and your husband?"

She shook her head. "My friend Judith and me. Saber led us to him by lifting a leg on the panel . . . over here."

George overheard Tom laugh. "Saber sounds like that cur you used to have, George."

"There wasn't a finer dog than Washington," he reminded Tom as Chris pointed directly at a panel beneath the staircase. He drew in his breath as it suddenly occurred to him there had been no covering before the war. "I'll fetch a crowbar to pry the boards apart." With the lantern guiding the way, he went into the adjacent room and searched through a toolbox. Most of his tools had been stolen during the war, but as luck would have it, he still possessed a crowbar.

After retrieving the tool, he returned to the main section of the cellar where Chris and his brother waited. He placed the crowbar beneath the first board and pried. Tom gave a slight tug and removed the board as George positioned the crowbar for the second board. It came away easily, but the final board resisted. He added more muscle, and the board gave way. A trunk rested behind the recess of the stairwell. He dropped the crowbar to the floor with a resounding clang.

With Tom's aid, George dragged the trunk from beneath the stairs. As soon as the trunk was on the cellar floor, Chris opened it. He had prepared himself with what they were likely to find, but he heard a woman's scream. Covering her mouth, Margaret stood on the stairs. A complete skeleton with a blue uniform rested inside the box. Red hair clung to a skull with a bullet hole where the left eye should have been.

As Chris slammed the trunk shut, Margaret raced down the stairs. "Nooooo!" Her lip curled, revealing her teeth, and her fists flailed at the lid. "He's dead! Let him stay that way!" She kept pounding the trunk.

George caught her bloodied, flying fists.

She continued to struggle against his grip. Finally her fire faded, and she lowered her fists. "Don't you understand?" she said, sobbing on his shoulder. "I shot him because he violated me."

Violated her? Anger welled inside him. He clenched his hands. "Margaret . . ."

Almost in a daze, she stared at him with tears streaking her cheeks. He reached for her, but she withdrew. She always pulled away. Now, he understood why.

"George . . . ," came Chris's voice.

He had forgotten about Chris and Tom's presence.

"Let me take Margaret upstairs while you and Tom rebury the scout. Take him as far away from here as possible."

Tom raised his arm that ended in a stump. "I need your help, brother."

Unable to move, George felt Tom tug on his arm. *Margaret.* He should have been there to protect her.

* * *

Time had changed, and Margaret had finally revealed part of the truth to George. Would it be enough to help her heal? She'd likely need to disclose how Georgianna had died as well. Chris guided Margaret to the drawing room.

"I've shamed George."

"You haven't," Chris insisted. "Now he knows one of the reasons why you've been so sad."

"But it was my fault."

Chris helped the trembling woman to a chair. "It wasn't your fault. Put the blame where it belongs—on Lieutenant Robert Howard. He is the one who beat and assaulted you. *You* did nothing wrong."

Margaret placed her hands to her face. Her lashes fluttered as if she might cry again, but she kept from weeping. Her knuckles were torn and bleeding from pounding the trunk.

"Here, let me get a cloth to clean you up."

"Where's Tessa?"

"I'm sure she's seeing to her chores."

Margaret's violet eyes held a haunting fear, as if she were a lost child without the servant's aid.

Afraid to leave her alone, Chris decided to forgo searching for a cloth. Heck, she had seen enough TV programs where the women ripped petticoats for bandages and the like. She lifted her dress. Fortunately, there was a small tear in her petticoat. The cotton weave of nineteenth-century fabric was much stronger than that of the twenty-first. With difficulty, she tore off a piece and dabbed Margaret's hands.

As she swabbed and dried the blood, the swatch made her think of Geoff's warning. Had she also torn the fabric of time? By helping Margaret she might inadvertently bring George and Margaret together again. In turn, couldn't that also affect her relationship with Geoff?

"There had been a lot of Yankees through here. I treated many of them when the house served as a hospital."

Margaret's voice had been monotone and distant, but she was talking. Really talking. Chris's choice was made. "Go on."

"Lieutenant Howard and his men stopped for a meal. We had very little food to spare, but Tessa and I served what we could. I told them to eat and leave. Lieutenant Howard got up from the table, swaggering from inebriation. He bumped me, and I accidentally spilled some hot coffee on him. He and his men tied me to a tree and tore my dress. Lieutenant Howard touched me in ways that only George had before—except George was always gentle. Then he whipped me. Tessa begged them to stop. I'm not sure how long he left me tied to the tree." Margaret lifted her gaze to meet Chris's. "He allowed Tessa to take me to the library. His men took Tessa, and he . . ." She placed a fist to her mouth and choked back a sob. "I got his gun, but I wasn't successful that time. I fought against him. I should have died. I didn't tell George because I was so ashamed."

"You're a survivor, Margaret." Chris wished she had access to a counselor from her time, but she had made a major breakthrough. "George will understand why you were afraid."

Margaret's eyes widened with terror. "He must never find out."

"But you told him . . ."

"No!" Margaret gave Chris a shove and bolted.

Tessa entered the drawing room, and Margaret fled to her arms. The servant shot Chris a harsh stare. "You leave Miss Margaret be."

"Tessa . . ."

"If'n you go to your room," Tessa said to Margaret, "I be straight up with your medicine." Margaret left the room, and Tessa focused on Chris. Her glare grew harsher. "I don't care if'n you white an' sharin' Mr. George's bed. You leave Miss Margaret be."

Deciding that Tessa was instrumental in Margaret's healing, Chris said, "She told me what happened with the Union scout."

"Ain't it enough dat she live through it again an' again in her head?"

"She has suffered enough," Chris agreed, "but she needs to heal. Laudanum isn't the answer."

Tessa placed her hands on her hips. "Da doctor say laudanum help her melancholy."

"Does it really? Is she any better than she was a year ago?"

The servant's eyes narrowed. "I already warn you." She made an about turn and followed Margaret.

What was she going to do? She was running out of time.

* * *

Near the stable, George and Tom loaded the trunk on the wagon. They took a seat at the front, and George flicked the reins to Raven and the mare. The wagon lurched forward and bumped along the dirt path toward the cemetery. Unable to rest until the bastard was buried, George asked the team for more speed. A wheel hit a pothole, nearly propelling the trunk from the wagon.

"Slow down, brother, or *we* may not arrive in one piece."

"You heard what he did to Margaret."

"His men did the same to Tessa."

George glanced quickly at Tom before returning his gaze to the lane. "You knew about this?"

His brother shook his head. "Tessa told me what happened to her, but she's so goddamned tight-lipped, she would never say anything that might shame Margaret."

Shame? And that was precisely the reason why Margaret had never told him what had happened. Up ahead came a cloud of dust. Sergeant Sullivan and a couple of his men rode toward them. George's forehead broke out in a sweat. If the Yanks discovered they were hauling another Yankee's remains, he and Tom would likely be hanged. Was that the death Chris had come to keep from happening?

Deciding to play it safe, George slowed the wagon to a halt and lowered his hat. "Good day, Sergeant."

Sullivan and a private stopped beside the wagon. He glanced from George to Tom, then back again. "Cameron, we would like to use your cabin."

The sergeant always phrased a request as an order. "Help yourself." Sullivan looked as if he was about to ride on, but he gave George a hard stare. George's hands grew so sweaty that the reins nearly slipped through his fingers. "Was there anything else, Sergeant?"

Sullivan nodded. "We're much obliged for your help. It's a long ride to headquarters." He squeezed his horse to a trot and waved for the private to follow.

George took a deep breath and cued the horses to resume walking. After a mile, he brought the wagon to a halt near the the family cemetery. Tom helped him unload the trunk, and he resisted the temptation to dump the damned Yank's bones on the ground for the feral curs to scatter to the four corners of the earth. They lugged the trunk past the brick wall. Wooden crosses marked the slave burial ground. Even though Tessa was the only remaining servant on the estate, he would never foul her family's hallowed ground with such a loathsome wretch.

"Wait." Tom set his end of the trunk on the ground and flexed his hand before gripping the handle again.

Sometimes he forgot that his brother was missing an arm. "Are you all right now?"

Tom nodded, and they continued well past the cemetery before setting the trunk down. George began to dig into the sandy ground, while his brother leaned against a tree. "George, if she's telling the truth about traveling through time, have you given thought to the meaning?"

With anger welling inside him, he flipped a load of dirt off to the side and sank the shovel into the dirt as if he could attack the dead Yankee with it. He shoveled harder and faster. "I've given thought to nothing else since finding out what that bastard did to Margaret. A quick death was too good for him."

"I didn't mean that."

Confused, George looked up, breaking his rhythm. "Then what?"

"That she came here to prevent your death."

George shrugged but continued shoveling. "We both faced death everyday during the war."

"True, but if she's telling the truth, she said that I'd live into the twentieth century. Does that mean I can court disaster, doing whatever I please and still live to see the next century without fear of retribution? But for you, she may know the exact day and time. She'd be unable to do anything about an illness. If she plans on preventing your death, then it must be an accident, or . . ."

Tom's insinuation made him shiver. He had already surmised that his death would be a violent one, and he had no doubt that Sullivan was involved.

"Aren't you even the least bit concerned on what her plan may be?"

"I've thought about it," George admitted, "but it's pointless to dwell on it."

"Pointless? If you know how and when, you may be able to help Chris in forestalling destiny."

Sometimes Tom could be a little too philosophical for his tastes. "If it's my time, it's my time."

"Apparently, Chris doesn't think so."

Halting his shoveling, George straightened. Could Chris really prevent a premature death? He shook his head. It was best not to dwell on it. He returned to the business at hand, digging the grave. Fortunately, Tom no longer interrupted and allowed him to finish. Covered in sweat, he rested a minute to catch his breath. The hole was shallow but deep enough for a few bones.

Together, they pitched the contents of the trunk into the ground. George picked up the shovel to finish the job. Instead of covering the bones, he pounded the shovel against the skull—again and again. The skull cracked. He whacked it another time. The crack lengthened. One more blow, and the skull shattered. He aimed at the remaining bones.

Tom seized his arm. "He's not worth it! He's dead. You're not."

"Does it really matter? I wasn't there for Margaret when she needed me, and now . . ." Thinking of Chris, George trailed off.

His brother gave a nod in understanding. "Let's finish here."

As George covered the bones, dark thoughts intruded. Lord forgive him, but he no longer cared if Margaret came out of her melancholy state. For now, he loved Chris.

Unable to concentrate, Chris fidgeted with a pen in the library. George and Tom had been gone for over three hours. She should have accompanied them. Then again, she had made progress with Margaret, but her time was growing shorter. She dipped the pen and continued writing to Geoff. What she wouldn't give for a simple ballpoint pen. Ink blotted, and she barely heard the door open as she muttered, "Christine Catherine."

"You have a lovely name."

Her head jerked up. Sergeant Sullivan stood with his hat in hand across from her. Immediately, she closed the ledger.

"Forgive me, ma'am. I didn't mean to startle you."

"What are you doing here?" she asked, hoping the waver in her voice didn't betray her fear.

"Cameron allowed us the use of his cabin, and I was hoping to find that he had returned. We found what looks to be a rather valuable piece of jewelry."

Her necklace. Her heart pounded. "Jewelry?"

"It appears to be a family heirloom." A condescending smile spread across his face. "I presumed it belongs to *Mrs.* Cameron."

Should she risk handling the matter herself? "He should be back momentarily if you wish to speak with him. Or if you prefer, I can relay a message."

"I'll catch him another time." He turned. As she started to take a deep breath, he faced her once more. "I don't believe we were ever properly introduced. Sergeant John Sullivan."

Although his tone had changed, she still didn't trust him, and dammit, what was the proper nineteenth-century introduction for a woman? Should she present her hand, or was that an upper-class custom? "Mrs. Olson," she replied, leaving her hand on the desk.

"And your husband served the Union?"

"He was a friend of the Cameron family before the war. He didn't serve the Union due to frequent epileptic fits."

His grin widened as he placed his hat on his head. "I see. Good day to you, ma'am."

"Sergeant." Once he closed the door behind him, Chris lowered her head to her folded arms on the desk. Should she ask for George's help to get her necklace back or try on her own? *Tell George.* She didn't know how long she had remained unmoving, when she heard tired footsteps moving toward her. Worried that Sergeant Sullivan had returned, she smiled in relief to see George.

His shoulders sagged from exhaustion, and his face registered weariness. He approached the desk and sank into the chair across from her. "The deed is done."

She would tell him about the sergeant's visit later. "Where did you bury him?"

"Past the slave burial ground, which is near the family cemetery."

Unaware that a slave cemetery existed on the estate, she hoped the scout was buried far enough away to never bother anyone again.

"Chris, I've been thinking. Georgiana was she . . . ?"

"She was your daughter." But Margaret might not have realized that fact. Even if she did, would it help her torment, since she was responsible for the baby's death?

His brow furrowed. "Why do I get the feeling that you're telling me only pieces of what you know? If you won't tell me how I will die, then at least do me the courtesy of letting me know how long I have left."

"The less you know, the better."

"Dammit, Chris!" With an angry scowl, he stood. "My wife is as good as dead because of what that Yankee bastard did to her. Not knowing what was wrong with her, I tried to help. Nothing changed. Now that I do know, I've discovered that I . . ." Closing his eyes momentarily, he swallowed hard. ". . . love someone else. If I have little time left, do I try to aid Margaret once more or follow my heart?"

"George, don't give up." Chris gestured to the ledger. "I've already proven that time can be changed."

"There's no way you can know that any of the changes makes a difference."

"It does. Geoff . . . *You* told me that it can be changed."

He leaned back in the chair, and the tension on his face relaxed as if he were contemplating what she had said.

"There's something else you should know. Georgianna . . . I'm not certain when Margaret found out that she was your daughter, but she . . ." *Stop stuttering and tell him.* "Margaret was responsible for the baby's death."

George stared at her, stunned. "Because she thought Georgianna was the Yank's?"

Chris managed a weak nod.

"That's not possible. Margaret isn't capable of . . ."

"Her depression, I mean melancholy, is caused by much more than what he did to her. Georgiana's death plagues her. The laudanum dulls her pain, so she never comes to terms with what happened." Chris came close to revealing how he would die but thought better of the idea. Nothing would be gained by it. "Don't you see? What happens now will affect *us* in the future."

"Are you saying I should forget how I feel about you?"

She got up and massaged his tense shoulders. "Not at all. We've been through so much together. It's part of who we are. But Margaret needs to find peace."

"Who we are," he repeated. "I have no notion who *I* am anymore."

Even though he wasn't afflicted by memories from a past lifetime like Geoff, he had difficulty absorbing all of the information she had given him. She moved around the chair to face him and clasped his hands. Kneeling down, she met his gaze. "I have no idea what my fate is during this time. I can't return to my own without the crystal necklace. Sergeant Sullivan found it."

"Sullivan?"

"He was here when you and Tom were burying the lieutenant. He thought the necklace belonged to Margaret. I remember a picture of her taken during the 1920s. She was wearing the necklace. I can only surmise that I won't make it back, except through the natural progression of time."

"I shall do my utmost to get the necklace for you." He placed his hands on each side of her face, then kissed her.

"Just as long as you don't do anything foolish about Sullivan." Wrapping her arms around his neck, she shivered. The prospect of living in the nineteenth century wouldn't seem so bad, if George remained alive. Where were her feminist convictions? Women had no freedom here. Yet she was with the man she loved. Right now, that was all that mattered.

Chapter Seven

ON GEORGE'S FIRST TRY TO CONTACT SULLIVAN, he had spent the entire day traveling to and from headquarters in Richmond only to discover the sergeant was on patrol. These days, the Yankees were few in number, and Sullivan had large expanses of ground to cover. Later in the week, Tom informed him that he had seen the sergeant at a tavern where locals were aware the Yank spent hours drinking, gambling, and frolicking with barmaids. By the time George arrived at the tavern, Sullivan had already left.

Returning to Poplar Ridge, George guided Raven to the path alongside the river. He gazed upon the waves and thought of Delaware Bay. Ice had formed on the water in the winter, and each man had been allotted only one blanket. Without a sound in the night, the officer next to him had frozen to death.

He blinked back the memory to gaze upon the peaceful waters. Unlike the bay, the James gave life. Raven fidgeted beneath the saddle. He was trembling, and the horse had detected his uneasiness. He may have survived prison for naught. At least here, he would be buried in the land he loved. He cued the stallion forward.

When he reached the house, four horses with U.S. brands stood tied out front. Two of Sullivan's men lounged on the grass near the horses. Resentment still lingered from the war, and none of them acknowledged the other when he tied Raven to the rail. As he ascended the steps, Sullivan and Captain Rhodes appeared on the veranda. "Cameron," Rhodes acknowledged. "I've been told that you were looking for my sergeant."

A hint of a smile tugged across Sullivan's lips. "If it's in regard to the necklace, I've returned it."

George had the feeling that he wasn't going to like what the sergeant had to say. "Returned it?"

His phony grin widened. "I presumed the little woman was pining for her family keepsake. The captain insisted we make a special trip from headquarters to give it to her."

Chris had warned him that Margaret would end up with the necklace. Now he knew why Sullivan hadn't simply pawned it. Deciding not to give the sergeant any satisfaction that he was outraged by his despicable act, George extended his hand. "It appears that I was wrong about you, Sullivan. I assure you that you'll be suitably rewarded for your kind gesture."

Without taking George's hand, Sullivan glanced at it, then met his gaze in a challenge. Good, honest *hatred*. George dropped his hand to his side. In a far from reunited country, war still waged within their hearts. *Don't waste your time with him. Get the necklace.*

As Sullivan stomped down the steps to his waiting horse, his spurs jingled. Rhodes lingered behind. "You have my apology, Cameron. I only learned about my sergeant's find last evening. The necklace would have been returned sooner, had I known."

"Thank you."

"The war is over. Can't *we* at least make peace?" Rhodes held out his hand.

War memories had biased his judgment. Not all Yankees were scoundrels. George shook the captain's hand.

"I don't know whether it will help, but I've given a recommendation to the colonel in hope that we can cut through the bureaucracy in Washington to issue you a pardon."

"You did this for me? Why?"

"To ease tensions. Our country needs to heal its wounds."

Thankfully, the war *was* over, and he could regard this man as a friend. After exchanging another handshake and "thank you," George went inside to the main hall. "Margaret?" A light sobbing echoed in the distance. "Margaret?" As he moved toward the sound, the crying grew louder. Margaret had retreated upstairs. He placed his hand on the banister and took the steps two at a time.

Upstairs, he halted. Her crying had ceased, but the door to her room was wide open. He hurried in that direction, only to find her room empty. Then, from her wardrobe, he heard a sniffle.

"Margaret?"

A muffled sob came from inside.

He opened the door to the wardrobe. Curled in a ball, she attempted to hide from him behind her dresses. When he extended a hand, she recoiled with a scream. "No one's going to hurt you, Margaret. It's me, George."

"George?"

He helped her to her feet. Her eyes were red and swollen from crying, and she trembled.

"You told me that he was gone," she cried on his shoulder.

"He?"

"You know—*him.*"

He took a linen handkerchief from his pocket and dried her eyes. "That was Captain Rhodes and his sergeant. Tom and I buried the . . ." He caught himself before uttering "bastard." "We buried the scout away from here. He'll never bother you again."

She grasped the handkerchief and finished drying her eyes. "Captain Rhodes?"

"You've met him before."

Another sniffle, and she twisted the handkerchief in her hands. "I saw the blue uniforms from the top of the stairs and thought . . ."

At least now he had some comprehension for the reason of her melancholy. "I know," he said, reassuring her once more that the scout would never harm her again. "Margaret, didn't you speak to Rhodes?"

She continued twisting the handkerchief. "Should I have?"

"No." For the first time since his return from the war, she didn't flinch when he hugged her. Tessa must have spoken with Rhodes. He'd question the servant later. Right now, Margaret needed him. His fingers stroked her hair, and she closed her eyes, relaxing in his arms. What in the hell was he supposed to do now? There might be a chance that she could get well.

* * *

Afraid of what she might find, Chris had held off visiting the cemetery. No spires or granite headstones existed, and the red-hued oak Geoff had been buried beneath was barely ten feet tall. The entire area of the new section was nothing more than wispy grass. She knelt to the ground and ran her hand along it. Why had she been expecting headstones with familiar names?

"Chris . . ."

For a second, she thought of Winston after the funeral. He would grasp her arm and lead her to the waiting car. She stood and turned to George. "The tree was at least sixty feet tall when I left."

"This place must have special meaning to you."

Should she tell him? "It's where we buried Geoff." Confusion registered in his eyes. She could read his expressions just like she had been able to with Geoff. Was that surprising? And he still probably didn't fully comprehend the dual life he would lead.

His gaze shifted to the four-foot red brick wall. He moved toward it. "Then you know where I shall be buried."

Concerned about his mood, Chris followed him.

When he opened the iron gate, the groan from its hinges that she remembered so well was absent. "My grandfather had the wall built to keep the livestock out."

As he went past several tombstones, the names leaped out at her. Joseph and Susan Alden Cameron. *His parents.* These were no longer mere names carved on stones, but people George had known and loved. People he had grieved for upon their deaths.

He came to a halt near a grave. Unlike the others, no fancy stone adorned the spot—only a plain wood headboard. *Georgiana.* Somehow the marker for her grave would disappear, and Geoff would eventually see that she received a proper headstone.

George's voice was soft when he spoke. "Now I understand why Margaret didn't initially tell me about her."

A daughter that he would never know. One that she had seen in a vision from beyond the grave. It made her yearn for Sarah. The only way to stop the madness was to prevent events from repeating. "Did you find my necklace?"

Her question broke his pensive mood. "Margaret was upset by seeing the Yanks. She didn't speak with them. I'll check with Tessa."

"How is Margaret?"

He shrugged. "Who can say? But I saw a tiny spark in her that I haven't seen since returning from the war."

That news gave her hope. She might have a chance of saving George's life after all. "Where did you bury him?"

He gestured to the ground beyond the wall. "Over yonder, a good distance beyond the slave cemetery."

Chris looked in that direction. Wood crosses marked the graves of the slaves. The markers were so fragile that they probably would weather rapidly with age. No wonder she had never known of its existence. She went through the gate, beyond the oak where Geoff would be buried to the slave cemetery. She'd write about the burial ground in the ledger. That way if the ledger reached Geoff, the area could be properly marked and preserved.

George joined her.

"Where have all of their families gone?" she asked.

"I don't know. They left before I returned from the war. It's just as well. If I can't afford a bookkeeper, I would have never been able to pay wages to farm the land."

So much history that she was ignorant of. But she was getting distracted again. She hadn't come there for a history lesson. "Take me to the spot where you buried him."

"Over here."

She put her arm through his, and he guided her to a desolate spot several hundred yards from the other graves. A fresh mound of dirt was the only sign there had been a burial. She hoped the grave was far enough away from the house to keep the scout from interfering with Margaret's life again. "Maybe we should put a clove or two of garlic on the grave."

George stared at her, perplexed.

"Never mind. It's a joke, but it would take too long to explain. I love you." She kissed him on the mouth. At first, he was a little hesitant, but then he took her into his arms. She felt resistance. As she had feared, he still loved Margaret. In the long run, would that affect her and Geoff?

* * *

For the next two weeks, Chris found concentrating on bookwork next to impossible. Margaret had remained unapproachable since uncovering the scout's body due to Tessa guarding her like a hawk. As she had feared, the servant had acquired the necklace from the soldiers and given it to Margaret. George gave excuses why he hadn't retrieved it from her. Worried and upset that history was about to replay itself, Chris occasionally rode over to Hester's. The kinship she felt toward the former slave woman was similar to the affection she had formed for Greta.

As she lay awake worrying about what action she should take next, she decided to discuss it with Hester in the morning. She felt the bed stir. George sat up abruptly. He trembled beneath her fingertips and his heart raced. "George?"

He touched her face as if checking to make certain she was real, then took a deep breath. "For a moment, I thought I was at Spotsylvania."

Disturbed by dreams of the war or Fort Delaware, he often woke suddenly in the night. Posttraumatic stress—years would pass before the term was even used. Chris stroked the stubble on his chin. "It's all right," she murmured.

Huddling next to her, he lowered his head to rest on her breast. Soon, he breathed easy again. Near morning, Chris thought that she should be returning to her room. Not that her keeping a separate room fooled anyone, but discretion was still the best policy. "I should be getting up."

He muttered a goodbye, and she slipped from beneath the quilt. She quickly dressed and shuffled sleepily down the stairs to the library and across the dark path to the main house. Upon returning to her room, she felt queasy to her stomach. She bent over the chamber pot and threw up. And her period was late—the symptoms were all too familiar. Her single experience of pregnancy with Sarah reminded her how miserable she had been during the first trimester. So much for time travel being an effective method of birth control. She should have known better than to trust fate. But what choice had she been given? It wasn't like she could have driven over to a drugstore and picked up a box of condoms.

Hester would be able to advise her. Unable to sleep, she lay on the straw mattress for a couple of hours. When the light of dawn arrived, she went downstairs. In order to avoid Tessa, she headed to the stable to wait for George. The spring day was clear and robins trilled, making her realize how little time she had left. May was nearly here.

As she crossed the grounds, she spotted George up ahead, carrying Jason, and Margaret had her arm intertwined with George's. A genuine smile beamed on Margaret's face. Her heart ached. Shouldn't she be happy seeing them together? After all, wasn't this the moment she had been working for? George would live if Margaret got better. She placed a hand to her abdomen. None of them had expected such a complication.

To remain undetected, she turned and made a beeline for the stable. Like everything else, the bricks were crumbling. She led Raven from his stall, snapped the stallion into a crosstie, and began to brush through his coat. George entered the stable and smiled upon seeing her. "Chris, I want to thank you."

Should she tell him? What would be the point? If Hester could help her, she didn't plan on keeping the baby anyway. "You're welcome."

Avoiding her gaze, he shifted on his feet. "Margaret is getting better. I see it in her manner. She's cut down the amount of laudanum she's been taking."

Chris continued brushing Raven. "That's good to hear."

"You don't understand . . ."

Finished grooming the horse, she turned to him. His eyes reflected indecision and confusion. "It's all right, George. She is your wife."

"If it were that simple . . ." He shook his head in frustration. "You're looking a little pale this morning."

"My stomach is feeling a little uneasy," she admitted. "I thought I'd ride over and see Hester. She might have a potion to help settle it."

He studied her a minute. *Did he suspect?* Finally, he said, "I'll accompany you."

"No," she said a little louder than intended. Collecting herself, she lowered her voice. "That won't be necessary. I'm sure you have chores to tend to."

"I do," he agreed, "but I want to make certain you're all right."

"I'm fine," she assured him.

"The least I can do is saddle Raven for you."

Queasy to the pit of her stomach, she massaged her belly. She hoped that she wouldn't have to throw up again. "That would be most welcome. Thank you." As he went to retrieve the tack, she touched the stallion's black hair. "Where was he wounded?"

He placed a blanket and saddle on the horse's back. "You know so much about me, yet I know very little about you." She opened her mouth, but he held up a hand. "I know. It's best if I don't know. Why do I have the feeling that the event you came here to prevent is near at hand?"

"George . . ." She inspected a jagged scar on the horse's shoulder.

He cinched the girth. "You've found where he was wounded. He nearly died."

And he had been returned by General J.E.B. Stuart. Margaret had thought George was dead. Chris blinked back the memory of Margaret's vision.

George finished tacking Raven. "Chris . . ."

"Don't say it." Grasping the stallion's reins, she led him into the courtyard. George boosted her onto Raven's back, and she leaned down in the saddle and kissed George on the forehead. "I'll return in a few hours."

Obviously perplexed by her behavior, he whispered, "Bye."

In an effort to keep her nausea under control, she squeezed the stallion to a walk. Two miles at a slow walk. What she wouldn't give for a faster mode of transportation. Ironically, in the twenty-first century, she had preferred horseback. Sycamore and poplar trees lined the road. Unfortunately, the lane was dirt and pitted with pot-holes. At least, on horseback, she could easily avoid them.

Forty-five minutes later, the green Victorian came into view. Hoping to avoid Tom, she brought Raven to a halt around back, near Hester's shack. "Hester?"

Chris dismounted, and the old woman lifted the rug and appeared in the doorway. She smiled her toothless grin and waved Chris inside. "Miss Chris."

Even after all her years of living in Virginia, Chris had never grown accustomed to being called "Miss Chris." She tied the stallion to a post and stepped inside. "Hester, I'm pretty certain that I'm pregnant. I can't have a baby. Not here."

The old woman pressed a withered hand to her abdomen. "Mr. George's?"

Chris nodded. "There is no one else. I love him."

Hester palpated her abdomen. "An' he love you. He take care of you an' da baby."

Did she really need to spell it out? "But I'm not from this time, and George..." She had nearly slipped that he might soon die. "George is already married. I can't live like that."

A grin crossed Hester's mouth, and she dropped her hand to her side. "You ain't got no choice. She be Sarah."

"Sarah?" She reached to her belly. Her daughter from her own time? "How is that possible?"

"I don' know how, only dat it is."

When Sarah had said that she'd help, she could never have imagined. Maybe they were meant to live as a family after all—in this time. Undecided whether to be sad or elated by her predicament, Chris thanked the old woman. As she left the shack, she nearly ran into Tom. Suddenly dizzy, she swayed on her feet. He grasped her arm to help steady her and aided her along the weed-filled path.

Once she was seated in front of a crackling fire, he gave her a tin cup, containing a mixture of chicory root and something she couldn't quite make out. The hot liquid tasted similar to an herbal tea. On a chilly morning, the drink was soothing—just what she needed to help settle her upset stomach.

"Chris, we need to talk."

His baritone voice intruded on her concerns, and she worried about how much he had heard before she left Hester's. "I have nothing to say."

"I'm a friend, and George is my brother. How much time does he have?"

"I'm not a fortune teller."

Stress wrinkles lined his forehead, and he sat across from her. "I can't help you or him if you don't tell me the details."

Sarah had foretold that she could trust Tom with the knowledge of where she had come from. Chris touched her abdomen. She believed in her daughter. With Tom's aid, they might be able to save George. Why hadn't she read Greta's journals more closely? "I don't know the date," she confessed. "Only that he died sometime in early May."

"That could be a couple of days or a fortnight," he said, letting out an uneasy breath. "How will he die?"

His blue eyes reminded her so much of George's. Heaven help her, but she *was* thinking of George now, not Geoff. "Do you remember the time that Margaret aimed the gun at you by the river?"

"She thought I was . . . If you hadn't been there . . . Margaret will kill George?" The worry lines etched deeper into his face. "Dammit to hell. No wonder you didn't share the details with him. He would never have suspected Margaret." His gaze grew fixed, as if he was contemplating the situation.

"Tom."

He blinked.

"Margaret won't realize what she is doing, anymore than she did with you, or—Georgiana. The family will attribute his death to suicide due to posttraumatic stress."

Genuinely confused, he arched a brow. "Post what?"

Wrong term. She quickly explained, "It's the melancholy suffered by a person that has been through a war or other stressful ordeal where their life has been threatened."

His facial expression relaxed in understanding. "Nostalgia."

She would have never guessed the term could have a negative meaning, but if someone kept reliving a traumatic event, she comprehended the origin. "I've gotten Margaret to talk about the rape, but I'm running out of time. She needs to accept the baby's death before she can come to terms with it. To do that, she must give up the laudanum. George says she has reduced the amount she's been taking, but I don't know whether it's enough. Tessa shields her from the real world and guards her accordingly."

"I can have Tessa brought here."

She shook her head. "If Margaret suffers another ordeal, it may trigger the event we're trying to avoid."

The empty sleeve of his coat raised slightly, then his left hand rubbed his chin. "Sometimes, I forget my arm isn't there. Chris, what details do you know leading up to George's death?"

"Not much, except..." In spite of her reluctance, she had to chance taking him into complete confidence. "Margaret has suspected George's involvement with me from the beginning. In one sense, she's relieved. In another, she can't help but be a jealous wife. Before George's death, she will find us together."

"I see." He exhaled slowly. "I can stay at Poplar Ridge," he suggested, searching her face.

"I'd like that," she responded in relief. At least with Tom's help, they had a fighting chance of changing time.

A day later, Chris and George ambled along the banks of the James. On such a warm spring evening the waters were calm. The sun glowed like a reddish ball as it was setting. How many times had she strolled with Geoff and taken the idyllic scene for granted? Such thoughts only reminded her how little time they might have. Still, she had to tell him about the baby. Would Sarah be another daughter that he would never know? Like when she had informed Geoff, she felt her palms grow sweaty, but George was a gentleman. He didn't say anything to embarrass her.

"I should have told you the news in the library where you could sit down."

Like a boy, he picked up a rock and skipped it off the water. "Tell me what?" He bent down and sought another rock.

"That I'm..." She had told Geoff over the phone, dreading the thought that he would propose to her. At least she had no such illusions with George. "I'm pregnant."

With his arm flexed to toss the rock, he dropped it to the ground. His face paled.

"George?"

He swallowed. "Are you certain?"

"Hester confirmed it."

"That was the reason for your uneasy stomach yesterday morning?"

She nodded, and he stared at her in shock.

"Say something," she said.

He cleared his throat. "I'm at a loss for words. Chris, I'm more than happy to see to your needs, but with such an uncertain fate ahead of me . . ."

She squeezed his hand. "That's why Tom has agreed to help. We *are* going to change time."

"Forgive me if I seem less optimistic, but you're right. Tom will help. He will see to your well-being. In fact, regardless of what happens to me, I know he likes you. I suspect he will marry you, so you don't have to suffer the shame I've brought upon you."

Her jaw dropped. She should have guessed his reaction. "Shame? Do you seriously think that I'm worried about my reputation? George, you fool. I don't want to marry Tom to save face. Besides, Tessa might have a thing or two to say about such a ridiculous suggestion."

"Tessa knows her place."

If she remained in the nineteenth century for the rest of her life, she would never get used to such attitudes. "Forget about it. The only man I'd marry in this time frame would be you, and since you're already married . . . well, I guess it's senseless to propose to you the way I did to Geoff."

"You proposed to him?"

"Things are different in my time. Women have more freedom."

He shook his head in amazement. "Some of the things you said soon after your arrival suddenly make sense." He put an arm around her and held her. "If you refuse to marry Tom, I shall find a way to see to your needs."

Wishing she could dismiss her dark thoughts, she shivered. The following day was the first of May.

Chapter Eight

THE NEXT DAY, CHRIS SLIPPED INTO THE KITCHEN and gathered fixings for a picnic. Bread, cheese, fish. She was getting so sick of fish, but the staple of their diets was provided by the James. During these times, any other meat was a luxury. A bottle of ginger beer sat on the sideboard. While she would avoid any alcohol, George might like the beer. She collected knives and forks. Funny, she was growing used to forks with three tines. She dreaded the day when she could say the same for a corset.

At the thought of spending the rest of her life in the nineteenth century, she closed her eyes. *No self pity.* Right now, she must focus on George's well-being. None of the baskets in the kitchen remotely resembled anything like a picnic basket. She made do with a wicker basket that had alternating green and yellow woven rows. The design looked African, and she suspected Tessa or her family must have made it.

As she packed the supplies into the basket, footsteps sounded on the stairs. "It time for me to make lunch," said Tessa, watching her prepare the basket.

Chris lifted the basket. Their relationship had been more strained than usual since unearthing the scout. Oh, to hell with it, she was going to ask straight out. "Tessa, why did you give my necklace to Margaret?"

"Da soldiers say it for Miss Margaret. I obey da white men and give it to her as ordered."

That one act had likely sealed her fate. Tessa's face exhibited no hint of wrongdoing, but Chris surmised the servant was a master at hiding her emotions. "Thank you, Tessa." Mulling the consequences over in her mind and ways to handle them, she headed outside and crossed the grounds to the stable. The warm spring air used to bring her joy, now it only brought sorrow. She found George with a hammer in hand, repairing a fence, while Tom held the board in place. She pasted on a smile and raised the basket for George to see. "Lunchtime."

"A picnic?" Tom responded with an amused grin. "I can't remember the last time that I've . . ."

"Sorry, Tom. I've only packed enough for two. Besides, I know you'd rather spend time with Tessa, and she's preparing your lunch back at the house."

Tom traded gazes with George and whistled. "She *is* a spirited one."

"Indeed," George replied with a growing smile. He set the hammer in his toolbox as Tom bid them a good afternoon and ambled along the path to the house. George's smile vanished. "I know what the two of you are doing."

"How do you mean?" Chris asked, pretending innocence.

"Upon waking this morning, I seem to never be alone." He grabbed a cloth from the fence rail and wiped the sweat from his forehead. "How soon?"

"I don't know."

He searched her face. "You really don't know, do you?"

She shook her head. "No."

His face paled. "But you know that it's sometime in May."

There was no reason for a response. He knew.

"Chris, at least give me a hint, so I can take action to help prevent it."

"I will, but first . . ." She held up the basket once more. "Let's saddle a couple of horses and have a picnic."

He nodded and accompanied her to the stable. After saddling Raven and the chestnut mare, they rode in the direction of the meadow. While most of the trees were gone, the spring grass had reached nearly knee high. They halted by a single dogwood and spread a linen cloth beneath it.

Chris cut the bread for sandwiches. "Where I come from the bread is already sliced."

Finally relaxing, George stretched his legs. "Tessa would certainly enjoy bread that she didn't need to slice."

The picnic setting reminded her of being with Geoff. On a similar occasion, he had been plagued with George's memories. And now, she might lose George too. They ate in silence.

"Chris, you've become quiet."

"I don't know what to do. I watched Geoff die, and I'm afraid that it's going to happen all over again."

His face grew pensive. "You said you would tell me. I'm already looking over my shoulder at the slightest sound, wondering what to expect."

Geoff had warned her that the fabric of time could be torn, but she would have been unable to live with herself if she hadn't taken the chance. That thought would keep her strong facing the difficult days ahead. She gripped his hand and squeezed it. "Margaret will shoot . . . you."

He stared at her in disbelief. "Are you certain?"

She managed a nod.

He exhaled slowly. "No wonder you didn't wish to inform me. I know she hasn't been well, but . . . Do you know the circumstances?"

She shook her head. "Only that it will happen in the library."

"Like your husband," he quickly noted.

"Yes, like Geoff," she said softly. The mood of the picnic had vanished, and she packed the plates and utensils into the basket. George got to his feet and shook the crumbs from the cloth. They loaded the supplies onto the horses. "George, I hate to bring the subject up, but I need my necklace."

"I'll get it from Margaret," he assured her.

"Why not let Tom? He could convince Tessa . . ."

"We're not sure enough of our facts. What if, as you keep hoping, that time has changed? I can't risk my brother or Tessa being in the wrong place at the wrong time."

She couldn't damn him for thinking of others first.

"Chris, I know the mood has been spoiled somewhat by your revelation, but I have something to show you." He led the horses along the path until the log frame of the cottage came into view. He tied the horses out front. Wondering what he wanted to show her, she followed him up the steps.

Inside, the knapsacks and coats had been cleared away, and the wood floor, repaired and swept. Against the far wall was a frameless feather bed.

"I wanted to restore it to the way it was before the war. Unfortunately, I don't have all of the supplies necessary."

Memories of Geoff and the time they had spent in this very spot came flooding back. "You've done a fine job," she said weakly. She thumped her fists against his chest. "Damn you! I can't keep watching you die!"

He caught her flying fists and held her, whispering that it would be all right. For ages, she clung to him. Tears streaked her cheeks as she listened to his heart beat. When she looked up, his eyes were moist. He kissed her.

She brushed away her tears. "I should have guessed why you put a feather bed in here."

His mouth formed a devilish grin, and he guided her in the direction of the bed. "I thought you might be growing weary of the straw mattress."

She sank to the bed with George atop her. Compared to the scratchy burlap, the feathers gave her a sense of floating. They kissed and caressed, almost in desperation, as if their time together might be their last. Their clothes fell to the side of the bed. Among laughter and tears, they rocked in rhythmic unison.

Wood creaked. Shadows mixed with light. Caught up in the moment, Chris barely detected a faint movement. A woman stood in the door frame, and she ducked to George's chest. Margaret bolted from the cottage.

Shaken, Chris rolled to George's side and covered herself with the coarse linen, while he got up and pulled on his trousers. "I'm sorry, George. I should have seen this coming."

His face was red with rage. "I'm going to kill my brother for telling Margaret."

Tom? She grasped his arm. "Tessa saw me packing the picnic."
"Why would Tessa . . . ?"

Still shaken, she swallowed hard. "If she thought she was protecting Margaret." And they hadn't changed a thing. Events were set
in motion. Margaret had been meant to find them together shortly
before George's death.

After finding George with Chris, Margaret had locked herself in her
room and refused to speak with him. For two solid days, George got
little sleep. His eating habits became equally irregular. No matter
what chore he engaged in, Tom lingered a few feet away. Even upon
his leaving the outhouse, he had caught his brother lurking nearby.
From a safer distance, Chris monitored his movements. In spite of
their constant presence, he suddenly felt *alone*.

In the library, he settled in the chair behind the desk and opened
a ledger. The loneliness was his own doing. He had known the consequences of caring for two women. As a result, Chris was with
child. For a second, he contemplated unlocking the case in the desk
drawer where he had stored the gun that Margaret used to kill the
Yankee scout and handing it to her himself. *Stop thinking like that.*

He checked his pocket watch—nearly ten. With a sigh, he dipped
the pen in ink and made a couple of entries in the ledger. A door
creaked. Expecting to see Chris or Tom, he looked up. No one had
entered. Certain that one of them lingered outside the door, he
stood.

"George."

He turned. Margaret stood near an open panel along the bookcase, wearing a blue silk gown with hoops underneath. She had
worn the same dress at a reception during the war. Was the occasion the last time he could recall the two of them truly being
happy? After the dance, they had retired to their room, where Georgianna had most likely been conceived. This was his chance to keep
the inevitable from happening. "Margaret, you surprised me. If you
wanted to speak to me, why didn't you use the main door?"

Her black hair glistened against her milky-white skin as she approached him. She even wore the perfume with the scent of honey-

suckle that he had imported for her as a gift. "Tom would have seen me. I wanted to apologize for my behavior."

A crystal necklace adorned her throat—the necklace that Chris had lost. He reached for it. "Apologize? Why should you apologize? It is I . . ."

Before he could touch the necklace, she grasped his hand and kissed his fingers. "I'm no longer afraid. I can be a good wife again. I want you to love me the way we used to love each other." He embraced her awkwardly, and her head came to rest on his shoulder. "George, you do love me?"

He swallowed hard. "Yes."

As she withdrew from his arms, a tear formed in the corner of her eye. "You love her, don't you?"

Another swallow. "Please believe me, I never meant to hurt you."

The tear spilled down her cheek. "I'm to blame. I've shamed you. It's only natural for you to find another."

"No, Margaret." He wiped the tear from her cheek with his thumb. "You have never shamed me. I should have been here for you. But why didn't you tell me about the Yankee scout or how Georgianna died?"

"I feared you would hate me, giving birth to that monster's child."

"I could never hate you." He clasped her hands. "Georgianna was my daughter—not the scout's. Her hair was red like my sister, Mary's."

Perplexed, she drew away from him. "I never told you what Georgianna looked like." Her voice grew soft—almost childlike—and full of grief. "I've never met Mary."

"She lives in Pennsylvania with her husband."

"George . . ." Her voice broke. "I'll return to our room from now on. If you no longer wish to join me, I understand."

The dutiful wife—he almost wished she would kick and scream in a fit of anger. *To absolve his guilt?* Nothing could release him from the burden, but her mood had improved since the unearthing of the scout. Even if his life was at stake, he owed it to her so see her through the ordeal. He gently took her hand and guided her to the door. Outside, Tom stepped toward them as they exited. George waved to his brother that everything was all right. Tears streaked

Margaret's cheeks as he showed her to the main house. Tessa and Chris stood in the front hall, both staring at them as if afraid to move.

With outstretched arms, Tessa took a hesitant step toward them. George waved the servant away. "Not now, Tessa." In complete obedience, she bowed her head. He aided Margaret up the stairs to their bedroom. The room had been closed off to the rest of the house since she had left his bed and was chilly. With a shiver, he lit a lamp. Now, he understood why she had seemed hesitant about sharing physical relations after his return from the war.

In front of the mirror, he helped her out of her gown and into her nightdress. From her neck, he unclasped the crystal pendant. For a moment, he held it. Was it possible for anyone to travel through time with the necklace? Perhaps, he and Chris... He silently chastised himself and set the necklace on the dresser. As soon as he returned it to Chris, she would travel back to the twenty-first century, without him. His responsibility lay with his wife. But what of the unborn child? Was the child part of the twenty-first century or this one?

"George?"

He should have let Tessa tend to Margaret. "Margaret, I . . ."

She sat on the bed and patted the straw mattress for him to join her. "Forgive me, please."

George closed his eyes to shut off his own tears. With some semblance of calm again, he said, "Forgive you? There is nothing to forgive. You're not to blame for what happened. Only that goddamn Yankee bastard." Unable to control his simmering rage any longer, he slammed a fist into the wall. He held his bleeding hand and cursed. *Focus, on the pain.* He preferred it. The pain would keep him from feeling anything else.

Margaret approached him and cradled his hand. "I never stopped loving you," she whispered.

Those weren't the words that he wanted to hear. "I don't want your love. You should hate me for the way I've treated you."

"I could never hate you," she said. "George . . ." She lowered her head into her hands and cried.

His first instinct was to draw away. His wife, his first love. He forced himself to stay. George put his arms around her, stiffly at first, and held her. He couldn't think. Unable to reach out to her grief, he felt weak.

With a tear-streaked face, she looked up at him. "Thank you."

"It's going to take time, Margaret. We've both changed after the war."

She swallowed but brushed away her tears. "I understand."

He kissed the back of her hand. "For the time being, I'm going to keep my room above the library. I'll see you in the morning." George grasped the necklace and placed it in his pocket before heading for the door, then thought better of the notion. He needed time to think. Chris or Tom would follow him if he retreated through the main section of the house. He ran his hands along a wood panel near the mirror until hearing a click. The panel popped open. As he entered the narrow passageway and closed the door behind him, he heard Margaret call for Tessa.

In the tight quarters, George had to duck to keep from hitting his head. He blindly fumbled through the darkness, feeling his way along the wall. He finally reached the stairway and descended to the brick floor of the cellar. Wind from the river whistled through the tunnel. He followed the sound until hearing waves from the James.

The ancient wood door stuck when he tried to open it. With a curse, he gave it a good, swift kick. It budged, then groaned on its hinges. The moon cast enough light for him to see the path back to the stable. After tacking Raven, he led the horse into the courtyard and mounted.

With a click of his tongue, he gave the stallion his head and shot off at a gallop. Hooves pounded against the dirt road. Not since the cavalry had he taken a night ride with such wild abandon. Yankees had been on his tail then, and he had allowed Raven to guide him through the darkness. He reined the stallion from the road, and the pair streaked across the uneven ground. The horse's mane whipped back in his face. Between the Yankees and Fort Delaware, how often had he cheated death? Even Raven had nearly died.

When they reached a fence, Raven sailed over as if he had sprouted wings, like the stallion's namesake. Unable to prepare for the jump in time, George flew from the saddle and collided with the ground. All over, his body screamed in pain until settling to a dull ache. Chris and Tom were trying to save his fool neck, and he could have broken it by taking a harebrained midnight ride. He began to laugh at the irony. What in hell was he going to do? He loved both women.

"George?" Sick with worry, Chris entered the library. George sat behind the desk, an empty glass before him. She breathed a sigh of relief. "There you are. Tom and I have been searching several hours for you."

The dark circles under his eyes warned her that he hadn't slept, and his rumpled shirt was streaked with dirt. He stood and limped over to the liquor cabinet, pouring himself a whiskey.

"George..." Her voice wavered. She moved closer. "That's not the answer."

Returning to the desk, he set the glass on the desktop and sank to the leather chair. His voice sounded distant when he spoke. "For so long, I wanted her to reach out to me, and now that she has I'm at a loss as to what to do."

She inspected a filthy, crusted cut above his eye, and he flinched.

"Let me get something to clean that up with." With no water easily available, she stepped over to the liquor cabinet and poured a small amount of whiskey in a glass. She withdrew a handkerchief from her sleeve and dabbed it into the whiskey. "This will likely sting."

He jerked his head back when she touched the cloth to the cut.

"You need to hold still if I'm going to clean it properly." She returned to cleaning the cut. He winced but held still. "George, there is no choice. Margaret is your wife."

"It's not that simple."

With a worried frown, she withdrew the bloody handkerchief from his forehead. "I came here to prevent your death. Now that Margaret has opened up to the truth, she will get better. You've been seeing gradual progress already. It means that I have done my job."

He pressed a hand to her abdomen. "You carry my child."

"Yes," she choked, nearly losing her voice.

George searched through a drawer and withdrew a crystal pendant on a gold chain. "It's time that you reclaim what is rightfully yours."

"My necklace." Now she had a way back to her own time. Chris lowered the glass with the whiskey to the desk, then clasped the chain in her hand. Tears entered her eyes as the crystal pendant caught the lamplight and cast a rainbow on the wall.

"Chris, before the war, I promised her to never love another, but . . ." His gaze met hers. "I knew when we first met that I loved you."

His dark mood worried her. No matter how much it hurt, she had to let go as the eddies of time revealed their true meaning. "What we shared was an echo."

"An echo?"

Fighting the tears, she spotted confusion and grief in his eyes. "I'm not of this time. You were meant to love Margaret. She is not part of the twenty-first century. I am, and you will be there too. We were meant to love each other at the right time."

"What of the child?"

A lump formed in her throat, and she unconsciously touched her abdomen. Sarah had said that she'd help. But what had she meant? "I don't know. Only time will reveal the answer."

"If you . . ." He cleared his throat. ". . . vanish the same way you arrived, how would I ever know if you were successful in reaching your time?"

"Because I'll love you again as Geoff."

His face was etched in pain, and he got to his feet. "I don't want to lose you."

"You won't." Unable to hold the tears at bay any longer, she felt like a fool. She brushed them away. "I hate it when I do this sort of thing. We made a pact, but it will be when you're Geoff. Even you said that you can't be *him*. You were right."

He embraced her and kissed her, then forced a smile. "Tell me more about what it's like in the twenty-first century."

She sniffed back her tears. "We no longer use horses for transportation. Even so, Geoff drove a car called a Mustang."

His grief gave way to curious confusion. "A railroad with the name Mustang?"

"No," she replied with a laugh. She had forgotten a car in the nineteenth century referred to a railroad car. "An automobile. At first, they will be called horseless carriages."

Chris described cars to him, and the library door creaked behind her. George's eyes widened. His hand connected brutally with her shoulder, shoving her and knocking the breath out of her. Pain shot through her left arm as she smacked to the floor. A woman screamed, and Tom shouted, then came a gunshot. Something warm spattered her face. George flew backward with his head thudding against the wood floor.

"Nooo!" she moaned. Without stopping to think, Chris crawled across the floorboards. She reached out her hand and extended her fingers, clinging to the sleeve of his shirt. She shook his arm. He didn't move. *Dammit George!* He wasn't supposed to save *her* life. "George, you can't die. We've changed time." Wrapping her fingers around his wrist, she checked his pulse—flighty—but he was still breathing. Thank God, he was alive. Where had he been hit? A small wound pierced his forehead. She bit her lip to keep from crying out. Could a person survive a head wound? She ignored the pain in her arm and drew him into her arms.

Blood pooled across the floor where his head had rested, along with something soft. When she realized that part of his brain lay on the floor, she screamed. "No, George, no!" Unleashing tears, she hugged him as if her grip could force the life from her body into his. He ceased breathing. *Just like Geoff*.

Chapter Nine

Near Charles City, Virginia
Late September 2002

Nearly eleven at night, Geoff drove the Mustang along the winding road from Williamsburg to Poplar Ridge. Familiar with the twists and curves like the back of his hand, he sped along ten miles faster than the speed limit. After a few miles, he passed his father's aunt's house. The house was dark. Greta must have already retired for the evening, which probably wasn't too surprising for a ninety-something-year-old woman.

Up ahead, a bolt of lightning struck the road, making him jump. Expecting to see smoke, he slowed the Mustang. The light radiated, intensifying, until nearly blinding him, then it flickered. A woman was trapped inside!

"Shit!" As he screeched the car to a halt, the light vanished. Only the Mustang's headlights illuminated the road. Charging from the car, he found the woman crumpled face down on the pavement. He took out his cell phone and called 911, then bent down to help. "Take it easy. Help is on the way."

Was she even conscious? He gently rolled her onto her back. Good, she was breathing. He pressed two fingers to her neck. Her pulse seemed a little fast, and her skin felt slightly warm. Her eyelids fluttered open, and she seized his hand. "George . . . hold me."

George? *Coincidence?* George was a common name, he quickly reasoned. She tried to rise, but he held her in place. "You shouldn't move just yet. Are you in pain anywhere?"

"A little tingly, but no pain."

Offhand, he didn't see any bleeding. "Can you wiggle your fingers?"

She complied.

"How about your hand?" In the distance, he heard a siren. He continued checking her for injuries.

"All of this fuss really isn't necessary."

Despite Geoff's warnings about not moving, she rose. He caught her in his arms, preventing her from hitting the pavement.

"Maybe that wasn't such a good idea after all."

"Does your head hurt?" he asked.

"No. Just tingly—like pins and needles—all over."

Flashing red lights halted a few feet from them. Paramedics rushed over with emergency equipment.

"I think she was struck by lightning," Geoff said, reporting her condition to the technician. He moved out of the way to make room for the medical personnel.

"George, don't go!"

George again. Now that the crisis was over, Geoff trembled. He spotted an object on the road. A crystal necklace. He sucked in his breath. *Chris.* Impossible. She wasn't supposed to arrive for another two years.

Chris woke with a start. A woman's face peered over her and gradually came into focus. She wore a stethoscope around her neck. Chris glanced around the room. White walls surrounded her, and a tube trailed from her arm to a plastic bag hanging beside the bed. A hospital. She had no recollection of being brought here. "Where's the man who helped me?"

"I think you mean the man who hit you with his car," the nurse responded brusquely.

"Hit me? That doesn't sound right. I was . . ."

The nurse taped the needle to her arm and began the intravenous drip. "Ms. Olson, you're one lucky lady. Most of your test results haven't returned yet, but you likely have a concussion. Now that you're awake, I'll send the doctor in to give you the details."

Her memory must be playing tricks. She couldn't remember any-thing leading up to the accident, but afterward, the man had helped her. Certain that he hadn't hit her, she asked, "What happened to the man?"

"He was charged with reckless driving and DUI."

DUI? But he rarely drank alcohol, much less drove while intox-icated. Where had the thought come from? "If possible, I'd like to see him."

The nurse peered down her beak-like nose. "Ms. Olson, you might want to consult with your attorney first."

Chris chuckled to herself. "I *am* an attorney. Please, it's impor-tant. I must speak with him."

"I'll see what I can do, but meanwhile—rest."

Exhausted, Chris obeyed, and after the doctor arrived she learned that she had been in the hospital for a few hours and would need to remain under observation until all of her tests had returned. She placed a call to her family in Boston. *No, she was fine. Don't get on a plane and fly to Richmond. She'd be in good hands with her friend, Ju-dith.* Damn it! She had forgotten to notify Judith. She was probably worried sick when she hadn't arrived on time. As she reached for the phone, a knock came to the door. "Come in."

A blond-haired man approximately in his mid to late twenties with scraggly beard growth entered. She had never known him to have a beard. Although his eyes were bloodshot, they looked famil-iar. Normally, they were a sparkling blue. *Where did these thoughts keep coming from?*

"Ma'am," he said, holding out a hand. "My attorney advised me against seeing you, but I had to know that you were all right. I could have sworn that you were struck by lightning, not my car." His grip was warm and robust, and he dropped his arm to his side.

"Let's not worry about attorneys," she replied. "I'm one myself, and I don't plan on filing any charges. While I can't seem to remem-ber what happened, I *know* that you didn't hit me. If you can lend some insight, I'd appreciate . . . Sorry, I'm so used to jumping right into matters that I forgot to introduce myself. Chris Olson."

He gave her a hard, disbelieving stare. In fact, his expression seemed to be one of shock. *An aftermath of the accident*, she told her-self. Finally, he spoke, "You're here early."

"Early?"

"Never mind." He shook his head. "I'm Geoff Cameron."

Judith's brother. Now she really felt foolish. Of course, she had seen him before—in Judith's pictures during college. "I was hoping that you could tell me something about what happened."

He cast his gaze to the floor and remained silent.

"Please . . ." She motioned for him to pull up the chair beside the bed.

"Here—I believe this is yours." He pressed something metal into her hand.

Her necklace. She clasped it next to her heart. "Thank you. I thought I had lost it."

"Glad to be of help," he muttered.

"The nurse said that you were cited with DUI. But you rarely drink alcohol because of a seizure disorder."

"I wasn't driving under the influence," he said, raising his voice, "and I don't have a seizure disorder."

No seizure disorder? Confused, Chris placed a hand to her head. "I could have sworn . . ."

Geoff pulled up a chair and sat beside her. He cleared his throat, but paused as if he were trying to make up his mind where to begin.

"The accident," she said, hoping to get him started.

He swallowed noticeably. "This is going to sound strange, but I saw what I thought was lightning. You were engulfed by it."

Tightening the grip on her necklace, she recalled flickering light. *Lightning?* "I saw it. The police didn't believe your story?"

Still hesitant, he fell silent again.

"Geoff, I should be able to help you, but you have to tell me what happened." When he failed to respond, she realized that he had no reason to trust her. "I'm an attorney for Christ sakes. If they've cited you, I'll explain what happened."

His eyes met hers—in familiarity. "I believe you, but if you don't remember anything, what good will it do?"

His gaze sent a shiver down her back. "*You* remember what happened, and I *know* you won't lie to me. Let's start with the basics. Did they cite you with reckless driving and DUI?" With some reluctance, he nodded. "Have you ever been cited or convicted on either of the charges before?" He shook his head. "Good, that helps. What was your blood alcohol level?"

"Point zero two."

"Well below the legal limit. Once I explain to the police that you didn't hit me and in fact came to my aid, I'm sure they'll drop the charges. Now that we have that settled, can you please tell me what happened?"

He laughed.

She blinked. "I don't believe I said anything funny."

"For some reason, I knew you would react the way you did."

A shiver tingled along her back again. She knew him, but from where? Her visit to Poplar Ridge might prove to be more interesting that she had anticipated. It had certainly started off with a bang.

When Geoff entered the drawing room at Poplar Ridge, Saber darted ahead of him to the tapestry sofa, jumping excitedly on Chris's lap. She wrapped her arms around the dog's furry neck. "Saber," she said as the dog licked her face.

"Saber, sit," Geoff commanded. The dog obeyed. "I'm sorry, I didn't expect him to jump on you. He's normally more reserved with strangers. Are you all right?"

With a nod of her head, Chris glanced to Judith sitting in the wing chair. "I'm fine, but I have no idea how I knew his name."

How much should he tell her? He stepped over to the liquor cabinet. "Can I get you ladies anything?" The women held up their drinks, stating they were fine. Judith had a soda, and Chris was drinking mineral water. He decided to bypass the alcohol and poured a glass of water for himself, then sat on the opposite end of the sofa. "Chris, I'm pleased to see that you're out of the hospital."

"My brother, the hero." With her hands clasped together, Judith flipped her hair over her shoulder and batted her eyelashes at him in cynicism.

Geoff ignored his sister's teasing and focused on Chris. Even though she looked weary, her smile was contagious. "How are you feeling?"

"Fine. The doctor says there's absolutely nothing wrong with me. They had never seen anyone walk away from a lightning strike the way I did."

He already liked being close to her. He should say something about the ledger. "That's good to hear."

"Relieved would be more like it," Judith said, intruding on his thoughts.

Suddenly annoyed, he glanced in his sister's direction. "Do you have something to say?"

His sister thumbed in the direction of the hall and huffed from the room. Geoff set his water glass on the mahogany table. "If you'll excuse me a minute."

"Of course."

Before he reached the hall, Judith waved her arms. "I can't believe you."

He glanced over his shoulder at Chris. She gave him a smile, politely pretending that she hadn't overheard Judith's loud voice. "About what?" he asked, returning his attention to his sister.

"Chris spoke to the cops on your behalf, saving your ass, and now you're hitting on her."

His jaw dropped. "Hitting on her? I haven't . . ."

"Oh, I know you're making small talk, but I can tell just by the way you look at her, *dear* brother. She's my friend, and I expect you to be on your best behavior. You can start by telling her that you're married. I'll give you the chance, while I check on lunch."

Geoff returned to the drawing room, and Judith fumed off in the direction of the kitchen. As Chris sipped from her water glass, he watched the curve of her mouth and the tilt of her head. "How much of that did you hear?"

When she looked up, the light captured the green flecks in her brown eyes. "Is it true that you're married?"

Had he detected disappointment in her voice? He sat in the chair vacated by Judith. "Beth and I have been separated for a over year now. At the rate we're going, it may take another year to settle things."

With his words, her shoulders loosened. "Any kids?"

"Neal is four."

"He has blue eyes like you and is a tow head." She shook her head in confusion. "Sorry, I don't know where these thoughts keep coming from."

Tell her. Not here. Besides, Judith would be returning momentarily. "Chris, if you're feeling up to it, I'd like to invite you to dinner this evening. I might be able to shed some light on your feelings of déjà vu, but I'd prefer to speak where we'll be uninterrupted."

"I'd like that. But I'm paying my own way."

Unsurprised by her insistence, he replied, "Absolutely. We wouldn't want anyone to think that we might be having a date—especially Judith."

"Did I hear my name being taken in vain?" Judith entered the drawing room. "Geoff, a Mr. Hollister is on the line wanting to know about leasing some land."

"Thanks, Judith." Finding it difficult to take his eyes off Chris, Geoff got to his feet. She had arrived two years early. He hoped that was a good sign.

The colonial tavern on a nearby plantation was a renovated carriage house. Lit by sconces that flickered like candles, the dining area held the ambiance from the era. Heavy oak beams spanned the ceiling. Pewter plates and goblets graced rustic wooden tables. Waitresses served in white caps and long dresses. Over Southern fried chicken and Virginia chardonnay, Chris told Geoff that she had taken the state bar over a year before and finally had landed an interview with the Virginia Commonwealth's Attorney Office.

"What would your job duties be there?" Geoff asked, seemingly pleased about the possibility that she might be moving permanently to the area.

"Prosecuting rapists." Talk about a conversation stopper. She damned herself for being so blunt. "Maybe I should explain."

Concern reflected in his eyes. "There's no need, but it sounds like you could be placing yourself at risk."

"The corporate world carries its own risks. Embezzling and money laundering aren't uncommon. Such people hold no qualms about hiring hit men. At least this way, *I* can make a difference. And before you ask, I've never been sexually assaulted."

"It wouldn't be my place to ask such a thing." He smiled at her with interest. "I admire anyone who can live by their ideals."

She took a sip from her wine glass and leaned back in the wood chair. "So, are you going to tell me why you think I'm having all of these weird feelings, or are you going to stare at me all evening, smiling politely?"

His smile widened. "I like looking at you."

"That's not why you brought me here," she reminded him. "Besides, if you're saying what I think you are, what would a country boy and city girl have in common?"

"What indeed," he whispered under his breath. He grasped a leather-bound ledger that he had kept by his side during the meal.

When he passed the ledger across the table, she suddenly trembled. "What is it?" she asked.

"Take a look inside."

She opened the book to her own handwriting—from 1867. The letters were addressed to Geoff. She glanced over at him in shock. "I don't understand. How did you manufacture this?"

"I didn't. I think you should read it. My father's Aunt Greta gave it to me shortly after I met Beth."

She scanned through a couple of the entries. Time travel? She and Geoff married with a daughter? "Preposterous!"

"I thought the same thing, but too many events came true."

Chris gestured to the ledger. "This says you have a seizure disorder. You told me that you don't. How do you explain something as significant as a serious medical condition?"

He leaned back in the chair and crossed his arms. "The car accident after which I was supposedly in a coma for a month never happened."

"Exactly my point. It's no better than TV psychics. They make some landmark prediction that gets blown out of proportion, then everyone believes they can predict the future." She examined the handwriting. It certainly looked like hers. "I would really like to know how you managed to produce this."

The waitress set a padded check holder on the table beside Geoff's right hand. He waited until she moved onto her next customer before speaking again. "Chris, if it's a fake, I'd like to know how it was accomplished as well. After you've read it, I'll say more, but I also dismissed it in the beginning. Then when Beth left . . ."

For some inexplicable reason, she trusted him. Temporarily forgetting the ledger, Chris reached across and grasped his hand. "It's none of my business, but if you'd like to talk about it, I'm quite used to confidentiality."

With a growing smile, he placed his free hand on top of hers. "Thanks, but the last thing I want to do is ruin the mood of our first date by talking about my soon-to-be ex."

"Date?" She withdrew her hand and snatched the check from the holder. "I've already told you that I'm paying my own way, so if you'd like to talk about her, by all means. Besides, if your 'soon-to-be ex' even suspects that you're having a date, trust me, her demands will escalate."

He watched her with amusement as she counted the bills for her portion of the meal. "I knew you'd be stubborn."

"In that case." She added enough cash to pay for the entire check. "I'm buying. After all, it's traditional in business arrangements."

"But I invited you."

She shrugged her indifference. "Details."

"Is it because my divorce hasn't been finalized that you're so insistent?"

"No. You . . ." Even though he had neatly trimmed his beard, it troubled her. Shouldn't he have a goatee instead? "You confuse me."

"Read the ledger."

"The two of us—married?" She pointed at him, then herself. "With a daughter? Get real. I'm married to my career and have no desire for children. I thought I had heard all of the lines before, but this one definitely wins the prize. You obviously went to a great deal of effort to concoct this scheme, but the answer is 'No.' Just because you wanted to treat me to dinner, doesn't mean that I'm blinded by your charm and willing to hop in bed with you."

He sighed. "And I suppose I knew ahead of time that I would find you on Route 5 in need of help? Believe me, after what I've been through with Beth, I'm not too eager to jump into another relationship anytime soon."

His face twisted, and she realized she had drummed up a raw memory. "I didn't mean to say anything hurtful," she replied, softening her tone, "but I'm having great difficulty believing your evidence."

"Fair enough. I'm only asking that you read it. You wanted to know why you are having strange feelings. The book may help explain them. If you still don't believe me after reading it, then we'll continue on with our lives the same as before we met. Can you think of anything simpler than that?"

Chris touched the leather book. A cold chill enveloped her. She started to open it, when the waitress returned to pick up the check.

Geoff slid the bills from the check holder and replaced them with a credit card. When the waitress thanked him and left the table, he pressed the money into Chris's palm. "Around here, a gentleman *always* pays for a lady's meal, whether it's business or otherwise. You may think my manners are quaint, but I truly hope that a little kindness between men and women never becomes old-fashioned."

She smiled slightly. "I hope so too, and I accept your hospitality. I rarely see people show such consideration in the city. Sometimes, I just need a gentle reminder to slow down a little. I will read the book."

"Good." The waitress returned with Geoff's receipt and credit card. He signed the receipt. With a pleasant smile, the server wished them a good evening before rushing from their table once more. Geoff stuffed the credit card and receipt in his wallet, then got to his feet. He held out his arm. "Ma'am, or are we still not having a date?"

"You win." Chris stood and laced her arm through his.

Carrying the ledger under his free arm, he escorted her to the darkened parking lot. Beside his vintage '67 Mustang, Chris was uncertain which of them initiated the kiss, but their lips touched.

"Wait." He set the ledger on the seat inside the car. Free of the book, he leaned down and sought her mouth in a burning hunger.

In spite of her previous skepticism, kissing him seemed so right, and Chris eagerly reciprocated. When their kiss ended, she laughed. "I think that makes it official. It *is* a date."

"But . . ."

"I should read the book before I say anything further."

With a nod, he opened the car door and closed it behind her after she got in. He went around to the driver's side and started the car. After a ten-minute drive, they pulled up to Poplar Ridge. Geoff accompanied her up the cascading steps of the brick mansion. Inside the hall, Saber greeted them with an excited bark. Instead of taking in the grandeur, Chris wrapped her arms around Geoff's neck and found herself kissing him again, but he drew away.

Glancing over her shoulder, Chris spotted Judith standing near the stairs. Geoff placed the ledger in her arms. "I'll see you in the morning. Good-night, Chris."

She hated seeing the evening come to an end so abruptly. "Good-night."

Geoff vanished through the room to her left with Saber trailing after him.

Uncertain whether Judith was angry, Chris approached her. "I hope you're not upset."

Finally, a smile appeared on Judith's face. "Of course not, but I worry. The two of you are very different."

Chris sensed that her friend was holding back. "I realize that his divorce isn't official."

"And probably never will be."

"What do you mean by that?"

"Because I'm not certain that Geoff wants one. Why don't we go into the other room?" Judith led the way to the drawing room.

Troubled by Judith's words, Chris followed her friend. She set the ledger beside her on the sofa and made herself comfortable while Judith poured brandy into snifters from a crystal decanter. She handed a glass to Chris, then sat across from her in the wing chair. "If you're beginning to see Geoff in the light that I think you are, then you'll need to ask him about the details, but Beth left rather suddenly."

Confused, Chris took a sip of brandy. "You're not making much sense."

"I know, and I'm sorry. I don't know much about the circumstances myself. Geoff is rather tight lipped, but what little I've picked up comes down to 'he said, she said.' I gather that he didn't know anything was wrong until she up and left. He hasn't been a very pleasant person to be around this past year. He's often in a foul mood, snaps a lot, and drinks too much. He pretends to hide it, but I was actually surprised that he passed the sobriety test."

No wonder he hadn't wanted to talk about his ex during dinner. He was still recovering from their parting. Chris set the snifter on the mahogany table. "Thanks for the warning, Judith, but I've got some reading to do." She picked up the heavy leather ledger.

"For your interview tomorrow?"

Surprised that Judith didn't recognize the book, Chris shook her head. "It's an old book that Geoff thought I'd be interested in."

"A book . . . ?" Judith laughed. "I can't remember the last time I saw him read a book."

And Geoff obviously hadn't wanted her to share the book with Judith. "Good-night, Judith." Chris went into the hall and up the stairs with the oak banister. Near the top, she spotted a person, kneeling on the floor as if looking for something. "Geoff?" No response. Perhaps it was Judith's father. She had only met the Cameron patriarch briefly. "Mr. Cameron?"

The person stood. A woman, and she had a dark skin tone. *Of course, the maid. What was her name?* "Laura?" By the time Chris reached the top of the stairs, the maid had vanished. *Odd.* She must not have heard her call. Chris looked up and down the hall to see where she might have disappeared to so suddenly. No sign of anyone. Tingling cold spread throughout her as she opened the door to her room. Her bag rested on the cedar chest at the foot of the canopied bed, and the sheets were turned down. Nothing was out of the ordinary.

Dismissing the weird feelings, Chris changed into her light-blue nightgown and stretched out on the bed. She opened the leather ledger and began reading. Time travel, reincarnation, ghosts. The story would certainly make a great novel. With a yawn, she glanced at the clock on the nightstand near the bed. 2:15. Thank goodness her interview wasn't until the afternoon. In any case, she had better make a quick trip to the bathroom and get some sleep.

Grabbing her robe from the end of the bed, she tied it around her. An image of a woman appeared in the heavy-bodied mirror. Her black hair was pinned at the nape of her neck, and her violet eyes were dark with pain. Chris reached out. "Margaret?"

The image vanished.

Chapter Ten

THE SOUND OF SABER BARKING WOKE GEOFF. Groggily, he snapped at the dog to shut up. Someone was knocking at the door. While middle of the night wakings were fairly common during the foaling and calving season, he usually got a good night's rest early in the fall. Half asleep, he switched on a night light and tugged on a pair of jeans. More knocking—louder and more frantic this time. "I'm coming," he grumbled. "If there's not a fire somewhere . . ." He opened the door and blinked. "Chris."

Barefoot, she stood in the doorway wearing a silk robe. "Sorry to wake you, but I need to talk."

He started to motion the way inside, then thought better of the idea. With her attired as she was, he wouldn't be able to concentrate. "Let me grab a shirt, and we can go down to the library." After throwing on a T-shirt, he led the way to the library and showed her to the sofa. "Would you like a drink?"

"Water, please."

He poured the drink, then sat beside her. "What's wrong?"

She trembled. "I've read a small portion of the ledger."

"And . . ."

She sipped the water before speaking. "If it's true, how can you even stand being in this room?"

"Because this is where George died?"

She nodded.

Thankfully, George had spared him from what those final moments had been like. He gestured to an area near the desk, covered by a round oriental rug. "There are still bloodstains on the floor-boards."

"That doesn't answer my question."

He should have known that she'd detect any diversions. "Chris, I've had visions all my life. Until I read the ledger, I had no idea where they were coming from. Once I understood... well, I was able to come to terms with some of the things I have been through. George is part of who I am. Sometimes his experiences torment me. Other times they help." He took her hand and kissed it. "It's also why I can't help but love you."

With another shudder, she withdrew her hand from his grip. "But I don't remember any of it."

"That's all right. You have arrived early, which gives us a couple of extra years."

"Don't joke about dying!"

"Sorry," he quickly apologized, "but if I started to dwell on what *might* happen in eleven years time, then I'd get very little accomplished each day." He grasped her hand once more. "Besides, simply knowing that you would come into my life has helped me get through the past year. I'm pleased that you're here early."

"Why did Beth leave?"

He let go of her hand and blew out a breath. "She accused me of having an affair."

Her gaze met his. "Did you?"

"No."

She raised a skeptical brow.

Suddenly annoyed that she automatically disbelieved him, he raised his voice. "I thought a person was innocent until proven guilty, counselor. I didn't cheat on her."

Chris took another sip of water. "Geoff, I'm not accusing you of anything, but you might want to ask yourself why you're so defensive about the subject."

Until she finished reading the ledger, she wouldn't be ready to hear the rest. Hell, at this rate, he doubted she'd ever believe what was written in it. "I guess I'm sensitive about being accused of something I didn't do."

"I believe you. Judith told me she wasn't sure you had known anything was wrong until Beth left. If that's the case, I'm certain you would have suspected something if you had been having an affair."

Even though more than a year had passed since his separation with Beth, the wound remained raw. "I doubt that you woke me in middle of the night to discuss my marital woes."

She shivered and pulled her robe tightly around her. "How did your mother die?"

The ledger stated that an auto accident had taken his mother's life when he was five. According to the same entry, he had been in the same unfortunate mishap and wound up with a head injury that had landed him with a seizure disorder. *Alternate history.* There were still times that he questioned it. "Judith never told you?" She shook her head, and he continued, "Leukemia. When I was nine. She had been ill for a few years. At least this time, both Judith and I were given the chance to know her."

Skepticism crossed her face. "This time?"

He cleared his throat. "I believe the journal has changed time."

Chris stood. "This conversation has been very enlightening. Thank you."

He got to his feet. "Are you going to finish reading the ledger?"

"I'm not certain. Right now, I need to get some sleep, so I won't doze off during my interview."

When he grasped her hand, she trembled under his touch. "I didn't mean to send you running."

Her lip quivered, and he couldn't resist kissing her. She responded enthusiastically but quickly drew away. "I really need to get some sleep."

"Good-night. I'll see you in the morning." He watched her as she headed for the door.

Before reaching it, she turned. "I will finish reading it—*after* my interview."

She closed the door behind her, and he glanced at Saber. "I don't think she was telling us everything, Saber." The dog pricked his ears in Geoff's direction. He waved at him. "Let's get some sleep, boy."

* * *

In the afternoon following her interview at the Commonwealth's Attorney Office, Chris took a quiet walk along the riverfront in the center of Richmond. Squawking gulls flew overhead. Confident that she would land the job, she liked the idea of moving to the area. Because of Geoff? Hadn't they just met? At breakfast, he had been friendly but kept a respectful distance. She definitely liked that about him. He was giving her space until she finished reading the ledger. In the meantime, she was certainly attracted to him. What a fool she was. Not only did she love the city life, but he was still married. *Only for a short time*, she reminded herself. It's not like she was the other woman. To be on the safe side, she stopped off at a drugstore on her way back to Poplar Ridge and bought a box of condoms.

At dinner, she was disappointed that Geoff's chair remained vacant. She relayed to Judith and her father how well her interview had gone, and afterward, they retired to the parlor, where Judith played Beethoven on the piano. When her friend finished the final note, Chris stood and applauded.

With her blonde hair neatly tied back in a silk ribbon, Judith smiled her dimpled grin, and Winston Cameron beamed with pride. "Let's adjourn to the drawing room for some brandy," he said, giving a slight bow and motioning for them to proceed. "Ladies."

Chris gave Judith a congratulatory squeeze. "If you don't mind, Judith, I'm a little tired. I think I'll retire early."

"We'll see you in the morning, then."

Together, they stepped into the hall. After a round of good-nights, Judith and her father went into the drawing room, and Chris headed toward the stairs. Putting her hand on the banister, she hesitated. Had she really seen a woman at the top on the previous evening? Something cold went under her skirt and nudged her leg. She jumped. It was Saber's wet nose. The dog barked and wagged a greeting. She pressed a hand to her chest. "You males are all alike."

"Should I be offended?" Geoff joined her.

With a growing smile, she held her tongue.

Pretending not to notice her amusement, he asked, "How did the interview go?"

"I think I'll get the job."

His eyes sparkled with the news.

"I missed you at dinner."

"I was helping a neighbor whose cattle got out on the road."

Farm work, and he loved it. She *was* a fool for falling for him. "I read a little more in the ledger before dinner. I was heading up to my room to finish."

"Then I'll bid you good-night." He lifted her hand and kissed the back.

The touch of his lips sent a shiver up her arm. "Good-night," she whispered. She withdrew her hand from his grip and climbed the stairs. Halfway up, she glanced over her shoulder. Geoff gave her a broad smile. *Damn him!* It was almost as if he could read her mind. *Concentrate. The ledger.* She focused on reaching her room. Fortunately, no eerie figure loomed at the top, and she easily arrived at the guest room. Without bothering to change, Chris took the leather ledger from the dresser drawer and made herself comfortable on the bed.

Although difficult to believe, the story was engrossing. Supposedly, her necklace was the time travel device. She clutched the crystal. An image of blinding light entered her mind. *Impossible.* But she continued reading. The last entry, dated May 1867, ended abruptly. Geoff had pointed out the bloodstain on the floor in the library where George had died. She fingered the rough edge of the ledger where a page had been ripped out. Had there been another entry? *Stop it!* She was now thinking of the journal as if it were fact.

The day had been a long one. She'd think more clearly in the morning. Closing the leather-bound volume, she drifted. Flickering lights, very similar to the crystal, appeared. Rapid eye movement. Suddenly aware that she was dreaming, Chris moved toward the light.

The dank cell reeked of urine from an overfull chamber pot. Chris's left arm was in a sling and it throbbed like hell from her fall. She paced the length of the ten-foot cell, then sat on the cot. A man in a blue uniform escorted a bearded man in tattered gray with his right sleeve pinned where an arm

*should have been. The guard rattled keys, and the iron door creaked. "You
have a visitor."*

*Tom entered the cell, and the guard closed the door behind him. "If you
don't mind, Sullivan, I'd like to speak with her in private for a few minutes."*

The sergeant nodded and left.

*Standing to greet Tom, she had difficulty fighting the tears. "I didn't kill
George."*

*His face remained grim as he removed his hat. "I know, Chris. I will get
you out of here." His voice cracked. "We buried him today."*

*A lump formed in her throat, and she sank to the cot. George dead.
How could that be? She had been sent to the past to change time. After the
shooting, she had passed out. Sergeant Sullivan had discovered the murder
weapon in her hand. This time, George's death wouldn't be labeled as a
suicide to cover for Margaret, but murder. She placed a hand to her belly.
There was only one person she could take into her confidence. "Tom, I'm
pregnant."*

His eyes widened with the news. "Are you certain?"

"Ask Hester if you don't believe me."

"I believe you. Chris, don't worry, the Yankees won't hang you."

*Hang? Not real. She would have never hurt George, but the prosecution
could easily pin her with all the motives of a jealous lover. Unable to hold
back any longer, she stumbled over to Tom and sobbed on his shoulder.*

Chris woke with her heart racing. She caught her breath. The digital
clock on the nightstand read 11:47. The dream had been incredibly
real. Her first inclination was to wake Judith and chat a while to ease
her nerves. Only Geoff would understand. She quickly changed into
a pair of jeans and a T-shirt and hurried down the steps leading to
the west wing. Thank goodness for the sconces lighting the hall, or
she'd be fumbling around in the dark.

At the end of the hall, she knocked on the door. "Geoff?" No
answer. She tried again. He might still be awake. Rushing down the
stairs to the first floor, she found the library door slightly ajar. Resting on a rug, Saber cocked his ears in her direction, and Geoff sat
behind the desk with acorn carvings, staring intently at the computer screen and tapping on the keyboard.

He glanced up, then immediately stood. "Couldn't sleep?"

"I've finished reading the ledger."

"And?" He motioned for her to have a seat on the sofa.

She approached the desk and remained standing. "I had a terrible dream."

He gripped her arm and escorted her to the sofa. "You're trembling. Would you care for a drink?"

"Water. No—make it something stronger."

Over by the liquor cabinet, Geoff poured a scotch, then returned to her side. He handed her the glass and sat beside her. "You're looking pale. What's wrong?"

The fiery liquid burned her throat as she gulped down the drink. "Did George die the way it was described in the ledger?"

His voice grew soft. "Yes. He died from a bullet wound to the head."

Chris snapped her eyes shut.

He grasped her hands. "Chris, what's wrong?"

"I had a dream that *I* had been arrested for George's murder."

His brow furrowed, and he tightened his hold on her hands. "*You?* Why would you have been arrested for his murder?"

"I don't know." Her hands trembled beneath his grip. She took a deep breath, hoping to calm herself. One trip to a spooky, old house and she was becoming a raving lunatic. Another deep breath, and she began to feel some semblance of composure again. "It was just a dumb dream brought on by reading the journal."

Geoff let go of her hands. "Are you certain?"

Chris stared straight ahead. The dream *had* been incredibly real. "What else could it have been?"

"You don't sound too convinced."

When she stood, he got to his feet.

"I'd like to thank you for being a sounding board," she said.

"Anytime." He watched her with concern.

"I'm fine now. Really, I am. Good-night."

"Good-night, Chris."

Turning swiftly, she envisioned the jail cell as she headed for the door. With no heat, she had paced the stone floor in an effort to keep warm. The captain had taken pity on her and scrounged up a moth-eaten shawl. Where had she dreamed up the visions? They hadn't been part of the dream. "They wanted to hang me."

"Chris?" Geoff was instantly by her side.

"They wanted to hang me for killing George." Suddenly sick to her stomach, she swayed on her feet. "Oh God, they were going to hang me."

Thankful that the rest of the family had gone to bed, Geoff aided Chris to her room. He assisted her with her shoes, then helped her to bed. He placed a pillow behind her back. "Can I get you anything?"

Still in distress from the dream, she barely managed to shake her head. "Even if the damned book is true, I wouldn't hurt George."

"I know that." He resisted the urge to take her into his arms and comfort her. She'd had enough pain for one night without him complicating her life further. "I should be leaving."

Chris grasped his hand. "Please stay. I'd rather not be alone right now."

Her tone hadn't hinted at anything sexual—only solace. Should he risk staying? She must have known that he wanted to touch her intimately. He glanced over his shoulder at the wing chair next to the bed.

She tightened her grip on his hand. "Hold me."

Unable to ignore her plea, he joined her on the bed. Fighting the urge to explore her body, he wrapped his arms around her as if that could absorb her pain. If he kept her talking, she'd eventually fall asleep. "What else do you remember?"

"A soldier in blue. His name was Sullivan."

"A Yankee."

She broke his embrace. "What would a Northern soldier be doing at a jail cell in 1867?"

He clenched his hand. At a time like this, he wouldn't dump the politics of Reconstruction on her. "They were the law of the land."

"Do you mean to say it would have been a military trial?"

"By 1867, the Yankees were pulling out, but martial law still existed in some areas. Are you admitting to believing the ledger?"

Lying back, she closed her eyes. "I can't. If I do, then I must accept the fact that I might have died there."

Death—maybe George shouldn't have sheltered him from the memory. He touched her necklace. "Or you could have found your way back to this time. Isn't that a possible explanation for your early arrival? You returned at the exact moment that time changed for you."

She pushed herself to a sitting position once more and shook her head. "That's not possible. According to the ledger, I didn't take the Virginia state bar until after we were . . ." She dropped the word "married" and continued, "I distinctly recall taking it last year in Roanoke."

Her gaze met his, and her face flushed slightly as if she finally realized they were in bed together.

"Chris, I, uh . . . need to be getting back to my bookwork."

"Must you?" She laughed and kissed him on the mouth. "Who would believe us if we say that we were in bed together without anything happening?"

He kept his gaze focused on her face, so as not to let it drift over the length of her body. "Who, indeed?"

She kissed him again—more intimately. "I may not believe everything in the ledger, but one thing seems right—you."

They slowly removed each other's clothing, kissing and fondling as they went. George's voice entered the back of Geoff's mind. *Don't rush. Cherish her.* Odd to have such familiarity with a woman he had just met. He fought his impatience and listened to the voice. Her eyes sank, lingering on his groin. He had never been overtly modest before, but he suddenly felt self-conscious. "You're not one of those feminists who bursts out laughing right about now, are you?"

"You tell me." She was touching him, teasing as she went. Not shy, she knew exactly where he was most sensitive.

When he felt her lips where her hands had been, he nearly lost himself. *Slow down*—George's voice, reminding him again. But hell—neither he nor George could stay cool when it came to Chris. Totally caught up in the moment, he nearly choked in frustration. He rolled to her side. "Damn!"

"What's wrong?" she asked.

He cleared his throat. "I don't have one in my wallet."

"One?" She blinked in confusion, then giggled. "Check in the nightstand."

He opened the drawer—a box of condoms. Withdrawing a foil-wrapped package, he laughed. "Extra pleasure for her?"

With a playful grin, Chris seized the package from his hand and tore it open. "I like spice in my life. Certainly, if you believe the ledger, you're already aware of that."

"I do, indeed. I only wonder if a simple country boy like me can handle a proactive city girl like you."

"Simple country boy," she muttered under her breath with a widening grin. "There's nothing simple about you."

Throughout the night, they made love—in a long and tender dreamlike state. Geoff caught a glimpse of her necklace. With the swaying of Chris's hips, the crystal captured the light and reflected it softly. He had given it to her as a gift. *When?* Somehow, the necklace was a missing piece to the puzzle, and they had eleven years to unlock the answer. Absorbed by the woman in his arms, he came in a satisfying warmth. Eleven years seemed like forever.

In the early-morning light, Chris dozed lazily with her eyes half-open. She felt a presence next to the bed and willed her eyes to open fully. In her drowsy state, they failed to obey. The feeling grew stronger. Someone stood over her. Breathing in sharply, she sat up. Saber stood at the end of the bed with his hackles raised. His eyes had fixated on a spot near her, and she heard a low rumble in his throat. When the dog saw that she was awake, he bounded over and gave her a sloppy kiss on the face.

"Saber!" At the sound of Geoff's voice, Saber only grew more excited, wagging his tail with frisky barks. Geoff glanced at the clock on the nightstand and threw a pillow over his head with a groan.

Chris lifted the edge of the pillow from Geoff's face. "I thought a country boy would be used to waking up by seven."

He opened one eye, then closed it again. "I am, but in case you've forgotten, I didn't get much sleep."

Saber trotted over to the door and scratched.

"Geoff, I think he needs to go out."

Another groan. Geoff failed to budge. Saber's scratching became more frantic.

"I'll let him out, if you'd like to rest." She started to get up, but a hand encircled her wrist.

"I'll do it." As Geoff groggily sat up, a smile spread across his face. He gave her an intimate good-morning kiss. "I hope you're not upset that we can no longer say we were in bed together without anything happening."

"Upset, no. Confused, yes. I can't believe that we're caught in some endless cycle of time. Do you have any records dating from the time of the ledger?"

"I've verified that George died exactly when and how the ledger states, if that's what you mean."

"No, I mean more than that. Something, anything that will tell us about the people and why it all happened."

"Greta's genealogical records might have something."

Greta? His father's aunt. Wasn't she also the one to give him the ledger? "Not only would I like to have a look at Greta's records, I want to meet Greta."

More frantic scratching.

"Your wish is my command. I'll gather the records together this evening, when I get back to the house. Right now, I had better see to Saber." He got up, quickly dressed, and vanished through the door with Saber. She had barely finished dressing when a knock came on the door.

"Chris . . ."

"I'm coming, Judith." Chris straightened the bed covers before answering the door. She motioned for her friend to come in.

Attired in green breeches and knee-high riding boots, Judith pursed her lips before speaking. "Is everything okay?"

Judith wasn't normally the sort to hedge. Obviously she had spotted Geoff leaving her room. Chris nodded. "I'm sure this comes as a surprise to you, but I'm . . ." Almost admitting to love, she caught herself. " . . . very fond of him."

Her friend's eyes widened. "And you need to take it easy."

How could she explain without coming across as sounding totally crazy? "It's like I've known him forever."

"It's an illusion. You've always been the rational one. When I met David two months ago, *you* were the one to tell me to slow down."

Chris laughed to herself. If the ledger was right, David would be the man that Judith would eventually marry. "What can I say? I was wrong."

"Chris..." Her friend grasped both of Chris's hands. "You're catching Geoff on the rebound. For heaven's sake, his divorce isn't finalized yet."

She withdrew her hands from Judith's grip. "I know all about it. Sleeping together doesn't necessarily equate to running off and getting married."

"Be reasonable. The two of you are so very different. What are you going to do if you don't get the job in Richmond?"

Chris shrugged, but something in her friend's tone bothered her. "I haven't thought that far ahead. Judith, what's really bothering you? Is it the fact that he's your brother?"

"No." Judith glanced away as if suddenly afraid to meet her gaze.

"Then what? Stop being so mysterious."

Judith wrung her hands. "Believe me, this is very difficult to say. In fact, we don't even talk about it among ourselves, but Geoff has a history of psychiatric illness."

"Psychiatric? As in..." Unsure what had hit her, Chris trailed off. "But he seems so..."

"Normal?" Judith continued to avoid eye contact. "He can be very good at hiding it, but it's something that he's had difficulty dealing with all of his life."

Would a *normal* person hand her a ledger purporting to be written by her during another time? But the dream had been incredibly real. Could Geoff have planted the seeds into her mind? "What sort of psychiatric illness?"

"Dissociative identity disorder, or in layman terms, split personality."

George was a second personality? Geoff had admitted as much in a more eloquent fashion. If he had somehow manufactured the ledger, how could he have known so many intimate details about her life?

"Thank you for warning me, Judith," she said, attempting to keep her voice even.

Judith squeezed her lightly on the arm. "I'm sorry that I didn't warn you sooner. I realized that you were falling for him, but I thought the fact that he's still married would deter you."

"Is that why Beth left?"

"I'm not certain. As I've already said, she left suddenly. Will you be all right?"

Disappointed and disheartened, Chris responded, "I'll be fine. We should be getting on with our ride."

Another squeeze to her arm. "Are you certain?"

Chris forced a smile. "Yes, Judith, I'll be fine. Just let me get my jacket." She threw a fleece jacket over her shoulders and accompanied Judith down the stairs and outside to the pillared steps. In heavy silence they crossed the neatly mowed grounds. *What an idiot!* Previously priding herself on level-headed restraint, Chris hoped her foolishness hadn't forced a wedge between her and her friend.

As they approached the red-brick stable with arches facing a stone courtyard, Chris envisioned crumbling bricks. *Where did these thoughts keep coming from? Time travel?* Maybe *she* was the delusional person with a split personality. No wonder Geoff had been drawn to her. They were more alike than different.

Inside the stable, Judith introduced Chris to a scrawny stablehand with a cleft chin and bobbing Adam's apple. She shook his hand. "Nice to meet you, Ken, but where's T.J.?"

Judith blinked in surprise. "I'm not sure. Why do you ask?"

"Right here, lass." The gray-bearded Scotsman carried a saddle from the tackroom. "Do I know ye?"

"Chris Olson." She held out her hand, and he eyed it curiously. "We met . . ." *Where?* "I mean Geoff has told me about you."

He shook her hand, then placed the saddle on a dark bay gelding's back. "Pleased ta meet ye."

"The pleasure is mine," she responded, rubbing the gelding's shoulder. "Will I be riding Ebony?"

"Aye."

How had she known the gelding's name? Chris overheard T.J. tell Ken to let the other horses into the paddock, while he helped her and Judith. The stable hand led a brown mare from her stall. *Tiffany.* Then Ken brought out a spirited gray—Geoff's favorite, *Traveller*, named after Robert E. Lee's horse. Why did she recognize all of the horses? Judith's hand went to her shoulder. "Are you all right?"

"I'm fine."

"The horses are ready to go."

They donned helmets and led the horses to the courtyard. On a chestnut mare, Judith showed the way to a dirt path. After following the path for a few hundred yards, they came to a meadow dotted with chicory and black-eyed Susans. They rode abreast in the waving hip-deep grass.

"Chris, I'm sorry if what I've said has hurt you, but I felt you should know the truth."

If she admitted to herself that Geoff might not have psychological problems, then she would have to accept the legitimacy of the ledger. She wasn't quite ready to make that claim. "You were right. I was falling for him in a big way."

Her friend gave her an empathic smile. "I gathered that. As I recall, Dan had to wait awhile before staying the night."

Dan had been her boyfriend for three years during college. "He didn't have to wait as long as you might think." With Judith's giggle, Chris felt like she was in college again. She should have known that something as impulsive as her spending a night with a man, even if he was Judith's brother, wouldn't jeopardize their friendship. "Judith, what am I to do?"

"Talk to Geoff. He's going to be furious with me for telling you, but now that you know, I'm certain he'll be upfront."

The meadow gave way to forest, forcing them to ride single file again. Chris halted Ebony.

Judith reined her mare back around. "What is, Chris?"

"Up ahead, the path isn't much larger than an animal trail. Later on, it opens to a clearing where there's a log cottage."

"Geoff must have told you about it."

According to the ledger, she and Geoff had often used the cottage as a private getaway. "He did," Chris lied. "I'd like to see it."

"Sure." Once again, Judith led the way.

The path grew narrower until the forest finally opened to a clearing. The rustic cottage was shaded by towering oak trees. *Many of the trees had been cut by soldiers.* They tied the horses out front to a hitching post. "Does Geoff come here?"

"I'm not certain. If he does, he hasn't told me about it."

The wood creaked under their feet as they went up the stairs. Inside, there were pegs on the wall for hanging coats. An old cupboard held tin plates. Along the far wall, there was a bed with a patchwork quilt. *Knapsacks and blue coats had been cleared away.* The soldier in her dream had been Sergeant Sullivan, but here was another soldier, friendlier than the sergeant. A captain, his name was Michael Rhodes.

He escorted her up the steps to the cottage. "We'll hide you here. I'll fetch Cameron."

"Why are you helping me?"

"No matter what happens, I'm not about to start hanging ladies. Besides, I believe you."

"Thank you," she whispered.

Rhodes removed his jacket. "Here. Take this in case I don't return before morning. It gets mighty chilly at night."

Taking the faded coat of blue, she thanked him again. She wrapped the jacket around herself and dropped to the floor in exhaustion. She tucked her knees to her body and drifted.

"Chris . . ."

Chris blinked at the sound of Judith's voice. "Sorry, I was lost in thought."

"Maybe we should be getting back."

They went outside to the waiting horses and remounted. As they retraced their steps through the forest and meadow, Chris thought about the vision. *What could it all mean?* The captain had helped her. He had said that he would get Cameron. *Tom?* Wasn't he the man in her previous vision? George's brother, according to the ledger.

Near the house, they curved around a sharp bend. Up ahead, a group of people roared. Ebony pricked his ears toward the sound, then began twitching nervously. The bellow grew louder, and she brought the gelding to a halt.

* * *

Lips curled and fists hurled for the sky. Others were heckling, pointing fingers. The leader of the angry mob motioned to the men beside the horse that she sat astride. They lashed her wrists behind her back. A misting rain mixed with her tears as she fought the ropes. A rock struck her in the ribs, knocking the breath out of her. A rope went over the branch above her head. Dear God, no!

More laughing from the crowd. "Die, bitch!"

As they slipped the noose about her neck, her eyes came to rest on Margaret, dressed in black. Her face remained emotionless in the blank stare of a laudanum euphoria. Then she spotted Tom. Several men held his arm and his stump, preventing him from reaching her. Tears streaked his face as he fought against them.

"I didn't kill him!"

Another wave of laughter, and skin sliced away as she struggled against the ropes. The man nearest to her tightened the noose. A sickening wave of terror gripped her. She urinated in the saddle and closed her eyes. The rain grew heavier, making her cotton gown stick to her body. She heard a slapping sound and a scream of victory from the crowd. She felt the horse in motion, hoofbeats, then nothing beneath her to break her fall.

Her neck twisted. The ropes cut into her twitching wrists, and her legs jerked in spasms. She tried to breathe. The rope squeezed her throat. Crushing pain. Pressure filled her head and eyes. Breathe! *But everything went black.*

"Oh my God! Chris!"

Judith helped her sit up, and she placed a hand to her throat. Pain. She rubbed it.

Her friend's frantic voice came again. "Are you all right? You took quite a fall."

"Fall?" Still massaging her neck, Chris glanced around with her gaze coming to rest on the tree where a branch extended over her head. "Margaret was part of the mob."

"Margaret? Chris, your neck."

Self-conscious, Chris stopped kneading her neck.

Judith stepped closer and examined it. "It looks like rope burns."

Chapter Eleven

THE CLOCK IN THE HALL STRUCK SIX TIMES. In the drawing room, Geoff reached for the scotch. When he heard Judith's voice call his name, he poured water instead. "I know about you and Chris."

"No 'Hi, how are you?' " He turned to face his sister. "So, you know about Chris and me. Do you want some sort of medal for your detective services?"

Red-faced, she fumed. "She's my friend, you bastard. Why did you have to go and sleep with her?"

To hell with it. No longer pretending, he poured the scotch and gulped it down. "I really think that's between Chris and me."

His response only made her angrier. "Damn you! I don't want to see her hurt."

He poured another drink. "I see. I'm suddenly so crazy that I couldn't possibly care for anyone. I went with Beth for a hell of a long time before I married her. I don't see you staying with anyone for any length of time."

"Geoff! We're not talking about me!" She pointed an index finger at him, but slowly lowered her arm. "You win, but you owe her the courtesy of telling her how difficult your other personality can be sometimes."

He left the second drink untouched and sank into the wing chair. "I will. I promise."

"There's one more thing." Judith sat across from him and frowned. "This afternoon Chris fell from Ebony. She was fine, but the odd thing about it was that she had what appeared to be rope burns around her neck and wrists afterward."

Rope burns? In her dream, she had been held in custody for George's murder. Could she have died for it?

"Geoff, I'm worried. Something happened when she fell, and she's not talking about it. She used to share everything with me, so I don't know whether she's frightened about something or if it's . . ."

He met her gaze. "Because of me."

With some reluctance, Judith nodded. "I'm trying not to intrude, but I think you know something about what's going on. She mentioned Margaret's name."

Due to the potential for public embarrassment, no one in the family ever referenced George by name, and Geoff had learned to keep his mouth shut as much as possible. "Are you asking me to consult with my alter ego?"

"If it will help Chris."

She *was* worried if she was begging him to let George surface. "I have a better idea. Why don't I just speak to Chris?" Without waiting for a response from Judith, he rushed to Chris's room and rapped on the door. When no one answered, he knocked louder. Saber barked to announce their presence.

"Geoff," Chris said, opening the door.

Around her neck was a fading pink ring. Self-conscious that he had noticed, she placed her hand there in an attempt to cover it, only to reveal a similar ring on her wrist.

"Can we talk?"

With a nod, she opened the door wide enough to allow him to step inside. "Judith must have told you about my stupid fall this morning."

"She did." He moved to take her into his arms, but she stepped back.

Silence.

"Do you want to talk about it?" he asked.

With a cursory smile, she shrugged. "What's there to talk about? I fell on my butt. I'm sure you have too. It goes with riding horses."

"I have," he agreed. "I've had some dandy bruises. I even broke my leg once, but I never wound up with rope burns around my neck."

Another strained smile. "Geoff, I appreciate your concern. I'm just not in the mood to talk about it. Now, if you don't mind, I'd like to get some rest."

Confused, he snapped his fingers. "Just like that. I get the hint, but I thought last night was more than . . ."

"It was. Between the ledger and strange happenings, nothing makes sense. And you seem to be the center of my confusion."

Suddenly comprehending her uncertainty, he blew out a weary breath. "What did Judith tell you?"

Without hesitation, she responded, "She said that you have dissociative identity disorder."

He should have known that he could count on Judith to warn Chris. "Why don't we go downstairs? I've dug out Greta's genealogical records as you requested. You can have a look through them, and we can talk."

This time, her smile seemed genuine. "It sounds like a good idea."

When he took her hand, it shook, but he led the way to the door near the fireplace. He closed the door behind them. Several stairs led the way to the west wing. At the end of the hall, another flight of stairs went down to the first floor beside the library. On top of the desk, he had stacked Greta's ledgers. He motioned for Chris to have a seat. She made herself comfortable in the leather chair behind the desk and took a ledger from the top of the stack.

He pulled up a chair next to her. "I have been treated for dissociative identity disorder. I've already told you that I've had visions all my life."

She glanced up from the ledger. "You said they were from George."

"Exactly, and the psychiatrists needed to give it a label. My mother believed that my visions, or 'memories,' if you will, were authentic. I envisioned things that would have been impossible for a small boy to comprehend."

She briefly returned her attention to the ledger. "Such as?"

"Such as, specific details of battles during the War between the States."

Her response was anything but what he expected. She giggled. "Forgive me, but I expected you to say the War of Northern Aggression."

"See, you have the memories too. We've been down this road before."

Chris flipped a page in the ledger. "I'm in a business that demands substantiated proof. I can't think in any other way. Submit the proof, then I'll truly believe."

"The ledger is written in *your* handwriting, and this . . ." He extended her arm to reveal the rope burns on her wrist.

Her brow furrowed, and she withdrew her arm from his grip. "Okay, then suppose for the sake of argument, everything is true. How did you make peace with these memories?"

"I'm not always at peace. Stress often triggers them, and after my mother died, I was on my own. My father thought I used them to get attention. First, they tried Ritalin, then they jumped to an assortment of antidepressants. All of the concoctions made things worse. I started hiding the pills, which paved the way for my first trip to the hospital."

She reached over and squeezed his hand. "First trip?"

"Two in all. The first time, I was ten. The second, sixteen . . ." Unable to meet her gaze, he glanced at Saber resting on the rug beside his feet. He clenched a hand. "The memories caused Beth to leave."

"Are you ready to tell me what happened?"

"Not really, but I'll do my best." If he just sat and stared into Chris's eyes, he would only think of her. Geoff got to his feet and paced the floor. "Beth and I went together in college. She doesn't have any family of her own, so I brought her home at Christmastime. That's when Greta gave me the ledger. Like you, I initially dismissed it as a fraud. Greta tried to tell me about Sarah."

Chris swallowed. "Your mother?"

He stopped pacing and met her gaze. "Her great aunt, Tom and Christine Cameron's daughter."

She stood. "Even if the ledger is true, there's no evidence the Chris of that time married George's brother. She wouldn't, not after watching George die. The diary wouldn't have ended so abruptly if she had survived."

Always the lawyer. The evidence had to be right in front of her. Geoff motioned for her to be seated again, but she stubbornly remained standing.

"Please, let me finish," he said. "I may not have the guts to tell you all of this later." Chris reseated herself, and he continued, "I didn't listen to Greta, nor did I pay any attention to the ledger. There were already many inaccuracies, so it was easy to dismiss. After college, Beth and I got married. We lived in Richmond for a while. No offense, but I've never liked cities. I've always preferred working outdoors and feel caged in a city environment.

"When we returned here, Beth was pregnant. With the battles I sometimes face inside me, I didn't think having kids was such a great idea. During her pregnancy, Beth started acting peculiar."

Chris raised an eyebrow. "Peculiar?"

"She always seemed sad. The doctor said that because of the stress of pregnancy, depression wasn't uncommon. When tension mounts, George has a habit of stepping in. There have been times where I've wakened in strange places and had no idea how I had gotten there. Hours and, on a couple of occasions, days were totally wiped from my memory. Beth accused me of seeing another woman. Even though I couldn't remember where I had been or what I had done, I was certain that wasn't the case. George never cheated on Margaret, until . . . Well, you weren't here.

"The stress only got worse after Neal was born. We pretended that everything was fine until one night she said that she'd had enough." A lump rose in his throat as he recalled Beth's tearful goodbye. "I don't remember much about the night. In fact, I keep wondering what I could have done differently, but, Chris, I wasn't having an affair."

"I believe you." Her words were like music.

"Thank you."

She stood and hugged him. "I'm so sorry."

"At least, you've learned all of the dirty little secrets around Poplar Ridge before they haul *you* off to the funny farm. I've already been there. It's definitely not a vacation spot that I would recommend."

Lowering her arms, Chris stepped back and frowned. "How can you joke about it?"

"It's the only way to get by around here, without truly going insane. Are *you* ready to talk about what happened this morning?"

Her lip quivered. "Not really, but I'll do my best," she replied, echoing his own words. Her hand went to the fading ring around her neck. "There was a mob of people. I was on a horse with my hands tied behind my back." She continued rubbing her neck. "The horse galloped away, and I . . . I couldn't breathe. Geoff, if that ledger is true, I think I died soon after it was written, so you see why the Chris married to George's brother couldn't have been me."

Her stubborn determination prevailed, and she returned to the stack of ledgers on the desk.

He reseated himself next to her and placed his hand over hers. "Let me help." He felt her tremble. Why hadn't he seen it before? Beneath her tough city girl exterior, she was afraid to admit the truth. "I can't know the events after George's death, but we'll find out what happened."

"Why would you want to discover the answers when you know what may be at stake?"

"Because you're part of who I am as much as George is." He withdrew a ledger from the stack and began searching for clues.

In the morning when Chris woke, Geoff was already dressing. Barely enough light filtered through the windows to see him in the shadows. She glanced at the clock—5:15. They had been in the library until nearly one poring over ledgers. Her head flopped back to the pillow. "Do you usually get up this early?"

Finished dressing, he bent down by the side of the bed and gave her a good-morning kiss. "It varies, but it's not unusual."

Ugh. Farm life. "That's why I live close enough to my workplace so I don't have to commute. If I don't have to be in court, I can go into work after rush hour."

He switched on a light and smiled broadly.

Self-conscious that she looked a fright, she attempted to smooth her hair. "Do I look that terrible in the morning?"

"As a matter of fact, I was thinking that you look beautiful." They kissed once more. "I'll be back early enough to take you to Greta's this afternoon."

"I appreciate that." After another round of kisses and a goodbye, Chris watched him leave the room. Saber bounded ahead of him. She really should have been returning to her own room. *Too tired.* At least in Geoff's room, she didn't hear strange noises nor see images in the mirror that weren't there. Content in relishing the quiet, she switched off the light and fell back asleep. When she awoke the second time, it was a little after seven. The sun had risen, but she heard the tapping of rain against the window pane. With a tired groan, she got up and dressed. After a quick trip to the bathroom, she padded down the hall of the west wing to her room.

Judith was exiting her room at the same time Chris arrived by the guest-room door. "I see how far my warning went," her friend remarked. "As long as you know what you're doing."

"I have no idea what I'm doing," Chris admitted, "but it's like I've known him all of my life."

Concern registered on Judith's face. "He's told you about Beth and why she left?"

"He did. Stop worrying, Judith. I'll be fine."

Judith hugged her. "I hope so. I thought of Beth as a sister. I can't imagine why she never said anything was wrong, unless she never felt that way in return."

The ledger warned that Beth had been possessed by Margaret. Determined to discover the underlying truth, Chris said, "Geoff gave me some ledgers last night. We only got through half the stack, and I'd like to finish looking through them after breakfast."

"Need any help?"

"I'd be delighted to have your assistance. I'll meet you downstairs."

After Judith gave a quick "See you later," Chris stepped into her room. A distinct chill permeated the air. Drapes swirled in the gusting wind, and rain lashed through the open window. She rushed over. The window stuck. With a little more force, the window gave and she managed to close it. She turned to the heavy-bodied mirror. Letters were scrawled in a jagged red.

BEHIND

Chris moved closer. Behind? Margaret had often worn the scent of honeysuckle. Chris sniffed the air. No honeysuckle. Did that mean the message couldn't be from Margaret? She touched a finger to the mirror. Sticky. At first, she thought it might be blood, but the texture wasn't right. She dabbed it to her cheek. Rouge. "Judith!" She dashed into the hall.

Both Judith and her father ran in her direction. "What's wrong?" Judith asked, out of breath.

"Look!" Chris pointed to her room. Winston Cameron immediately charged inside. Judith and Chris went in together. "What does it mean?"

The elder Cameron pulled the dresser away from the wall. Nothing was behind it. "It's just a practical joke," he said.

"And who was in my room to do such a thing?" Chris asked.

Doubt crossed the elder Cameron's face, and he left the room without responding.

Chris turned to Judith. "He thinks I did it. What motive could I possibly have for playing such a silly prank?"

"Chris, don't worry about what Daddy thinks. He can be stubborn when admitting to what might be behind some of the creaks and bumps in the night of this house. Let's go down to breakfast, so we can get a start looking through the ledgers."

Still annoyed that Winston Cameron believed she was capable of having pulled a stupid stunt, Chris agreed. It was more important for her to focus on the answers to her questions.

After breakfast, Chris and Judith proceeded to the library. Seated in Geoff's chair behind the desk, Chris examined one of Greta Cameron's genealogical ledgers.

"What specifically are we looking for?" Judith asked, sitting across from her.

"Anything from the Civil War era or shortly thereafter," she responded, flipping another dusty page.

Judith shook her head. "Most of the records from the war were lost."

To an extent, Judith was right. Greta had meticulously recorded names and dates from public records. Chris scanned through Cameron after Cameron. She found Geoff's entry. Below his name, his son was listed. Beside Neal's name, another name had been etched in by pencil, but erased. "Judith, did Beth lose a baby?"

"Not to my knowledge. Why do you ask?"

Chris pointed to the entry.

"I bet Aunt Greta just recorded it in the wrong place. Even as tight-lipped as Geoff is, he would have mentioned something if Beth had miscarried." Judith squinted her eyes. "I can't quite make it out, but it looks like the name begins with an 'S'."

"S?" Sarah? Chris forced a smile. "You're right. I'm sure she put the name in the wrong place." She returned her attention to the ledgers. A picture of the house at the turn of the twentieth century caught her eye. Three buildings stood in the place of one grand mansion. A black stallion had carried her to the front steps, and the entry hall had been barren of furniture. She had called the man with blue eyes and blond hair, "Geoff."

"Chris? Is everything all right?"

Chris blinked back the vision and swallowed. "Yes."

"Something has been bothering you since arriving. Granted, even your arrival was under less-than-ideal circumstances. Are you sure you didn't hit your head when you fell from Ebony yesterday?"

"Positive." She flipped a page in the ledger, continuing with the entries.

"Chris . . ." Judith handed her the ledger she had been reading. "Entries from the time of the War between the States and Reconstruction."

Chris scanned through the pages. Margaret Harrison had married George Cameron in 1861. His brother, Thomas, had married a woman by the name of Christine in 1867. Coincidence? The ledger had supposedly been written in 1867, the same year as George's death. Recalling the hanging, she placed a hand to her throat. There was no mention of Thomas's wife being hanged, or anyone else, for that matter. In fact, Christine and Thomas had lived into the twentieth century. They had one daughter by the name of Sarah. Intrigued, she was looking forward to meeting Greta.

* * *

The Mustang pulled beside a Gothic-style, off-white Victorian. Even though the rain had halted, Chris stared out the window. Shouldn't the house be a gaudy green? Geoff opened the door. "I'm surprised you let me get the door for you."

She blinked. "I was lost in thought."

"Does the house look familiar?"

Continuing to stare at the house, she got out of the car. "Should it?"

He closed the door after her. "You tell me. The night you were struck by lightning, you were on the road out front."

"Geoff, if I admit to believing the ledger, then I admit to time travel, ghosts, reincarnation, and who knows what else?"

"Us." He drew her into his arms. "I think it seems just right."

She pulled away from his embrace. "Yes, but . . ."

"But what?"

"If I've watched you die twice already, how can I possibly face it again?"

"By finding answers. If time has changed, maybe we can prevent what seems to be inevitable. I only know we were meant to be together. I'd like to grow old with you this time around."

She nodded that she was ready to continue, and he clasped her hand, showing her along the brick walk to the steps. Saber reached the porch before them.

Another brick path lined with black-eyed Susans and purple asters led in the direction to the back of the house. There wasn't supposed to be bricks and the path had been edged in weeds. Around back was a shack. The former slave's name had been Hester.

Geoff knocked, and a wrinkled, bone-thin woman answered. She smiled a broad, welcoming grin. "Geoff, what a pleasant surprise."

"My friend, Chris . . ."

"Olson," the old woman finished. "I'm Winston's aunt, Greta." She waved the way inside.

Chris kept her feet firmly planted on the porch. "How do you know my name?"

"Please come inside. We'll talk." Once more, Greta gestured for them to come inside.

With some hesitation, Chris stepped forward. The interior of the house was decorated with antique tinware and glass knickknacks. Expecting to see furniture made from scraps, she shivered.

"Make yourselves at home, and I'll get some tea," Greta said, motioning for them to have a seat.

"The bother really isn't necessary," Chris insisted.

"It's no bother." Greta continued shuffling in the direction of the kitchen.

Geoff indicated to the sofa. "When Greta says she's making tea, she makes tea."

"I guess I'm still growing accustomed to Southern hospitality." She got comfortable on the sofa, and Geoff sat beside her. When Greta returned, he stood and helped her with the tray holding the teapot. Chris smiled to herself. While his manners were quaint, she realized that unlike so many people in the city, he was genuine. And he was right. They needed to discover what happened in the nineteenth century.

Finally, the silver-haired woman sat in the rocking chair across from her. Only then did Geoff reseat himself. Greta took a deep breath. "I've been waiting a long time for your visit, Chris, but aren't you here early?"

"So, you believe the ledger?"

"I do," Greta responded without hesitation.

"Why?"

"When Aunt Sarah gave me the ledger, she told me that it belonged to Geoff. She even accurately predicted the year he would be born."

Sarah again. "When did Sarah give you the ledger?"

Greta tapped her knobby fingers against the arm of her chair. "I'm not certain. It was a long time ago, and she died shortly after. Let me see . . . 1924 or '25. I was just a girl myself."

Was it possible that Christine hadn't died after George's death, and Sarah *was* her daughter? Could she really have married Tom? She glanced over at Geoff. "Then you believe that Geoff is your grandfather?"

Greta glanced in Geoff's direction. He gave her a nod to continue. "*Was* would be a more appropriate term."

Geoff fidgeted in his seat. In spite of his brave front, he was at odds with his previous life. *Think like an attorney and gather all of the evidence before drawing conclusions.* "How did your grandfather die?"

"A woman murdered him."

Someone *had been* hanged for George's murder. In her dream, Chris had been jailed and on the run. She got to her feet, and Geoff immediately stood. "Thank you for your time, Greta," she said.

"But your tea."

With a sick feeling in her stomach, Chris headed for the door. "I'm sorry to have been such a bother. Bye, Greta." Once she reached the Mustang, she took deep, gulping breaths.

"Chris," Geoff said, joining her, "you look like someone who has just seen a ghost."

"If I was really there, why would I have married George's brother?"

He touched her on the shoulder. "I think that answer is rather obvious. Sarah Cameron was born seven months after George's death."

Finally facing him, she shook her head. "I wouldn't marry someone that I didn't love because I was pregnant."

"Hell, if I know, but you're thinking in modern terms, not the late 1860s."

She trembled. "Then how do you explain my dream where I had been arrested for George's murder, then the hanging?"

"I don't have all the answers, and I can't consult with George on that detail. It was after he died." He grasped her hand. "What I do know is that we've been given another chance."

His calm was what she needed. The following day, she'd be returning to Boston, and she wanted to make the most of the remaining hours.

Spires and headstones—a graveyard. Chris felt as if she should know the place. Dogwoods bloomed near the four-foot brick wall. A woman stood near one of the graves. Locks of gray streaked her short auburn hair. She wore a low-waist dress that looked more like a sack, with the hemline falling at her calf. As Chris approached, the woman raised her head. Trying to remember who she was, Chris placed a hand to her temple. "I should know you."

"I'm your daughter, Sarah."

"How is that possible?"

"Time isn't linear." Sarah motioned to the grave.

Chris gasped. Christine Cameron. *Beside the stone marked with her name was another stone—Thomas Cameron. She whispered his name.*

"Mama, please listen."

How could this old woman possibly be her daughter?

"Mama!"

Chris glanced in her direction.

"I gave Greta the ledger. Only time will tell if Papa receives it."

Geoff? "He got it. I've read it, but . . ."

The smile spreading across Sarah's face was one of peace. "Then my work is complete."

"Are you trying to tell me that we have succeeded in changing time?"

"Yes," she stated matter-of-factly. "Isn't that what you wanted? I wasn't able to arrive in time to help him when he was George, but we should be able to make a difference this time." Sarah hugged her. "I love you. We shall be a family."

"No!" Chris sat up in bed, shaking. A light went on and strong arms went around her. *Geoff's room, not a graveyard.* She took a breath in relief.

"You're trembling," came Geoff's soothing voice.

"I had a dream about Sarah, not your mother, but our . . ."

He brushed the hair away from her face. "Sarah in the ledger."

Even he couldn't say "daughter." Calmer now, Chris continued, "She was an old woman, dressed in a 1920s-style dress. She said that her work was complete."

"Complete?"

"Because you had received the ledger, she said that we had succeeded in changing time."

"That's what I've been saying all along."

Chris drew away slightly from his embrace. "I'd like to visit the graveyard."

"Tonight?"

"I'll be leaving in the morning," she reminded him.

With a groan, Geoff left the bed and tugged on his briefs. "Visits to a graveyard at three in the morning," he grumbled under his breath. "My father was right. I *do* need my head examined."

"Thank you."

A slight grin formed on his mouth as he zipped his jeans. "You haven't bothered asking what I accept in repayment."

So many events seemed to keep replaying in her mind. Had they really changed time? "The fact that we'll eventually get married and have a daughter isn't enough?" she asked, getting up to dress.

He laughed. "So, you do believe."

"No," she snapped.

Another laugh. "I should have known that you'd remain stubborn. What are we going to do with her, Saber?" The dog wagged his tail, and Geoff finished dressing. "I see you're taking her side. In that case, I'll get a lantern and meet the two of you in the library."

Saber sat and attentively watched Geoff as he headed for the door.

"He was kidding, boy." Chris shooed the dog on, and Saber bounded after Geoff. As the pair vanished from the room, she shook her head in amazement. It was eerie how much the dog seemed to understand.

She quickly dressed and went downstairs to the library. Geoff had yet to arrive, and she went over to the circular rug that hid the bloodstains and bent down. *Was I present when George died?* She heard a soft clicking of nails against the hardwood floor and turned. Saber jumped on her and planted a wet tongue on her face, knocking her flat on her back.

"Saber!" Geoff gave the dog a hand signal and he immediately sat. He reached out a hand to help her to her feet. "Sorry about that. If we haven't been down this road before, I don't know what's come over him. He is not that friendly with strangers."

She brushed herself off and scratched behind Saber's ears. "That's all right. It must be his sad brown eyes. Usually I'm not taken in by overt male advances like that."

The amusement that crossed Geoff's face told Chris he was biting his tongue.

"I think you're right," she said. "We have been down this road before. How else would you know not to respond to that kind of statement?"

"George warned me. Now, shall we go?"

"Lead the way."

He escorted her to the door at the corner of the library. They stepped outside. So much had changed in 135 years. Once they reached the main section of the house, security lighting illuminated the way to the garage. Geoff showed her to the Mustang. He opened the door for her and Saber, then drove a mile along a dirt road to the cemetery. No moon helped to brighten the path. Except for a few twinkling stars, the night was pitch black. The florescent lantern cut through the darkness. In the broken light, the spires and headstones cast tall, imposing shadows, and Saber's silhouette gave the appearance of a stalking wolf.

Geoff raised the lantern, and Chris spotted his mother's grave.

Sarah Cameron
October 15, 1954–July 2, 1984

"Over there," Chris pointed to her left.

He shuddered visibly. "I was afraid you were going to say that."

"You're afraid? Is that where George is buried?"

"It is," he responded.

"I thought you said you had come to terms with George being a part of you."

He edged in the direction that she had indicated and hesitated at the gate. "I *do* accept that George is part of me, but I don't care to see his grave."

Could she blame him? The dream with Sarah had been incredibly real. Chris broke out in a cold sweat. Why was *she* suddenly shaking? Normally graveyards never bothered her. The iron gate groaned when Geoff finally opened it. He held the lantern high so she could read the names on the tombstones. *Thomas Cameron*. He had died in 1910. *Oh, Tom*. A paralyzing iciness gripped her. Beside him lay . . . She felt dizzy. "It's not possible."

Christine Cameron
?–May 12, 1901

Nearby was Sarah. She had died in 1925. The ground swayed beneath her feet. Chris clenched her hands. "It's true! All of it. Geoff..."

Telling her that things would be all right, he set the lantern on the ground and held her.

"Tom... Sarah..., they're all dead," she said, sobbing on his shoulder. She caught her breath and glanced into the darkness. Wiping the tears from her face, she picked up the lantern. "Georgianna is buried over here, Margaret and..." *George.* She fell to her knees. "I called you George when you thought I had been struck by lightning. It wasn't lightning, but..." She reached up to her necklace.

Geoff inched toward her and cleared his throat. "I think we should be getting back to the house."

With her discovery, she felt numb. Always so practical in life, she had no explanation for what had happened, except that she had loved him.

Chapter Twelve

In the drawing room, Geoff handed Chris a brandy. With regret, he sat beside her. "I shouldn't have shown you the ledger."

Her hands trembled as she sipped the drink. "You know as well as I do that I needed to know the truth. But Geoff, what do we do now? I don't want to see you die . . ."

Again. Even though she hadn't said the word, he heard it all the same. "Trust Sarah. She risked everything to get the ledger to me. I have to believe that your arrival two years early has to mean something positive."

She set the brandy snifter on the table. "Funny, before my arrival, I couldn't imagine anything but my career. Were those memories even real?" Her hand went to her necklace. "What if we *are* caught up in an endless cycle?"

Geoff shook his head. "I can't know the answer for certain, but time has already changed for the better. My mother lived longer as a result. George's memories can be a pain in the ass to deal with sometimes, but I doubt they're worse than a seizure disorder."

"We'll have to face what lies ahead sooner or later."

"I know." For so long, he had kept the ledger a secret. Now, Chris was here, truly sharing the ordeal with him. He embraced her. "Don't go back to Boston."

"You know that I must."

Why did he suddenly feel wounded? Had she come into his life, only to walk right out again? There had to be a reason. Time held the key. It always had.

* * *

After packing her bag, Chris wandered to the library to say goodbye to Geoff. They had spent the last few hours sitting on the sofa, holding and comforting each other. When she reached the library, the door was slightly ajar. She went inside. Saber lay on the rug beside the desk, and Geoff stood near the fireplace with his back to her. She overheard his heated voice on the phone.

"I'm growing very weary of your delay tactics. You accuse me of . . ." He caught sight of Chris. "I'll call you back." Obviously embarrassed that she had overheard, he hung up the phone. "Sorry you had to hear that."

"I presume that was Beth."

With a nod, he sank into the leather chair behind the desk.

"I didn't mean to intrude."

"Intrude?" He finally smiled. "You're a welcome diversion, and it's definitely not the memory I wanted to imprint on your mind before you leave."

She approached the desk and ran her fingers through his beard. "There's no need to worry. I'll recall the nights, holding each other and making love. But what are we going to do now?"

He stood and put his arms around her. "Hope that you get the job in Richmond."

She ached at the thought of leaving. "Even if I get the job, it may take several months before I can move to Virginia. Will you come to see me?"

"Absolutely." He stroked her cheek before kissing her.

Neither of them made any mention of what would happen if she failed to get the job. Like Geoff had said, there must be a reason for her arrival two years earlier than expected. They shared another intimate kiss. "It's time that I leave," she said, stepping back but not quite breaking their embrace.

"Stay here."

She successfully fought the tears. "I wish I could, but you know as well as I do that things aren't quite right yet."

With a sigh, he returned to the desk. "Beth."

"A finalized divorce would definitely help, but I think we need to think things through with a clear head."

"And you suddenly sound like a lawyer."

Chris detected annoyance in his voice. "Geoff, if we've truly been given another chance, we must use it wisely. I can't believe that I would have to suffer watching you die, only to keep repeating the same mistake throughout eternity."

"I'll try to be more patient."

"Good." She clasped his hand. "I need to be leaving. I have a long drive ahead of me."

With a nod, he accompanied her down the hall into the main section of the house until they reached the entry hall, where Judith stood beside Chris's bag. Geoff picked up the suitcase. "I'll take this to the car for you."

As he and Saber stepped outside, Judith said with a smile, "I hope you'll visit again soon."

"I will. I promise."

Her friend laughed. "I won't know whether you'll be visiting me or him."

"Both of you."

Judith hugged her. "I was hoping you'd say that."

Chris glanced at the Colonial table, vase, and gold mirror. Things didn't matter. People were what made a household. "Then you're not upset by what happened?"

"Upset? Why would I be upset? I'll admit—I don't normally give my brother credit for having good taste, but this time is definitely an exception."

They went down the mansion's cascading steps, where Geoff and Saber waited beside her car in the circular drive. Judith gave her another hug. "Bye, Chris. I'll give you a call."

As Judith disappeared back into the house, Chris unlocked the trunk. "How soon can you come to see me?"

Geoff placed her bag into the trunk and slammed it shut. "Two, maybe three weeks, but I'd prefer that you . . ."

She placed two fingers to his lips. "Don't say it. I would stay. Then what? You know the timing must be right."

He laughed. "My patience must have lasted all of five minutes. I can't help it. I love you."

"And I, you. We will make it right—in good time."

They exchanged a final, parting kiss, and she got into the Integra. She started the car and waved. Her eyes misted when she drove down the lane. If they had precious little time together, why was she driving away?

In the week following Chris's departure, Geoff struggled with the idea of confronting Beth. In the thirteen months since Beth had left Poplar Ridge, she had carefully arranged his visitations with Neal through third parties, so his only communication with her had been on the phone or through attorneys. Concerned about what reception he would receive, he parked along a Richmond street in front of a yellow Victorian.

Maybe a face-to-face meeting hadn't been such a good idea. He stared at the door a minute, debating with himself. *Stop being a wuss.* Straightening his shoulders, he grasped Saber's leash and strode up the brick walk. The gabled roof looked vaguely familiar. *A sword clanked at his side. He wore a gray uniform with a yellow sash.* It had been Margaret's home with her family before she had married George. Geoff halted by the door. According to the ledger, Beth had been possessed by Margaret. *Continue on.* He knocked.

The door opened. Beth blinked back her disbelief. "Geoff. Whatever you have to say can be relayed through my lawyer."

He put his foot in the door before she closed it. "I've come to tell you that I agree to your terms."

She relaxed slightly and let him into the foyer. "Why now?"

For some reason, seeing her again brought no emotion—no animosity, or, the opposite, love. "I just want it over and done with."

Regarding him with suspicion, she crossed her arms, when Neal burst into the foyer.

"Daddy!"

Geoff picked up his four-year-old son and gave him a bear hug.

Neal stared at him with his big blue eyes. "Will you read me a story about King Arthur?"

"Before I leave." Geoff put Neal down. "Saber's been looking forward to playing with you. Why don't you take him out back, while Mommy and I talk for a few minutes?"

With a childish giggle, Neal grasped the dog's leash and led him away. Saber was larger than Neal, but he accompanied the boy.

Beth continued to scowl. "I don't like the way you just showed up, without warning."

"If I had asked for a meeting on neutral ground, would you have agreed to it?"

Her gaze softened. "Probably not. Still you have no right barging in on me like this. I never wanted to see you again."

"I missed you too." So much for lacking any feeling. Even before the words were out of his mouth, he regretted them. He had promised himself not to say anything hurtful.

Tears entered her eyes.

"Beth, I'm sorry. If we can talk and get things settled, I'm out of here."

"I'll put on some coffee. Come into the kitchen."

As he followed her to the kitchen, he thought of sconces on the wall, flickering a shadowy gas flame. In the kitchen, a blocky wood table stood in the center of the room, and a black servant tended the cook fire in the fireplace. *Tessa.*

"Geoff?"

He blinked back George's memories. Beth added a scoop of coffee to the coffeemaker and motioned for him to have a seat at the table. "We'll have coffee in a few minutes. So, you'll agree to my terms?" She pulled out a chair and sat.

He sat across from her. "I will, if you'll tell me what happened."

"Hold it right there. If you want conditions, then we can just start bickering through our lawyers again."

He successfully fought the urge to hurl an angry retort. "Maybe you've forgotten, but we used to talk our troubles through. I merely want closure. Nothing more."

She clasped her hands together. "I got tired of competing with another woman."

"Another woman?" He raised his voice. "And I'm tired of being accused of something that only happened in your mind. I *never* cheated on you."

Her eyes narrowed. "Dammit Geoff, and you keep giving me the same, tired response. How do you explain the late hours where you'd go missing? Or the time that you vanished for two days? Toward the end, when we made love, it was obvious you wanted to be with someone else. You even called me Chris."

George's memories. He was damned, no matter what he said.

"I see that you recognize her name."

"It's not what you think," he replied weakly.

"Of course not. It never is." With tears in her eyes, she got up for the coffee.

"Beth, I knew Chris before I ever met you." *An entire lifetime before.*

She brought two steaming mugs over to the table and reseated herself. "When we first met, we agreed to be upfront about our pasts. Are you now saying that was a lie too?"

"No."

"Then stop denying there was no one else."

And now that he had met Chris, Beth would never believe otherwise. "If I told you the truth, you wouldn't believe me, so I don't see the point in discussing it further. I guess I still don't understand why we couldn't have talked it over before you left."

Tears trickled down her cheeks. And if the ledger was correct, she would kill him in eleven years time as a consequence of Margaret's possession. Had there already been signs that he had missed? "Or did something else happen that you're not telling me?" he asked.

Averting her eyes, Beth wiped her tears away. "No."

Convinced that he had suddenly hit on something, he said, "Beth . . ."

"I said, 'No.' " She raised her voice. "If that's not good enough for you, then you can leave. I didn't ask you to come here to dredge up old wounds in the first place."

"Fine." Geoff held up his hands in surrender. "Then we're agreed. We can get this over and done with."

More tears. She gave him a nod.

Only with her agreement did he realize that she had been stalling the divorce proceedings for a reason. She hadn't really wanted the separation in the first place, and whatever she was keeping from him was a clue to her actions.

* * *

Chris's days had returned to normal. The hectic pace of her corporate, high-tension job helped her concentrate on something besides what had happened during her recent trip to Virginia. But dreams of her graveyard visit plagued her, and lack of sleep was catching up. Her stomach churned, and she popped a couple of antacid tablets into her mouth. Her intercom buzzed. "Yes, Nancy," she said to her secretary.

"A Mr. DeBolt is on line two."

"Thanks, Nancy." With nervous anticipation, Chris pressed the button for line two. "Mr. DeBolt, thank you for returning my call. I was wondering if you've made a decision about the position . . ."

"As a matter of fact, we have."

When he hesitated, Chris anticipated the worst.

"We decided it was best to go with someone with a little more experience."

Knowing she was perfectly suited for the job, Chris read between the lines. He had meant they wanted someone older than she was. "Thank you for your candor, Mr. DeBolt." The ledger had stated that she would work for an all-female firm—three years in the future. As she hung up the phone, she was strangely relieved.

"Chris, is something wrong?" asked her secretary.

She looked up at the silver-haired woman. "Nancy, I hadn't heard you enter." Nancy had been the only person at the office that she had confided in about the job prospect. "I won't be moving to Virginia just yet."

"I'm sorry. I know how much you wanted the job."

Chris frowned. "That was until . . ."

"Until?"

"I met someone."

Nancy waved at her for the details.

Chris shook her head. "I'd rather not talk about it. Things were happening a little too fast, is all."

"I detect something amiss." Her secretary's eyes widened. "Good heavens, he's not married?"

"As a matter of fact . . ."

"Chris . . ."

"Spare me the lecture. I know what you're going to say, Nancy. It's foolhardy, but Geoff is in the process of getting a divorce. The fact that he's still married is the least of our problems."

"How do you mean?"

Now Chris's head hurt as much as her stomach. "It's this little problem that I had of time traveling to 1867 and watching Geoff's first incarnation die in my arms. If I'm not careful, we're doomed to repeat the whole scenario."

Nancy arched a brow. "If you don't want to tell me, just say so."

"Sorry, Nancy. I didn't mean to be rude. I'm a little stressed, right now."

"Men, especially married ones, often have that effect on women. Take care of yourself and get some rest."

Before Chris could respond, Nancy bid her good evening. She checked her watch—4:53. She needed to let Geoff know that she didn't get the job. Her best bet would be to try his cell phone. She picked up the phone and dialed.

"*Hello.*"

"Geoff, it's Chris."

"*I was just thinking of you. I've agreed to settle with Beth. We're just waiting for a court date.*"

"That is good news." So why were her hands shaking? "Unfortunately, I have some not-so-good news. I didn't get the job."

"*There will be others.*" Sympathy registered in his voice.

"I was hoping to live near you, sooner rather than later," she stated, in spite of her misgivings.

"*You could move in with me. Besides Saber, no one would ever notice in a house as big as Poplar Ridge.*"

She laughed. "I doubt that would help your divorce proceedings. If Beth finds out about us, she could change her demands."

He sighed. "*Warning duly noted, counselor, but she already thinks I was involved with someone by the name of Chris. You can imagine how much she'll believe me now when she does find out about us. I was hoping to drive up to Boston next weekend. If you'd rather that I didn't come . . .*"

"Of course I want you to come see me. My feelings haven't changed. I think I'm just a little bummed out about not getting the job."

"Then I'll be there next weekend to help cheer you up."

After a series of goodbyes, Chris hung up the phone. She should be elated by the prospect of seeing Geoff again, but the ledger's warning remained imprinted on her mind. The truth haunted her. If she made Boston a safe haven, instead of uprooting to Virginia, she wouldn't have to watch him die—again.

By the following Friday, a brisk October chill was in the air. Eagerly anticipating Geoff's visit, Chris had bought theater tickets for Saturday evening, then worried if she had done the right thing. Would a country boy even like the theater? Near five, she returned to the warmth of her office. After picking up her messages from Nancy, she dropped her briefcase on her desk and sifted through them. Geoff had called while she had been in court. She dialed his cell number.

"Hi, Chris, I'm going to be late."

She recognized the metallic hum of his cell phone. "Traffic?"

"No, I made a side trip. I'll tell you about it when I get there."

Chris checked her watch. "How late do you think you'll be?"

"It'll probably be around eleven."

Her excitement fizzled. "That late?" Then she caught herself. It's not like he was canceling the weekend. At least he had called to warn her. "All right. I'll pick up dinner on my way home, and we'll warm it up when you get here." He sent his appreciation before saying goodbye. Well, there was no reason to hurry home.

Disappointed, Chris hung up the phone.

Nancy stepped into her office. "I thought you had planned on leaving right after court today."

"There's no rush to get to an empty apartment. Geoff called to say that he'd be late."

"If you'd like to pass some time, we can go out for a drink."

"Sure. I'd like that." After packing her papers in her briefcase, she joined Nancy for a couple of drinks before heading home. It was nearly eight by the time she arrived at her apartment. She wondered if she should call Geoff. If he had run into any difficulties, he would have called again. Chris kicked off her shoes and began flicking TV channels with the remote control. After she sat through a boring documentary about the latest theory on Atlantis, a movie, *The Two Worlds of Jenny Logan*, about a woman who could travel through time by wearing a Victorian dress caught her attention. She grasped the necklace about her throat.

Pain spread throughout her arm. Beside her, blue eyes revealed their agony. Blood flowed across the floor. "George!"

Through a flood of tears, she drew him into her arms and held him. Whispering her love, she stroked her fingers through his hair. His hand fell away with a thump to the floor, and his eyes opened to the sightlessness of death. "George, you can't die. We've changed time."

A scream echoed in Chris's mind, waking her just in time for the tail end of the movie. Not only had the woman in the film traveled time, but she saved her lover in the past from a premature death. And the couple lived happily ever after. *Hollywood.* She had been unsuccessful in helping George. Only now was she coming to grips with what had happened. She had been arrested for his murder, and a noose had been around her neck. Yet the gravestone had marked her death in 1901. The pieces didn't quite add up.

A knock at the door drew her from her gloomy thoughts. *Geoff.* She hurried to the door, made her way through the locks, and opened it without checking through the peephole first. With a tired smile and wearing a jacket more suited to Virginia's autumn, rather than Boston's, Geoff held out a bottle of champagne. Her arms went around him, and their mouths met. She grasped his hand and pulled him inside. Suddenly self-conscious that her entire apartment was smaller than the library at Poplar Ridge, she said, "I realize you're used to more spacious surroundings."

He kissed her again. "I didn't drive all the way to Boston to criticize your apartment."

"Hungry? I'll warm some dinner . . ."

His mouth pressed against hers, cutting off her sentence. Obviously, another hunger required satiation before eating. As she showed him to the bedroom, clothing trailed behind them. Three weeks apart seemed more like three years.

In an enthusiastic reunion, they touched and teased each other on the bed. Out of control, she felt like she was spinning in an endless cycle of grief. With a shudder, tears formed in her eyes. "Geoff, you mustn't leave Boston."

Still caught up in the moment, he kissed and held her. Finally regaining his senses, he moved to her side. "Why? What's happened?"

"I had a dream that I held George when he died. I can't watch you die like that—not again."

He sighed. "Even if I stayed in Boston, we may not change anything, only the circumstances. I could be hit by a bus tomorrow. Besides, what would I do in Boston? I doubt there are too many job openings for plantation managers around here."

His sense of humor was what she needed. She rose up on her elbow and stroked his chest. "Thank you for putting things in perspective."

He grasped her hand and kissed it. "Anytime, ma'am."

She loved the sound of his accent. " 'Ma'am.' If anyone said that around here, his motives would be suspect."

With an impish smile, he kissed each of her fingers individually.

Chris snuggled next to him. "Now, are you going to tell me why you were late?"

Rat call! Rat call! The sergeant in blue tossed rats from the platform. *The starving prisoners scrambled for the rodents.* "I was late because I visited Fort Delaware."

"Fort Delaware?"

"George spent nearly a year there during the war. I warned you that he sometimes draws me to places. At least this time I remembered enough details to realize I had been there so I could give you a call that I'd be late."

"You did warn me," she agreed. "Wasn't Fort Delaware a prison camp?"

Once salted and fried, rat meat was tender. "It was, and he nearly died there."

She shivered beneath his fingertips. "What do you remember about the trip?"

Geoff blinked. "That the fort is closed until spring."

He stroked his fingers through her hair, and she settled her head on his chest. "What's it like when you have George's thoughts?"

"The memories are more like a dream. Sometimes they're fuzzy. Other times, he just takes over. A hypnotist once tried to bring his memories to the forefront to purge them from me. That was just before my second visit to the hospital. If I remember them too clearly, it's like my head goes into overload."

She hugged him.

A dim recollection of a brown-haired woman looking out of place in a long dress came to Geoff's mind. "He loved you."

"If it stresses you to talk about it, then don't."

He traced his fingers along the length of her back. "I'm too relaxed right now to be stressed by it. He felt as if he should know you. Now, I understand why."

"Do you recall anything about that day?" she asked with a quaver in her voice.

"Over the years, I've been able to piece a number of the details together. Margaret was upset. She was wearing . . ." He touched Chris's necklace. ". . . this. I took her to our room. She wanted forgiveness."

"For what?"

He couldn't recall why Margaret had wanted forgiveness. "I'm not certain. Anyway, I got the necklace from her and was going to give it back to you."

"Geoff, you've started using I for George."

Unaware of the slip, he placed a hand to his temple. "It wouldn't be the first time. Now you see why the shrinks have diagnosed me with dissociative identity disorder."

She gave his arm a sympathetic squeeze. "I didn't mean to interrupt, but I think your memories may help me unlock my own."

"Do you think it's wise? You may end up divided, like I am."

"It's a risk we have to take."

For some reason, the thought unsettled him. Angered voices—his parents argued over his mental stability. His father had claimed that he used George to get attention. But the ledger had brought Geoff peace, even though he had learned his likely fate. "I took one of the passageways through the house."

"Passageways?"

"Secret passageways behind panels throughout the house. My ancestors were paranoid about British attacks. I saddled Raven and nearly broke my neck taking a midnight ride. I had to walk back to the house. You met me in the library. I gave you the necklace, and that's the last thing I recall. George has spared me from the final minutes."

"You've switched to third person again."

"At least now you have some idea how he can take over."

She gripped his hand. "I'm not frightened anymore. It's who *we* are."

"Together." He tightened the grip on her hand. All this time, she had been the simple answer to what he had been missing.

Chapter Thirteen

Almost two weeks later, Laura helped Judith ready the guest bedroom. Chris would be returning to Poplar Ridge for the annual Halloween ball, and Judith wanted everything immaculate before her friend's arrival. On second thought, she should have asked Chris about her intentions. If she planned on staying with Geoff, all of the preparations would be for naught. Doubting that Geoff would freely volunteer the information, she'd simply have to ask him herself. The months following Beth's departure had been especially rough, but Geoff had been pleasant to be around of late, not to mention his alcohol consumption had dropped significantly since meeting Chris. She highly suspected he was in love. Imagine that, two such opposite people perfectly suited for each other.

As Laura made the bed, Judith dusted the dresser of the heavy-bodied mirror. The message "Behind," had been written in a sticky rouge. Daddy had dismissed it, but Judith knew that her friend wasn't the sort to play wacky tricks. When she bumped one of the hand-carved horse heads in the frame, the mirror wobbled. It must have come loose when Daddy had moved the dresser. "Laura, can you give me hand? We need to move the dresser a little, so I can tighten the mirror."

The maid joined her at the opposite end of the dresser.

Even with Laura's assistance, Judith struggled to move the solid oak antique dresser. She should inform Geoff about the mirror. But if she waited for her brother's help pertaining to anything inside the household, Chris's visit would be over before he attended to the problem. She heaved, and the dresser budged. Combining their strength, the two managed to push the dresser away from the wall. The mirror rocked, and a support strut cracked. Bits of glass went flying when the mirror crashed to the floor.

"Are you all right, Laura?"

The maid nodded. "I'll get something to clean the mess."

Judith sighed. The mirror hadn't seemed *that* loose. She bent down and carefully collected the larger shards. Paper poked between two fragments of glass. As she removed the top layer, a sharp edge pierced her index finger. "Damn," she muttered under breath before sucking on her bleeding finger.

Yellowed with age, the paper had been folded to fit neatly between the mirror and frame. *Behind?* Judith reached for it and unfolded the paper. It was dated May 1901 and addressed to Geoff. What's more, it was in Chris's handwriting. How was that possible? She began to read:

> *Dear Geoff,*
>
> *This will likely be my last entry in the ledger. I hope you'll forgive my lapse over the years, but after I watched you die a second time, I had difficulty carrying on. It's been over thirty years now, and I have seen the turn of two centuries. How different they are. Causes that I might have championed if I had been born in this time, I have let slide. I know that women will soon gain their right to vote, without my involvement. I have seen the first automobile and electric light bulb.*
>
> *Seven months after George's death, I gave birth to a baby girl. I named her Sarah. She is Sarah Cameron. Tom convinced me that during this time any child born out of wedlock would be at a true disadvantage. I couldn't impose extra hardships on her due to my time displacement. After all, she is your daughter. Tom and I were quietly married shortly after George's death. Don't laugh at what may seem to be my fading ideals. It distressed me to marry Tom, but Sarah's livelihood is more important than my feminist goals. Of course I instilled women's rights in her head, and with some luck, she will live long enough to have the joy to finally cast a ballot.*

As for Tom, he has raised Sarah as if she were his own. We never had children of our own. I guess in that sense time was playing a cruel joke because I couldn't have asked for a more devoted and loving father, except of course to have you here. But that wasn't meant to be. Tom helped me when I needed it most, and for that I'm truly indebted. I do hope you will forgive me, but after a few years, I grew to care for him. It's love based on friendship and has never had the intensity of my love for you. Both of us struggled to get past those early days after your death, so it was only natural that we'd eventually share our lives.

Sarah looks very similar to our Sarah. In her childhood, she had the same reddish hair and on the bridge of her nose, she had freckles. As a result, I can easily imagine what she will look like when she's grown. She also possesses the gift of being able to communicate with the dead. Unfortunately, she was only successful in reaching you once. Believe me, we have tried on numerous occasions, but our bridge to you was never crossed again.

After your death, Margaret's laudanum addiction worsened. Unlike the previous time line, she is very aware of your death. She has never stopped wearing black, and I know she secretly visits your grave, as well as Tessa's. If only I had been a psychologist rather than an attorney, because I have never been able to reach Margaret. All of us have tried.

Tessa, her faithful servant, suffered the consequences for your death. Whether she pulled the trigger on Margaret's behalf or simply took the blame for Margaret, none of us knows. It grieves me that a potential innocent party from the original time line may have died, who shouldn't have. You had warned me about the fabric of time being torn, but after you were shot, Tessa placed the gun in my hand to make it look like a murder and attempted suicide. If only she had realized that you had already agreed to return to Margaret, both of your lives could have been spared.

I was unjustly accused of killing you and spent nearly two weeks in jail. Tom and Captain Michael Rhodes came to my aid. By the time Tessa was captured, she had hidden my necklace.

*A Negro woman in the nineteenth century had no chance of
receiving any other sentence but death for killing a white man,
even if the fatal bullet was meant to hit me. Before the trial, she
escaped and a mob got to her first. Tessa hanged for George's
murder.*

*In any case, I never saw my necklace again. If Margaret
knows its whereabouts, she's not speaking. Even though Sarah
says I shall find it soon, it is no longer a priority for me as I am
much too old to return to my original time.*

*Sarah promises that she will make certain Greta receives
this ledger. She is our link in time to you and will convince Greta
of the ledger's validity. Time can be changed. My time grows
short, and I can rest with confidence that you will eventually
read my words. I have loved you as George and look forward to
loving you again as Geoff.*

Always,
Chris

The letter made no sense. Judith reread it to try and absorb
the information. *Time travel?* Temporarily forgetting about the broken mirror, she went into the hall to the nearest phone and dialed
Geoff's cell number. When he answered, she asked, "Can you meet
me in the library? I've found a rather peculiar letter. It's addressed
to you, from Chris, but it's dated 1901."

"*I'll be right there,*" he responded excitedly.

The phone went dead, and she replaced the receiver. She nearly
went charging down the stairs but caught herself. At this time of
day Geoff would have been working outside, and it would take him
at least ten minutes to get to the library. Someone had carefully hidden the letter in the mirror. She would make certain the intended
recipient would finally receive it.

By the time Geoff arrived, Judith was already waiting for him in
the library. Saber greeted her with a wagging tail, and without a
word, she passed him the yellowed paper. The missing page from the
ledger, dated 1901. He eased himself into the leather chair behind
the desk and read Chris's final letter from the past.

Tessa might have killed George? In the original time line, it had been Margaret, mistaking him for the Union soldier who had raped her.

"Well?" Judith asked, obviously dying with curiosity.

His head suddenly ached. "I'm trying to absorb it."

"That can't possibly be from Chris."

"It was." For thirty years she had been stranded in the past. *Wait.* She had the necklace in her possession. Somehow, she must have found a way to the present. The two didn't add up.

"Geoff?"

He glanced across the desk at Judith.

"All these years when doctors diagnosed you with an alternate personality, *he* was real?"

She still couldn't say George's name. "Our great-, several times removed, grandfather, George Cameron. If you'd like to meet him, I can oblige anytime."

Shaking her head, she sank into the chair across from him. "Reincarnation isn't possible."

Geoff cleared his head and picked up a pen with his left hand. "Meet George, little sister."

"Holding a pen in your left hand is no proof."

He lowered the pen to the desk. "Would you care to hear stories about the War between the States or Fort Delaware that would curl your hair naturally, instead of using that girly gunk you put on it?"

"Geoff!" But she didn't chastise him on the point further. "Are you saying that you knew Chris in the past?"

He withdrew the ledger from the desk. "I think it's time that you read this. It explains it better than I ever could."

She flipped through several pages of the leather volume. "Where did you get this?"

"From Greta. Her Aunt Sarah gave it to her."

"Just as the letter stated would happen. But why would anyone go to so much trouble of ripping out the last page and hiding it?"

"Good question." He shrugged that he didn't know.

Judith picked up the ledger and stood. "I'll read it."

"Be aware that it contains some very personal information."

"I will, and I'll treat it with respect."

"Thanks, Judith."

A smile crept to her face. "Which reminds me. Do I finish getting the guest room ready, or am I wasting my time? After all, I presume that Chris will be spending her time in your . . ." Her face reddened slightly.

He laughed. "You had better ask Chris. I wouldn't dare to presume."

She echoed an agreeing laugh.

"So, you approve?"

"I'm just relieved that you've finally gained some decent taste in women."

As soon as she finished reading the ledger, she'd realize that he had been attracted to Beth because she looked like Margaret. "Me too."

She waved on her way out of the room, and he returned to studying Chris's final letter from the past. Why would anyone go to great lengths to hide it? Burning would have been more practical. Unless it was meant to be found.

Geoff had been unable to meet Chris at the airport, so Judith had picked her up. On the drive to Poplar Ridge, her friend shared the fact that Geoff had given her the ledger to read, along with finding the letter behind the mirror.

By the time, they arrived back at to the house, Chris was eager to read the discovery for herself, but she contained herself enough to ready for the ball. She straightened her long black wig to better cover her cinnamon-colored hair in front of a full-length cheval mirror. She tilted it slightly to get a better look at her costume. Black laces tightened the bodice of her thigh-length, leather dress with flowing sheer sleeves and a floor-length overskirt. Her lipstick and nail polish were blood red. Fishnet stockings and black boots finished the look. She grasped her tall, pointed hat and placed it on her head, then went into the hall.

At the bottom of the stairs, Geoff, dressed in gray uniform with gold embroidery on the sleeves, waited. For the occasion, he had shaved his beard, leaving a goatee, and looked as if he had stepped right out of the pages of a history book. Alongside him stood Saber, wagging his feathery tail. Geoff peered at her favorably as she descended the stairs. When she reached the final step, he kissed her full on the mouth. "I have something to show you, Chris."

She bent down and scratched Saber behind the ears, and the dog planted a wet tongue on her face. "The letter?"

"I have something else to show you first."

With the enthusiasm of a schoolboy, Geoff grasped her hand. He led her through the parlor and down the wood-paneled hall to the library. From the desk, he withdrew an official-looking paper from a drawer. A divorce certificate. She had thought it might be risky attending such a public event without his divorce being final. Now, there was no need to worry. She threw her arms around his neck and kissed him until the sound of a throat clearing came from behind them.

"I don't mean to interrupt," came Judith's voice, "but I was wondering if the two of you are ready to go. I can always send your apologies, if you'll be late."

"That won't be necessary, Judith." Chris turned to her friend, who was dressed in a gauzy white costume with an equally white wig. "We'll be along soon."

"Good. I'd like for you to meet the man I'm going to marry." With a giggle, Judith left the room.

Chris met Geoff's gaze. "She warned me on the way back from the airport that she had read the ledger. Am I the only one who doesn't know what the final letter says?"

"Tessa may have killed George. She was the one you saw hang."

"Tessa? What do you mean 'may have?' " Never suspecting the servant, Chris thought that might also explain the apparition she had dismissed as being Laura at the top of the stairs upon her first arrival. "I would like to see the letter."

As if expecting her request, he withdrew the letter from the top desk drawer. 1901. She *had* lived out her life in the past. *A woman dressed in black slipped the page from the desk and hid it behind the mirror.* Why would Margaret have hidden the letter there? *Stop dwelling.* She read it. Numbed by the account of Tessa's violent death and her marriage to Tom, she set the letter on the desktop. "It explains almost everything, except how I got this." She clutched her necklace.

"I think we can solve that little mystery later."

He held out his arm, and she laced hers through his. She should have worn a period costume to complement Geoff's. They retraced their steps down the hall until reaching the drawing room. Judith led a round of introductions to her dark-haired boyfriend dressed as a pirate. As the ledger stated, David lived on a horse farm in northern Virginia. The glaring difference from the ledger was the ever stoic patriarch Winston Cameron also had a date. A seemingly pleasant woman by the name of Barbara, who appeared to be in her fifties. Attired as a ghost in a shroud for the ball, she could have been almost any age.

Maybe time had worked out for the best. Geoff and Judith's mother had lived longer, and as a result, Winston carried no guilt over Sarah's death. But what of Tessa? Even though Margaret may not have pulled the trigger on George in this time line, she had never recovered mentally, which meant that Geoff's life could still be in danger. She felt a sympathetic hand on her shoulder. Geoff's eyes flickered as if he knew exactly the torment that was churning through her head.

"Care to ride with us?" Judith offered. "You'd never fit your hat in Geoff's Mustang."

Determined not to let her discovery spoil the evening, Chris agreed. Following Judith and David, Geoff escorted her from the drawing room. Once outside, they went down the steps to the drive where the car waited. Ever the Southern gentleman, Geoff helped her into the backseat. Removing her witch's hat first, she got in. Soon, he sat beside her, and she breathed in the spicy scent of cologne. Anytime they were apart was agonizing. Weeks were like years, and she had come to the conclusion that in spite the hand fate might play, they were destined to be together. Now that his divorce was final, would he ask her to stay?

While Judith and David chatted in the front seat, Geoff's arm went about her waist. When the motion of the car halted, he drew away and aided her from the car. Unlike Poplar Ridge, the manor home was a white frame house, approximately the length of a football field. The ballroom extended half that length.

At the end of the room, an orchestra played. Wizards and ghouls danced with medieval princesses and fairy tale Sleeping Beauties. If Chris had thought fast enough, she would have costumed Saber as her black cat.

"Geoff!" A woman dressed as a seductive vampire waggled her fingers and approached them. "You weren't here last year. Good to see you again, and Beth . . ."

"This is Chris," Geoff replied with some awkwardness. After introducing them, he continued, "Beth and I have divorced."

"I see . . . ," the woman stated, giving Chris a slow, appraising glance. "I must admit that comes as quite a shock. You always seemed such a happy couple."

Ready to rip the woman's hair out by the roots, Chris narrowed her eyes, when Geoff drew her in the direction of the bar. "Sorry about that, but you shouldn't have to suffer through it again. She'll spread the word around."

Chris relaxed slightly. "And someone will report back to Beth, I'm certain."

He halted by the bar and handed her a glass of champagne. "Beth doesn't matter. She's the past. She's my ex now."

If only life were that simple. Others would likely see her as Beth before the evening was over. Chris sipped the champagne. "Are you going to ask me to dance?"

He shot her a grin. "I'm waiting for the right moment."

She finished her champagne and set the empty glass on the bar. The orchestra began playing a slow waltz, and Geoff extended his arm, escorting her to the dance floor. Nineteenth-century music. She should have guessed that Geoff would be drawn to it. Once on the dance floor, they drew close. In his arms, she could almost forget about the letter and her own double life.

Throughout the evening, they danced and mingled. As she surmised, a couple more people mistook her for Beth. Each time, she spotted annoyance in Geoff's eyes. Around eleven, she asked, "Do you mind if we leave early? I wouldn't mind a stroll back to the house."

"It's a good three miles. You're hardly dressed for the terrain by the river."

"Or we could take the road," she suggested.

"That lengthens the hike by a quarter of a mile, city girl."

"I'm game."

An impish smile crept to his face. Who was she fooling? A hike dressed as a witch! At least she had the good foresight to wear black boots instead of stiletto heels. Still, Geoff was looking forward to the prospect of rescuing her.

She wouldn't give him the satisfaction. "I've clomped around miles of city streets. I *can* make it."

"Of that, I have no doubt." He bowed slightly at the waist. "Ma'am."

She grasped his arm. When she informed Judith of their plan, her friend was a little surprised. In the hall, Chris collected her black cape, and they went outside. Fortunately, a full moon guided the way as Geoff showed her along the cobblestone path. The night was unseasonably warm for late October.

A half mile passed before they reached the road. Although she felt awkward in her costume, Geoff adjusted his pace to hers. "You've been quiet since leaving," he said.

She remained annoyed by the the number of times she'd been called Beth. And she couldn't get the contents of the letter out of her mind. The ledger had warned that Geoff had difficulty putting the past behind him. "Do you still love her?"

Surprised by the question, he halted and faced her. "I'm relieved the divorce is finally over."

"That doesn't exactly answer the question."

He shoved his hands in his pockets. "What do you want me to say?"

"You should know by now that I respect the truth."

"And what you need to realize is that George was the one who fell in love with her."

Because Beth looked like Margaret. "You're still avoiding the question. George is a part of you."

"I'm not avoiding the question," he insisted. "I'm just finding it difficult to explain. Beth was a lot like Margaret before the war. George couldn't help but love her. I admit I was hurt when she left, but something between us never seemed quite right. I think it's because the past can never truly be recaptured. I'm a little numb, but love her? I haven't loved her in quite some time, but I was only able to admit it to myself after your visit."

"Thank you for answering honestly." Hand in hand, they started walking again. "What about us?"

"I was hoping that you would decide to stay."

Half-expecting him to ask, she felt her heart pound. "I haven't found a job yet."

He shrugged that it didn't matter. "You'd have an easier time finding one if you moved here."

"I can't afford an apartment until I find a job." He opened his mouth but before he could speak, she continued, "Before you suggest it, I won't sponge off you. I make my own way in this world."

"I was suggesting that you move in with me."

While his proposition had been anticipated, she hesitated. "I'll have to think about it. It's all very sudden."

He laughed. "Like over a hundred years sudden." He halted once more and grasped both of her hands. "If there's one thing that George has taught me, it's that life is too short. For whatever reason, you're here two years early. Why waste the extra time that we've been granted?"

She trembled beneath his grip. "What if my being here early shortens the time you have left?"

He squeezed her hands. "Then we're like everyone else, not knowing when that time will come."

As she had expected, his argument was pragmatic. "You're right. Besides, I'm sure in a house as big as Poplar Ridge, no one would notice, except Saber."

At hearing the echo of his own words, he laughed once more. "Chris, I didn't mean move in with me as in shacking up. I meant . . ."

"Don't say it." With his divorce now final, she should have seen his proposal coming. "We've only known one another for a month and a half."

"Do you seriously believe that?" he grumbled.

"No, and if anyone else had asked the question, I'd be running back to Boston as fast as I could. I thought career was everything, but you've revived memories, showing me that isn't the case."

"Does that mean I should propose in nineteenth-century fashion?" He gripped her hand and got on bent knee, placing his hat over his heart.

Chris stifled a laugh. "That won't be necessary." She did laugh when a car passed them. In the dim light, she saw the passengers rubber-necking. What a sight they must be—a Confederate soldier on his knee, proposing to a witch. "I had better say yes before we cause an accident."

Geoff regained his feet, and they continued along the road to Poplar Ridge. "Now that we have that settled, when can you move in?"

Never having been the impulsive sort, she was amazed at herself for agreeing so quickly. But everything seemed right. "Judith will want us to have a large wedding."

"We can elope."

"Let's do it right this time around. With Judith's organizational skills, I bet she can help me plan a smaller wedding than she'd like within a few weeks." To this suggestion, he agreed. As they continued along the road, they approached a Gothic Victorian—Greta's house. A light on the porch and in her sitting room had been left on. Even the old woman hadn't returned from the party yet. "Tom lived here."

"I know," Geoff replied softly.

"How could I have lived in that house for thirty years and not remember?"

"Because it was a lifetime ago."

"You said that you always had the memories but were unable to make sense of them until reading the ledger. I've never had memories like that until . . ." Clutching her necklace, she moved forward. "The night I was struck by lightning. I wasn't hurt, but poof, I'm remembering things from a previous life. It's almost as if that incident unlocked the memories." Once they were past Greta's house, she asked, "Do you have a picture of him?"

"Who?"

"Tom."

"I think so."

His voice had grown unusually quiet since she had first mentioned George's brother. "Geoff, are you jealous of Tom?"

"No."

He answered more abruptly and loudly than she would have expected. She couldn't help but snicker. "There's no reason to be. I don't even know what he looked like."

"You'll eventually remember."

"Even if I do, he's long dead." She grasped his hand. "Besides, the letter explained everything. It's you that I love."

He stroked her cheek. "I know, and it shouldn't bother me. Tom apparently went out of his way to help you and Sarah after George died."

But . . . Even though he hadn't said the word, she heard the hesitation in his voice. Maybe he had an inkling of how she felt being in Beth's shadow. And she had spent *thirty years* with a man that she couldn't remember. At twenty-six, she found the thought of marrying for convenience or for that length of time incomprehensible. Now, she was marrying Geoff. That's why she had arrived two years early. Her gloomy thoughts faded, and as they made their way back to Poplar Ridge, she bubbled with enthusiasm.

Near the entrance, a dog barked from the top step. Another bark, and Saber raced down the steps to greet them. "That's odd," Geoff said.

Chris reached down to pet the dog. "What is?"

"There shouldn't be anyone home to have let him out." He went up the steps to investigate.

Saber bounded after him, and she followed the pair. The door was ajar. In a house so large, an intruder could be hiding almost anywhere. She grasped Geoff's elbow as he was about to enter. "It might be better to call the cops."

He shook his head. "Saber would have stopped anyone that he doesn't know."

"It still might be better . . ."

"You can stay out here until I give the all clear."

"Not on your life. If you're going inside, I'm going with you." She clung to his sleeve. "Men," she muttered under her breath, "why do they always have to play a hero?"

"Chris, if I truly thought the house had been broken into, I'd do as you suggest."

The lighting remained low as they entered the main hall. Geoff turned up the lights. No one lurked in the shadows, and Saber gave no indication that someone might be hiding behind any of the furniture. First, they checked the parlor, then the drawing room. No one. They went down the hall to the library. Suddenly uneasy, she swallowed hard as Geoff opened the door.

He switched on the lights. "It's clear."

Chris breathed out in relief, until spotting a pistol on the desk. "Geoff..."

He picked up his pace. "I see it."

She moved closer. The pistol was an antique weapon. "George's?"

With a nod, Geoff checked the chamber to see if it was loaded. He made a quick search through the drawers. "The ledger is missing."

"That book would make little sense to anyone else, except..."

"Margaret," he finished for her.

And Margaret had possessed Beth. Her early arrival *had* pushed the confrontation forward.

Geoff locked the gun away in a desk drawer. Thankfully, it hadn't been loaded, but why would Beth have returned it in such a secretive manner? Unless...

"Geoff..."

He met Chris's gaze, her eyes wide with worry. "I know what you're thinking, but it doesn't mean a thing. I don't recall any instances where I thought she was being influenced by Margaret, except..."

Quick to pick up his hesitation, Chris asked, "Except what?"

"Her house in Richmond—it's where Margaret lived before she married George." With the revelation, Chris bit her lip. "I'll talk to Beth about it. Meanwhile, let's not spoil the weekend because of this. We should be celebrating." Hoping to distract her, he moved around the desk and swept her into his arms. "I'll get a bottle of wine from the cellar."

Apparently still unsettled by their discovery, she grasped his hand as she accompanied him along the hall to the stairs to the cellar. Wine bottles lined the wall. Saber trotted ahead of him as he crossed the stone floor to choose a special vintage, while Chris touched the panel behind the stairwell. *The trunk rested in the recess. A skeleton with a bullet hole where his left eye should have been lay inside. Chris had opened the trunk after George and Tom had dragged it from beneath the stairs.* "Are you recalling something?" Geoff asked.

Perplexed, she faced him. "I'm not certain."

Should he tell her? "You have been here before."

She returned to the panel and placed her hands on it. Her eyebrows knitted together. "A soldier was buried here."

"The Yankee bastard who raped Margaret."

Chris turned to him. "Is that all you remember?"

For some reason the memory was unusually clear. It was best to be upfront. She wouldn't respect anything else. "You said that you had found his skeleton in 2004, which would have coincided with your original arrival. When we unearthed him, Margaret finally admitted to what he had done. Tom and I buried him away from the house, so he would stop haunting her."

She appeared to mull over what he had said. "You've switched to first person again for George."

"So I have," he agreed.

"Do you mind if we find that picture of Tom?"

Why was it when he thought of Tom, he bristled? He *was* jealous. George's brother had spent thirty years with Chris when he had been shortchanged. And right now, she looked extremely appealing in her low-cut black leather. "Then you'd rather I didn't get the wine?"

"Go ahead and get a bottle. We'll save it for later."

Her tone was suggestive, and he nearly lost himself. *Think.* He returned to the wine racks, choosing a vintage chardonnay. She clasped his hand as they returned to the hall of the west wing on the main level. He couldn't let her slip through his fingers again. He cleared his throat. "Chris, I've been thinking . . ."

"The picture of Tom," she reminded him.

"Right." As he guided Chris to the library, he attempted to access George's memories. Although they remained murky, nothing indicated that George had ever been jealous of his brother. Then why did he get the feeling that if Tom were present, he'd beat the crap out of him? He set the wine bottle on the desk and searched through Greta's ledgers. He handed Chris the ledger that had several period photos. "Here."

A hint of a smile crossed her lips. "You're angry with me."

"I'm not angry. I merely thought we might have a more romantic evening."

She stroked his cheek with her fingertips. "We will. But it's like when you say George takes over. I need to know what happened." She set the ledger on the desk and flipped through the pages.

Glancing over her shoulder, Geoff saw Margaret. Her black hair and violet eyes. *Damn, I loved her.* If only she had told him about the Yankee scout and Georgianna.

Chris turned another page. *Tom.* Upon seeing the photo of George's brother, he clenched a hand.

Chris glanced up at him. "He lost an arm near the end of the war."

As he feared would happen, she was remembering. They both had to face the past and make their peace. "What else do you remember?"

"It's like you said, recalling a dream, but I remember . . . Funny, I lost the thought." She stood and encircled her arms about his waist. "I never loved him the way I do you."

Relief spread through him, and he let out the breath that he hadn't realized he was holding in. At last, this truly was *their* time.

Chapter Fourteen

The following morning, Chris traipsed down the hall to the guest room. As she reached the door to her room, Judith turned the corner, attired in her gauzy costume from the night before. Her friend's beaming face made her look like anything but a ghost. "It looks like neither of us made it back to our rooms last night," Chris said.

Startled, Judith jumped and pressed a hand to her chest. "I didn't see you." Then, her friend gave a hearty laugh. "I guess not. I never expected the two of us to fall in love at the same time."

"We're getting married."

Judith blinked as if she hadn't heard correctly.

"Did you hear what I said?"

Squealing with delight, Judith hugged her. "After reading the ledger, I should have seen this coming, but . . ." She stepped back and gave Chris an appraising look.

"I'm not pregnant, Judith. I'm nervous and excited about the prospect. I never thought of myself as the motherly type, but I'm kind of hoping that Sarah may make an earlier appearance."

Her smile was reassuring. "I'm looking forward to becoming sisters. Now, when is the big day?"

"As soon as we can make the arrangements. I was hoping that you might be able to help. I have to return to Boston to tie up loose ends, but I'll be back as soon as possible. My being here will make it easier to look for a job, not to mention the fact that we want to take advantage of the extra time we've been granted."

Judith clasped Chris's hands. "Of course, I'll help."

"Just keep it small. We only want family and a few friends."

Judith's smile widened.

"Judith . . ." Chris extended an index finger. " . . . small."

Her friend's smile vanished. "I'll do as you ask, but I can't help but get excited. Soon, we'll be sisters."

Another hug. For the first time in her life, Chris felt content.

After dropping Chris off at the airport, Geoff drove into Richmond. He parked the Mustang in front of Beth's house and strode up the brick walk. *On the street came a clatter of horses' hooves.* Fighting the urge to look behind him, Geoff knocked on the door. *Tessa answered.* He blinked, and Beth stood before him.

"You're not supposed to be here until next weekend for Neal," she stated curtly.

"I didn't come here for Neal. I wanted to know if you've been out to Poplar Ridge recently."

She quickly averted her eyes. "No."

"Beth, you're not a very good liar."

"Unlike you."

Weary of the accusations, he ignored her snide remark. "Why?"

"To return the damned gun of yours."

If it was the gun that had killed George, maybe she had done them a favor. "What about the ledger?"

She narrowed her eyes. "What ledger?"

"From 1867. It's more of a diary than a ledger."

She finally opened the door, allowing him to enter. "Neal's playing at the neighbor's right now. Let's talk."

A man with a beard and wearing a gray pin-stripe suit greeted him. Geoff blinked back the vision. George's memories were strong in the house.

She showed him to the parlor and indicated for him to have a seat. He stubbornly remained standing. She withdrew a leather volume from a bookshelf and handed him the ledger. "Why didn't you ever tell me about it?"

"Because when we first met, I didn't believe it myself. After that, it no longer mattered."

"It does matter. We may have our differences, but I could never . . ." She averted her gaze to hide brimming tears. When she looked back, her eyes were clear, but her voice was soft. "I can't be the cause of so much pain."

"Then you believe it?"

"*She* told me to read it."

Surprised by her confession, Geoff sank to the sofa. "How much does Margaret influence you?"

Beth sat across from him in the Bentwood rocker. "Enough. Even before reading the ledger, I knew that she was afraid because of what had happened to her during the war. It seemed like her mind was in a fog. Now, I understand it was because she was addicted to laudanum. I also comprehend what happened to us."

"I never lied to you."

"Please forgive me." She pressed her hands to her face and her sides heaved. "And I promised myself that I wouldn't do this when I saw you again."

When they were married, he would have taken her into his arms and comforted her. That was then. He remained where he was. "Perhaps, it's best if I leave."

"Not yet." She brushed away her tears. "Geoff, I admit, if I had known the truth, I would have never asked for a divorce, but what's done is done. I don't want to become like the woman in the book."

Alone, and in a psychiatric ward. He couldn't blame her. Such a fate sounded worse than his own premature demise. "Time can be changed."

She stared at him as if trying to absorb his words. "That's why she wanted me to return the gun."

An ally—Beth was going to help them in order to try to prevent the future described in the ledger. "Then she must have been the one to shoot George."

Another intense stare. "She doesn't remember."

"Dammit, Beth." He stood. "How can she not remember?"

She waved at him to calm down. "I can't tell you any more. If I could, I would."

Composed again, Geoff reseated himself. "I didn't mean to raise my voice. While I'm here, I might as well tell you that Chris and I are getting married."

Her face paled, and when she spoke, her voice sounded distant. "Not unexpected, I suppose."

As Geoff got to his feet, he thought she might cry again, but she remained collected. "I'm sorry that it didn't work between us."

She forced a smile. "We both know that it was meant to be this way."

Her words sent a shiver down his back. Exactly how much of the ledger was "meant to be"?

Upon her return to Poplar Ridge, Chris stayed in the guest room. Not for appearance's sake, but she hoped to discover the reason behind the unusual happenings before moving in permanently with Geoff. A week passed, and she was no closer to finding a job. As she had expected, Geoff was unbothered by her unemployed status, yet she grew frustrated. To break the stress of searching for a wedding dress and looking over food menus, she accompanied Judith to Greta's.

The thin woman answered the door with a broad grin, motioning for them to come inside. Almost as soon as Chris stepped in the foyer, she felt a chill. As on the previous occasion when Chris had visited with Geoff, Greta shuffled off to make tea, while her guests got comfortable on the sofa. Upon the elderly woman's return, Judith chatted about wedding plans.

Even the tea failed to warm Chris, and she sipped frequently. During a moment of silence, she returned her china cup to a coaster with the James River on it. "Greta, did you know Tom Cameron?"

"I met him, but I was a small child when he died. As a matter of fact, he died upstairs."

"Upstairs? Do you mind if I see the room?"

"Judith, why don't you take her up? I'm much too old to be climbing stairs."

Judith waved the way. Unlike in Poplar Ridge, the stairs were narrow with a turn. As soon as Chris reached the second floor, she was drawn to the room on her right. Beside the brass bed was a marble-topped dresser. Lace curtains lined the windows.

Hester bent over the bed, sponging Chris's sweaty forehead. She groaned. "This isn't the way it was before."

"Each birth be different."

The time before Chris had wandered into the bathroom and given birth standing. Geoff had been in attendance, and now here she was flat on her back with a withered russet face hovering over her. "That crowded city hospital still sounds mighty nice, right now."

"Miss Chris?" Hester responded, arching an eyebrow.

"Doctors will become more common than midwives." Another contraction caught her off guard, and the breathing exercises she had been taught with the birth of Sarah were all but forgotten.

"Cry out, if'n you feel like it."

As the pain eased, Chris gave a tired laugh. "Tough city lawyer types aren't allowed to show weakness."

Hester sponged her forehead once more. "You be speakin' nonsense again. You needs to get on with birthin'. Da pain stop when da baby born."

Her plain nightdress was soaked in blood, but Chris bent her legs into birthing position. "It's time to push." She wrinkled her face in pain.

The former slave continued to encourage her. "I see a head, Miss Chris. Your baby be here soon."

Suddenly, Chris felt as if she were on fire, and she let out a cry.

"Keep pushing." Another push, and the baby dropped into Hester's waiting arms. "It be a girl. Miss Sarah arrived."

"Sarah," Chris said in an exhausted whisper.

Hester's wrinkled hands cleared the baby's nostrils and quickly massaged her until her skin turned to a healthy pink. A squall pealed through the room. "Mr. George be proud."

Tears streaked Chris's cheeks as she snuggled the baby in her arms. "George, we have a beautiful girl." But George wasn't here. He'd never see their daughter, unless . . . Sarah could speak to the dead. When she was older, maybe she'd be able to reach him. And now Chris was linked to this time.

Hester shuffled from the room. "I fetch Mr. Tom."

Her heart ached. Legally, Tom was Sarah's father. Unable to think any further on the subject, she cast her gaze on her perfect daughter. She started counting fingers and toes. Tom's bearded face appeared in the doorway. As he came closer, tears of pride were in his eyes. "Chris, she's beautiful."

She yearned to respond to him in a way that he hoped to hear. After George's death, he had been her salvation. So, why was she unable to feel anything for him? It was too soon, she reminded herself. But would she ever come to love him? Instead of reaching out to Tom, she clutched the baby tighter. "Please leave. I'd like to be alone with *my daughter.*"

His shoulders slumped and his tears changed to grief. As soon as he left the room, she wailed. George, why did you have to die?

Swallowing hard, Chris blinked back the vision. *Her vision*—from another time. She stepped inside the room. "Sarah was born here. I just relived her birth."

"Did you see Tom?" Judith asked.

Chris nodded. "He gave me a home and a name for my daughter, but I turned him away."

"You were grieving. The letter stated that you eventually came to love him."

Geoff had told her that Beth had taken the ledger and read it. How much did Margaret already possess her? "Geoff's jealous of Tom. I wish I could convince him there's no reason to be."

"I'm sure he understands." Judith grasped Chris's elbow. "Maybe we should be getting back."

Chris sighed. "To do what?"

"I know you're bored, but you will find a job soon. Or is it something deeper? Are you having second thoughts?"

"Second thoughts? Certainly not. For the first time in my life, I feel as if I'm home. In fact, I think we should see if we can find my wedding dress." They retreated down the steps and Chris relayed what she had envisioned to Greta.

The old woman frowned. "If you think it will provide answers, you're welcome to come here and look around any time you like."

Greta was as kind and warm-hearted as the ledger had stated. "I appreciate that," Chris replied. After finishing their tea, she and

Judith said their goodbyes and headed into Richmond. The countryside gave way to gleaming high rises. Judith parked in the refurbished downtown area next to a trendy bridal boutique. Chris pressed traditional lace gowns and sensual white dresses against her and looked into a full-length mirror.

"Nothing?" Judith asked.

Disappointed, Chris shook her head. "For some reason, they're not right."

"You'll know it, when you see it." Her friend squeezed her arm in reassurance. "I know of another shop at the north end of the city."

Exhausted and foot weary as they left the boutique, Chris waved a hand. "Not today—please." As they made their way along the sidewalk back to the car, they passed a shop with a mint-green low-waist dress from the 1920s on a mannequin in the window. She pressed her hands to the glass.

"Chris?"

"It was Sarah's." Chris blinked. "I'm going to buy it for her." When she opened the white multi-paned door, a bell jingled. Racks of clothes held vintage garments, and glass display cases contained precious brooches and pendants. Hats with feathers and flowers were perched atop mannequin heads.

A young woman with friendly turquoise-blue eyes and short-cropped hair like a flapper greeted them. "May I help you?"

"Where did you get the green dress in the window?" asked Chris.

The saleswoman smiled and walked over to the window display. "From a woman in the city."

Obviously, that was the only detail she was going to receive. Details didn't matter. It was Sarah's dress. "I'll take it."

"Splendid," the saleswoman said, widening her smile.

Judith nudged Chris. "Look over there."

Chris glanced in the direction that her friend had gestured. At the back of the store were white dresses. Why hadn't she thought of it sooner? A vintage wedding gown. She negotiated her way around the clothing racks and display cases and rummaged through the bridal dresses encased in plastic garment bags. A gown from the 1940s had a high ruffle around the neck and a long train. An 1880s dress had a bustle, while a turn-of-the-twentieth-century gown had a high back waistline with a dropped front. The final dress on the rack, an ivory satin gown with a wide-gathered skirt and a low-cut neckline trimmed in handmade lace ruffle, caught her eye. Even without reading the tag, she knew it was from the mid-1860s.

"Getting married?" the clerk asked, unzipping the garment bag. "This dress is from the Civil War era. It's in excellent condition with only a couple of small spots on the back. No one will even notice them." She held up the fabric so Chris could inspect the damage. "I have a veil to go with it." She withdrew a box from a nearby shelf and carefully unfolded a lace veil edged in floral motifs. "Would you like to try the gown on? You'll likely need a corset. The fashionable women tended to like tiny waists during the era, but I'm certain you can get an idea of how it will fit."

"Yes, I'd like that." Ecstatic, Chris was certain that she had found her wedding dress.

Chris felt the bed shift and nearly whispered George's name. She blinked sleep from her eyes.

Tom's bearded face hovered over her in the flickering light. "I didn't mean to wake you," he apologized. He unbuttoned his patched gray jacket with the adeptness of any two-handed individual.

Deep down, she admired how he had overcome his handicap, still he hesitated when it came to removing his shirt. Realizing that he was self conscious of her seeing the stump of his right arm, she said nothing. Over the months, her silence had kept him distant, and he had attributed it to her grief. More than a year after George's death, she still grieved, but she had Sarah's welfare to think of now.

He clutched her hand. "You can't keep turning me away."

"You're right," she murmured. "I've been unfair to you. You've lost two that you cared for." She invited him to join her.

He removed his shirt. His right arm ended halfway between his shoulder and elbow. Unlike smooth-looking stumps she had seen in the twenty-first century, his was jagged, though it was perfectly healed. When he lowered his threadbare pants, she looked away. The bed jostled from his weight as he climbed in beside her.

His hand caressed her neck, and she looked at him. His eyes reflected the same deep blue as George's. "Chris, God forgive me, for any good coming from their deaths, but I love you." *She opened her mouth to say something, but he continued,* "I don't expect you to return it. I just want to be a good husband and father."

Because of his kindness, Sarah would never shoulder the label of bastard. How could she ever make peace with her feminist ideals? "When the time comes, she must know who her real father is."

"Of course," *he agreed.*

"She must also be raised to have a mind of her own."

To this request, he was more hesitant. "I'll abide by your wishes."

"Tom, do you realize what it entails? You were raised with the idea that your wife and daughter would obey you. Women from my time question things when the rules don't make sense. At some point, she will likely embarrass you."

With a smile crossing his face, he laughed. "Strong-willed women are common in the South. I reckon I can get used to two women telling me that women should have the right to vote."

For the first time, Chris felt tenderness for Tom. She wrapped her arms around him and kissed him on the mouth.

In the subdued light before dawn, Chris sat up in bed, short of breath.

"Chris?" came Geoff's sleepy voice.

She hushed him and kneaded his shoulders. "Go back to sleep."

He murmured, and as she felt his muscles relax, she snuggled next to him. Tom was the one subject that she was hesitant to discuss with Geoff. She'd confide with Judith when it was light. She drifted and had no idea how long she lay there when she heard an escalating rumble in Saber's throat. Her eyes snapped open to a dark-skinned face looming over her. She sprang toward the face and the woman vanished. "Tessa."

"Tessa?" Geoff sat up with the blanket falling away from him.

"Margaret's maid."

"I know who Tessa is, but why would she be here?"

Donning her robe, she hopped out of bed and went over to the dresser. Instead of oak, it was made of poplar, and the simple mirror had no hand-carved horse heads. In its reflection she saw Geoff. "I saw her once before. That time, I thought she was Laura."

"That doesn't answer the question."

"Search your memory, Geoff." She faced him. "I take that back. Ask George. What's the significance of this room?"

He shook his head, then his eyes widened. "This was Margaret's room after . . ."

"After she moved out of the room she shared with George. Tessa was a dutiful servant." And Tom's lover. On that point, she remained silent.

Stress lines formed around his eyes, and he placed a hand to his temple. "Who spent a lot of nights in here tending Margaret and Jason."

Margaret's room. Why hadn't she realized it earlier? "If it strains you too much to think about it, then don't."

Getting up to dress, he muttered that he was fine. After putting on a pair of jeans, he joined her. "Tessa was Margaret's servant before we were married. They grew up together. Even though there was strict protocol in those days, they were friends. She was a strong-willed woman, but I never thought she'd . . . I suspect there's a reason why George has never revealed those final moments to me."

Geoff's gaze met hers, and she said, "She's still taking care of Margaret."

His expression turned thoughtful as if he were pondering her words. "You could be right." He drew her close. "I wish you'd move in with me now."

"After the wedding," she assured him.

"Which is two weeks away."

"And in that time, I may learn something useful."

He kissed her. "Very well. Right now, I need to see to my chores. I'm a phone call away should you need anything."

She eagerly reciprocated with an intimate kiss of her own. After Geoff finished dressing, he and Saber left the room. Chris barely had changed into her long-sleeved T-shirt and a pair of jeans when a knock came to the door. "Chris?"

Judith. Just the person she wanted to see. "Come in."

Dressed in breeches and riding boots, Judith opened the door. "I waited until Geoff left, but I was hoping that you might be up for a ride this morning."

"Most definitely." She got a fleece jacket from the wardrobe to break the morning November chill. When Judith turned to leave, Chris drew her back. "I saw him."

"Who?"

"Tom."

"And?"

"He was kind and caring, but I kept turning him away. A year after George's death, I didn't love him. Still, he stayed by my side. I told him that Sarah would have to know who her real father was, and he agreed."

"Chris, I think you should visit Greta more often. Isn't that where you feel Tom the strongest?"

"It is," Chris agreed. "But I don't want to upset Geoff."

"How is it any different than you knowing about Beth? Even if you only loved him as a friend, you spent thirty years married to him. I've often heard that divorce is as painful as having your spouse die. Before you came along, Geoff grieved for Beth. You require the same space. Tom needs to be laid to rest once and for all."

Judith's words made sense. But what would Geoff say about it? "You're right. Let's go for that ride."

Together, they made their way down the stairs to the main hall. Once outside, they crossed the lane to the stables. As they passed a colossal three-hundred-year-old oak, Chris heard a shouting mob. Bile rose in her throat. A woman's body swung from a rope tied to a branch. *Tessa.* Now she understood the vision where she felt herself hanging. The servant had caused George's death.

Determined to uncover answers, Chris spent more and more time at Greta's. Leaving Judith to the wedding details, she rode Ebony along the river path to the Victorian house. She tied the horse to a hitching post, but before she went up the steps, the path to the back of the house was edged in dry and shriveled winter flowers. They almost looked like weeds. Curious, Chris followed the path. No slave shack existed where Hester's tumbledown hovel once stood.

The wind blew in Sarah's face, and she giggled. "Mama."

"Sarah?" Mama bent down and straightened her hair.

It seemed like Mama always fussed with her hair when she was upset about something. Sarah held out her black cloth pony. "I've named him Raven after Aunt Margaret's horse."

"That's a nice name. I wanted to tell you about the former slave woman who used to live here."

Sarah played with the pony's mane until it lay flat on its neck. "Hester."

"She attended your birth." Mama frowned. "I'm sorry you never got to know her. You were only two when she died."

Her mother always seemed sad when she talked about dead people, especially when she told Sarah about her real papa. Papa Tom had said that people go to heaven when they die. Where was heaven when she could see people who went there, but others couldn't? "Don't look so sad, Mama. She talks to me."

"What does she say?"

"She gives me a big grin, like a crescent moon." Sarah wiggled her loose front tooth. "She's missing her teeth. She says you came from a great distance. Where did you come from, Mama?"

Her mother closed her eyes before smiling.

Mama rarely smiled. Sarah was pleased that she could make her mother happy.

"I'll tell you where I came from when you're old enough to understand. Do you think you could talk to Papa too?"

"My real Papa?"

"Yes, Sarah, your real Papa. I miss him."

"What does he look like?"

"He was as tall as Tom. They were brothers. He had blond hair, a moustache, and eyes the same color of blue as yours."

"Does he use Papa Tom's desk at Poplar Ridge?"

Tears were in Mama's eyes. "That's him."

Once Papa read her a story. It was about a black horse like Raven. A lady came with a gun. Papa was covered in blood. Sarah tensed, clenching her hands at her sides. "I can't talk to him, Mama. I'm scared."

Mama's tears rolled down her cheeks, and she hugged her. "I didn't mean to frighten you."

"Was it my fault that Papa died?"

Mama hugged her tighter. "No, Sarah. It wasn't your fault."

When her mother drew away, Sarah saw Papa Tom with a big scowl on his face.

"How much of that did you hear?" Mama asked.

"Enough," Papa Tom snapped.

"Tom . . . I only wanted to see if Sarah could speak to the dead."

When Papa Tom looked at Sarah, he had a mean look in his eyes. Was it wrong to speak to people if they were in heaven?

"Sarah." Papa Tom reached out with his left hand because his right one was missing. He gripped her arm. "I don't think it's good for a little girl to speak to the dead."

"Didn't my papa love me?"

"He didn't even know you!" Papa Tom stomped back to the house.

"Oh, Sarah." Mama kissed her on the forehead. "It's not your fault. Your papa died before you were born. Tom isn't mad at you. He gets angry because he feels he should have been there to prevent your father's death."

"Did the lady with the gun kill him?"

Mama started to cry. Sarah didn't like seeing her mother cry, and she wished she could make her stop. She handed Mama her cloth pony. "If it'll make you happy, I'll talk to Papa."

Her mother took the pony, sniffled, and smiled, before fussing with Sarah's hair again. "Maybe we'll try when you're a little older. You have a special gift, and I don't want it frightening you. Your papa loved you, and that's what I want you to see for yourself when you speak to him."

Sarah fancied the notion of speaking to Papa when she was bigger. She hoped he would read her a story.

Chris blinked back the vision. More and more of her life during the nineteenth century was being revealed. Her life seemed to be re-volving in a never-ending circle. Judith was right. In the nineteenth century, she had been faced with burying George. Now, it was Tom, and somehow Sarah was the link.

Attired in a charcoal-gray tuxedo, Geoff paced the length of the library, then back again. He didn't think having a Victorian wedding as being healthy, but he had conceded to wearing a cravat. Fortunately, George had known how to tie the archaic neckwear.

"Calm down, lad, or ye'll scour a rut in the floorboards," said T.J. Dressed in a suit similar to his own, the crusty old stable hand had neatly trimmed his beard for the occasion.

Without halting his pacing, Geoff checked his watch. "What's taking her so long?"

"A bride is always late ta her weddin'. It's one of those unwritten rules aboot women. Ye should remember that from the last time."

Beyond a fancy church wedding, he barely recalled the ceremony when he had married Beth. What's more, he didn't care to. He was marrying Chris now. Why couldn't she have agreed to something simple? Bride's prerogative, and it was her first, he reminded himself—at least in this lifetime. Why did he bristle anytime he thought of Tom? He stopped pacing long enough to realize that nerves had gotten the best of him. He needed to relieve himself. "I'll be back in a few minutes, T.J."

"Where ye goin' now? The lass could be ready any minute."

"I need to take a leak."

T.J. waved him on. "I'll warn ye, if they come fer ye."

"You make it sound like an execution."

T.J. bellowed in laughter. "Now ye know why I ne'er got married."

After a quick trip to the bathroom beside the library, Geoff decided to see what was keeping Chris. He went upstairs and traveled the hall to the guest room where Chris was dressing. When he knocked, Saber barked.

Judith, dressed in a gown the color of claret, answered, "Geoff, you can't see her now. It would be bad luck."

Over her shoulder, he caught a glimpse of Chris clad in a silk corset and gartered stockings. He suddenly wished the wedding festivities were over and done with, so he could escort Chris to his room.

Realizing that he had spotted Chris, Judith stepped into the hall. Saber shot out the door before she slammed it behind her in annoyance. "I said you'll have to wait."

"What's taking so long?"

"Makeup, hair. She's getting dressed and will be along soon." She inspected him and straightened his cravat. "I see what it takes to get you to wear something other than jeans." Finished with the cravat, she lowered her arms. "You will treat her right? After all, she is my best friend."

"You know I will."

Judith gave him a hug. "I need to get back to Chris. Where did Saber go? Saber..." She looked up and down the hall for the dog and called for him again.

With a silk dog coat the same color as Judith's gown and his long black hair fluffed and teased as if ready for the show ring, Saber pranced over to her. Instead of a collar, a garland of tiny white flowers surrounded his neck, and he reeked of a sickeningly sweet perfume.

Aghast by the sight, Geoff pointed. "What have you done to my dog?"

"Chris wanted to include him. He's the flower dog."

"But he's not a girl."

Judith smiled sweetly. "Unless he lifts a leg on one of the guests, who is going to notice? Save your testosterone poisoning for something that matters, *dear* brother. Saber doesn't care. Besides, Neal is the ring bearer. I imagine you'd squawk louder if we switched the roles. Now, I really need to be getting back to Chris." She shooed Saber back into the guest room and closed the door behind her.

Patience had never been his best virtue. Hoping that Chris might actually come over to the door, he watched it a few minutes before making his way back to the library. Once more, he paced. Finally, someone knocked, and his father came in. "The bride will be down soon." Geoff and T.J. moved toward the door. When they reached it, his father continued, "Geoff, I have a feeling about this—a good one. For some reason, it seems right, and I know your mother would be proud."

Stunned by such an admission coming from his father, Geoff stared at him a moment. He extended his hand. His father grasped it and shook it, sealing a bond that he had never expected to see. Together, they went down the hall.

As they neared the parlor, the piano tinkled the tune "Walking in a Winter Wonderland." He should have known that his sister would script a theme for the entire wedding. He only hoped that she had maintained her promise in keeping the guest list small. His father held the door to the parlor open, while T.J. and he entered.

The room was ablaze with candles, giving it the appearance of what the parlor would have looked like during the nineteenth century. *Before the war,* George reminded him. Geoff shook hands with the justice of the peace. The guests sat in folding chairs, adorned with magnolias and white and claret-colored ribbons. With his appearance, Chris's parents were escorted to the front row. He had met them on his trip to Boston. Her father could be a bit overbearing at times, and Geoff wondered how he felt about not being allowed the opportunity to give the bride away. Then again, par for the course, he respected Chris's decision for ousting obsolete customs, which is why the whole traditional wedding idea had surprised him.

Ushers unrolled the ivory aisle runner, and the woman at the piano started playing another tune that he didn't recognize initially. The melody was light. He *had* heard it before, played by fiddles. After Judith walked down the aisle and took her place, Neal led Saber on a flowered leash. When the dog spotted him, Saber gave an excited bark and jerked on the leash, nearly toppling Neal over. Fortunately, Judith snatched the leash from Neal and brought the dog to her side before he got overly rambunctious.

Amused, Geoff exchanged an "I told you so" glance with his sister. Judith suggested that he pay attention by looking in the direction of the aisle, then back again. Without his noticing, Chris had entered the parlor. The flickering candlelight framed her beaming face. Along with the vintage gown she wore, he had the feeling that he had been transported to the nineteenth century. He now understood why she had chosen the mix of modern and traditional. She was attempting to make peace with her past life.

Her smile was radiant as she joined him. He was so focused on her that he hadn't heard the justice begin to speak. The words were a blur for he could only see Chris. Finally, T.J. jabbed him in the side, holding out Chris's ring. Grasping the ring, he hoped he didn't stutter on his vows. They joined hands. "Like the seasons, this ring forms a circle. It has no end. Neither shall my love for you. I commit myself to you always." He slid the ring on Chris's finger.

Judith handed Chris his ring. "The binding of life and love are truly eternal. It is more than the lives we have chosen to lead together. It is my mind to your mind; my soul to your soul; in this world and the next. I commit myself to you always." She slid the ring on his finger.

"I pronounce you husband and wife," the justice said. "You may seal your pledge with a kiss."

They kissed, and Geoff realized that he, too, was making his final peace to the past by marrying Chris.

Chapter Fifteen

Elegant crystal and silver polished to perfection set the table in the dining room for the reception dinner. Magnolias and roses adorned the room. Caterers served oysters, filet mignon, roast duck, vegetable quiches and salads, éclairs, wedding cake, brandy, and fine wine. Even though Chris restrained herself from eating too much of the decadent food, she consumed more calories than she dared to think about. She should have known that Judith would go all out for the occasion.

After dinner, they journeyed to the main hall, turned into a ballroom where a small orchestra played. She laughed and danced the evening away. The woman who had previously prided herself on being career oriented and remaining single delighted in the fact that Geoff was her husband. During a slow waltz, they drew close. Under the candlelight, he kissed her. When she responded, someone tugged on Geoff's suit jacket. Neal rubbed tired eyes. "Will you read me a story about a castle?"

Chris laughed at the interruption.

"I could have Judith put him to bed," Geoff suggested.

"Don't you dare. I'm not going to turn into an evil stepmother."

Geoff gathered Neal in his arms. "It's way past your bedtime. Let's make the rounds and say good-night to everyone."

She grasped Neal's hand and bid him good-night. As Geoff took his son around the room, Chris smiled to herself. He was going to make a wonderful father to Sarah, too. She only hoped . . . She caught herself. *No dark thoughts. Not on this night.*

Judith joined her. "You're positively glowing."

Chris watched Geoff vanish up the stairs with a sleepy Neal in his arms. "I was thinking of Sarah. How can you love someone who isn't even born yet?"

"Because you know her essence. You've been given a rare privilege."

But along with that privilege came knowledge. Knowledge of which few people ever wanted to be cognizant. Once again, Chris chastised herself for allowing bothersome thoughts to intrude on the occasion. To take her mind off Geoff's absence, she danced with Winston Cameron, then her father.

He shook his head. "My daughter, married to a Southern gentleman. Who would have ever guessed?"

Suddenly a bit concerned, she asked, "Does that mean you don't approve?"

"Oh, I approve." He laughed as they flowed across the floor together. "I had wondered if he might wear his jeans to the ceremony."

"Dad," she grumbled.

"Christine Catherine," he responded in a mocking tone that made her feel like she was twelve again. "I'm joking. I'm sure we'll get along fine."

"As long as the two of you don't discuss the Civil War."

"I'll try and remember that."

Oh, shoot—what had she done? Now her dad was likely to go out of his way to bring the subject up with Geoff. The music stopped playing, and her dad thanked her for the dance. Geoff joined them and bowed. "Would you do me the honor, Mrs. Cameron?"

"Ms.," Chris corrected.

His eyes glistened. "As I suspected. If you don't care to dance, we could always slip away." He held out his arm.

She placed her arm through his. "I think this is one occasion where we can't just slip away. Let's mingle a little, then say goodnight. By the way, where's Saber?"

"Neal is at the age where the creaking of the house scares him. He won't fall asleep unless Saber stays with him, which is fine with me. Saber needs a bath before he's allowed in our room again."

Chris wrinkled her nose. "Judith did overdo the perfume."

"T.J. and Ken will never let me live it down."

She laughed as they strolled over to her parents and gave her mom a hug. "We're going to be leaving soon."

"And no honeymoon?" her dad said in an overly loud voice.

"Dad," Chris said, reminding him to be civil. "Geoff suggested one, but I . . ."

"She didn't like the idea of jetting off to Europe, taking in thirty countries in five days."

She elbowed Geoff in the ribs. "That was four countries in fifteen days."

To her relief, her father laughed. "On our next visit, I think we should sit down and talk about General Grant's strategy in Virginia."

"Ah yes, the Butcher."

Before the discussion heated up, Chris tugged on Geoff's arm, so they could see to the other guests. After a number of goodbyes and people wishing them well, they slipped into the west wing. Once they were out of sight of the other guests, Geoff drew her into his arms and kissed her with a burning desire that he must have been holding at bay all evening. He clasped her hand and escorted her along the wood-paneled hallway. "At least we got away without everyone throwing rice at us."

"Judith wanted to. Heart-shaped rice," she said as they turned the corner to the stairs.

His face wrinkled in distaste. "I'm surprised you talked her out of it."

They reached the top of the stairs, and Chris replied, "I told her that we didn't need any ancient fertility rites. Sarah will arrive in due time." Once outside his room, he picked her up in his arms. She squealed with surprise and wrapped her arms around his neck. "I'm sure this is a custom that we don't want to know the meaning of."

He carried her into the room and put her down beside the bed. She turned and lifted her hair and veil for him to unbutton her. He unfastened her dress and the cool air nearly made her shiver. His warm fingertips caressed the bare skin of her back, then came the brush of his tongue. She closed her eyes. With great difficulty, she pulled away. "Unfortunately, I need to hang my dress. Why don't you make yourself comfortable?"

She gave him a kiss and went into the bathroom. After removing her veil, she unpinned her hair and sensed someone standing behind her. "Geoff?" In the mirror's reflection was a young woman with auburn pin curls on her forehead. "Sarah?"

Sarah led her mother through the hidden passageway at Poplar Ridge to the library. As a girl, she had often played hide and seek in the catacombs with her half-brother, Jason. Now, she wished she had known the nature of their venture ahead of time so that she would have worn something more practical than her sheer overskirt and bustle.

Upon reaching the library, she closed the panel behind them. Mama's face wrinkled in pain when she cast her gaze to the floor. Sarah squeezed her hand. "Have you visited here since Papa's death?"

Taking a deep breath, Mama shook her head. The worry lines faded from her face as she attempted to conceal her anguish. "I thought you might be able to reach him upstairs."

Seventeen years had passed since her mother had confronted this place, and Sarah sensed a whirlwind of emotions. But Mama said nothing. The strong outward appearance was either a consequence of her "other life" in a man's world as an attorney, or the years of practice at hiding her feelings from Tom.

They moved toward the stairs. At the top, they fought their way through a tangle of cobwebs to a room where there was no furniture besides a sagging straw bed. Mama bent down and touched the mattress with a bittersweet smile crossing her face.

Gray streaked her mother's otherwise light-brown hair, and the little wrinkles around her mouth were noticeable when she smiled. She smiled so rarely that Sarah hadn't noticed that Mama was growing older.

"I never realized how much you still love him."

Mama's smile widened. "I could never stop. Can you reach him?"

Sarah knelt beside her mother and ran her hand along the mattress. She had been conceived here. This place was special, not simply because of Mama's love for Papa, but it marked the beginning of their love as well.

"The whispers are usually stronger when I'm near their physical space." On this occasion, Sarah heard no voices. Frustrated, she continued touching the mattress. Why did Papa always elude her? She had no friends because she communicated with everyone else's departed relatives and friends. Even

Tom reprimanded her for doing what came natural. Only Mama accepted her abilities. Finally, Sarah gave up and stood. "I'm sorry."

"You tried. There's another reason why I brought you here. I have something to show you." *Mama lifted her long skirt and retreated down the steps to the library. As Sarah joined her mother in the library, Mama rubbed her arms with a fixated gaze on the floor.*

He died here. *"Mama, stop putting yourself through this."*

"It's important." *Mama went over to the bookcase, searched it, then her brow wrinkled.* "It must be here somewhere. Thank God, here it is." *Standing on her tiptoes, Mama reached to an upper shelf and retrieved a leather-bound ledger.* "Tom didn't want it in the house. You're old enough now to understand. It explains fully how I came to be here." *She handed Sarah the book.*

Sarah cradled the ledger. Images and voices bombarded her. Papa. *Struggling to isolate the voice, she went over to the desk and touched the fine grain wood.* "He read to me. I can hear him. His voice was soothing and comforting. It was a story about a black horse like Raven."

Mama's eyes misted. "That was Geoff. Sarah, you don't just hear voices from the past, but from the future as well."

"The future? That can't be."

Mama grasped her hand. "Read the book, and you'll understand fully."

"I shall," *Sarah agreed.*

A key turned in the lock of the door. Her mother snatched up the book and hurried toward the panel in the wall. Sarah remained behind. No one would question her presence as she often helped with Poplar Ridge's bookkeeping while Jason was away at the university. She moved to the door to run interference until Mama was safely out of sight. The door opened, and Tom entered. "Sarah? I hadn't realized you were going to be here today."

She grasped his arm to keep his attention on her, then she heard the click of the panel door, letting her know that Mama had reached safety. "I had a few transactions that I wished to check."

He shook his head. "And I wish you'd pursue more appropriate callings."

Annoyed, she let go of his arm. "Such as finding a husband?"

"You know that's not what I meant."

Sarah held firm. "Why shouldn't I have the same freedom as Jason?"

At first anger reflected in his eyes, then they softened. "Your mother warned me that it would sometimes be difficult having two strong-headed *women in the family. I'll teach you all that I know about running the farm."*

Her arms went around Tom's neck, and she planted a kiss on his cheek.

"I only wish . . . ," he began.

She lowered her arms. "Yes, Tom?"

He winced at the use of his given name. "That you could find it within your heart to call me Papa again."

Although her mother had never said anything derogatory about Tom, she couldn't bring herself to grant him his wish. Despair crossed his face. Was she wrong to discover who her real papa had been? She had heard his voice, reading to her. Mama had called him Geoff.

"Chris . . ." Concerned that she had been taking an overly long time, Geoff stripped off his shirt and went over to the bathroom. He knocked. When no answer returned, he opened the door.

Still in her wedding dress, Chris stood in front of the mirror as if hypnotized. Finally, she blinked.

"Are you all right?" he asked. "I became worried when you didn't return."

"I'm fine," she answered with a slight waver in her voice. "I'll be there in a minute." She whooshed him away so she could ready in privacy.

He returned to the bedroom and stared into the empty fireplace. A few more minutes passed. *What could be taking her so long?* Impatient, he headed for the bathroom once more. Before he reached it, the door opened. She stood in the frame, dressed in a calf-length black gown with a deep V-neck and a thigh-high side slit. Her neck and chest flushed gorgeously.

Lace, mesh, and velvet lent her modest but provocative covering. She pirouetted, revealing her slender bare back. Frozen in place, he absorbed the shape of her leg and the curve of her buttocks. She faced him again. The word "wow" formed on his lips, but he remained tongue-tied.

She batted her eyelashes in a teasing manner. "You like?"

He cleared his throat. "That . . ." He swallowed and cleared his throat again. "That would be an understatement."

She licked her lips and strutted over to him. "Then why are you still half dressed, silly?" With a laugh, she reached for his zipper.

His heart hammered as his pants and briefs hit the floor. She sank to the bed, pulling him with her. Settling herself into a perfect position, she wrapped her legs around him. With one hand on his shoulder, she reached down with the other and guided him in with ease. He gripped her tightly, thrilling in the sensations—downy-like velvet brushing his chest, the warmth of her skin contacting his belly, the feel of her all around him. They hugged and kissed until spiraling to orgasm.

When Chris went downstairs for breakfast the following morning, Judith and Laura were scouring floors and gathering trash in the main hall where the dance had taken place.

"Chris," Judith said, stuffing a wadded napkin and several plastic cups into a garbage bag. With a wry grin, she glanced at her watch. "It's nearly ten-thirty. I trust you slept well."

"Very well, thank you." Chris attempted to sound nonchalant.

Her friend's response was a giggle. "I take it the little black number was a hit."

Chris glanced over her shoulder and spotted Laura's smirk. "It *was* my wedding night," she reminded them.

"Why you refused to go to some romantic getaway spot, I'll never understand."

Chris shrugged. "I have everything I want or need here. Besides, I have a job interview on Wednesday."

"And face everyday life. Daddy's in the library, seeing to farm things while Geoff takes a few days off. Neal's outside playing with Saber. I can drive him back to Richmond, if Geoff prefers."

"That can wait." Chris grasped Judith's elbow and guided her in the direction of the breakfast room and said in a low whisper, "I need to speak with you."

Once out of Laura's earshot, Judith asked, "What's wrong?"

They continued through the dining room to the breakfast room. "I saw Sarah."

"Did you tell Geoff?"

Upon arriving in the breakfast room, Chris stopped and shook her head. "I didn't want to spoil the evening. She's trying to tell me something. In the vision, she was about seventeen years old. Judging by the clothing she wore, it must have been from the 1880s, but she saw Geoff. Somehow her communication skill works both ways."

Judith's eyes widened in amazement. "Both ways?"

"I need to find a way to speak with her directly."

Judith reached up and touched Chris's necklace. "This seems to be a connecting force to that time. Do you suppose?"

"I've thought about it, but I'm not certain how the crystal works."

"Then you'll have to wait until Sarah communicates what she can, when she can."

Sarah had said the whispers were stronger when she was in the same physical space. She'd make certain to frequent the places that Sarah likely had.

"Chris . . ."

"I was just thinking about what Sarah said."

"Sarah?" Geoff asked, entering the breakfast room.

"Yes, Chris was telling me that if you're not more careful, Sarah might put in an earlier appearance than expected." With a teasing laugh, Judith ducked out of the breakfast room.

He crossed his arms and stared at her.

Uncertain whether he was angry or confused, Chris said, "She was kidding. Do you think I'd actually tell her intimate details of our love life?"

He lowered his arms—slowly. "To be honest, I don't know what women talk about. After all, she *is* my sister."

"And if I hadn't known her first, we would have never met." She put her arms around his waist and kissed him on the cheek. "We do talk about sex, but not the specifics of our personal lives. Feel better?"

His tense muscles relaxed. "I wish you had agreed to go away for a few days."

"Nonsense. This place is so big that we rarely run into one another. Here, you sit down and relax." She led him to the table and motioned for him to have a seat. "And I'll fix brunch."

With a smirk, he did as she asked. "I'll have to see this to believe it. You somehow learned to cook overnight?"

She waggled a finger at him. "Oh ye of little faith." Relieved that he had been distracted from the mention of Sarah, she went into the kitchen. Hand smudges covered the stainless surface of the stove near the counter where she had told Laura to leave the muffins. Beside the stove, Neal sat cross-legged on the floor, happily gobbling down a muffin, with blueberries smeared over his face. Saber wagged his tail while licking the boy's face. Neal stuffed another portion of the muffin in his mouth, when the dog snarfed a piece for himself. "Saber!" Chris shouted.

Near the doorway, she heard Geoff's laughter. "A large house also lends itself to kids and dogs getting into trouble without being heard."

Saber seized the rest of Neal's muffin and wolfed it down. The boy looked up with round, blue eyes and a tear rolling down his cheek. Geoff went over and collected his son in his arms. "I had better clean you up, or your mother will have my head."

"Geoff . . ." Chris held out her arms. "Let me. From what I remember in the ledger, we will become close. I'd like to start off on the right foot."

"You might think otherwise, when he screams about having his face washed." He placed Neal into her arms.

How strange it seemed, holding a four-year-old, tow-headed boy. It was magnificent in a way. A smile spread across her face as she headed for the bathroom, never believing that she had possessed any maternal instincts. Sarah had changed her feelings.

"Oh, and if he has to pee, just remember his aim isn't always the best."

"Dad," Neal protested.

Geoff was testing her. Even without looking at him, she knew he had an ear-to-ear grin. "I know some grown-ups who could use a few lessons on how to aim."

His laughter filled the kitchen. *Welcome to an instant family.* But for now, she was content.

* * *

Over the next two weeks, with the exception of her job interview, Chris spent the majority of her time with Geoff. Some days, they went sightseeing. She enjoyed touring Colonial Williamsburg. Geoff also showed her the nearby Civil War battlefields. On one occasion his eyes glazed over, and she realized George recognized the battle site. Other days, they would take long horseback rides through the woods to the cottage. Once there, they'd pile the goose down covers over them or start a roaring fire in the fireplace and make love.

In the late afternoon, Chris dozed beside the toasty fire with her body next to Geoff's. His hand rested on her thigh, and their legs were intertwined.

"Mama?" Sarah called.

Her mother blinked. She had her hair tied back and was wearing a split-skirt riding habit with a top hat and veil.

Similarly attired as her mother, Sarah felt Mama's swell of emotion that she usually held in check as they entered the cabin. "You accompanied him here, didn't you?" Without waiting for an answer, Sarah continued, "That's why you never wanted to bring me here."

Her mother grasped both of Sarah's hands. "He's been gone for twenty years. It's time that you stop worrying about me and make a life for yourself."

A life for herself? Not quite comprehending, Sarah withdrew her hands and lowered her arms. "But I have Poplar Ridge."

"Sarah, Jason will be returning soon. He'll take over running Poplar Ridge from Tom. Your papa never had time to make any provisions for you in his will."

And Aunt Margaret would never acknowledge her as anyone but Tom's daughter. Upon Jason's return, Tom would take over her duties, and she would likely be asked to leave. Tom must have known when he had agreed to teach her how to run the farm. "What else am I capable of doing? I'm already considered a spinster by many." A nostalgic smile crossed Mama's lips. After Sarah had read the ledger, her mother confided more about her "other life"—one that she now realized was in a future time. "We could search for the necklace," Sarah suggested.

Mama's smile faded. "I gave up hope of ever finding it long ago. Even if I found it now, I couldn't use it, unless there was a way to bring you with me."

At least that thought was comforting, for Mama was the only friend she had. "I long for when women can freely be doctors and lawyers."

In a stubbornly determined voice, Mama said, "We shall send you to college where you can be whatever you wish."

College? Sarah had often dreamed about what it would be like—books and classes—and when she finished, she could get a job like any man. She dared not hope. "What will Tom say?"

Mama shrugged. "Does it matter as long as he agrees?"

The dream vanished as quickly as it had begun. The whole notion was impractical. She couldn't leave Virginia. She had made a promise to Mama. "What about the ledger?"

"We'll put it in a safe place where only the two of us will know. How will things be any different than it is already? Sarah, you must have your own life. I refuse to let you sacrifice everything for me."

Sarah had never thought of getting the ledger to Jason's future daughter as a sacrifice. It was part of who she was. "My sacrifice is a selfish one."

Confused, Mama asked, "How could you possibly be selfish?"

Sarah went over to the fireplace and stared at the layer of ash at the bottom. In the library, she had felt Papa's presence. "Do you remember the day you gave me the ledger?"

"That was almost two years ago."

"After reading it, I suddenly understood why I hear the whispers in my head. On that day, I saw him."

"Your papa," Mama stated.

Sarah faced her mother. "I want the chance to know him—really know him."

"You will get that opportunity, but that doesn't mean you have to give up everything now. You can have a career and a family if you like. Women from the twenty-first century do it all the time. Things are more constrained here, but don't give up your dreams."

An attorney—like her mother. Sarah fancied the notion. "Tom laughs when I say women should have the right to vote. What do you think he'll say when I tell him that I'd like to continue my schooling?"

"He'll grumble and scowl, but he'll say yes because your papa would have wanted it that way." Mama hugged her. "Sarah, I'm proud of you."

Without opening her eyes, Chris nestled closer to Geoff's warm body. She reached out to touch him and stroked fur. Saber curled next to her instead of Geoff. "Saber!" She whooshed the dog away, only to hear Geoff's laughter.

"I didn't have the heart to wake you."

With the dream still fresh in her mind, she looked around the cabin to locate him. "You could have warned me. Usually you're the one who falls asleep."

Fully dressed, Geoff got up from the chair beside the bed and bent down to her. "I didn't mean to upset you."

Upset? No, but she didn't care to relay the dream to him—not just yet. In the past, Sarah was too connected to Tom, so she refrained. "I'm not really. Saber took me by surprise, is all."

"We should be getting back to the house." He extended a hand to help her up.

"I'm not coming out until I'm dressed," she said, waving him away and reaching for her clothes from beneath the safety of the covers.

He grinned in amusement. "You've never been shy before."

"It has nothing to do with being shy. Staying warm is more like it." She fumbled with her clothes. Once dressed, she threw back the covers.

Geoff helped her to her feet. With the air definitely chillier than when they had arrived, she shivered. The fire had burned down to a few glowing embers. He held up her jacket, and she placed her arms through the sleeves. Hand in hand, they stepped outside to the gray January day where the horses stood tethered to the hitching post.

He boosted her onto Tiffany's back, then handed her a helmet. He strapped his own helmet on and mounted the gray gelding. They reined their horses around. The path narrowed to the size of an animal trail, and she dropped her mare behind Geoff's horse, Traveller.

Except for a layer of dead leaves on the ground, the woods were barren this time of year. By the time they reached the stone courtyard outside the barn, the sun was sinking in the sky.

While T.J. and Geoff saw to the horses, Chris went up to the house. Each time she passed the tree where Tessa had been hanged, she shivered. And she was no closer to discovering what it was that Margaret's former servant wanted now. She sprinted up the steps and into the main hall.

Judith rounded the corner from the drawing room, waving a piece of paper. "A Ms. Warren called." She handed Chris the slip of paper.

The woman who had interviewed her the previous week. "Maybe it's not too late to catch her."

Judith nodded and ducked back into the drawing room.

With her heart pounding, Chris picked up the phone in the hall and dialed. "Ms. Warren, please."

A woman came on the line, and in a friendly, but firm tone explained the job. *"Can you start Monday?"*

"Yes." As she thanked her and hung up the phone, Geoff entered through the main door with Saber jogging beside him. She threw her arms around Geoff's neck and gave a jubilant shriek. "I got the job at the all-female firm in Richmond!"

"This calls for a celebration. Isn't that the same firm as in the ledger?"

"It is," she replied, stepping out of their embrace. According to the ledger, she had gotten the job not long after giving birth to Sarah. Now, she would be working at the firm close to three years earlier. "I'll be one of the assistant attorneys."

"This is good news."

The ledger also stated that soon after she had landed the job, Geoff had admitted to having an affair with Beth.

As if reading her thoughts, he said, "I hope you won't hold what's written in that book against me. I haven't even been tempted. Except where Neal is concerned, that part of my past is closed."

If only life were that simple. She raised up on her tiptoes and gave him a kiss on the mouth. "I believe you." Thrilled with the prospect of returning to work as an attorney, she had forgotten in the excitement that she might have little time to uncover what Sarah was trying to communicate to her. Even though they had changed time, Geoff's life might still be at risk. She had eleven years, she reminded herself and would find a balance as she hoped Sarah had.

Over the next few weeks, Geoff rarely saw Chris. On weekdays, she spent most of her time in Richmond at her new job. In spite of the long hours, there was a new energy about her. She loved the work, and it seemed to keep her from dwelling on the writings in the ledger. On a Sunday afternoon in March, he accompanied Neal up the brick walk lined with daffodils. Anytime he dropped his son off with Beth, he felt like a "weekend dad." Still, Neal chattered on about his time horseback riding and playing with Saber. In a hurry to tell his mother, Neal darted up the walk only to be met by a locked door. His son pounded on it.

Before Geoff reached the door, a man, approximately thirty with shortly cropped brown hair, answered. Neal gave a quick "hi," then scampered past him, shouting for his mom.

The man extended his right hand. "You must be Geoff Cameron."

Geoff eyed his hand before reluctantly shaking it. "And you are?"

"Al Fisher."

"Geoff, you're early." With tousled hair and a rumpled blouse, Beth widened the door for him to enter.

"That's obvious," Geoff replied, stubbornly remaining where he was.

"It's not what you think."

Geoff sized up Fisher—about six feet two inches, athletic build. "Does it matter? You're free to do as you please. Although if he's moved in, *he* can pay your mortgage."

Beth's lips were pursed and her face, pinched. She seized his arm and dragged him inside. "If you'll excuse us, Al, I need to remind my half-witted ex that he's behaving like a stupid bastard." Once in the kitchen, she grew red-faced. "Geoff, how could you! I've only gone out with Al a couple of times. He's a gentleman, not pressuring me in anyway, but I shouldn't have to explain that to you. You've re-married and made a new life for yourself. Shouldn't I have the same right? Or do you want me to become that crazy woman described in the ledger?"

Suddenly feeling foolish, he lowered his gaze. "You're right."

She raised a finger to continue her rant, then blinked. "Did I hear right?"

"You did. I'll apologize to him."

"Thank you." As he turned, she said after him, "It really is for the best. I haven't heard *her* voice since I met Al."

"That's good to hear." And shouldn't he be happy? Beth was achieving something that she apparently never had in the previous time line—acceptance of what had gone between them. It's time that he did as well. Fisher had remained in the foyer, looking as if not knowing whether he should stay or shoot out the door.

"I told Beth that I'd apologize. I shouldn't have said what I did."

Fisher nodded. "I've been through it myself."

Geoff resisted the temptation to ask Fisher any personal questions. It was none of his business. Instead, he shook the other man's hand.

Beth joined them and took a deep breath in relief. "Geoff, can you pick Neal up a couple of hours earlier next Friday?"

Don't ask. "Give me a call on Thursday to remind me." Without looking back, he went out to the Mustang parked along the curb. Maybe Beth moving on with her life was a good thing, especially if she no longer heard Margaret's voice. So why was he concerned? *Jealous was more like it, you idiot.* No, it wasn't jealousy, but protectiveness. Beth deserved a full life. He only hoped that Fisher didn't let her down as he had.

Chapter Sixteen

WITH THE HECTIC PACE OF WORKING as an attorney again, juggling time between career and family became difficult for Chris. Late in April, a week had passed before she realized that her period was late. In nervous anticipation, she stared at the test strip. Negative. *Stress.* She had thought for certain that she was pregnant.

Geoff's reflection appeared in the bathroom mirror behind her. "Is that what I think it is?"

Disappointed, she flicked the test strip into the waste basket. "There's no need to worry. I'm not pregnant."

"Chris, I'm not against having a baby. I just think it may be a little soon yet. Sarah will appear when the time is right."

With all of the diversions from the ledger, how could any of them be certain of the timing for anything? "Maybe we should have let Judith throw the heart-shaped rice after all."

His eyes narrowed in uncertainty. "I doubt ancient fertility rites would make any difference, but if you're really concerned about it, see a doctor to help ease your mind."

Her hands went to her hips. "So, it's automatically my fault."

"Maybe I should go back out and come in again. I don't think I said that."

She lowered her arms. "Sorry, I didn't mean to snap. I'm disappointed. I had hoped . . . well, I thought maybe Sarah might put in an earlier appearance. She said that you will read *Black Stallion* stories to her."

"When the time comes, I'll look forward to it, but have you also given thought to the possibility that if you got pregnant now, it might not be Sarah?"

No. "I don't think that'll happen."

"A feeling?"

"Yes, a feeling."

He took her into his arms. "Okay, I trust your feeling. Since you have the day off for a change, maybe we should go for a ride."

"A little later. Judith and I promised Greta that we would stop by. I haven't seen her in a month."

His face expressed disappointment, and she kissed him on the cheek.

"You could always come with us. You haven't seen Greta since the wedding."

"Another time. I have chores to tend to."

Chris detected apprehension in his voice. "Does seeing Greta bother you?"

"No."

But she had plainly heard a waver. "Geoff..."

"No, Chris. You can't understand. She is my... George's grand-daughter."

His confession confirmed her suspicion. "Why did you pretend that it didn't bother you when we first met?"

"Because I wanted to help you, not have you end up divided, like me." Obviously distressed by the conversation, he vanished from the bathroom.

"Geoff." By the time she reached the bedroom, the door closed. Her concern mounted when she went downstairs and only Winston and Judith sat at the breakfast table.

Upon her arrival, Winston stood.

"Where's Geoff?" she asked.

The elder Cameron helped her with her chair. "He grabbed a cup of coffee and said he had some chores to tend to."

Generic chores again. Usually Geoff was more specific. "Did he seem upset about anything?"

Judith and her father exchanged a glance, both shaking their heads. Calming, Chris debated throughout breakfast whether to postpone her trip to Greta's. For the time being, Geoff would be fine. Right now, it was imperative that she discover what had happened in the past.

An hour later, she accompanied Judith to Greta's house. After their prerequisite tea and a long chat to bring everyone up to date, Chris wandered upstairs to the room where she had given birth to Sarah, hoping for a vision. *Nothing.* She hadn't sensed anything since her return to work.

Disappointed, she returned to Judith and Greta. Perhaps, she should use a different tack. "Greta, what can you tell me about your father?"

Greta's pale eyes glistened. "My father? He was a kind, gentle man. His first wife died in childbirth. Nearly a decade passed before he married my mother. I remember him lifting me on my pony. One day, she bucked me off. Like all of the Cameron men, he was temperamental, but he had a special way with horses. She never did it again."

The old woman beamed, making the wrinkles on her face seem to fade. Chris could almost imagine Greta in her youth. *Did I know Jason, as well?* "Do you have any pictures of him?"

"In my bureau." Greta pushed her thin frame from the chair and went over and retrieved the pictures from the bureau. Chris leafed through them. While she had hoped to see what Jason looked like in his youth, a photograph of him in his sixties was enough to tell her, that with streaks of gray through his dark hair, he had taken Margaret's side of the family in appearance.

Still, no answers. Why did she keep running into a dead end? She checked her watch. "We should be getting back. I promised Geoff that I'd take a ride with him."

They thanked Greta for the tea and bid her goodbye. On the drive back to Poplar Ridge, Judith asked, "What's wrong, Chris?"

She should have guessed that her friend would sense her distraction. "I haven't had any visions about my previous life in weeks."

Judith turned onto the paved lane leading to Poplar Ridge. "Did you ever stop to think that things are now as they should be?"

Staring out the window at the pine and oak trees, Chris shook her head. "Or it could be the calm before the storm."

"Think about it. You and Geoff are married. You have a career again, and Beth has a steady boyfriend. I think Margaret is truly at rest."

"Possibly." The road turned into a single, graveled lane, and Chris continued, "Or I haven't been in the right place at the right time to get anymore impressions."

At the top of the ridge, a zigzag fence lined the road. Judith drove between the brick pillars topped by prancing bronze stallions. "I think you're being too pessimistic."

"Do I really have to remind you what's at stake?"

"Geoff's life," Judith said, glancing in the rearview mirror and breathing out. "You needn't remind me. I'm only trying to say that if Beth is capable of moving on with her life, then maybe Margaret is at peace."

"I can't take that chance. I need to know what happened back then that might affect us now. If it's nothing, then that's great. We can get on with our lives like every other couple, but if something is unresolved, then we must find out what it is."

As they approached the garage, Judith pushed the button for the door opener and parked the car beside Geoff's Mustang. On their walk to the house, Saber barked and circled them. Aware that Geoff couldn't be far behind, Chris turned and waited. His eyes twinkled as he neared them. Judith said a quick "bye," and he gave Chris a welcome-home kiss. "How's Greta?" he asked.

"She's doing well. You seem to be feeling better."

"I am. Should I saddle the horses?"

"I've got to look up one thing for a case I'm working on, then I'll be right with you."

He stared at her dubiously.

"I promise. It won't take more than a minute." After exchanging another kiss, she headed to the west wing and the library. She stepped inside.

Although her friendship with Jason had remained steadfast over the years, Sarah hadn't gone into the library since attending Howard University. She and Mama approached the desk. Jason stood and motioned to the chairs across from him. "Aunt Chris, Sarah, please be seated."

His eyes were a paler blue than her own, and his hair was black like Aunt Margaret's. Almost hidden behind a handlebar moustache, he had a kind, but mischievous smile, very much like the one she remembered in the photographs of her father.

"You wanted to see us?" Mama asked, seating herself.

His smile vanished, and he cleared his throat, giving Sarah a nervous glance. "It has recently come to my attention that Sarah isn't my cousin, but my sister."

Mama exchanged an intense gaze with her. Sarah felt that she was trying to tell her something. Her mother's lips failed to move, but she clearly heard her name. Sarah. The voice had been a whisper like when she spoke with the dead. How could that be when Mama sat right beside her?

Sarah reached for her mother's arm, when Jason said, "Please, Aunt Chris. I don't mean to embarrass you. I only want to know about my father. What was he like?"

Jason's voice broke the connection, and Mama turned her attention to him. "Who told you?"

"My mother. She didn't mean to, but you know how she rambles sometimes." He glanced at Sarah. "You knew, didn't you?"

For nearly thirty years, Sarah had kept her secret from Jason. As children, they had played side by side. They had shared a special bond, and only he stood behind her when other children had poked fun of her gift. "I've been brought up knowing who my father was," she admitted.

Jason's eyes narrowed in confusion. "Why didn't you tell me?"

"Because I thought it best," Mama answered for her. "Jason, I'm sorry if our silence has hurt you, but I had to think of Tom and your mother as well."

"My mother," he grumbled under his breath, "she's always been melancholy. I doubt my father's indiscretion has been the source of it."

Mama's eyes clamped shut. When she opened them again, they had misted.

"Mama, why don't you tell Jason about Papa? I'll let him know the rest."

Her mother squeezed her hand in thank you, then returned her attention to Jason. "Your father, he was . . ."

As Mama told Jason about their papa, Sarah beamed. With the truth finally revealed, she could finally welcome him to the family in the way she had always felt—as her brother.

Clutching her necklace, Chris stared at the empty leather chair behind the desk. For a brief moment, she was certain that Sarah had been aware of her presence in the vision. If only she could break through the time barrier and speak to her daughter. The communication had to be two way. Perhaps the answer had been staring her in the face, without her realizing it. Sarah spoke to the dead. She sprinted toward the outside door. When she opened it, Geoff was about to enter.

"Ready to go?" he asked.

"I need to talk to George."

His brows furrowed. "Why?"

"He may hold the key to communicating with Sarah."

"Sarah?"

She tugged on his arm and pulled him inside. "Sarah speaks to the dead like the rest of us talk to each other. She can communicate with George and in turn, you."

Rejecting the idea, he shook his head adamantly. "I can't. If I let him through, I never know if I'll be able to regain control. He loved you. He may not want to let go."

She hugged him. "For that very reason, he will let go."

The tension in his muscles faded. "All right, but not here. I don't want to relive any memories of his death."

"We'll go upstairs," she suggested.

"That should be okay."

Chris shivered. The letter from 1901 had stated that Sarah reached George once.

Why had he agreed to such a preposterous proposition? Geoff hesitated upon reaching their room.

"It may give us the answers we need."

Face it. "You're right." As they stepped inside their bedroom, he chose the overstuffed chair near the fireplace. If he relaxed on the bed, George would think of Chris sexually. Hell, he might anyway.

"What happens now?"

Getting comfortable, he leaned back and placed his arms on the armrests. "I clear my head, then concentrate on the things I know about his life, and he'll take over. I have one request."

"Name it."

"I'm not likely to remember what happens. You must be honest with me."

"I will," Chris promised without hesitation.

He closed his eyes and focused on his breathing. Deep, relaxing breaths. *In. Out. Now think of George.* Chris wanted him to speak with Sarah. Nothing. He tried again. *Concentrate.* A scratching at the door distracted him further, and he opened his eyes to Chris walking over to the door.

"Do you want me to let him in?" she asked.

"He'll keep scratching if you don't," he replied.

As soon as she opened the door, Saber bounded over to him. Geoff scratched the dog under the chin, then signaled for him to lie down. Saber curled on the rug beside the bed, and he closed his eyes once more. *Focus. Deep, even breaths.* Darkness. In his mind's eye, he thought of leather reins sliding through his fingers as a black mane whipped into his face. Powerful muscles strained beneath him and hooves pounded through the grassy meadow. Alongside him, Tom raced on a brown horse.

"Tom!" he shouted.

"George?"

The woman's voice seemed distant. Unable to locate her, he clicked his tongue to Raven for more speed. The stallion accelerated with a new burst, but Tom remained by his side. They streaked across the grassland with yellow and blue flowers.

"George."

He recognized the woman's voice and opened his eyes. "Chris?" She stood next to him. Her hair was longer than he remembered, and she wore trousers. And there were no little wrinkles near her eyes. He reached a hand to her face to see if he was dreaming. "It really is you." Unable to hold back, he swept her into his arms.

"George, please." She stepped away from their embrace. "I need your help."

"I haven't seen you in ..." *How long?* " ... ages. Where have you been all this time?"

"It's difficult to explain, but I don't know how much time we have."

To see and touch her again. The last thing he remembered ... His room was *different*. The straw mattress was gone. In its place stood a four-poster bed with an arched headboard. An unusual-looking lamp sat atop the night table. He went to inspect, when Chris's voice drew him back.

"George, please, I need help."

He blinked in confusion. "How can I help?"

"Do you trust me?"

On her finger was a gold band, and she wore her crystal necklace. He touched it. "You found it."

"You're in my time."

"Then this ..." He held up Chris's left hand. "You're married to Geoff."

"I am," she admitted. "Your essence lives in him. As you warned me, decisions I made in your time have changed this one. I need to know what happened then to move forward in this time."

His leg didn't hurt from the war wound. He examined his hands. They looked the same. He went over to the mirror above the dresser. The face staring back was his, but different. Instead of a simple moustache, he also had a small, neatly trimmed beard with no side-burns. His body was muscular, but not quite as thin. He *was* in Chris's time. A memory flickered through his head. He faced her and pressed a hand to her abdomen. "You were with child."

Her voice grew soft. "I named her Sarah."

They had a daughter. "Sarah? Why can't I remember what she looks like?"

"I can't tell you everything because it might affect Geoff, but she's the reason why I've asked you to come here. She's been trying to tell me something, and you're the only one that I know of who can speak with her."

Him? Only now was he coming to the true realization that he was a ghost from the past. *Dead, you fool.* How had it happened? "I don't know how to communicate with Sarah."

"Try. It's all I ask."

"I'll do my best." But he was at a loss. Contact a daughter that he hadn't known? *How?* Chris was counting on him. He must try. She wouldn't have summoned him, if the circumstances were unwarranted. For some reason, he was compelled to go to the library. He glanced around the room. There were no stairs. He spotted the door and strode for it, when a black dog rushed after him. *Saber.* Where had the voice come from? He bent down and patted Saber, and the dog licked him on the face. "He's sleeker, but otherwise, he's like Washington."

"Saber is a Belgian sheepdog," she said. "I don't think the breed came to this country until early in the twentieth century, but he's Geoff's constant companion."

George straightened. "We are a lot alike."

"Of course," she whispered.

He opened the door to a hallway. Puzzled at first, he saw stairs leading the way down. He followed them. The stairs led to another hallway. He tried the door to his left. As he had guessed, he found the library. The desk with acorn carvings sat in the middle of the room. *Chris had run her hand along the surface as though she were caressing a lover.* He had loved her from the moment they had met. That was due to Geoff's influence? On top of the desk was a thin metallic-looking object and some sort of board with letters and numbers on it. He touched one of the letters, but nothing happened.

"*A computer,*" said the voice in his head.

"George." Chris joined him.

"I died before Sarah was born?"

She gave a weak nod.

"Chris, I'm so sorry for not being here." He swiveled the chair around and eased in. *His chair.* It molded to him as if he had never been absent. "Tell me about her."

"As a girl, she had reddish curls like your sister Mary. She grew into a beautiful young woman who believed in suffrage for women."

He laughed. "She sounds like your daughter."

"Our daughter," she corrected.

"Our daughter," he agreed. But to contact her? Where did he begin? He was dead. Shouldn't it be easy? But he was in Geoff's body. He closed his eyes and imagined what Sarah must have looked like. All of the years she had been growing up, he had been absent from her life. "Sarah, your mother wishes for me to speak to you."

"Papa?" The man in the chair before Sarah opened his eyes, staring at her as if he should know her.

He slowly got to his feet, standing about six feet tall. He was around her own age. "Sarah?"

Tears filled her eyes as she rushed around the desk and hugged him. "Papa, you don't know how long I've been trying to reach you. We had almost given up hope." As he took a step back and examined her, she wanted to ask him all of the questions that had formed in her head over the years. Now that the moment had arrived, she couldn't think of where to begin.

A smile spread across his face. "You've grown into a lovely woman, Sarah."

"I'm an attorney. It was difficult at first, but people are finally accepting the fact that I can do the job as well as any man. Jason was the first to send business my way."

His eyes misted. "I'm sorry I've missed the two of you growing up."

She grasped his hand. "You're here now, even if it's only for a little while."

He lowered his hand and snapped to attention. "Your mother thinks you're trying to send her a message."

"Mama," she said in confusion. "Why would I send her a message? She's right here. She wants to see you."

"Right here? Sarah, what year is it?"

Afraid that if she fetched Mama she'd lose her connection with Papa, she turned and called for her mother. "1898."

His forehead wrinkled as if he were mulling the date around in his head. "I spoke to your mother in the twenty-first century."

"*Where she came from originally?*" *He nodded.* "*I haven't tried to communicate with her, and as far as I know . . .*" *She* had *felt her mother's presence once, in this very room on the day that Jason had confronted them about her parentage.* "*Papa . . .*"

The library door opened. Mama, with her nearly silver hair parted in the middle and a gentle wave in her bangs, entered. She wore a white blouse with puffy sleeves near her shoulders, a thick belt about her waist, and a bright-red skirt. "*George?*" *Tears streamed down her cheeks as she moved toward him.*

He stretched his arms. Drifting to the side, Sarah felt like an intruder as they kissed and hugged each other. Seeing Mama so happy, she smiled. Finally, both of them looked over at her with tears in their eyes. "*Sarah.*" *They drew her in their arms and embraced her.* "*Thank you.*"

For so long, she had dreamed of this day. Papa gave her a kiss on the forehead, and she felt the connection between the two worlds begin to fade. He gazed wistfully at Mama a moment, then he moved to the area covered by the braided rug. The spot where he had died.

"*George!*" *Mama cried.* "*Don't!*"

He lifted the rug to faded stains. Mama stood across from him, wringing her hands as he spoke. "*You were telling me about Geoff driving a Mustang. Naturally, I thought about a horse, but you said it was a car. Even then, I didn't understand. Tessa stood in the doorway. She had a gun. I must have reached you in time. Chris!*" *His face grew transfixed with disbelief and horror.*

Mama tried to reach him, but Sarah knew it was fruitless. The link had been severed.

A dog gave a high-pitched bark. Saber rushed at George, grasping his arm in his mouth.

Blinding pain. A woman's voice shouted his name as he collapsed to the floor, striking the back of his head. Light shimmered. He drifted toward it. *Noooo!* He tried to reach Chris. She cradled him in her arms. He struggled to speak, but he couldn't breathe. Darkness carried him under, then nothing.

* * *

In exhaustion, Chris folded her arms and lowered her head to the surface of the bed. Thank goodness, Geoff seemed to be all right. Or would he be George when he woke? The vision of George recalling how he had died had been very real. Too tired to be afraid any longer, she closed her eyes and drifted until the bed jiggled. She raised her head to the drab white walls, blinked, and rubbed sleepy eyes. She held her breath as he stared at her in confusion.

He glanced around the room. "Where am I?"

"The hospital," she responded with some hesitation.

"Please tell me that it's not the psycho ward."

He *was* Geoff. "It's not the psychiatric ward. You passed out in the library. Since then, you've been drifting in and out of consciousness. Sometimes George spoke, but I couldn't make out what he was trying to tell me. The doctors have taken blood work and ran a CT scan."

"Then they could still admit me?"

She detected fear in his voice. "I didn't tell them about George. They won't try to admit you. Do you remember anything that happened?"

He pressed two fingers to his temple. "No. You promised to tell me everything."

She swallowed. "What's the last thing you remember?"

"Sitting down and thinking of George. Saber interrupted, then . . ." He shook his head.

Sometimes Geoff and George almost seemed like two separate entities, but she would never forget the look of disbelief on his face, then shock, pain, and complete terror. "I'll never ask you to go through that again. George remembered his death."

"I don't."

"Which is a good thing." And she finally understood. The fact that he forgot George's traumatic experiences protected his own health.

"You look like you could use some sleep. How long have you been here?"

She brushed stray hairs away from her face. "All night, but I'm fine."

"Chris, you don't need to nursemaid me. Someone will call when I can be released."

"Geoff..."

"Please, go home and get some rest."

He was looking better, but still she hesitated. "You'll call me when the test results return?"

"I will," he promised.

Slowly, she stood, then she kissed him on the forehead. Judith and Winston remained in the waiting room, also giving her promises they would call if there was any change. Finally convinced Geoff would be in good hands, she drove back to Poplar Ridge. As she left the garage, a bronze Mercedes pulled into the lane. A woman with long black hair got out of the car. A breath caught in Chris's throat. *Margaret.* Even without being told, she knew the woman was Beth. *And Beth would murder Geoff.*

Uncertain of her facts, Chris got a grip on herself. *They had changed time.* Tessa had killed George in this time frame.

Beth gathered Neal in her arms from the safety seat in back. "You must be Chris."

"I am." Chris held out her hand. "And you're Beth."

"The ex," Beth said with a laugh. She shook Chris's hand, then glanced around the grounds. "I presume Geoff is off doing chores somewhere?"

Chris shook her head. "He's in the hospital."

Beth's violet eyes widened. "Is he all right?"

The fear on Beth's face warned Chris that she still cared for Geoff—a lot. "He should be fine. He passed out in the library, and they're running some tests as a precautionary measure."

Beth's features relaxed somewhat. "I wanted to speak to him and hoped he could look after Neal for a little while."

Her fear faded, and Chris stretched out her arms. "I'll look after him."

"Are you certain? What if Geoff calls?"

"There will be someone here to watch him if you don't return by the time I need to pick up Geoff."

As Beth placed Neal into her arms, Chris longed for Sarah. Neal would play beside Sarah, just as Jason had. At least there would be no need to hide the fact they were siblings.

* * *

The following day, Geoff pulled the Mustang in front of Beth's house. He unbuckled Neal and went up the brick walk with his son and Saber. Bristling slightly, he wondered if Al would be present. He knocked. *A woman with neatly pinned black hair at the nape answered.* He blinked back the vision of Margaret to see Beth.

"Geoff." She smiled and welcomed Neal and him inside. "I'm relieved to see that you're out of the hospital. Are you all right?" She motioned for him to proceed to the parlor as Neal scampered toward the kitchen with Saber.

He glanced around the foyer.

Her grin widened. "Looking for Al? He's not here."

She obviously delighted in the fact that he had reacted. "I'm fine," he finally said. "Chris said you wanted to talk to me about something."

"Just like that? I thought you'd tell me what happened."

Not about to reveal his experience concerning George, he answered, "No one knows, and all of the tests came back fine. What is it you wanted?"

"Would you like something to drink?"

Her evasive tactics were growing annoying, and past experience warned him that he wasn't going to like whatever it was that she wanted to talk about. "No."

Once more, she motioned to the parlor. Obliging her, he moved in that direction. In the parlor, she gestured for him to have a seat.

He remained standing. "Spill it, Beth. Even if what's-his-name is moving in, I'll handle it in a calm manner. We went our separate ways over a year ago."

She giggled and sat on the sofa. "Al's not moving in, but . . ." Beth turned serious. "I feel like I'm repeating my mistake."

"Mistake?"

She failed to meet his gaze. "Us."

With no desire to reopen old wounds, Geoff let out his breath slow and easy. "It might be best if I leave now."

"Please don't. I blamed you for something that never happened."

"True, but I understand where you got the wrong impression. What's that got to do with repeating your mistake?"

"Because if I had known what I do now, I would have never asked for a divorce."

Her confession wasn't what he wanted to hear, and he sank to the leather chair beside the fireplace. "I think you know by now that it was meant to be. If we hadn't split, I would have done the very thing you accused me of when I met Chris."

Beth managed a weak nod. "Maybe it was for the best."

He gestured for her to back up. "You still haven't explained why you think you're making the same mistake."

Frowning, she waved a dismissal. "It wasn't important."

"Beth, no matter what we've been through, I still care about what happens to you."

"I don't know why. Not when I could ... could potentially ..." Her voice cracked, and tears filled her eyes.

Kill him. "I think we've changed that event."

"How do we know for sure?"

His own sanity depended on the belief. "Only time will tell, but *she* didn't kill George. And you've said that you haven't heard her voice since meeting Fisher."

Quickly averting her gaze, she stared into the dark fireplace.

"You've heard her again."

"No," Beth replied with a shake of her head. "I haven't. It's just that things don't *feel* right."

"In what way?"

Her brows furrowed. "It's not a topic that a woman can discuss with her ex."

His gut nudged at him to leave. If he didn't, the raw wound of how much he had loved her would resurface. He thought of Fisher in bed with her, trespassing her body, and he wrestled with an increasing discomfort. Forcing himself to stay and console her, he sat on the sofa beside her. "We used to be able to talk about anything."

She forced a smile. "You forget, I can read you like a book. I know what you're trying to do, and that was when we were married, you idiot."

He shrugged. "Hasn't enough time passed that we can bury the bitterness and be friends?"

"No." She stood and stared into the fireplace with her back to him.

"Beth . . ." He got to his feet and placed a sympathetic hand on her arm.

When she faced him again, tears streaked her cheeks. "You don't understand. Ever since reading that journal, I can't live with the thought of what I may become. Al has merely been a diversion, so I don't think about it too much."

He inhaled sharply. "I see."

"You don't," she insisted. Her tears were gone, and she was in control of her emotions once more. "*She* has never stopped loving George."

"I thought you said you didn't hear her voice anymore."

"I don't, but I *feel* a numbing presence. She's confused about what happened."

When he first arrived, he had seen Margaret. Was it due to George's memories or something more?

"Geoff, I refuse to become that woman, and I'll do whatever is necessary to prevent it."

Surprised by her uncharacteristic resolve, he stepped back and met her gaze. "Okay. I understand."

"Thank you," she replied, her voice remaining decisive.

"Then I'll see you next weekend when I pick up Neal?"

She nodded, and he turned to leave.

Chapter Seventeen

I N A MONOTONOUS RHYTHM, MAMA ROCKED *her chair on the front porch. It had been over a month since making the breakthrough to Papa. While Sarah rejoiced in finally meeting him, sometimes she regretted making the connection. She had felt him relive the horror of his death, and with his memory renewed, her mother had grieved ever since. She no longer even made her weekly journey to visit Papa's grave. "Mama."*

With red-rimmed eyes, Mama blinked, not really seeing her.

Sarah knelt beside the rocking chair. "You can't go on like this. I hear you crying when you think no one else is around."

Another blink, and her presence seemed to register. "Is my only destiny to keep losing him?"

Throughout the years, Sarah had always admired her mother's tenacity, but she was at a loss. Mama had already watched Papa die twice. How much more could any person endure? "This time was my fault. He spoke through me."

"Through you? He seemed so real. I held and touched him."

Her mother's mood worried Sarah. "It was an illusion. He spoke through me," she repeated.

Mama gripped her hand. "Sarah, I'm sorry. It wasn't your fault. You gave me a gift. I thought we would never reach him because we have tried for so long without success."

And now Sarah understood why. Papa's whispers could be heard in the library, where he had died in both time lines. Still, she felt he had been attempting to communicate something to them. She hesitated before asking her next question, "Should we try reaching him again?"

Mama halted rocking. "We should always continue to try, but he won't be back. I'll not see him again until . . ."

After more than thirty years, her mother rarely talked about her previous life in the twenty-first century. In times past, Sarah had often grown absorbed in her tales. The thud of hooves in the lane distracted her. She pointed to the road. "Mama."

A man with muttonchop sideburns trotted up on a sleek bay stallion. He dismounted, removed his derby to reveal gray hair, and gave a bow. "Ladies. I'm looking for Mrs. Christine Olson."

Sarah had never heard anyone call her mother by her maiden name. The man had a nasal-sounding accent. A Northerner?

Mama stood. "You've found her. Do I know you?"

Dressed in charcoal trousers, a black coat, and a bright red vest with a silk tie to match, he stood beside his horse, holding the reins. "I believe so. Michael Rhodes, ma'am."

Rhodes? Sarah recalled her mother's story of a Captain Rhodes helping her when she had been accused of Papa's murder.

Mama descended the steps. "Captain Rhodes? What could you possibly want after all of these years?"

"Please, I'd like a chance to speak with you."

Her mother motioned for him to have a seat. Satisfied that Captain Rhodes meant no ill will, Sarah turned to leave them to their privacy, when Mama grasped her arm. "Please, stay."

"Yes, Mama."

Captain Rhodes tied his horse to the rail and joined the women on the porch. "Mrs. Olson . . ."

"Cameron," Mama corrected. "I'm Mrs. Cameron now, and this is my daughter, Sarah."

"Mrs. Cameron." He turned to Sarah. "Pleased to meet you, ma'am."

Sarah nodded an acknowledgment, and as they took their seats, a heavy silence hung between them.

"I never had the chance to thank you, Captain," Mama said, attempting to break the awkwardness.

"Much obliged, ma'am, but please, call me Mike. I haven't been in the military since the summer of '67."

"Mike," Mama agreed. When the uncomfortable silence returned, she continued, "I presume that you have sought me out because of that incident. Why did you help me?"

His tormented gaze met her mother's. "I knew you were innocent. The Negro gal was too."

A gasp escaped Mama. "Tessa was innocent? How do you know?"

He clenched his hand so tightly that his knuckles nearly turned white. "Because my sergeant, you remember Sullivan, found her hiding in the woods near Poplar Ridge. She told him that she was protecting the Missus."

That's what Papa had been trying to tell them. He had specifically mentioned Tessa. Missus? Did he mean Aunt Margaret?

Mama paled with the news. "Why would she have offered your sergeant this information?"

His hand remained clenched. "Because he had promised to help her in return for favors, but the mob got to her first."

Clamping her eyes shut, Mama swayed in the chair. Sarah reached out to help steady her. "Are you all right?"

Mama reopened her eyes. "My God. Tessa died for nothing. And Tom . . . all of these years, he must have known."

Sarah glanced from Mama to Mike in confusion. His face had gone ashen from withholding his knowledge for so long. But Tom? She returned her focus to her mother. "How would Tom have known?"

"Dammit, they were lovers!"

"Tessa was innocent!" Gasping for breath, Chris sat up in bed. Beside her, Geoff startled awake and his arms went around her. The early dawn cast enough light for her to see that she was in her own bed at Poplar Ridge. Relieved, she pressed her hand to Geoff's bare chest and felt the rapid thumping of his heart. He was alive and with her now. "Tessa covered for Margaret."

He brushed the hair from her face. "What do you mean that she covered for Margaret?"

She could no longer hold the tears at bay. "The only thing that has changed is George's death was listed as murder, rather than suicide. Just like before, Margaret killed him." Keeping an arm around her, he drew away slightly, trying to absorb what she had said. She continued by relaying the dream. His face remained calm, almost serene, as she spoke. "Say something."

"What would you have me say?" he responded with a shrug. "We both knew it was a long shot that time had changed for the better.

Let's not worry about what may happen. It's ten years away."

"Is it?" she asked, unable to believe his casual response. "I arrived two years early. How do we know that everything else hasn't shifted?"

Geoff let out a weary breath. "If it has, it has. What's going to be gained by worrying about it? Besides, Sarah hasn't made her presence known yet. There's time."

Now she was pissed—really pissed. Her whole body trembled. "What has gotten into you? How can you possibly ignore how all of this ends?"

As he gripped her hand, she felt it shake. A brave front. She should have known better.

"Chris, I don't want to die, but what can I do? Accuse Beth of something that hasn't happened yet. You're an attorney. You know that I can't. I can't cut her out of my life, unless I'm willing to give up my son. That's not an option either. I can only hope the fact that with the knowledge Beth possesses, she will prevent it from happening."

The ledger had caused more grief than it had solved. If only she could slip back in time and tell herself not to write the damned thing. "You're right. We'll talk about this later. I've got to get ready for the office."

Caught in an endless time loop, she had to break the cycle once and for all. After changing and a quick cup of coffee, Chris called the office that she would be late for work. Instead, she drove to an older section of Richmond to gabled Victorians, stopping along the street in front of a yellow house. She hesitated. Should she involve Beth? She was already involved, and Geoff's life was at stake. Chris went up the walk and knocked on the door.

"Chris?" Beth said, upon answering the door. "Is Geoff all right?"

Beth's concern told her what she needed to know. She still cared for Geoff. With a slight shudder at seeing Margaret's face in Beth, Chris reminded herself of why she had come. "He's fine, but Beth, I was wondering if we could talk? It's important."

"Come in. Can I get you some coffee or tea?"

"I'm fine. Thank you." Chris stepped into the foyer and spotted Neal.

The boy gave her a wide grin. "Did you bring Saber?"

Chris bent down to his level. "Sorry, but I didn't think to bring him along. He's home with your dad. I think they're busy mending fences today."

Neal's grin vanished, and Beth picked up the boy. "Let me take him to his room. You go ahead and make yourself comfortable in the parlor, and I'll be back when I've got him playing quietly." She indicated the direction of the parlor.

"Thanks." Chris went into the parlor. Instead of making herself comfortable, she paced the floorboards. *Was she doing the right thing by coming?*

Ten minutes passed before Beth reappeared. "Now, what's so important?"

The wait had only made her more nervous. "I probably shouldn't have come."

"I presume that it's about Geoff," Beth said, seating herself on the sofa.

Clasping her hands together, Chris sat at the opposite end of the sofa. "Yes, and I doubt that he'd tell you himself."

"Tell me what?"

Beth had read the ledger. Why was she continuing to hesitate? Straight out would be the best way. "I don't think we've changed anything. Margaret killed George. Tessa covered it and took the blame."

Stunned by the news, Beth stared at her with her eyelashes fluttering. Her voice was barely a whisper when she spoke. "Please believe me, I've considered every scenario I can think of to try and change the outcome. I'm scared to death of becoming that woman. I'd move if I thought it would help, but you know that Geoff won't let me take Neal far enough away to make a difference."

In regard to Neal, Chris trod a fine line that she didn't dare cross. Nor would she want to. "Would running from the problem truly solve anything?"

"I don't know," Beth responded weakly.

Chris stood. "Beth, I'm sorry. I shouldn't have come. I'll let myself out."

By the time she reached the foyer, Beth called after her. "Please, Chris, I'm glad that you had the courage to see me. You were correct when you said that Geoff would never say anything."

"Courage?" She faced Beth, whose violet eyes flickered thought-fully. "I'm hardly courageous. Desperate would be more like it, and I'm used to taking action. Sometimes inappropriately. I won't bother you again."

A smile lit up Beth's face. "Your action is hardly inappropriate. If our roles were reversed, I only hope that I could face the situation as rationally as you."

Why hadn't she realized it before? Beth didn't just care about Geoff. She still loved him. While the thought was a bit unsettling, it could work to everyone's advantage. Chris sifted through her purse for a business card. "If you think of something that might work, no matter how bizarre it may sound, or just need to talk to someone, feel free to call me."

Beth accepted the card. "Thank you for not blaming me."

"You're not at fault. We'll find a way to keep history from repeat-ing itself." As she went down the walkway to her car, she felt hope. With Beth on their side, at least they had a fighting chance.

When a floorboard creaked, Saber raised his head from the rug. The dog's tail wagged, and Geoff looked up from the monitor on his desk. Chris entered the room, and he stood to greet her.

"I'm sorry that I missed dinner," she said, easing into the chair near the desk and kicking off her shoes. "I grabbed a bite at work because I was late getting into the office this morning."

He reseated himself behind the desk and keyed in a couple of entries. "Late? You left at the usual time."

With a slight grimace, she rubbed her feet. "I went to see Beth."

He stopped typing. "Why?"

"Because I knew you wouldn't tell her about my dream."

For better or worse, he *had* made a habit of sheltering Beth be-cause George had treated Margaret in a similar manner. Should he be angry or relieved that Chris had interfered? "How did she take the news?"

"Fairly well. She wants to help."

He glanced at the rug that covered the stain where George had died. The ledger hadn't changed anything. Where *he* would die. "Chris, I've been thinking about it all day. I'm at a loss as to what to do."

"Beth says she's willing to move away from Richmond."

"If I agreed to that, I'd lose my son."

"You wouldn't lose him. You'd be alive to visit him."

Always so practical. Unable to consent to the proposal, he rubbed his forehead. "There has to be another way."

Chris moved behind him and kneaded his tense shoulders. "We'll find the answer—together."

To her soothing touch, he closed his eyes. He nearly drifted. When he reopened his eyes, Chris stood before him. He got to his feet, and they held each other for a long while.

"I have a special feeling about tonight," she whispered in his ear.

In her desire to conceive Sarah, she'd had the feeling before. *Humor her.* "Why tonight?"

"I arrived two years early, so will she." Suddenly giddy, she tugged on his hand. "Let's either lock the door or go upstairs."

"Upstairs would be . . ."

In her blind enthusiasm, she nearly dragged him up the stairs to their room. Once there, they undressed and hustled under the covers. *What if this time she was right?* A daughter. Until now, he'd thought of Sarah in the abstract, not a living, breathing baby. For a second, he detected a faint glow from her necklace. The crystal had always held the key. Lost in a maze of light, he surrendered to her.

Worried that something was terribly wrong, Sarah climbed the stairs to the second floor. Once outside Mama and Tom's room, she stopped. Her heart pounded so hard that she had to catch her breath. When she raised a hand to knock, the sense of dread vanished as quickly as it had overcome her. She tiptoed down the stairs, hoping she hadn't woken anyone.

By the time she reached the parlor, she was still shaking. She thought about making some tea but decided against it. She had an early appointment in the morning and needed to get some sleep. As she padded down the hall to her room, she heard someone bump into a table. A lamp rattled from the jolt.

"Sarah?"

"Mama?" Sarah turned back. "I didn't mean to wake you. Are you all right?" She lifted the hourglass globe and lit the lamp.

Mama hugged her as if she hadn't seen her in years. "Sarah. I was so afraid that you were gone."

"Gone? Where else would I be?"

Mama placed a hand to her head. "I don't know. I'm confused. I had a dream that I was with your father—in the twenty-first century."

With a mix of emotions, Sarah now understood her feeling. "The time must be getting close."

"Close?"

"For your return," Sarah stated, matter-of-factly.

Mama put her hand to her throat. "But I don't have the necklace."

Her mother would soon be gone, and she would need to carry on alone. Sarah forced a laugh. "Have you forgotten that I can hear the whispers through time? You shall find it. Weren't you wearing it in your dream?"

"I was, but Sarah, there's no way that I can leave without you."

According to the ledger, Greta would be born in a couple of years. When her niece was old enough, it was Sarah's duty to see that she got the ledger. "You won't be leaving me behind. I thought you knew by now. Like you, I'm part of both times."

"But you've barely lived in this one."

Sarah shrugged. "I have my law career."

"And you have never desired anything more?"

"Not really. I didn't wish to make do, like . . ."

"Tom and me."

Her mother had sacrificed so much in order to give her what she needed. Sarah regretted saying anything hurtful. "Yes," she answered softly.

With a gentle smile, Mama reached a hand to her face. "It's all right. I understand. I need to make one more entry in the ledger. Will you accompany me to Poplar Ridge?"

"You know that I will." Sarah gripped Mama's hand. Her father would receive the ledger, and in the twenty-first century, they would be a family.

* * *

A deep, even breathing came from beside Chris. With a tremble, she touched him, lightly tracing over the lines of his face. He had a goatee. *Thank God.* Tom had a full beard. He was Geoff. His nose twitched, and she withdrew her hand before waking him.

The year had been 1901. She had yet to find her necklace, but she was getting close to whatever it was that Sarah was trying to tell her. Relieved that Geoff was near, she slipped her hand in his and snuggled next to him, hoping no more dreams awakened her.

Over the next month, Chris had no further dreams from Sarah. She tried not to dwell on it. Her career kept her busy. One morning in early May, she barely finished her breakfast of dry toast and a poached egg before having to make a mad dash for the bathroom in the reception room. She bent over the toilet and threw up. When she thought her stomach was empty, she vomited again.

"Should I hazard a guess as to why you're praying to the porcelain god so early in the morning?" Geoff handed her a glass of water to rinse her mouth.

Swirling the water around her mouth, she spit into the sink. "I've been afraid to take the test. I've been disappointed before. What if I'm not pregnant?"

With a mischievous grin, he playfully patted her on the behind. "Why else would you be puking your guts out like that?"

"Do you have to be so crude?" she asked, whooshing his hand away from her butt. "How would I know what it's like to be pregnant?"

"Pregnant! Did Chris say she was pregnant?" Judith squealed with delight outside the bathroom door.

Chris shushed Judith, only to discover Winston also stood a few feet away. Nothing like having an entire audience observe her losing her breakfast. "Listen, everyone. I'm not certain yet. Besides, I've got to be getting to the office."

"The office?" A frown appeared on Judith's face. "Shouldn't we go shopping?"

"I think we need to verify that I'm pregnant before you start spoiling her." Judith opened her mouth in protest, but Chris pointed a finger before her friend could speak. "No pink!"

Judith giggled a tentative promise, then hugged her, followed by Winston doing the same. When she was finally alone with Geoff again, he embraced her with a kiss to her cheek. "Under the circumstances, you'd think that I'd be the first to get to hug you."

"You were," she responded lightheartedly. "How do you think I got into this condition in the first place?"

"As I recall, that consisted of more than a hug."

The joy of the moment faded when her knees wobbled.

"Chris, are you feeling all right?"

"I'm a little queasy."

Geoff escorted her to the settee and sat beside her, holding her hand. "Can I get you anything?"

With a shake of her head, she took a few deep breaths as a terrible thought occurred to her. She touched her abdomen. "What if it's not Sarah?"

"Then she'll have an older brother or sister."

She blinked in disbelief. "You want me to go through *two* pregnancies?"

"I was trying to reassure you. I have no illusion of you remaining barefoot and pregnant in the kitchen."

"Illusion?" Her hands went to her hips. "Exactly what do you mean by having 'no illusion'?"

He held up his hands in surrender. "I think I'll quit while I'm behind. I meant nothing by either statement, okay?"

His comment made her laugh as she got to her feet. "I didn't mean to overreact. I'm not sure whether I've truly absorbed the idea yet."

He stood and kissed her hands. "If it's Sarah, I may need to find something to read to her besides medieval knights. What do little girls like? Didn't you say that I would read something about a black stallion?"

"*The Black Stallion* is a classic. I'm certain she'll enjoy it," she said weakly. "Geoff, I really need to be getting to work." With a hasty goodbye, she picked up her briefcase in the main hall. Her necklace—she had forgotten to put it on. She checked her watch. Already late, she decided not to run halfway across the house to retrieve it. She needed to take comfort in Sarah's words that they would be a family, not worrying about what might happen. Thankfully, she didn't have any client appointments until eleven. That gave her time to get her head together and gain some semblance of professionalism.

Without noticing the transition of the countryside dotted with swamps to high rises, she drove to her office in Richmond. Barely had she reached her desk when her boss, Denise Warren, entered and placed a brief on her desk. "Good morning, Chris. I have a case that I think you might be interested in."

She glanced through the papers when queasiness returned to her stomach. Thinking that she might barf again, she looked away to catch her breath.

"Are you all right, Chris?"

The nausea passed. "I'm fine. I think I'm pregnant."

"Congratulations! We have excellent daycare in the building, which is especially handy if you should decide to nurse."

How different Denise was from her boss in Boston. Instead of congratulating her, he would have been complaining about how much time she'd eventually need to take off. "Thanks, Denise. The convenient daycare was one reason why I initially wanted to work here, but now I have the best of everything, friends too."

Beaming, Denise seemed pleased. "I'm glad you feel that way."

As Chris returned her attention to looking over the brief, the phone rang. Denise told her that she'd catch her later, and Chis gave her boss a nod.

By five, she was beat from taking calls and meeting with clients. When her last client of the day left, she sank back in her chair, wishing she could take a long, hot bubble bath. She was looking forward to a quiet weekend.

The phone to her direct line rang. Presuming it was Geoff, she snapped out of her daydream and answered it.

"Chris," came Geoff's voice. "Could you do me a favor and pick up Neal on your way home? One of the stallions got loose . . ."

"Not to worry," she assured him. So much for a quiet weekend.

She had forgotten Neal would be visiting. With him spending many weekends at Poplar Ridge, sometimes it was difficult to keep track. At least his visits gave her a sample of what it would be like to have a small child running around the house. By the time she packed up and pulled in front of the yellow Victorian, it was nearly six.

Beth showed her into the foyer. When she heard a childish squeal come from the parlor, Beth escorted her in that direction. A man, on all fours, played horsey with Neal. He pretended to buck Neal off, and the boy's howl of delight echoed throughout the room. Maybe it had been a good thing Geoff had been unable to pick up his son. His heart would have ached at seeing another man taking on his fatherly role.

The man spotted her. He stood to over six feet tall. Chris stuck out her hand. "You must be Al."

He sent her a dazzling smile before grasping her hand. "I am, and you're Chris."

As they shook hands, she realized that Judith could be right. With Beth moving on with her life, maybe Margaret was finally at peace.

Dressed in mourning black, Aunt Margaret exited the library. After her aunt's tragic history, Sarah had never known her to go near the library. She had more pressing matters than to analyze her aunt's constant state of melancholy. "Have you seen Tom?"

"He's inside." Without giving Sarah so much as a second glance, her aunt scurried along the path to the main house.

Without knocking, Sarah stepped inside. Near the fireplace, Tom lit a match to some kindling. "Tom?"

He immediately straightened and faced her. Even though his bushy gray beard hid most of his features, his face was pale with remorse. As she approached him, she spotted Mama's ledger on the desktop. She glanced from the growing flames in the fireplace to him. "You followed us when I brought Mama here the other day. Tom, how could you? She's dying."

He wandered over to the desk and slumped into the chair.

She seized the ledger from his reach and hugged it to her breast. "Why?"

He closed his eyes and shook his head.

She set the ledger on the desk and flipped through. The last page, where Mama had admitted what sort of feelings she had for him, was missing. She glanced at the growing fire. "It appears I'm already too late to save that entry."

Tom gripped her wrist. "I didn't burn it. Sarah . . ."

She shook free of his hold. "Never mind that now! Mama needs us by her side."

He gave a weak nod. Together, they went outside to her waiting horse and buggy. Tom helped her into the buggy and climbed in beside her. As he cued the horse to a fast trot, Sarah worried they might not make it in time. And she had lied to Mama. She had been unable to find the necklace. A cry of anguish escaped her. "She can't travel without it."

"Without what?" Tom looked in her direction before returning his attention to guiding the horse along the road.

"I promised Mama that she would have the necklace to return to the twenty-first century."

"She shall have the necklace," he said in a low voice.

Sarah decided not ask him his reason for keeping the necklace's whereabouts a secret. Now was not the time. Mama needed them. "Thank you."

They traveled the rest of the trip in silence. When they came to a halt outside the house, Sarah clambered from the buggy before Tom could help her. As she hurried up the steps, he was beside her.

"Let me explain," he said.

"You don't need to tell me anything. Just get the necklace." Once inside, Sarah dashed up the stairs to Mama and Tom's bedroom. "Mama, I'm here. Tom will be along soon." She bent beside the bed to her mother's prone form. Her breathing was ragged, and her pulse was growing weak.

"Sarah . . . ," Mama gasped.

Sarah patted her mother's hand. "Save your strength."

The door creaked behind her and Tom entered. Tears were in his eyes. He placed the necklace in Sarah's hand, then turned to leave.

She grasped the sleeve of his jacket as a signal for him to stay. "Mama, I have something for you." She held up the necklace to the light, and a prism reflected off the wall.

"My necklace. Where did you find it?"

Without answering, Sarah exchanged a glance with Tom. "Let me put it on you."

Almost as soon as the stone rested on her mother's chest, her breathing became easier. Tom stepped forward. "Sarah, please, I'd like to speak with your mother."

Sarah whispered in her mother's ear. "Mama, I love you. I'll keep our promise." The long ago pact of seeing that Greta would receive the ledger.

With confidence, Chris clutched Sarah's hand. She could finally let go of a life that had never really been hers. Only twice in her life had she ever seen Tom cry—when George and Tessa had died and on Sarah's birth. All these years, he had stood beside her, cared for Sarah, and she had kept him at an arm's length. She grasped his hand. "I've been unfair to you. Please forgive me."

"There's nothing to forgive," Tom responded, squeezing her hand. "Chris, Tessa placed the gun in your hand to protect me, not Margaret."

Suddenly feeling betrayed, she managed to wiggle free of his grip. "Protect you? Why?"

Tears of grief rolled down his cheeks. "She wanted you dead because you carried George's child. She felt you were disgracing Margaret. I tried to stop her." He held up his shaking left hand. "I was still awkward without my right hand. George saw us. He pushed you clear at the same time I tried getting the gun from her. George took the bullet. I'm responsible for my own brother's death."

A stupid accident—all of these years without knowing the truth. "Why did she want me to take the blame?"

"Because she was afraid that if either of us were implicated, we would hang. She knew the Yankees wouldn't hang a white woman."

Until the end, Tessa had remained the dutiful servant to Margaret and lover to Tom. "Then you've known all this time where my necklace was?"

He gave her a weak nod. "Tessa had hidden it in her room. After she died, I meant to return it. Chris, I didn't think I could ever love again." His voice broke. He clutched her, sobbing on her breast. "Lord forgive me, but I grew to love you, and it was the only way I could keep you here."

Tom. Totally numb from his revelation, she could think of nothing to say. Her breathing grew difficult once more. Too exhausted to absorb the truth of his words, she reached up for her necklace. Her hands shook as she unclasped it. Chris curled her fingers around the crystal. An intense warmth radiated inside her hand, and light reflected from between her fingers. The time had come. Even Tom realized it. With no animosity toward him, she sat up. Her arthritic pain faded. It was almost as if the years were melting away.

"Chris, I don't expect your forgiveness, but I love you."

Tom's voice momentarily drew her toward him. "It's an illusion. I loved George, and you loved Tessa. We both wanted what we could not have." She got to her feet and opened her palms to the shimmering light. Sarah reappeared. With difficulty, she said goodbye and stepped toward the lighted passageway.

"Chris . . ." A man with a moustache stood in the middle of the light.

Immediately, she moved toward him. "George." Already she had that feeling of being restricted and free as a bird at the same time. George had the same appearance as the day of his death. How long ago had he died? Yesterday. Her joints no longer ached, and she could walk with straight shoulders. As when she had traveled the passageway before, the light intensified. She reached a branch and waited for George to tell her whether to take it.

"Go forward."

Chris followed the light—on and on, until she came to another branch and another. George guided her through the maze of light. At each turn, his words echoed inside her head. Go forward. Finally, the light faded.

Up ahead, she spotted the road outside the house she had shared with Tom. Her journey had been successful. The road was paved. A woman stood a few feet away from her, staring in confusion. She stepped toward her. In the darkness, she was unable to discern the woman's features. As she got nearer, Chris blinked. She was staring at herself. Light flickered, and she gripped the crystal in her hands as their bodies merged.

Chapter Eighteen

When Geoff entered the library, the rug had been moved and Chris stared at the bloodstains where George had died. "Chris?"

She bent down. "It was an accident. It was nothing but a stupid accident!"

As he put his arms protectively around her, he felt the racing rhythm of her heart. "What was an accident?"

"Tom shot George," she cried on his shoulder. "He didn't mean to, but he was afraid to tell me."

Tessa stood in the doorway with a gun aimed at Chris. He shoved her, trying to get her out of the line of fire. Tom wrestled Tessa for the gun. Then blackness. Geoff brushed Chris's tousled hair away from her face. "It's over, Chris. Margaret wasn't responsible for George's death in this time line."

Calming, she reached a hand to her throat. "Over? Geoff, where's my necklace? I didn't put it on this morning because I was late for work again."

"Upstairs?"

He accompanied her to their room, where she made a quick search through her jewelry box on the dresser. "It's not here."

"I'll help you look."

What he had originally thought was a sign of relief turned ominous. For the rest of the night and much of the weekend, he helped Chris search for her necklace to no avail. By the time he pulled the Mustang in front of Beth's house to drop off Neal on Sunday evening, he was exhausted. Before leaving the car, he gazed up the brick walk. How many times had he lived through George's memories? He unbuckled his seatbelt and got out. Just one more time. He helped Neal from the car. With childish giggles, the boy scampered up the walk, tugging on Saber's leash.

Beth greeted them on the steps outside the door as Neal chattered about his weekend. While she laughed at the dog walking the boy, she sent him a pinched smile. She made no motion to invite him inside.

"I'd like to speak with you," he said.

"Not now," she responded in a clipped manner.

"I take it that Fisher is here."

Neal dashed inside with Saber, and she waited until he was out of earshot before speaking. "If it's any of your business, no, but I see Chris has told you that he was here on Friday."

"She did." Scorn crossed her face, and he instantly grew tired of having to justify his actions. "Goddammit, Beth, I don't give a rat's ass that you're screwing him. I just want to speak with you for a minute. Or do I have to call and make an appointment?"

"No, but I will thank you to watch your language. Neal might overhear." Taking a deep breath, she motioned for him to step inside.

For some reason, he felt uneasy when he went into the foyer and followed Beth to the kitchen. Neal rushed in, complaining that he was hungry.

Afraid of being accused that he hadn't taken proper care of their son, Geoff said, "He ate supper just before we left Poplar Ridge."

Beth stood on her tiptoes and grabbed a bag of potato chips from the cupboard's upper shelf. "You know boys. Grown-up men, too. Their stomachs are bottomless pits."

He pointed at the bag of chips. "I always get fussed at for feeding him things like that."

Telling Neal to go into the parlor and watch TV, she handed him the bag. As he disappeared from the kitchen, she said, "They're an instant distraction, only used for special occasions. I thought it would give us a chance to talk. Now, would you like a cup of coffee?"

He waved that he'd pass. "Not this late in the day." They stared at each other with neither knowing where to begin. Straight out would be best. "Tom killed George."

She clutched her belly like she might vomit and sank to a chair at the table. "He didn't mean to."

She knew! In horror and disbelief, he asked, "What do you mean?"

"*She* was there that night. She saw everything from the panel near the passageway."

"Why didn't you tell me?"

"Because *you* triggered the memory. She never recovered from the tragedies in her life. So you see, we haven't changed anything. I will become that woman in the ledger, unless . . ."

Finally comprehending her initial reluctance to speak with him, he reached across the table and gripped her hand. "If nothing has changed, that gives us time to work out a solution."

A hesitant smile appeared on her face. "Thanks for trying."

He let go of her hand. "Have you thought of moving out of here? Away from her influence?"

"I have, but dammit Geoff, as I told Chris, you're not going to let me take Neal far enough away that would make a difference."

Lose his son or his life? Some choice. "Where would you go?"

"Scotland. T.J. could help me make the contacts, and with an ocean between us, the cycle would be broken once and for all. Neal can visit you during the summer once he's in school, and we can alternate between the holidays."

His heart sank. He supposed Scotland was fitting. The Camerons had traveled by sailing ship to tidewater Virginia in the early-eighteenth century, but Scotland was over three-thousand miles away. Contemplating her proposition, he ran a hand through his goatee. No matter what he decided, he was damned. His son would be absent from a major portion of his life. "Let me think about it for a while."

"Sure," she said weakly.

He got up to leave.

"Geoff, I'm not trying to keep you from Neal."

Without facing her, he replied, "I know." He went into the parlor. Neal munched potato chips while watching Cartoon Network, with Saber curled on the floor beside him. A lump formed in his throat. Instead of a weekend dad, he'd be reduced to a holiday dad. Was it too much to ask? He'd be alive and Beth would remain sane. At least, Neal would have both parents. He bent down to his son's level. "Mommy's thinking of taking a trip to Scotland."

Neal stopped crunching the chip in his mouth. "Will there be castles?"

He ruffled Neal's hair. "Lots of castles."

The boy's eyes grew round with adventure. "Oh, boy! Can Saber come too?"

"He'll stay here with me."

Tears suddenly welled in Neal's eyes.

Geoff nearly lost it himself. "We'll talk on the phone, and you'll come . . ." His voice cracked. "You'll come back for visits."

Neal's arms went around his neck, and he clung to him. His son's grip tightened, and he screamed as if in pain. "I don't want to go! Daddy, please don't make me!"

Geoff patted him on the back and reassured him, all the while struggling to keep his own emotions in check. Over his shoulder, he saw Beth. When she realized that he had seen her, she hustled from the room with tears streaming down her cheeks.

Monday morning, Chris fidgeted with a pen on her desk. After what had transpired over the weekend, she was uncertain how she'd get any work done. With Geoff distraught over the thought of Neal moving to Scotland, she had almost called in sick. Unfortunately, she was due in court in two hours. Even then, she had nearly been late because of searching for her necklace—with no luck. Her direct line rang. *Geoff.* Thinking he needed someone to talk to, she answered quickly.

"*Chris,*" came a female voice.

"Beth?"

"*You told me to call if I thought of anything that might help.*"

Her heart pounded. "Geoff told me that you've decided to move to Scotland."

"*It's one option, but I can't bear keeping Neal and Geoff apart. Besides, I think Poplar Ridge is as much a part of Neal as it is Geoff. I can't repeat what I have in mind over the phone. I'll meet you at Poplar Ridge this evening."*

Beth's voice sounded anxious. "I'm scheduled to be in court in a couple of hours, but you can stop by to see me at the office before then."

"It's important that I see you at Poplar Ridge."

Before Chris could respond, Beth hung up.

When T.J.'s frantic call came in the late afternoon, Geoff raced to the barn. The Scotsman was going from stall to stall, inspecting each one. Expecting one of the horses to have been injured or taken ill, Geoff asked, "What's wrong, T.J.?"

"Traveller is missin'," T.J. explained, waving his arms excitedly.

"Missing?"

"Aye, when Ken went out ta get him from the pasture, he couldna find him. He's out lookin' fer him now, but there's no sign of a horse breakin' loose."

"He must have jumped the fence," Geoff reasoned. "How long has he been missing?"

T.J. checked another stall. "Maybe an hour. I saw him meself around three."

"I'll help with the search," he reassured T.J. "Where have you looked already?"

"The barn an' nearby pastures."

He'd need to look further afield. To cover more ground quickly, Geoff saddled one of the other horses. Hopefully, the presence of a pasture mate would help attract Traveller. He checked the outlying fields. Black Angus cattle grazed, but no horse. He rode on. Maybe the gelding had gotten in with the neighbor's horses. Bays, chestnuts, but no gray. He watched them a moment before continuing on. Soon he found himself in the grove of sycamore and oak trees. Green spring leaves topped the trees leading to the meadow. Up ahead in the clearing, thigh-high grass waved. He was heading toward the cottage, where he often rode Traveller to meet Chris. He cued Tiffany to a trot.

Outside the cottage, Traveller stood tethered to the rail. He now understood. With T.J.'s help, Chris had been planning the rendezvous all along. Aroused by the idea of a secret tryst, he tied the mare alongside Traveller and went up the steps to the cottage with Saber at his side. The door opened, and he stood frozen in place. "Beth? What are you doing here?"

She wore Chris's crystal necklace. "George, I've been waiting for you."

He should have guessed that Beth had taken the necklace. "Beth, you're not Margaret. She influences you, but you're not her. Let's get back to the house." He held out a hand.

Surprised that she offered no resistance, she grasped his outstretched fingers. As they mounted the horses, he notified T.J. from his cell phone that he had found Traveller. On the return ride, Beth remained silent. They tied the horses to a rail outside the house, and he escorted her to the sofa in the library.

He sat beside her. "Beth, we have to end this once and for all. None of us are free to live our lives until it is settled. I think it would be best if you and Neal move to Scotland as soon as possible."

Her violet eyes glittered in an odd sort of way. "That night, I came to you through there." She pointed to the secret panel near the bookcase. "I didn't want Tom or Chris to see me."

Margaret wore a silk dress with hoops, with her black hair glistening against her creamy white skin. So, this was how it would end. They'd replay George's final night. "You wore a blue gown."

She sent him a bittersweet smile. "I wanted you to recall the last time we had been happy."

"I did." Like now, the necklace had adorned her throat. He reached for it, then withdrew his hand. "Where did you get it?" Even before she replied, he knew how she would answer.

Her smile faded. "Tessa."

Everything revolved around the servant. He glanced at the rug where George had died. But Tom and Tessa weren't present. Is that why Beth had brought Fisher into the picture?

"I asked you if you loved me."

She had been his wife—his only love—until Chris had arrived. He *had* loved both of them. "I never stopped loving you."

"I know." Her voice nearly broke. "But I killed Georgiana." Sobbing, she bolted.

Geoff now understood what kept her from finding peace. He attempted to catch her retreating arm, but it slipped through his fingers before he could get a solid grip. Saber raced after her as she fled from the library. By the time he reached the door, Beth had vanished, and Saber returned to his side, wagging his tail. "Where did she go, boy?"

If she wasn't anywhere in the hall, then she had to have taken the stairs. Racing up the steps two at a time, he went up to the second floor. No sign of Beth. He looked in the room he shared with Chris. Empty. Margaret would have led her to the main section of the house. He hurried down the hall to the room where Chris had stayed on her first visit.

Upon entering, he smelled honeysuckle. On that final night, Margaret had worn the scent. *Of course.* She had agreed to return to *their* room. Geoff went into the main hall and hesitated before the door. He hadn't entered since Beth had left. Swallowing hard, he slowly opened the door.

Beth stood in front of the full-length mirror, staring at her reflection. When he had helped Margaret get ready for bed, he had gotten the necklace for Chris. She turned from the mirror and faced him. "She carries your child."

Like now, Chris had been pregnant, and George had suffered from the guilt of loving two women. But he held no guilt now. All along Chris had been right, *this* was their time. "Yes," he finally responded.

When she smiled that eerie look returned to her eyes. "Jason shall have a sister. He was meant to have a sister."

"Margaret, please release Beth. She's an innocent party in all of this."

"You loved her because you couldn't let go of the past."

On the first day of classes, he had spotted Beth crossing the University of Virginia grounds. It wasn't until Greta had given him the ledger that he understood why George was attracted to Beth. "I realize that now."

"She hasn't stopped loving you. Nor have I."

Those weren't the words he wanted to hear. "That's why we have to do whatever is necessary to end this."

"Whatever is necessary," she repeated. Her hand went to her throat. "I watched Tessa die. The mob dragged me from the house so I could watch my faithful servant hang. She died for something she didn't do."

Distraught that the servant had paid for his death, he whispered, "I realize that now. Tom killed George. It was an accident."

"Tom tried to burn the ledger. I managed to save a piece of it for Chris to find."

So Margaret was the one who had hidden the letter behind the mirror. "Margaret, what can I do now to make things right?"

"Follow the same path as on the night you died."

Easier said than done. George's memory was hazy. "If it'll bring you closure, I'll do it, but I don't remember."

"You held me in your arms and told me that it was going to take time, for we had both changed since the war."

Her words triggered nothing. He motioned for her to continue.

"You ducked out the passageway, so Chris or Tom wouldn't see you leave. After that, I don't know what happened, except that you were in the library several hours later."

He grasped her hand and kissed the back, then turned. He felt along the panel near the mirror until hearing a click. The panel popped open.

"Goodbye, Geoff."

The finality of her farewell made him pause. To hell with it, he forged forward and entered the narrow passageway with Saber on his heels. In the tight quarters, he had to duck to keep from hitting his head. His hands felt the way as he fumbled through the darkness. Beside him, Saber panted, and his nails clicked against the wooden floor. Geoff reached the stairway. Which way had George taken from here? *To the cellar.* He made his way carefully down until reaching the brick floor.

Although it was still daylight, not much light shone through the tiny cellar windows. A breeze from the tunnel made his face tingle. No longer needing to be told which way, he grabbed the skeleton key hanging on a nail. As he neared the end of the tunnel, he heard the lapping waves of the James.

After climbing six steps, he reached a heavy wood door. The lock had rusted long ago, and he fumbled with the key, hoping the door would budge. Nothing happened. He swore, trying yet another time. The hinges groaned, and he stepped into the fresh river air. While Saber snuffled ahead and marked a tree, Geoff cast his gaze to the river and stood mesmerized watching the waves.

He blinked. That night, George had ridden Raven, and he must follow the same footsteps. He circled back in the direction to where he had left the horses tied. In a few hours, he would return to the library. Chris would be home from the office by then, and the two of them would talk. *"We were meant to love each other at the right time."*

Why hadn't he seen it before? Suddenly comprehending her words, he jogged across the grounds to the horses. Out of breath, he reached the spot out front where he had left them tethered. Tiffany stood calmly, but Traveller was gone.

Saber growled and raised his hackles.

"What is it, boy?"

Cautious with his ears twitching, the dog moved forward, and Geoff followed. Near the front lawn, Traveller galloped by. Saber's growls gave way to frenzied barking. Geoff thought he saw a figure near the oak tree. *Beth!* A rope twisted around her neck, and her body thrashed inches from the ground. Shouting her name, he ran toward her. By the time he reached her side, her face had turned blue, and her tongue protruded. More thrashing. Supporting Beth's weight, he withdrew his pocketknife from his jeans and hacked through the rope. Her eyes bulged with blood spots filling the whites of her eyes.

The rope snapped, and he eased her to the ground. *Dammit, what should he do?* Check her breathing and heart rate. Her pulse was flighty, and her breathing, irregular and raspy. But she was alive.

A woman screamed. Judith stood on the steps of the house.

"Call 911!" he yelled.

His sister dodged inside.

"Beth, it wasn't meant to happen this way. You can't die." Panic gave way to measured reason. Careful not to injure her further, he cut the rope around her neck. The crystal in the necklace glowed, and she stopped breathing. Hoping that she could hold on until help arrived, he bent over her and administered mouth-to-mouth resuscitation. As he did, the whispers from George that he had so often heard at the back of his mind vanished.

Traveling down the lane, Chris suddenly braked at the end of the drive. The grounds were covered with police cars and flashing lights. "Geoff!" Fearing the worst, she stopped the car and shot out, racing toward the squad cars. Then she halted.

Although his face was ashen, Geoff stood talking to a square-jawed detective with a receding hairline. She recognized him from working with him on a couple of cases: Detective Jim Franks from the homicide division. Geoff was very much alive, but visibly shaken.

A siren blared and a rescue truck sped past her as Judith joined her. "What happened?" Chris asked.

"Beth, she . . . uh . . . she hung herself."

"What? She was supposed to meet me here." When Chris moved toward Geoff, a uniformed police officer stepped in front of her, refusing to let her pass. "I'm Christine Cameron, Mr. Cameron's wife."

Judith vouched for her, and the officer allowed Chris to pass. "I'm going to pick up Neal."

"Thanks, Judith. Geoff, what happened?" She took his hand.

Beneath her grip, he trembled. "The tree where you . . . you," he stammered. "I found her . . ."

Recalling the vision, Chris placed a hand to her throat. Another detective called to Franks, and he stepped aside to converse with the other. "Will she be all right?"

"I don't know," he replied weakly.

"Mrs. Cameron," Jim said, returning. "If you don't mind, I'd like to speak to your husband alone. I'll talk with you in a few minutes."

Chris returned to her car and watched while Detective Franks questioned Geoff. At one point, Geoff appeared to be nearly in tears himself. *What would have made Beth do such a thing?*

As Geoff strode for the library, the detective spoke to T.J. and Winston Cameron each in their turn. Finally, he approached her. "Chris," he said, less formally. "You're familiar with the routine. You know I need to question you without your husband present."

"She called me earlier in the day." Only after she blurted out the words, did she realize she was shaking.

"The victim?" He scribbled into his notepad. "What did she want?"

Calm down. Any good cop needed to find out if foul play was involved. "She wouldn't tell me. She said that she'd meet me here after I got off work."

"How well do you know her?"

Summoning the control of an attorney in the courtroom, she managed a collected appearance. "Only casually. She visited on occasion when she dropped off or picked up my husband's son."

"Are the victim and your husband having an affair?"

Shocked by the question, she blinked. "Jim, level with me. Are you implying . . . ?"

He looked up from his notepad. "I'm not implying anything. I'm merely trying to find out what happened. Chris, as you may or may not realize, women rarely try suicide by hanging. I also have reason to believe that your husband isn't being totally honest with me."

Geoff not being honest? "He's in shock from what's happened."

"Maybe." He placed his notebook and pen inside his suit jacket, then headed for his car. "I'll be in touch, Mrs. Cameron."

With a sick feeling, Chris skirted the yellow police tape. The dangling rope tied to the limb of the oak made her shiver. Beneath the tree, the forensics team scoured the ground for possible clues. She went in the library door.

Geoff sat behind the desk, staring with a vacant expression at a blank monitor. "I'd rather be alone," he said brusquely.

"I'll bring you something to eat a little later." *Unreal.* This couldn't be happening. Had Beth meant for *her* to find her? Chris joined Laura in the kitchen and took a roast chicken out of the oven for dinner. Due to Chris's inability to cook and lack of general domestic capabilities, the maid normally protested any time she tried to help, but Laura remained uncomfortably silent.

When the phone rang, she nearly jumped through her skin. Laura wiped her hands on her apron and answered, but immediately hung up. "Geoff already got it," she explained.

Fearing the worst, Chris cut some breast meat from the chicken and placed it on a plate. After adding a baked potato, she returned to the library. Frozen in place, Geoff remained seated, continuing to stare at the monitor. What she wouldn't give for his usual quaint manners. "I brought you some chicken."

He waved that he wasn't hungry.

"Who was on the phone?"

"Judith."

When he offered nothing further, she prompted him. "And?"

He avoided looking away from the blank monitor. "Neal was with a neighbor, and she's on her way home."

At least they could be thankful for one small favor. "Are you all right?"

His eyes met hers. Their usual spark was absent. "Chris, I didn't reveal everything to the cops."

Jim's suspicion *had* been correct. "Like what?" she asked, placing the plate on the desk before she dropped it.

"I spoke with Beth before I found her . . ." His voice trailed off, and he clenched a hand. "She had your necklace."

"What did she want with my necklace?"

He pounded his fist on the desktop with a resounding crack. Saber jumped from the rug by the desk and scurried with his tail tucked to his padded dog bed near the wall. "I don't know!"

What a fool she had been. He still loved Beth. "Did you sleep with her? Goddamn it, Geoff."

"No, Chris." He stood and grasped her elbow before she could leave the room. "I have *never* cheated on you."

Calming slightly, she lowered her arm and searched his face for any signs that he might be lying. There were none. "I didn't mean to accuse you unjustly, but the ledger . . ."

He withdrew the ledger from a desk drawer. With bold, confident steps, he carried it over to the fireplace and reached atop the mantel for a match. He struck it against the bricks and placed the flame to the pages of the book. Wisps of smoke rose, and flames fluttered. He tossed the ledger into the fireplace. His face was dark with pain, and when he spoke, he struggled to keep his voice even, "All my life I've heard George's voice. Sometimes he took over, but generally, I learned to tune him out. He's gone."

"What do you mean gone?"

"I no longer hear his voice."

Before she could respond, the phone rang. Geoff answered. His face twisted in shock, then anguish.

"What's wrong?" Chris asked.

He dropped the phone and eased into the leather chair behind the desk. "Detective Franks. Beth . . ." His voice cracked. "She died on the way to the hospital."

Died? Beth couldn't be dead. The ledger had stated . . . Damn the ledger anyway! She watched the flames in the fireplace. It should have been burned long ago. "Geoff . . . Oh God. Are you all right?"

He closed his eyes. "I should be the one dead, not her."

"Don't say that. You did everything you could to save her."

"I did nothing!" Calming slightly, he lowered his voice. "Months ago, she told me that she refused to become that woman in the ledger, and she would do whatever was necessary to prevent it. How will I ever tell Neal that I let his mother die?" He placed his head between his hands and trembled.

Chris bent down and held him. "There's no way you could have known what she meant. It's not your fault." She felt dampness on her arm and realized he was crying. First, Tessa, now Beth. Two innocent people had died because she had dared to change time. As they clung to each other, their tears mixed. "I love you," she whispered.

He wiped the tears away and met her gaze. "Thank you."

"We'll get through this together." She gripped his hand, and he squeezed it. She only hoped her words were more than a brave front.

Geoff had insisted that Beth be buried in the family cemetery. With no immediate family of her own, she was interred in a plot near where Neal and any future family would rest. Besides the family, only a few of Beth's acquaintances attended the funeral. The overcast day spit rain. Chris spotted Winston paying his respects to his wife, Sarah. Sarah had lived longer due to the diary. Her stomach churned. Could the fact that some people had lived and some died in a different time frame justify what she had done in writing the ledger? They *had* changed time, and Beth was no longer a threat to Geoff's life.

With Beth's death, Chris's necklace had vanished. None of the paramedics had remembered seeing it, and it had most likely been lost in the hurried shuffle of transporting Beth to the hospital. Maybe it was for the best. Chris no longer searched for it.

Geoff grasped her arm. As they walked to the waiting car, she saw a man with a bowed head lingering near a towering oak. She blinked, and he was gone. Wondering if she had truly seen him, Geoff helped her into the car. He sat beside her, and Ken drove them the mile to the house. Near the steps stood the man she had seen at the cemetery. No ghost, he was over six feet tall, muscular with dark hair. Al. His face was red with rage.

"Cameron! You bastard! She's dead because of you!" When Al lunged, Geoff pushed Chris aside, throwing her clear of any blows. As she tumbled to the ground, she heard the sickening crunch of Al's fist connecting with Geoff's face. Another crack, but it was Geoff fighting back. Ken jumped into the fray, trying to separate them. The stable hand seized the first swinging arm and received a punch in the stomach.

Gathering her feet beneath her, Chris stood. "Stop it!"

Ken pinned Al's arms behind his back and struggled to maintain his hold. With Geoff's eyes seething, he stalked his opponent.

Chris stepped between them and held up her hands in each of their directions. "Enough!" She glared at Al. "Leave now, or I'm calling the cops."

Al jerked himself free of Ken's grip, muttering barbed insults under his breath. But he was leaving.

Chris took a deep breath and lowered her arms. "Are the two of you all right?"

The stable hand nodded. "I need to get back to work."

"Thanks, Ken." She turned her attention to Geoff. "What about you?"

"What about me?" A dark puffiness was already forming near his left eye, and blood streaked from his nostrils. He cradled his right hand in pain.

She grasped his arm and tugged him in the direction of the house. "Let's get inside, where I can see how bad it is. You may need a doctor."

"I don't need a doctor," he responded gruffly.

"I'll be the judge of that."

No longer resisting, he accompanied her up the stairs. Inside the door, Saber met them with his tail wagging.

"Where were you when we needed you?" Chris asked. Seeming to understand, the dog lowered his head, while Geoff inspected his injuries in the hall's mirror. In the time that they had climbed the stairs and walked through the door, his eye had swollen larger. She guided him to the drawing room and motioned for him to have a seat in the wing chair. "Let me get some supplies to clean you up."

Saber remained with Geoff as she hurried to the kitchen and collected a first-aid kit, along with a bowl of water, cloth, and an ice pack. Upon her return to the drawing room, she gave him the ice pack for his eye, then started dabbing away the blood. "You haven't said anything about what happened."

"What's there to say? He was right."

His mood worried her. She continued swabbing the blood, but more trickled down. "Geoff . . ."

"Chris, I know what you're going to say. You know as well as I do that Beth's death doesn't change anything."

She pressed the cloth a little harder than she intended, and he got to his feet, swearing.

"You need to hold still, or I won't be able to get you cleaned up."

He muttered an apology and reseated himself.

She wrung out the cloth in the bowl, turning the water red. "You've suffered a loss. She may have been your ex, but I'm well aware that you still loved her." He opened his mouth to protest, but she continued, "First, you need to admit it to yourself, then grieve for her. Neal's young. He'll get through this quicker, but she'll live on because you'll tell him about her."

In appreciation, he gripped her hand. If only she believed the words too.

* * *

Due to the fact that Beth had no living relatives besides Neal, Chris and Judith had received the chore of sorting through her belongings. Geoff had opted not to accompany them, and a week after her death, they parked on the street in front of the gabled Victorian. While Judith tagged the furniture for auction, Chris went through personal items, keeping an eye out for things that Geoff or Neal might want to hold onto for keepsakes.

Most of Beth's clothes they would donate to charity. In a dresser drawer, Chris stumbled across a box of letters. She recognized Geoff's handwriting. She unfolded one dated from July 1993. A love letter. Without reading it, she returned the letter to the box and closed the lid. She would ask Geoff if he wanted them.

By late afternoon, they climbed the steep stairs to the third floor. An old brass bed was in the center of the room. An antique mirror and dresser stood off to the side. On the far end of the room sat an old trunk. "We might as well get started," Chris said with a sigh, hoping the attic would be empty.

"It's getting late. We could always come back tomorrow," Judith suggested.

Chris shook her head. "I'd rather get this over with."

Judith gave her a hug. "This can't be easy for you."

Moving over to the dresser, Chris started sifting through the drawers. "It's Geoff and Neal that I worry about." She uncovered Neal's baby book. It contained the usual announcements—date, time of birth, weight—along with first accomplishments—crawling, walking, first tooth. Among the pictures, Beth had included an ultrasound.

She touched her abdomen and thought that she should purchase a baby book soon. A light touch on her neck, tickled her. She glanced over her shoulder to see Geoff and Saber standing behind her.

"I should have been here to help," he said.

Chris handed Geoff the baby book. "I don't mind, really. I have a few things stashed in the foyer that I thought you might like to look through."

With a nod, he glanced through the book. A sad, nostalgic smile formed on his lips. "What do you have left?" he asked, closing the book.

"Judith . . ." She looked around the attic for Judith. Her friend had vanished. "I didn't hear her leave."

"She's downstairs, putting your stash in the car."

"I guess I got too involved. The only thing I have left is that huge trunk. Maybe you can give me a hand hauling it out of the corner and into some light."

Geoff grasped the brass handle and pulled the black pine trunk into the center of the room near the bed. Ornate, sweeping nineteenth-century script initials, E.R., were painted on the front. "I didn't know she had this," he said, opening the lid.

They shuffled through several old petticoats, shawls, and dresses. The little shop where Chris had bought her wedding dress in Richmond would most likely be interested in the vintage clothing. "I think that about covers everything."

Geoff removed another dress. At the bottom of the trunk was an oak jewelry box with fluted columns on the corners and leaf carvings at the bottom. Chris reached for it. Moss-green velvet lined the drawers, where brooches and gold necklaces rested. In the second drawer was a letter and a key. She unfolded the brittle, yellow paper.

Dear Geoff . . .

Gasping back a breath, Chris closed her eyes. *Beth's suicide note.* He took the letter from her trembling hand and began reading. His furrowed brow slowly relaxed, and confusion rested in his eyes. When he finished reading, his gaze met hers before he handed her the letter. He grasped the key and lifted a small pine box from the bottom drawer. "Damn lock," he muttered, struggling with the rusted lock.

Chris read the letter. It was dated April 1872. How was that possible?

Dear Geoff,
    I returned to Poplar Ridge in 1867. With all of Margaret's memories intact, I was able to pass myself off as a distant

cousin. *No one could deny the family resemblance, and the Cameron family welcomed me into their home. As a family member, I was able to gain Margaret's confidence. I also made friends with her servant, Tessa.*

With Tessa's guided assistance, I was able to help Margaret come to terms with her tragic past. She is now laudanum free. As a result, she and George are no longer estranged. In this era, Tom and Tessa can never marry and truly share what is in their hearts. Still, they make the best of their time together, in spite of cruel remarks from polite circles, I might add. All in all, they appear to be happy.

After the death of Margaret's parents, I moved into her childhood home with my husband, Captain Michael Rhodes. He is retired from the army now and has taken up banking. I hope you can find it within your heart to forgive me for abandoning Neal. Not a day goes by without me thinking of him and missing the precious moments of him growing to manhood. He is part of Poplar Ridge. It runs in his veins as much as it does yours, and he shall be happier living in the place that he loves.

This is my time. I go by my formal name, Elizabeth, and feel as if I have always belonged here. Finally, I am returning what rightfully belongs to Chris. You were meant to give it to her. You were my first love, and I will always treasure the memories.

Love,
Beth

"E.R.—Elizabeth Rhodes," Chris said under breath.

Geoff dangled a crystal on a fine gold chain in front of her.

Fighting the tears, she clasped the necklace in her hand. "She risked everything for . . ." She exchanged a long look with Geoff. "She loved you."

His eyes glistened as he gave a nod.

Chris clutched the crystal tighter, then wrapped her arms around Geoff. "Thank you, Beth," she whispered.

Epilogue

April 2008

From behind the desk, Geoff stared at the computer screen, checking through the day's email. The door cracked open, and he heard a giggle. Without flinching a muscle, Saber remained upside down on his dog bed with his legs splayed. Another giggle. Clad in powder blue My Little Pony pajamas, his four-year-old daughter skittered into the library with a book under her arm. "Will you read me a story?"

"All right, Sarah."

She handed him *The Black Stallion* picture book and climbed onto his lap. Her round blue eyes looked up at him inquisitively. "Daddy, who's Beth?"

All of the curious childish questions, and he still found speaking about Beth painful. "I've told you before. I was married to Beth before your mommy. She's Neal's mommy."

"Oh." Her long eyelashes fluttered. "She's dead, isn't she?"

"Yes." His voice broke. Even though Beth's letter had brought him inner peace, the memory of her hanging from the oak tree would always linger in his mind and haunt him. "Why do you ask?"

"You get sad. Why do you get sad, Daddy? She speaks to me."

With any other four-year-old, he could easily dismiss her words to the difficulty of separating make-believe from reality. But with Sarah, she claimed to hear voices that he couldn't cast aside as daydreams. "What does she say?"

"That she has a pretty little girl too. Her name is Victoria." She held up the picture book. "Do you think Victoria would like *The Black Stallion?*"

Relieved that Beth had definitely made a new life for herself in the nineteenth century, he laughed at Sarah's enthusiasm. It would be a few years before she could truly understand how she spoke to the dead. "I'm sure she would."

"I hope I'm not interrupting." Chris entered the library with a light-green dress draped over her arm. She pressed the low-waist dress resembling a sack against her. "I found this dress stuffed at the back of the closet. I bought it at the same place as my wedding dress, but for the life of me, I can't remember why. I've never had any interest in the 1920s."

Geoff shrugged that he hadn't the faintest idea why she had made the purchase. But then, he suspected that along with the bringing of peace to George and Margaret, Beth had changed other aspects in time. Would they notice if she had?

Sarah pointed at the dress. "My dress. I'll wear it when I'm big."

Her dress? He exchanged a confused glance with Chris. She laughed. "I'll be sure to save it for you, Sarah."

His daughter clapped in delight. The key to the mystery always belonged with Sarah. Because of her gift, only she could translate the whispers through time.

Acknowledgments

A special thank you goes to my editors, K.A. Corlett and Catherine Karp, my cover designer, Mayapriya Long, Charley Holley of Holley Photography for providing a photo for the cover art, and my seven-year-old technical advisors, Meggie Karp and Sean Riddle. And of course, I mostly wish to thank my family: my son, Bryan, and especially my husband, Pat; both are now wondering which century I will end up in next.